TASK FORCE LONE BANDIT

A NOVEL OF THE BATTLE OF THE BULGE

ROBERT S. BILLINGS

Cover by Maia Ballis

Poppy Lane Publishing Company
Fresno, California

Poppy Lane Publishing Company
P.O. Box 5136
Fresno, CA 93755

ISBN 0-938911-18-X

For orders by individuals or groups, write to the following address
(a substantial discount is offered for orders of 10 or more copies):
Vice President of Special Markets, Poppy Lane Publishing Company,
P.O. Box 5136, Fresno, CA 93755. E-mail Bette1234@aol.com

This book
is dedicated to
my wife Elizabeth Peterson
without whose help it could never
have attained publication

and to
my fellow members
of Battery B's O.P. crew,
187th Field Artillery Battalion,

Henry "Hank" Boiselle
Paul "Huck" Hull
Ralph "The Old Man" Swisher
(who was all of 30 at the time)

whose steadfast and courageous support
enabled me to make it home and write it.

A glossary of World War II terms and a map of the immediate battlefield area are placed at the end of the book.

Roadblock Outside St. Vith

Does time entomb your midnight madness still?
Do eyes quite dead still stare down burning streets,
All hope despaired of, knowing all retreats
For you have ended? Out there the fiery hill
Crawls with swollen-headed monsters. The past
Devours the present. Courage, fear, elan,
Panic riding piggyback on man,
Were these felt, and are they frozen fast?

You stayed while others fled. Too late to roar
Down narrow midnight roads, down fog and fear,
Resurrecting with each tank's tred clanking near
Hope for dead men. We strike the ice no more...
Too late...too cold. Yet somewhere sound of war,
And I see at midnights what that midnight saw.

R.S.B.

staff job, but at least it would get his foot in the door. The trouble was, in trying to keep him at tank school they'd given him two quick promotions only months apart. Now he had too damn much rank to command a tank company — and nobody in his right mind was going to give a fresh young punk a whole battalion of armor. So he'd grabbed at the staff job, figuring once he was in combat something would open up.

Well, he'd been right there. Something sure as hell must have opened up while he had been flying over the Atlantic. And he was beginning to suspect that "something" had very little to do with the plodding American offensive north of the Ardennes. For months now the Hurtgen Forest and the difficult terrain around the Roer River dams had been gobbling up American infantrymen by the hundreds — with little to show for it. Colonel Berrigan had begun to feel uneasy himself about how bogged down things had become. When you're up against an army as well-led and innovative as the Wehrmacht, you'd damn well better not think you can just plod along to a sure-fire victory. The Germans had written the book on how to snatch victory away from the plod-along boys..

The General was just setting down the field phone as Colonel Berrigan strode in, still uncomfortably conscious of his brand new battle gear. He stopped at attention and snapped a salute. The General swung his tired eyes toward him. The newcomer could see the mildly startled look in the General's eyes at his sudden appearance. It was apparent the General knew immediately who he was — and what he had probably overheard. After a moment the General smiled slightly, returned the salute, and reached out his hand.

"Welcome to combat, young man. Maybe it's just as well you heard. Now I won't have to bullshit you for the sake of your 'morale.' We got something going here I'd love to see them work out a solution for back in armored school. They'd probably say there isn't any and send everyone back to the barracks for a hot shower. Well, I can't give you a hot shower, but I think I've got something else hot enough for you. It's plenty hot for me, anyway."

After a moment the General appeared to cast off the blanket of gloom that had enshrouded him ever since Colonel Berrigan had entered. He rose from his chair and walked quickly to a large map laid out on a table.

"Okay," he said, his voice now briskly efficient, "Let's see exactly what you've got. Here's where I want you to set up for business. A little place called 'Monville.' Right here." He tapped the spot on the map with his finger.

"You'll be stuck out there on your own," the General said, watching him closely. "As you can see by the overlay, there's nothing out there now. And that damned hard-surfaced road that runs through the town leads straight back here. So we can't afford to leave it open. I think the Krauts have concentrated most of their force in this area down these two roads — one to your east and one to your west. Here...and here. But I've got some pretty heavy stuff blocking those roads — and though they've had a helluva rough time, so far they've been running a model operation. Taking some bad losses, but holding things together and giving ground slowly — considering the heavy stuff that's hitting them. I can't guarantee anything, but I think there's a good chance they can take their losses without panicking and hang on through today and tonight — maybe.

"As long as they hold out, you've got at least something on your flanks. But I can't guarantee anything on the smaller roads. You'll just have to stay alert for all kinds of catastrophes. If they get down some small road to this main hard-surfaced road that runs in your rear, they can shoot along it for miles in a few minutes. But don't try to set up initially on that road. With what you'll have, you'd never be able to hold it. Up here's where you'll have to set up — you can see why."

The General traced his finger along a line that passed through the cluster of buildings labeled "Monville." Colonel Berrigan's depressed spirits rose slightly at the thin blue line on the map that paralleled the line the General's finger was tracing.

"Yeah," the General said as he noticed the colonel's slightly improved expression. "It ain't much, it damned sure ain't the wide Missouri, but it's water — and from the jammed-up contour lines I'd guess it has banks a bit too steep for armor to cross without some help. That's all that's giving us a prayer. Because we've got to keep that road through Monville plugged. And you're the little boy with his finger in the dike — for blocking that road, and at least a couple miles on either side. And you've got to realize that, despite what the map shows now, either flank may suddenly end up hanging in the air.

So what the hell do I do after I realize it, the colonel wondered — bring it to the Lord in prayer?

He knew the General was watching him carefully, seeing how he was taking it.

Well, what the hell did he want — a few words of patriotic confidence? The hell with that noise. Colonel Berrigan knew exactly what was being asked of him and how bad the odds were — even if he were being given a unit of reasonable size. And from the hints dropped so far, that was mighty damned unlikely.

"What can I count on having for strength, sir — minimum?"

The General's mouth twisted into a tight smile.

"You asked that the wrong way, Colonel. I can't tell anybody what's 'minimum' any more. You'll have what's left of Task Force Doyle — as much as makes it back that far. They had a full tank company when they left here. God knows what they have left now. About all we can tell you is a Sergeant Bradovitch had some surviving tanks and was headed back to rendezvous at Monville. We're just hoping the hell they make it back. So never mind 'minimum.' Maybe we better talk max — and call it half a company. It damn well better be close to that — because that's the backbone of your whole task force."

Colonel Berrigan thought it best to say nothing. So this is what you gave up a soft training job in the States for, he thought. Well, you asked for it, buddy — so don't complain.

"I guess I've told you the worst," the General went on. "There's a few positives I was saving — but they're not much. First off, there'll be stuff coming back through your position. After all, there were some large units up ahead — or they were large units till they got the shit kicked out of them by something ten times their size. But there'll be a lot of bits and pieces that make it back. There always are. A lot of them will be funneled down that road through Monville. So get set up to short-stop them. They're all yours — for what they're worth."

And I can just imagine how much that is, Berrigan thought grimly.

"Now," the General went on before the colonel could reply. "I did have one platoon of Stuarts left here at headquarters. That was my last combat armor reserve. It's not much of a gift, considering your mission — but they're yours. You can pick them up on the road to Monville."

Thanks a lot, the colonel said to himself. Stuarts: high silhouettes that stick up, prominent as a barn door with purple stripes — and blessed with all the firepower of a rusty BB gun. Thanks a million.

"I know what you're thinking," the General said patiently. "But in this mess we have to make use of any damn thing we've got."

"Didn't Task Force Doyle have any of its armored infantry with the tanks?" Berrigan asked, fearing he knew the answer already.

"Their infantry lost almost all their half-tracks in an action yesterday, and I had to send them out on some supply trucks this morning to reinforce another roadblock. For infantry, I'm afraid you're stuck with what you can salvage from the stragglers. I know the problems of trying to fit stragglers into a strange unit — but at least there should be quite a lot of them. And you're authorized to attach anyone and anything that passes through your position. You may even have some artillery support. I understand there were two or three battalions still operating in your area. Though they may have flown the coop by now. Our armored artillery is all parceled out to road blocks, I'm afraid. It's crazy, but we're even at the point of using them for direct fire. I know what the book says about that — but what we've got here's not even in the god-damned book."

Colonel Berrigan was trying to absorb what he had just heard. But he kept coming back to one thing — what a mess it was going to be trying to patch together some kind of defensive force out of a collection of stragglers. After they'd been hit by a devastating panzer attack and run for a couple of days and nights, those boys were going to be a real help. He hadn't expected a perfect situation — but to start his combat career with this? His disappointment got the better of him for a moment.

"A platoon of light tanks and some infantry stragglers. How long were you figuring on me holding out, sir?"

The General looked at him seriously. "If you were a reasonably competent officer with battle experience, and I sent you up with no more than I'm giving you — about ten minutes, I guess. That's a reasonable military estimate. Only we left reasonable estimates behind us when we came up to this god-damned mess. I don't know how long you can hold out. I just know that road has to be blocked for the rest of today and tonight, and part of tomorrow. There's a fresh division moving up behind us. But the best estimate on their arrival time is tomorrow. And if a panzer column gets down that road before then, they'll cut off most of my battle groups from getting anything out — and hit that new division before they get into position. See what I mean?"

Colonel Berrigan saw what he meant. "Yes sir," he said. "I'll get up there right away and do all I can."

"Good," the General said. Then a glint of humor came back into his eyes. "We've got to use whatever we've got any way we can. You need something to fight eighty-eights and I'm giving you Stuarts with thirty-sevens. Maybe you can use them for slowing down your infantry stragglers. Oh, I have got a bit of good news I was saving for last. We just got five new T.D.'s from somewhere. M-18's. Everybody's begging for them, but they're yours. Their seventy-sixes will give you a bit more striking power against the Panthers or Tigers you can expect."

Colonel Berrigan's spirits lifted slightly.

"Thank you, sir. That will help a lot." He knew it must have been a big concession from the General, and it did make him feel somewhat better. "By the way, sir," he asked, "what are you calling my group?"

The general's tired face creased slightly in a half-smile.

"Until people get to recognize your name, I thought we might as well take a name that describes your situation out there. I thought we'd just call you 'Task Force Lone Bandit.'"

Private Lucas Hatfield raised his head cautiously and peered down the empty tree-lined road. It was a dismal sight — all dark trees and gray sky. Not a soul in sight — not even the blasted hulk of a knocked-out Sherman. But he sure knew where there were some, if anyone was interested. Straight down that road about two miles to a crossroad — he'd seen at least five that weren't going anywhere. One with half the driver hanging out the escape hatch was still burning as they hurried past. Whatever it was that had got them was long gone too. By the width of the tank tracks he'd bet they were Tigers. Lucky break seeing them tracks. At least they could tell which way the Tigers had gone and take the other direction. From the look on the lieutenant's face when he had tried to find the crossroad on his map, he didn't have any idea where in hell they were. "Couldn't find his ass with a whole roll of toilet paper," Sergeant Forte had muttered disgustedly. Not that Private Hatfield had any better idea. Starting as part of an organized battalion, they'd been fighting and then running for it seemed like a long time. And they were down to less than half a company now.

He'd tried his best to follow orders, even when they didn't seem to make much sense. There'd been a major at first giving the orders, and he at least seemed to know what he wanted everyone to do — and sounded like he expected them to do it. Then he was gone and there was only a shrill-voiced captain who gave so many contradictory orders nobody could tell what the hell he wanted. Then this lieutenant.

Earlier they'd been trying to find the spot where they were to rendezvous with some Shermans. They never did find the rendezvous. And after the German armored column got through blowing holes in them and most of the surrounding landscape, they'd lost the shrill-voiced captain, at least half the formation, and there was only the one lieutenant and his blank look when he tried to find anything on the map.

It hadn't mattered so much when the shrill-voiced captain had been in command, because Sergeant Forte had still been there. But now....

When Private Hatfield had first joined the outfit in the hell of the Hurtgen Forest, Sergeant Forte had told the whole bunch of replacements, "Just remember, none of youse guys know diddly shit, so just keep your eye on me, and when I dive for the ground, you be sure you're down there lookin' up at me before I hit. Then maybe some of you will still be alive in the mornin'."

Private Hatfield had taken that advice to heart. All during that shadowy hell of slicing machine-gun bullets and shuddering mortar explosions, he'd stuck close to Sergeant Forte, done what he was told as well as he could, and after a while he sensed Sergeant Forte was keeping an eye on him, trying to give him every chance to stay alive one more day. He didn't have to go on patrol unless Sergeant Forte was going along too, and they'd stuck close together and always made it back. Then they'd left the Hurtgen and come down here for a rest. They'd got some new replacements, but he and Sergeant Forte had continued to stick together, digging their foxholes side by side, even going back to the rest area once together.

And then just this morning as they had stopped for a breather, a shower of artillery had struck them and a tank had come down the road toward their position, machine gun spraying and cannon blasting away, and they were up and running for shelter in the edge of a forest fifty yards away, with men screaming and falling all around. In the trees they'd paused only a moment to look back at the still bodies left behind before plunging deeper into the wood. He'd made it to the trees all right, but when he looked around, a clammy hand grabbed his insides as he realized Sergeant Forte wasn't there. He'd looked wildly around for him, even started back to where the fallen bodies were — but somebody had grabbed him, told him it was no use, and the tank was now passing the bodies and coming toward them, with another three or four tanks on the road behind it. So with a terrible empty feeling inside him he had finally turned and run with the others — anywhere to get away from the earth-shaking blasts of that tank's cannon. Later they'd struck a small dirt road and followed it west

Now they were just a scattered bunch of lost-looking men huddling together, with only that lieutenant who Sergeant Forte had said....

He stopped and shook his head, as if to clear it of old cobwebs. That lieutenant had taken over only a few hours ago. And Sergeant Forte had been gone since early this morning. Yet he was sure it had been Sergeant Forte's voice he had heard telling him the damned lieutenant "couldn't find his ass with a whole roll toilet paper." The same gruff, always half-humorous voice, muttering to him as it had so often done before. Something wasn't right. But hell, nothing was right any more. Everything was wrong, and the longer it went on the worse it got.

Suddenly there was the whish of an incoming shell, followed by an explosion a few hundred yards to the left. He groaned as he heard the lieutenant's excited voice ordering them back on the road again. Wearily he got to his feet, slung the M-l over his shoulder, and joined the ragged column trudging disconsolately toward the rear.

Sergeant Bradovitch pulled the hatch of the Sherman shut above his head and rotated the turret so he could see the road to his rear. That sound of something slicing the air had probably been just a stray shot from somewhere off yonder — but just because they'd written you off back at headquarters was no reason to make it easy for the bastards.

Of course they were almost written off in his own mind as well. Not a god-damned officer left. Back there at the crossroads he'd seen Colonel Doyle's tank go up. Doyle left us in position too long, he thought. But Colonel Doyle would never have made that mistake on his own. It had to be something like a direct order to "hold your position at all costs." Probably so some god-damned rear-echelon bastards could finish breakfast and pull out ahead of them. They'd held all right — till the Krauts had got a couple of heavies around a flanking road and into their rear. Doyle must have seen them at the same time he had, because while Bradovich was putting three rounds of armor-piercing into the second one, he'd heard the gun from Colonel Doyle's tank fire twice and saw the rounds hitting the lead tank. It must have been a Panther, because the shells from the Sherman's short-barreled seventy-five just bounced off it like hail off the sidewalk. The Panther had already rotated its turret to fire, so Doyle had to hit it head-on where the armor was thickest. Luckily Bradovich had got his first shot in at the second tank while its turret was pointed straight down the road it was using to get behind them. So Bradovitch's first shot had hit his Panther in the side where its armor was thinner. He wasn't sure it had penetrated, but it must at least have jammed the turret — or maybe rung the gunner's bell so loud he didn't know which end was front for a couple of seconds. That was enough for Bradovitch to get the second round of armor-piercing off—and then a third he knew damned well had penetrated and made mincemeat of whatever was left of the gunner.

Then he'd swung over to the lead tank — only to find it had backed behind a rise and out of sight. But it had sure disposed of Colonel Doyle's tank first. Bradovitch could see the Sherman burning furiously, and only one man had scrambled out.

Just then the Kraut column they'd been holding up took advantage of the distraction in their rear to pull a go-for-broke attack straight at them. The lead tank must have been only a Mark IV because Bradovich's platoon leader got him from the front with only one shot. That blocked the roadway for a minute. But Bradovitch knew the tanks following the Mark IV would soon work around the obstruction — and the Panther that had backed into cover behind them might get brave any

Then they'd been stuck out there so far the god-damned radios couldn't pick up headquarters. So they had continued back the road they were on, stopping once on a hilltop to throw a couple of rounds at the distant German pursuit. Finally they'd got Division on the radio, though not very clear, and they'd received instructions to proceed back to a little town called Monville. An officer would meet them there with orders, they were told. And headquarters wanted to know what officer was now in command of the force.

"Don't have an officer," Bradovich answered. "Fact is, ain't got much force either."

"All right," the radio squawked faintly, "then you're in command. Until you pick up your new commander. Good luck."

Thanks a lot, Bradovich thought. You sound like Errol Flynn in a British army movie. I wonder what kind of a rear-echelon hero they're sending to chew up what's left of this miserable outfit.

"What the hell's going on?" his driver asked.

"Division's sending up Errol Flynn to lead a cavalry charge," he said grimly. "Betty Grable's going to be his loader.

"Screw Errol Flynn," his driver snorted. "You can send Betty up though. I got a load she can handle."

Bradovitch smiled without mirth and continued to watch the empty road recede behind him under the leadened sky.

2

Lieutenant Colonel Berrigan shut his mind firmly to everything except what had to be done before he pulled out for the little town he had circled on his map. Back at advanced armored school he'd always lectured his students about the necessity for "making do with what you have."

"Don't expect to have all the things the Tables of Organization and Equipment say you'll have. Much of the time you won't. Even if you start out at full strength in weapons and personnel, a few minutes of combat will change all that. Theoretically you can draw replacements for everything — men, tanks, vehicles. But outfits all around you will be screaming their heads off to replace their losses, and even if you work your way up to number one on the list, the replacements just may not be available. So in actual combat, gentlemen, scream for all you can get — but go ahead planning to complete your mission with what you've got. Because much of the time that's all you're going to get. And replacements not arriving on time is *not* an excuse for failing to carry out orders. If you've been given a mission you can't possibly succeed in with what you have available, your job is to go ahead and do your best anyhow. Then if you use all your resources well, you may even succeed. Warfare isn't a hard science. Miltary history is full of great leaders who took on the impossible and simply went ahead and did it. If you fail, you fail. Success is not a requirement, gentlemen. In fact, you may not even be able to say for sure *whether* you've succeeded. You may appear to lose everything — and your loss may have held up the enemy just long enough for the other units in the larger battle to succeed.

"But even when you think there's no hope — remember, the great battle leaders in history have been those who refused to lose hope when the odds against them were insurmountable. General Lee, gentlemen, knew the horrible odds against sending Stonewall Jackson's whole force in a vulnerable flanking march right across the front of Hooker's Union forces. But bad as the odds were, he reasoned they were his only hope for success. And Jackson didn't question the order but went ahead and did it anyhow. The result was Lee's greatest victory."

Lieutenant Colonel Berrigan had always enjoyed giving that lecture. But somehow he'd never expected to be forced to live up to it in a situation as ridiculous as this — and in his first chance at combat, too. In fact, this little action could well make up his total combat career. But he'd given the lecture, and he still thought there was an important truth in it. So now by God he wouldn't waste time bewailing the odds. He would just have to follow his own advice and make do.

He glanced down at the map resting on his lap as the jeep bounced along the rutted dirt road only a few hundred yards from the Division C.P. This side trip had been a hard decision. He wanted desperately to get up to the little town he had circled, yet he knew how easily, even on maneuvers, small units could go astray on strange roads and take hours getting to a prearranged spot. So he had decided to take the few minutes to find his meager "reinforcements" and lead them personally up to the line he was to defend. That was the only way he'd be sure they got there.

"How much farther?" he asked the sergeant driving the jeep.

"Just around that bend up ahead," the sergeant answered quickly. "If they're still there, that is."

The colonel looked at the sergeant questioningly. He was the same non-com that had not quite smothered his smile at sight of the new officer's sparkling-clean battle gear. Berrigan wondered if this sergeant was going to be such a wonderful gift after all. The General had thrown him in at the last minute — a kind of personal offering in lieu of an adequate staff.

"Oh, I'll let you take Sergeant McClanahan," the General had said as he had walked back through the C.P. with Berrigan. "He's the best master-sergeant in the Division and I hate to let him go — but you'll need him up there more than I will back here."

Colonel Berrigan had wondered how the sergeant had felt at hearing the news. His face hadn't shown any emotion. But Berrigan knew it would take a rare master-sergeant to find much pleasure in leaving a nice safe slot at Division HQ — to get shoved out in this bitter December weather into a patched-together task force under a totally unproven officer. Well, he thought, welcome to the club, Sergeant — and you're not the only member inducted today.

"You think maybe they won't still be there, Sergeant?" he asked, keeping his voice noncommittal. He'd be damned if he'd let this sergeant pry any emotion out of him.

"Well, sir — I'd say they were a gift of...questionable value. As of right now, that is."

He knew the sergeant was referring to his obvious gratitude when the General had thrown in, at the last minute, the five M18 tank destroyers. They had seemed like manna from heaven — after the General had told him how little was left of the command he was to assume.

"Just what is that supposed to mean, Sergeant? Five M18's — with the new higher muzzle-velocity seventy-sixes — they sound like a useful addition to a rather…depleted force."

"Well, sir — yes, and then again, maybe no. Not these jokers, anyway."

"And what's the matter with these 'jokers,' Sergeant?"

The sergeant smiled slightly. At least it wasn't a smile of ridicule. He actually seemed amused at something.

"They weren't exactly attached to us, sir.

"Oh?"

"No, sir. In fact, they've only been with us about an hour and a half." He paused for a moment, smiling again at some scene he was remembering.

Colonel Berrigan waited for him to go on.

"You see, sir, they came barrel-assing through here early this morning. I was driving the General back to the C.P. 'Stop the jeep right in front of these bastards,' he told me. So I did. The jeep had the General's two stars on it, and they didn't dare push on through. The General made the lieutenant climb down and tell him where he was headed so fast. Well, you ought to have seen that lieutenant try to make up a reasonable story on the spur of the moment. It's obvious what had happened. They'd been attached to another outfit up ahead. They'd only been with them a few days. The tank destroyer battalion commander couldn't have been worth much, because they'd been shifted around so often they didn't know who they belonged to. Then the shit hit the fan and outfits all around them were collapsing. There wasn't any clear line of command and they said they were forgotten — left behind and nearly cut off and only got out at the last minute by luck. You can believe as much of this as you want to — they looked like they didn't know what to believe themselves. Anyway, they had started pulling back, claimed they lost all contact with their own outfit — and you can guess how it went then. The further back they got the faster they went. Until they hit the General.

He took over fast enough. Said he had authority to attach all stragglers to his division, and he was happy to see them in such good shape, and just follow him to their new positions. They didn't like it worth a damn — but what else could they do? He had me run them up here because it didn't look like there was any other way out without going past the C.P. But you can't tell — when you get the running shits as bad as these guys had it, you don't know how ingenious they can be. Here we are, sir."

They rounded a sharp turn and Berrigan saw the M18's parked in a small cleared space in the forest. They looked in pretty good shape — the vehicles, that is. They obviously were brand new and hadn't received any battle damage yet. But the men — that was a different matter.

Most of them were clustered around smoking fires in three disconsolate groups. Some of the men were heating water for coffee, others were trying to warm themselves at the slight amount of heat generated by the fires, and still others were sitting glumly near their vehicles — staring at nothing, waiting without hope or anticipation. Their new commander saw immediately what the sergeant had meant. Turn your back on this disorganized bunch long enough for them to find a clear route to the rear — and they'd be gone. Some gift, he thought.

A tight smile was playing over the sergeant's features as Berrigan motioned for him to stop at the second fire. Damn his smug superiority, Berrigan thought. I don't know which is going to be worse — this disorganized bunch of babies, or the "best master-sergeant in the Division," with his barely concealed contempt for all novices – including, no doubt, his new commander. Well, to hell with him. There was work to be done here and they'd better get at it.

"Where's your commander?" Colonel Berrigan asked sharply as he jumped out of the jeep and stood erect before the group by the middle fire — as they were still in the process of rising unenthusiastically to stand at a lame-looking attention.

For a moment no one in the rag-tag group answered. They really were a mess, Berrigan thought. Many of the men had stubble-growth beards covering their faces, and they all had that hopeless, hollow-eyed look of men who had either been seeing too much combat — or seeing too little and worrying about it too much.

No one spoke for a moment. It was as if merely taking the initiative of speaking out first was too much for any of them. Finally a staff sergeant with the flattened face of an over-the-hill boxer roused himself to answer.

"He went...back there," he said, gesturing toward the thick trees that crowded the edge of the open space where the M18's were parked.

Berrigan glanced where he had pointed and saw nothing. He looked back at the sergeant questioningly.

"He's...he's sorta sick," the sergeant said — then added quickly, "he had to go...back there."

"Here he comes now," another man said — his voice containing just a trace of contemptuous humor.

Everyone turned to stare at the sorry apparition emerging from the trees. It was a small, almost shrunken figure — plodding along wearily, hopelessly, head down and feet shuffling like an old man in hospital slippers. He held an entrenching tool in one hand, dragging it listlessly behind him. In his other hand he carried a roll of toilet paper. Never once did he raise his head to see more than three feet in front himself.

As the plodding figure came closer, the colonel was surprised to see his face looked extremely young. He had curly, close-cropped blond hair and wore gold-rimmed spectacles with lenses so small they gave him a squinting look. His lips, though nearly as ashen as the rest of his face, had the soft slackness of a young child's. He looked barely old enough to be out of high school.

Jesus, Berrigan thought, what in hell are they sending over here now.

But there it was — the single gold bar on the shirt collar under his over-sized all-weather officer's coat. Somehow this specimen had got into (and out of) officer candidate school.

He shuffled to within three feet of the colonel, stopped when he saw the strange pair of shined boots, and slowly raised his eyes until he was staring into the face of the officer confronting him.

For a moment in his misery he failed to attach any meaning to what he saw. Then when the bleary eyes spotted the silver oak leaf pinned to the colonel's shirt, his eyes widened slightly. First the entrenching tool and then the roll of toilet paper fell to the ground. He appeared to be manfully trying to draw himself to an approximation of attention. Then, after a moment's pause, he raised his hand to salute.

"Lieu-ten't Hood..sir."

Berrigan heard two or three repressed snickers. My God, he thought, what the hell do I do with this?

But he was at a loss only for a moment. Then he snapped an answering salute and spoke sharply.

"I'm Colonel Berrigan. You've all been assigned to my task force for T.D. support. We're pulling out to go forward immediately. Do you have a full load of ammo?"

The baby-faced lieutenant blinked once, then answered.

"Yes, sir. We didn't...get to fire at anything."

"Great," the colonel replied enthusiastically. "Because in just a little while you're going to have plenty to shoot at, and you'll need every last round you've got. Now get your men march-ordered and follow me."

The lieutenant blinked twice this time, then turned to the staff sergeant with the flattened face and said in a slightly quavering voice, "March order, Sergeant."

The sergeant seemed unhappy about something. Before giving an order he spoke in a low voice to the lieutenant.

"Remember that transmission problem I told you about, sir? If we try to move that one before it's fixed it probably won't last more than a few miles. Then it'll really be shot to hell."

The diminutive lieutenant turned vaguely toward the colonel, obviously not sure what to do.

"It's perfectly all right, Sergeant," Berrigan said confidently "We're going to need every gun in this action. It hasn't got far to go. If the transmission goes out, you can tow it with one of the other T.D.'s. I'm sure you can get it up there somehow. And you don't have to worry about getting it back. So snap to it. Have your lead T.D. follow me. And Lieutenant, you bring up the rear. I don't want anybody dropping out. Drag, push, or pull — do anything you have to, but just be sure they all get there. Now let's go!"

"Let's go-oh," the young lieutenant tried to echo with equal force, though his voice cracked right at the end.

Colonel Berrigan jumped into his jeep, turned to see the men piling onto their T.D.'s, and motioned to Sergeant McClanahan to take off. I sure do get the luck of the draw, he thought. And this is supposed to be the best part of my outfit.

"Stop here," Colonel Berrigan said sharply to his driver. They had just passed a demoralized group of eight or ten infantrymen plodding toward the rear, backs hunched against the wind driving the cold into their frozen joints. He had been too preoccupied with the immensity of his task to be much aware of the miserable conditions the foot-soldiers would have to fight in. But he knew he'd better become aware of it in a hurry. He had somehow to construct a defensive position out of flotsam and jetsam like these pitiful creatures. He knew he couldn't take the precious minutes to get these men turned around and moving forward. With no transportation to take them with him and no organized unit for them to join, he was sure within minutes they would have reversed directions and once again be fleeing toward the rear.

But when he reached his intended position, he would have to take fleeing men as miserable as these or worse — and somehow get them to stand with him against terrible odds. And just how was he to accomplish that little miracle?

There had to be at least some temporary — respite if not actual reward — to offer. Something to once again make them see themselves as soldiers capable of action other than panic and flight. Well, he had to hope he would find some leaders capable of getting such hopeless-looking specimens to rise to the occasion. But first of all he had to find something to stop their mad rush to the rear. And that was when he had seen the line of two-and-a-half-ton trucks pulled off to the side of the road. He knew it was a long shot, but considering the lack of alternatives, he had to grasp at it and hope. So he had told the sergeant to pull over and stop by the lead vehicle.

He jumped out of the jeep and ran to glance inside the first truck in the column. By God — he had been right! And if these were more fleeing trucks the General's men had stopped, he could surely use what some of them were bound to have.

"Get this truck ready to roll," he shouted at the two men standing in the back of the truck and looking at him dazedly. The piles of unopened boxes crammed into the bed of the truck convinced him they might be just what he needed for his little miracle.

Before the dazed men in the truck could protest, he had spun around and was shouting to Sergeant McClanahan, "Get me a quick rundown on what each truck is carrying."

"Yes, sir," the sergeant said, leaping out of the jeep and starting back along the column as he took a notebook from his pocket.

"We have to be getting back to our outfit — " a hesitant voice spoke up behind him. Colonel Berrigan turned and saw it was a pudgy-looking captain speaking. He had obviously been riding in the cab of the leading truck. Berrigan wondered what had kept this obviously reluctant warrior from following his clear desire to be barreling toward the rear. It had to be someone with a lot of rank. Remembering what the master-sergeant had told him about what had stopped the T.D.'s head-long retreat, he took a stab in the dark and prayed he was right.

"Is this the outfit the commanding general had pull over to await his orders?"

"Uh...well...yes, but I didn't get a chance to tell him how important it was for me to get these vehicles back to their battalion headquarters — "

"The Commanding General sent me here specifically to make sure some of your vehicles were diverted to a mission of the greatest importance," Berrigan said reassuringly, taking a chance the general would approve his slight embellishment of the truth. Then he noticed the captain glancing at the silver leaf on the colonel's shirt and come grudgingly to a rather sloppy attention.

"I have orders to get these trucks back to — "

"At ease, Captain," the colonel snapped, as if too pushed for time for such formalities. He figured the best way to handle this pudgy-faced joker was fast and furious — with no time for questions. "I've just talked to the General about your column," the colonel went on quickly. "We're lucky you made it here — and just in time, too."

" Sergeant McClanahan," he added quickly as the master-sergeant came running back from his mission," what have we got?"

"Kitchen truck and seven supply trucks, sir. Each one pulling a trailer. One truck carrying new clothing — mostly socks, some underwear. Three trucks loaded with gasoline. One truck with boxes of rations, and one carrying miscellaneous company gear. One truck loaded with mostly small arms ammo."

"The trailers?" Colonel Berrigan asked quickly. The captain's mouth was beginning to move in protest but no sound had yet emerged.

"All loaded with gasoline cans," the sergeant replied.

"Filled or empty?"

"All filled, sir.

"I'll be needing most of that gasoline for our trucks when they — "

"Right," Colonel Berrigan said. "The General and I figured to leave you enough for that. Now, here's what the General wants. Let me have a page out of that notebook, Sergeant."

He took the page the sergeant hastily tore out and handed him, placed it against the door of the captain's truck and made some quick notes.

"This is a crucial operation, Captain. Top priority. Now, I'll need the kitchen truck, the ammo truck, the one with socks and underwear, and the truck with the rations. I probably should take all the gasoline too — but I'll just take the four trailers loaded with gas cans and try to make that do. You can keep the other four trucks under your own control. Here's the authorization. The General said to be sure to give a receipt for what I needed. So in case anyone questions your actions, this gives you a full seat of ass-cover. Sergeant, tell the drivers of our four trucks to pull out and follow us when we pass. Thanks a lot, Captain, for being so cooperative. The General won't forget it."

"But I have no — " the captain began.

"Don't mention it," Colonel Berrigan said graciously, as if he thought the captain had been about to thank him. "This is a crucial time — firm control of all units is required. Your trucks and drivers will be playing an important role in the defense being set up. Carry on, Captain."

The colonel started to raise his hand as if answering an expected salute. The captain had to rush to get his hand up to salute before the colonel's answering salute. Then the captain's mouth moved in continued protest — but no sound came out.

"All right, men," Colonel Berrigan shouted back at the vehicles behind his jeep, "let these four trucks pull right in behind me, then you all follow."

He jumped into the jeep as Sergeant McClanahan raced back from notifying the supply-truck drivers. The colonel raised his map board to study it carefully, as if he had already screened out the captain and all other local distractions to concentrate on his more important combat problem.

"This is very irregular — " the captain muttered in hopeless protest, looking down at the scribbled paper he'd just been given, and then raising his eyes to stare at the colonel despairingly. The colonel smiled, waved briefly, then like John Wayne at the head of a cavalry column in a Hollywood movie, drowned out the captain's protest with a dramatic "F'ward, HO-ooo!" Sergeant McClanahan pulled the jeep out to pass the column of trucks. Colonel Berrigan glanced back to see the four trucks he wanted pull out one by one to follow him. The five M18 T.D.s came close behind, while the pudgy-faced captain stood bewildered, his lips still moving in soundless protest as the vehicles roared past.

3

Sergeant J. C. Washington watched as the six cannoneers struggled to dig out the huge tires on the wheels of the one-five-five howitzer. He'd been trying to free up the artillery piece for the last forty-five minutes. They'd had it free for a moment — then it had slid off to the left and into another muddy morass as bad as the one they'd just freed it from.

He was desperate for time. They'd been given march order forty-five minutes before, and he could already hear the tractors of Able Battery pulling out onto the main road.

They said the damn Krauts were coming right down this road — and nothing much to stop them. The cannoneers had been stealing worried glances down the road all morning. Little clusters of infantrymen had been rushing past on the road ever since dawn. A few of them, hurrying by, would glance down into the draw where the guns were located. But most of them just trudged along with their heads lowered, their backs hunched under the weight of their loads. They didn't see or care who was down in the draw.

But he knew what the few who looked down at them would be saying.

"Hey, look at those scairty-ass niggers down there. Eyes big as saucers. Jeeze, do them black bastards wanta shag ass. Gun stuck or unstuck — you ain't gonna hold no scairty-ass niggers around here f' long."

They were too far away for him to hear — but he knew what they'd be saying. And though he'd long ago accepted it and written it off, the thought of it could still make his eyes burn with tears of shame and anger.

They had claimed they were forming all-black combat battalions. Not rear-echelon outfits, like they were putting all the other blacks in. Strong backs and weak minds —that's how the army classified them. His great-grandfather had told him, when he was a little boy, how there had once, long ago in the Civil War, been whole regiments of black soldiers — real soldiers, infantrymen. His great-grandfather had been one. He'd charged forward with the others of his regiment in the brave, mad attacks against the gray-clad lines. He'd even been wounded outside Petersburg, and been given a medal for "gallantry under fire" in the face of the enemy.

His great-grandfather had told him about it. He'd been a very old man then with bleary eyes and a back that wouldn't straighten up properly. As a boy JayCee had told his friends about it, but they wouldn't believe him. "They din't let no niggers fight in that war," they had told him, so he'd tried to look it up in the history books, but even though the books told a lot about gallant men standing bravely under the burning sun at Little Round Top and the Sunken Road — never was there one word about Negro troops as a part of that gallant band.

He felt sure his great-grandfather had been telling him the truth, but he never could prove it to anyone. He'd had to take it on faith. And when the old man had finally died, one bitterly cold and rainy winter day, JayCee had known what he was going to do. That night he stole into the "whites only" cemetery, searched around in the scary dark until he found a grave with one of them on it. He knew it by the feel. Hard cold iron underneath —still holding the faded flag placed there on Decoration Day. He knew no one would believe him if he asked for one in the proper way. Because that was one of the "everyone knows" things. "Everyone knows" the niggers didn't fight in any war. "Everyone knows" a nigger might get into a fight with another nigger over a woman or a bottle of whiskey, and maybe slice that other nigger up with a razor. But stand proudly in line of battle with white men? Who you kidding, boy?

So he'd stolen that flag and flag-holder from the white soldier's grave. Hell, they could always get another one to plant over him. But they'd never believe it about his great-grandfather, so he didn't even ask, he just took the damned flag and a few nights later sneaked in to stick it up on the new-mounded earth beneath which his great-grandfather lay. In peace, he hoped. If that's what soldier-heroes did. Or if they lay there fighting again those glorious moments of shell-shattered heroes — then his great-grandfather would be fighting right alongside them, as he had the right to.

That's the way he had thought of it then. And even though he had grown up and left those crazy dreams behind him, when the war came he'd tried to enlist in a combat outfit.

"Go on home, boy," they'd told him indulgently. "They'll get around to drafting you sooner or later. Put you in one of those quartermaster or engineer outfits. Rear-echelon. Have yourself a real good time, and no danger getting your ass shot off."

They'd finally drafted him — but he'd found out about the few special all-black "combat" outfits being set up, and he'd got into one.

Of course they weren't "all-black." That is, they were —

except for the officers. Those had to be white. The Army had been willing to try out a few selected black soldiers in special "combat" outfits. But "everybody knew" they had to have white officers. After all — would you trust one of "them" to command men in the heat of battle? So it wasn't as he had hoped — it sure wasn't like his great-grandfather had told him. The white officers were mostly from the deep South and knew how to "handle niggers" and keep them from getting biggity ideas.

But he had worked to master the simple details of firing and caring for the big one-five-five howitzers, he'd kept his mouth shut and his bitterness to himself, he'd played the game of "soldier" so they couldn't fault him — and they just had to make him a chief of section.

He didn't think Lieutenant Ransom really wanted to. That was one white officer JayCee really had no use for. Vain, foul-mouthed, always trying to prove he was a tough son-of-a-bitch — but JayCee suspected he'd cave in among the first if things ever got rough. He was a tall man with the beginnings of a pot-belly, and his face had that soft, doubled-chinned look of a man who liked his ease too much.

And though JayCee had always kept his mouth shut before him, Lieutenant Ransom must have felt the contempt this "uppity nigger" had for him. The lieutenant would have prevented this 'uppity nigger' from ever being promoted if he hadn't been more interested in saving his own ass. The lieutenant was having all kinds of trouble with his fourth section and had been really reamed out by the battalion commander after a bad error on a firing problem. The gunner had dropped a hundred mills in elevation and the shell had landed a thousand yards short of the target — and only a hundred yards away from a group of visiting dignitaries observing on a hill-top. Scared the shit out of them, and they raised so much hell they scared the shit out of Lieutenant Ransom. So in desperation he'd made JayCee chief of section. And his problems with the fourth gun section suddenly ended. JayCee knew more about that damn howitzer than anybody else in the battery — including the captain himself.

But JayCee knew Lieutenant Ransom had no feelings of gratitude toward his new chief. If anything, he resented the fact that he'd had to give in and promote an uppity nigger to save his own ass — and to continue to depend on him for inspections and field problems, and finally in combat itself.

So they'd struck an uneasy truce. But there was one thing Lieutenant Ransom could do to show he was still in the driver's seat. JayCee was his best chief of section and certainly should have been given the staff-sergeant rank that went with the job. But JayCee was still just a three-stripe buck sergeant. The lieutenant had wanted to "reserve judgment" on him until he had "definitely proved himself." That was what JayCee knew he had told the captain. And JayCee was sure he was going to withhold that one little stripe as long as possible — just to let JayCee know who was still top-dog, no matter how well this uppity chief ran his section.

As if JayCee gave a shit about his one little extra stripe. JayCee was going to go through this war in a way to make his great-grandfather proud — if there was any way the old man could know how his great-grandson was following in his footsteps. That was what mattered — what the old man knew, and what JayCee himself knew. Not what some weak-faced horse's ass of a white officer thought. He could take his extra stripe and shove it, as far as JayCee was concerned.

"Haven't you got that damn thing out yet?" a voice behind him shouted.

JayCee didn't have to turn to tell whose voice that was. But what surprised JayCee so much was the edge of panic in it. Lieutenant Ransom was obviously as desperate to get out of there as any of his "scairty-ass niggers."

JayCee turned slowly to look up at the lieutenant sitting in the right-front seat of the executive officer's jeep.

"We had it coming out once, sir," he said in that carefully neutral voice he always used with the lieutenant. "But the slope was too much, and it just slid off again toward that depression."

"Well, for Christ's sake hurry up. Able Battery's already pulling onto the road. The colonel wanted us to go next, but because we couldn't get ready, Charlie Battery's going in our place. The word is we've got to fall in right after Charlie — ready or not. What we can't get out we'll just have to leave. You got maybe five minutes more. Then we're hauling ass with what we've got."

"I'm sure we can get this piece out," JayCee said, trying to sound confident. The task was a real bitch — but he knew he could get it out somehow, if they'd just give him a little more time.

"I don't give a shit what you're 'sure' off," the lieutenant said, his voice breaking slightly. JayCee knew what that was for. The tough-talking Lieutenant Ransom was scared shitless of being left behind and getting his ass shot off by a Kraut panzer.

"Hell," the lieutenant went on, "I don't think you'll ever get that thing out that way. Hitch the god-damned tractor onto it and goose it for all she'll take."

"I don't want the tractor hitched onto it while it's hanging there right on the edge. If it starts sliding down again she's liable to go over the edge and right into the draw — and pull the tractor over with it. That bank's too steep and slippery — I don't think the tractor can even get traction enough to keep itself from going over."

"Well, Jesus — if that's the way it is, we'll just have to go off and leave it. Able Battery had to leave two of theirs. Charlie

Battery says they'll have to leave one too. If you can't do it, throw a damn thermal grenade down the tube, and load your men up and let's go."

JayCee hated to have his struggling cannoneers hear this. They were scared enough already — they didn't need this horse's ass getting them into a panic. They wanted out as much as the lieutenant did.

"This is a valuable weapon," JayCee said, trying to keep his voice calm. "The Army ain't going to take kindly to it if we run off in a panic and leave it. Not when I feel sure I can get it out."

The lieutenant glared at him. He'd like to be pissed off at me, JayCee thought — but he's too busy being scared of what may be coming down that road.

"All right," the lieutenant said, his voice strung so tight it quivered on the last word. "We're getting out of here. If you want to try one more time with the tractor, go ahead and do it quick. Otherwise get your men loaded and pull up to the road. That's a god-damned order, Sergeant. The battalion's having to abandon three guns anyhow — so we'll make it four. It's better to save the crews and the tractors than nothing. So hop to it."

"If we hitch the tractor to it now it's sure to --"

"I told you that's a god-damn order, Sergeant. And one more bitch out of you and it's going to be 'Private' Washington."

Jesus, JayCee cursed disgustedly to himself — so now we've got to lose a fifty-thousand-dollar howitzer *and* a prime mover. Just to prove you're at least not scared to give orders to a nigger.

Boiling inwardly JayCee had the tractor back up to hitch the gun on. Just the motion of raising the trails to attach the gun to the prime mover almost started it sliding into the draw.

The struggling cannoneers finally managed to complete the job with the gun slipping back only a few inches more.

"All right," the lieutenant said. "Let's get loaded up and pull it out."

"Wait a minute," JayCee said hastily as two of the men started to climb onto the tractor. "Nobody get on that tractor until we see what's going to happen. If the damn tractor goes over, we don't want a gun crew crushed under it.

JayCee didn't wait for the lieutenant to approve. Getting a bunch of men killed for this bastard's stupid vanity is just too god-damn much, he thought.

"Everybody stand clear," JayCee continued quickly. "And Vince, pull it ahead ver...y slow. Don't jerk it. If the tractor starts to go over, you take off over the high side. Jump as clear as you can — but be damn sure you don't go off the low side. If you do, that damn thing may come right down on top of you.

"No sweat, Sarge," the tractor driver answered cheerily. JayCee knew Vince was a damn good driver and had enough sense to jump clear. But JayCee didn't like this worth a damn. And if he had to lose his gun and prime mover, he didn't want any crushed bodies under that god-damned mess.

"All right," the lieutenant said testily. "Don't get everybody in a god-damned panic before they even start. Now let's see if she'll come out. Goose the bastard."

"Easy now," JayCee cautioned, raising his arms and gesturing for the driver to pull ahead slowly. He didn't want Vince to pay any attention to that stupid-ass lieutenant's chattering. "Slow...steady...easy does it now."

The tractor strained forward, the tracks digging in enough to move a few inches forward. It looked as if it might even work — the gun wheels couldn't grip but were sliding forward slightly in the muck. Another few inches and the gun's tires could get purchase enough to pull the howitzer out.

"Okay," the lieutenant shouted triumphantly. "You got it! I knew if you stopped all this stalling — now give the bastard full throttle!"

JayCee had been watching the wheels carefully. He knew it was still touch and go. "Easy does it—" he started to warn. He knew Vince was not dumb enough to follow that lieutenant's order.

But maybe the lieutenant's shout had made the driver step down harder on the gas than he had intended. The motor revved up just slightly — but that was enough. The tracks began to spin without getting a purchase, the tractor began to slide...slowly at first, then more...then the limbered cannon slid back a full foot, stopping just short of the drop-off, with Vince helplessly gunning the motor. Then the wheels slipped back another six inches, dropping over the edge onto the very steep part of the slope.

JayCee knew it was all over.

"Gun it! Gun it!" the lieutenant was shouting hopelessly.

"Set the brake, Vince!" Jaycee shouted loud enough to drown out the lieutenant's silly chatter. "Cut the motor and get the hell out of there! Now!"

JayCee was glad the driver heeded his command. Vince set the brake, reached up to turn off the motor, and clambered up over the heavily tilted right side of the prime mover. He slipped backward as the gun and tractor together began the inexorable slide backward.

"Get over that damn side!" JayCee shouted desperately. "Now! Jump clear!"

Vince reached again for the side, pulled himself up on it as it tilted nearly horizontal, got one foot up and over to stand on the tilted outside panel, got his second foot over the side panel and pushed hard with it against the side. Then as the gun and tractor tipped fully on the side and slid over into the draw, he jumped, one foot catching against the track and making him stumble, his other foot coming down on the track. Then lunging, pushing with both hands and feet, he was suddenly clear of the whole mass of stricken metal, landing just at the top of the steep part of the slope and starting to slide back. JayCee caught one arm and pulled him up and onto the safe ground.

"Good boy, Vince," JayCee said softly, putting an arm around his shoulder and patting him briefly.

"I almost had it, Sarge," Vince said disgustedly.

"I know," JayCee said reassuringly. "It was god-damned stupid to make you try it —and you almost did it anyway."

"If you had just goosed it when I told you!" the lieutenant shouted, "you could have had the god-damned thing outa there. Now get your men loaded up Sergeant, wherever you got room. We're getting the hell outa here!"

The lieutenant looked down at the sergeant and saw him glaring up with angry eyes. The officer started to speak, hesitated, then turned quickly to his driver. "Let's go!" he ordered. The driver put the jeep in gear and raced it up the slope to the road.

There was a moment of suspended silence among the cannoneers. JayCee knew they wanted out of there as badly as the lieutenant did. But they had all stayed and done their best. Now it was right they should get out with the others. It was all over. They'd had a chance to get out as a good combat outfit should — *with* their guns. Not like "scared niggers " — leaving their weapons in a mad rush for safety to the rear. But now there was nothing for it but to go ahead and leave them.

He glanced down into the draw. There they were — prime mover and gun, still hitched together and lying on their sides.

A thought suddenly came to him. Was it still possible...?

"You thinking what I'm thinking?"

He started slightly at the voice behind him. Turning he saw

the short, square-bodied motor sergeant standing behind him. Sergeant "Hooley" Jenkins was, in JayCee's opinion, the best non-com in the whole outfit. JayCee knew Hooley had badly wanted to be assigned to a gun crew when they got into combat. In fact, he'd told JayCee that the captain had promised him he would be. But the captain had got too used to depending on him for handling the motor pool during all those training inspections. Now there was no one else the captain would trust with the job, and so Hooley had been screwed. "What a god-damned war," Hooley had told JayCee recently. "All I'll have to tell my kids about is how many times I saved the captain's ass on Saturday morning inspection."

Now he was looking down at the lost gun and prime mover with interested eyes.

"I suppose it's a long shot," JayCee answered "And the orders are to pull the hell out of here — before the god-damned Kraut tanks come barrel-assing down the road."

"Supposed shit! You got the guts to try it or you ain't?"

JayCee felt his heart surge upward at Hooley's snorted question. By God, there were some men — niggers or no — who could still measure up to his great-grandfather.

"Hell, yes, you ol.' black son-a-bitch. I got the guts. But can we do it? That's about a twenty foot drop — more than forty-five degrees. And they're both tipped over on their side."

"Shit! That just makes it a little more fun. What d'ya say?"

JayCee felt as if something had blossomed in his chest.

"I say all right, god-damnit. Let's do it. But what do we use? I saw the battalion wrecker go past already. All our other tractors are waiting up by the road. That god-damned lieutenant wouldn't let us use one anyhow. He's only interested in saving his ass."

"He has to be," Hooley grinned. "It ain't worth a damn to nobody else."

"When you get through the big talk," JayCee reminded him, "you got to have something to work with. You got anything?"

"I got my own three-quarter ton."

"So you gonna pull a gun up outa a damn canyon with a three-quarter ton, when the only reason it's down there is a god-damn tractor couldn't even pull it up?"

"Hell, yes, I'm gonna. An' you're gonna help me."

"Well...all right, then. Just let me get these men some transportation outa here."

He turned to the cannoneers who had been standing and watching them. "All you men take on up the hill. Pile on the kitchen truck, the supply truck — whatever has room. Hurry up and you'll catch them before they pull out. If anybody asks, Sergeant Jenkins and I'll be along later."

Jaycee was surprised to see nobody moved.

"Hurry up," he urged. "You just got time. Otherwise you got a long walk —.with maybe a Tiger tank's eighty-eight shoved up your ass."

"How 'bout we ride outa here on the Sarge's three-quarter ton — like you two?" one of the cannoneers asked.

"Yeah," a second man added. "How come you bastards get all the fun?"

JayCee looked over at them in surprise. He knew they were all good cannoneers, no goldbricks and game to do their share — but he also knew how anxious they had been all morning to get the hell out of there while there was still time. He could tell some of them were still nervous — but now nobody seemed to want to be the first to go.

This was a little beyond his expectations. What was getting into them all of a sudden?

Well, never look a gift horse in the mouth, he told himself. And what makes you think you're the only nigger with a great-grandfather — or great-somebody-else to make proud? Maybe you're as bad as all those white soldiers going by on the road, looking down here and making their cracks about scairty-ass niggers.

"Okay," he said, feeling suddenly light-headed. "Anybody wants to go, get on up to the road fast. But if you stay here you're gonna get your ass worked off — or shot off, one. And maybe," he added with a grin he couldn't suppress, "what the hell — maybe both."

4

Colonel Berrigan glanced down at his map and checked the position of the major crossroad they had just reached. The road he had been traveling was narrow but hard-topped. The intersecting road was obviously a major highway — much wider, its asphalt surface smooth and in good repair.

"I want you to remember this crossroad," Colonel Berrigan said to his sergeant. If he'd had even a minimal staff he could have left a field-grade officer here with responsibility for this major crossroad. But at the moment all he had for staff was the enigmatic (and probably resentful) Sergeant McClanahan.

"Sir?" the sergeant answered — his voice far from friendly, but well short of insubordinate.

"Our position is going to be only a couple of miles down the road," the colonel said, "and I damn sure don't like this major highway running behind our position. It means if anything collapses either to our left or right, a few panzers can shoot down the damn thing and have us cut off in a few minutes. What the hell is that coming down the road?"

Colonel Berrigan stared at the two strange-looking vehicles which had just heaved up from a dip in the road about three hundred yards to their left.

They were tracked vehicles — that much was certain. Beyond that, it was anybody's guess. They apparently had objects tied outside the vehicles — but a huge tarpaulin was pulled over the top and down the sides of each, so that the bundles tied to the sides bulged under the tarpaulin like a woman eight and a half months pregnant.

"It's American, I guess," Sergeant McClanahan said doubtfully. "That's about all I can say. Looks like a god-damned Barnum and Bailey's circus wagon. If those are tentpoles, that is."

He was referring to the long pole-like devices which were suspended horizontally the length of the vehicles but completely concealed by the tarpaulin.

The vehicles proceeded steadily toward the colonel's column stopped at the crossroad. Colonel Berrigan decided he wouldn't be much surprised if either of them suddenly blared forth with the loud reedy whine of a steam calliope. Circus wagons were as good a guess as any.

The first vehicle continued to within five feet of the colonel's jeep and pulled to a stop. Down from it jumped a tall, gangly creature as strange-looking as his vehicle.

The colonel could see that his smudged and greasy coveralls bore on the arms the insignia of a master sergeant.

The man had a long, cavernous face with hollow cheeks puffed out in one spot by what must have been a wad of tobacco. He wore wire spectacles under a shock of unruly, greasy brown hair. In his left hand he carried, apparently unconsciously, a huge wrench.

Arriving before the colonel's side of the jeep, the gangly creature drew his bony figure up to an exaggerated attention.

It was a pose he obviously wasn't much used to striking, as every bone and joint seemed to want to slouch, and his head naturally bent forward so he could look down from his lofty height on whomever he was talking to.

As a final touch of military formality, the apparition raised his bony right arm in what must have been intended as a salute — though it was a motion the arm was apparently unused to, and the whole operation came off a little more like a dirt-farmer putting his hand to his head on a hot day to wipe off the sweat.

"Sergeant MacKay, sir, reporting as ordered."

The colonel stared back a moment speechless — before he remembered to bring up his own arm to return the salute. His surprise must have been readily apparent, for the sergeant rushed on to further explanation.

"That is..." he corrected, "they didn't tell me exactly who I was to report to. But I was told to get these two babies ready if I possibly could. So we worked all night on 'em — and this morning we find our god-damned Ordnance Company pulled out and left us sometime during the night. Just as well, I guess. From what I hear's going on, these babies'll be more use up here than wherever the hell that Ordnance Company ran to."

"Just what are these 'babies,' Sergeant?" the colonel asked hopefully

"Experimental models, sir. Regular M18 T.D. chassis. Only these babies can take on any damn Tiger they got. I been tellin' 'em for a long time they oughta stop puttin' out pop-guns when they need an elephant gun. So they let me try out a couple to see how they work."

"And just what do these 'babies' mount, Sergeant?"

The sergeant drew himself up and spoke with all the pride of a new mother anouncing the birth of sextuplets.

"Ninety millimeters, sir. Got 'em from an AA outfit."

"Sergeant," the colonel said quickly, "welcome to the First Ordnance Testing Range — ETO division. You and your babies have struck a home. Have you got crews for them?"

"I kept a few of my own men, sir. All volunteers. They know more about these guns than any damn AA mechanics — theory *and* practice. And when it comes to firing these babies, I'd back 'em against any tank or anti-tank men. Anyhow, I don't think anybody else'd know how to operate these babies. I had the steering mechanism apart on mine and didn't have time to reassemble when somebody said the Krauts were comin' in the other end of the village. So I had to take off steering with this here wrench. But it works fine — long's you know where to put it and how to turn it. I hope you're not one to be too fussy what branch of the service we come from — long's we can do the job on those Panthers and Tigers."

"Fussy we're damn sure not, Sergeant. You and your 'babies' have struck a home. Just pull in at the end of this column and we'll be only too happy to give you an ideal testing grounds."

"Thank you, sir," the gangly man said enthusiastically. He turned and ran back to what the colonel still thought of as his "circus wagon."

"All right," the sergeant yelled as he threw his huge wrench up into the vehicle and clambered after it. "No more rear-echelon, you guys — we joined up with a fightin' outfit."

"We're sure getting a wide diversity of personnel in this task force, sir," the sergeant said, his voice screened to reveal only a mild amusement. "I'd hate to see a chart of our Table of Organization."

Colonel Berrigan wasn't sure how much derision lay under that amusement.

"We're going to look like a god-damned circus, all right," the colonel agreed. "But what the hell — it's how we fight that counts. And I just might be willing to bet that elongated Huckleberry Finn will pan out top-quality in a tight spot. But let's go before somebody comes along with a lion act or a cage full of monkeys."

"Yes, sir," the sergeant said, shoving the jeep into gear and leading the strange column across the intersection.

"Tanks !"

Private Lucas Hatfield felt the cold hand close around his insides again at the panicky cry.

"God-damnit! Tank's coming up behind us! Take cover!"

Private Hatfield saw it was a sergeant doing the shouting this time. But this was no Sergeant Forte. You could see this man was so filled with fright all he could do was holler and run.

Private Hatfield found himself racing with the others for the doubtful safety of the tree line ten yards back from the road. It wasn't a planned move. Even as he ran he knew what was pulling him — the terror in that first shout of "Tanks!" and then the fear-stricken sergeant stoking the panic with his useless words. He ran past the first few trees and threw himself prone on the wet ground. He lay there for a moment, shoulders hunched and expecting to hear the crashing blast of a tank shell exploding nearby.

Nothing happened.

He held his breath, waiting.

Still silence — then he heard the panting wheeze as he finally let his desperate lungs suck air.

"Tanks hell, they're only Shermans," the voice came, as if from a great distance — yet somehow directly into his ear.

His racing heart slowed and some of the panic seemed to wash out of him. He began to squirm around so he could see the road. He looked carefully along it, back in the direction from which they had come.

The road was empty. The infantry had scattered at the first shout and were now hidden among the trees. Everyone had been as ready to panic as he had. Maybe more so. That was a strange thought. Since his first time in combat — weeks, even months ago now, maybe it was — he'd always seen himself as the most terrified replacement in the outfit. It had always been just stick close to Sergeant Forte and hope to hang on somehow, however bad it got. But now suddenly he began to realize that the fear and panic was not all his. Nearly everyone felt it. Even some of the sergeants — like that terrified one he had seen echo the panicky tank warning a few moments ago.

Well, he'd never had any illusions about being a hero. He knew the thought of having his body blown to bloody bits or ripped by machine-gun bullets made him cringe inside. But all that time with Sergeant Forte had made him aware that there were things that had to be done, you couldn't just cringe in a hole, as much as your body cried out to let it. And if you kept tight hold of yourself, it was possible to make yourself do those necessary things even as your body screamed in protest.

His glance fell on a crumpled body a few feet to his left. For a moment he almost thought it was dead — it lay so still in such an awkward position.

But he saw the shoulders shudder slightly — then the whole back moved at the intake of a gulping breath. After a moment the head turned and he caught a glimpse of a young face squinched into a tight mask of fear.

He heard the tank motors on the highway approaching fast. A moment more and they were racing past. He made himself look at one, saw the short-barreled gun, the markings on the turret.

"It's all right," he shouted, his voice filled with a sudden relief. "They're only Shermans."

He put a reassuring hand on the hunched-up figure lying beside him.

"It's all right now," he said reassuringly as the face looked up at him and the eyes flicked open for just a moment. "They're only Shermans. Let's get back on the road."

He rose, picked up his Ml rifle, then grabbed the soldier lying beside him by the arm and helped him up. He could feel the arm tremble under his hand. He noticed how young the face was. Now that it had begun to relax from its tight mask of fear it looked to be hardly more than the face of a boy. And as the young soldier raised a trembling hand to adjust his helmet, Hatfield saw the curly shock of tow-colored hair spill out.

"It's okay," he told the boy again. "Just Shermans. We better get back on the road."

The boy followed him automatically — almost, he thought, like that old dog when I first found her, just a puppy, wet and cold and skinny as a rail fence. She was so damned happy to find somebody who gave a damn, she went running around and jumping up on me and acting half crazy for joy. The two of them walked slowly back toward the road.

Others were stirring now and beginning to come out from among the trees. Private Hatfield looked ahead where the front of the column had been. No one was moving up there yet. He walked a few steps in that direction and saw the lieutenant — still hunched up on the ground and hardly stirring.

Without thinking Hatfield walked over to where he was lying and, after a moment's hesitation, placed a hand on the lieutenant's shoulder. The lieutenant slowly turned his face so he could stare up at the soldier who had touched him.

Private Hatfield's first impulse was to draw back. Officers had played a very small part in his experience — he had been in awe of them. But this one seemed as scared as all the enlisted men. He was staring up at Hatfield with nearly blank, fearful eyes.

"All right now, sir," Private Hatfield screwed up enough courage to say. "Just some of our own Shermans."

The lieutenant slowly raised himself on his hands and knees. He grunted something unintelligible that might have been an expression of gratitude or displeasure or even shame. Private Hatfield thought it best to turn away and walk with his companion back to the road.

He hardly knew what to make of all this. He did know he had been panic-stricken like all the rest — at first. But something had pulled him out of it. Then he remembered the voice in his ear.

Yes...it was all very funny and didn't make any sense. He was sure he had recognized the voice in his ear. Yet he knew that could not be. He'd left Sergeant Forte's lifeless body lying in that field miles behind them. Was he going loco?

As the infantrymen were assembling in a ragged column, Hatfield noticed a small sign by the side of the road. It pointed straight ahead and read simply "Monville 4 Kilometers."

Lieutenant Clarence Huntington Stallingsworth, U.S. Field Artillery, was disgusted. He was also cold, tired, and nearly asleep on his feet. But most of all he was disgusted. He'd been watching infantry units break up for a long time now, and whenever he had arrived on a scene where he could have helped them out and plastered some beautiful targets with his battalion's one five fives, the damn battalion was "displacing to the rear." Or they were so far back already his radio couldn't reach the battalion Fire Direction Center. But now maybe things were finally going to be different.

He had just convinced the leader of a small infantry unit he should leave his men in position in their roadblock for at least another few minutes. He'd done it by promising that his battalion of one-five-fives would devastate any tank attack coming down the road across the long half-mile stretch of open ground in front of them. The infantry lieutenant had been trying to get permission to withdraw for over half an hour. But he'd had trouble getting through to his commander. He'd been about to withdraw on his own. "Bastard's gone off and forgotten all about us," he had muttered loud enough for the artillery lieutenant to hear.

But Lieutenant Stallingsworth had been desperate to bring his one-five-fives into action. He had been late in getting shipped to the European theater. His OCS class had graduated in the spring, well before the Normandy invasion — but he had been posted to a division that had been doing so poorly in maneuvers the higher brass had obviously decided it was not ready for combat duty. No one knew for sure whether it would be shipped in the very near future, or merely cannibalized for replacements. So D-Day on Omaha Beach had found the lieutenant still fighting the battles of the Tennessee Maneuver Area.

After D-Day he'd given up on that outfit and concentrated on trying to get shipped out as a replacement. But nothing had gone right. His commander had been trying to keep his best people from leaving — and when it came to adjusting fire in difficult terrain or under adverse circumstances, Stallingsworth was clearly the best observer he had.

After the lieutenant had cajoled and threatened for a transfer to a replacement depot, he was held up again: first by a sprained ankle, then by an abscessed tooth, and finally by his whole group being quarantined after exposure to measeles.

Only then had he finally managed to get himself shipped to England — but on a former United Fruit Lines banana boat that had to be put in the slowest convoy available so it could keep up. Arriving in England in October, he'd found the replacement depot chock-full of artillery second lieutenants. It had turned out that the casualty rate for forward observers had not been anywhere near as bad as it had been in North Africa. So it had been the beginning of December before he had finally arrived at the outfit with which he would go into combat.

It was a separate battalion of corps artillery, and the commander was a somewhat over-age national guard officer — a cautious man primarily desirous of living through the war and escaping charges of incompetence.

Despite all the commander's caution, his first firing position had been squarely in the middle of the big mid-December German panzer attack. With no experience in combat (and little desire to gain any at first hand), the colonel had nearly been caught in the sudden German advance. Just barely escaping with all three firing batteries intact (though leaving behind many hundreds of rounds of ammunition in the rush to safety), his goal now was to "displace to the rear" many miles ahead of any perceived threat. And in this, at least, he had been having marvelous success.

Consequently Lieutenant Stallingsworth, eager to send his battalion's hundred-pound shells in waves of supporting fire for some hard-pressed infantry unit, had not once to date been able to fire his guns on a real target. In fact, his firing experience had been limited to adjusting the guns on a crossroad just once — so successful had the commander been in keeping his guns well back out of range. And just as it looked as if enemy traffic would soon be coming through the crossroad, the lieutenant had received a message to move back, as the guns were soon to "displace to the rear" again.

But here at last the lieutenant thought he had his opportunity. The battalion was in position where their guns could reach; he definitely had radio contact with them; and he had just picked up in his B.C. scope a glimpse of a small column of armored vehicles passing over a ridge some distance behind the open area in front of him.

So the nervous infantry lieutenant had agreed to stay at least a few more minutes — on the promise of having available instant and heavy artillery support to counter any panzer attack that might come charging against him.

Lieutenant Stallingsworth had already made his plans. He knew using medium artillery to hit armor racing down a good highway was not considered a high-percentage game. But he had found a spot on that open stretch of highway — about halfway to their position — where he was sure any approaching tanks were going to have trouble. The road had been raised slightly to pass over a culvert, through which ran a small stream of water. If he could block that one spot, the panzers would have to leave the highway and try to cross the rocky little stream that spread out on both sides of the culvert. The land was not only rough and rocky in places, but much of the area was obviously a wet morass. Heavy tanks would have trouble navigating there if they had to leave the road.

So he had sent back his fire commands to adjust on the spot and was awaiting the first round when the message crackled from his radio.

"Cease fire on the problem, Baker Three. We just received orders to displace. Pulling out now. Advise your pulling back too."

The infantry lieutenant looked over at him with disgust.

Stallingsworth's stomach seemed to drop a foot. Not again!

This time he thought he had had it for sure. And a large German tank was just coming over the top of the rise a half-mile away.

"No!" he yelled despairingly. He grabbed the microphone from his driver and shouted into it. "No! Not now! There's plenty of god-damned time to shoot this mission first. It won't take more than a couple minutes — and you can have a chance to blow up a whole column of Jerry panzers. Just hold on a couple minutes!"

There was a moment's silence. Then the answer came back clearly.

"Sorry, Baker Three. March order's already been given. Able Battery guns already limbered. Others about to hook up."

"Well...hell, *un*-limber them, for Christ's sake! Or at least shoot with Baker and Charlie. You can't just go off and leave these people up here without support!"

"Sorry, Baker Thr -" came from the speaker, followed by a number of crackling noises. A voice in the background said sharply, "Give me that thing." Then an older, more authoritative voice spoke up.

"This is Valiant *Six*, lieutenant. *Six* speaking to you. You have received your orders. Obey them. And I never want to hear you disregard radio discipline like that again. In fact, I think it would be best for you to return to your battery immediately. This is the final transmission you will receive from this position. That is all. Over and out."

Lieutenant Stallingsworth stared despairingly at the dead mike in his hand.

"All right, we're pulling the hell out of here!" the infantry lieutenant shouted to the men clustered around him. "Pronto. Those tanks are going to be here in a few minutes, and we can't take them on all by our lonesome. The god-damn artillery's running already — and they're probably five or ten miles behind us. Let's go!"

"Want me to try one round on the lead tank?" the gunner behind the roadblock's anti-tank gun asked.

"Hell, no!" the lieutenant shouted. "That's a god-damned Tiger tank. Your little fifty-seven'll just bounce the hell off —

and they'll answer you with an eighty-eight down your throat. Let's go!"

Lieutenant Stallingsworth's jeep driver looked at him questioningly. "We taking off too, Lieutenant? Nothing we can do here, is there?"

The lieutenant tried to swallow his diasppointment. "Yeah — I guess we might as well. We'll try again as soon as we find out where they're going into position."

"Valiant Six said for us to return to the battery," the driver pointed out diplomatically.

"No," Lieutenant Stallingsworth said, trying to sound confident. "He didn't *order* us to return — he said he thought it would be *best* if we did. That means it's what he *thinks*, on the basis of the information he has available. Worded that way," he said in what he hoped was a convincing explanation, "he means do what he says *only* if events on the ground don't indicate another action would be better."

"Okay," the jeep driver said. "If you say so, Lieutenant. It's your ass."

Lieutenant Stallingsworth examined his map closely, looking for a likely spot for an O.P. He wondered how far back the colonel would take the battalion this time. And where would a resistance line be likely to form? Perhaps, he thought, by that little river a few miles back. The road he was on ran back and crossed the river — right at a little town called "Monville."

5

"Okay — slow and easy, all together when I signal. Stop immediately if I give you the cut sign. Are you ready?"

"Ready here, JayCee," Sergeant Jenkins shouted from his three-quarter-ton a few yards away.

"All set," Vince yelled. "Now all you guys pull together when I tell you," he added to the cannoneers standing in line holding the rope.

JayCee and Hooley Jenkins had talked it over and decided this was their best bet. The main power source they had was in the winch coiled to its drum at the front of Hooley's three-quarter-ton. The army had figured it had enough power to pull out stuck vehicles — but they probably hadn't figured on such a small vehicle handling anything as big as an MS tractor.

"It just has to have enough power to tilt the tractor back upright," Hooley had said. "Never mind pulling it out. That comes later."

"The trouble is," Jaycee had said, "that damn gun on back.

Jammed in and turned over like that, the men'll never be able to uncouple it. And with all that weight behind it holding it down, either the tractor won't budge — or it may pull upright but tear the gun hitch all to hell. Then we might save the track, but we'd have to leave the gun. And the real point of this, Hooley, is we want to save that god-damn gun."

"We'll save your god-damn precious gun, JayCee. Trust me." Hooley's voice sounded both exasperated and amused at the same time.

"Okay. How?"

"Look," Sergeant Jenkins explained patiently. "We'll put an A-frame beside the tractor and run my winch cable to the A-frame. We'll run a chain I got in my truck from the A-Frame down to the side of the tractor. I know damn well I got power enough to tip it upright. Now...I got some heavy rope in my truck too. We'll tie that to the gun, then put all your cannon-eers along that rope. We got enough muscle to tilt the gun up — while you synchronize the pulling, so they both come up-right together. No strain, no sweat. I tell you, Jaycee, it'll work."

So they had done it. In less than fifteen minutes they had cut off two heavy branches from a tree, lashed them together at one end, cut two smaller limbs for the cross-pieces of the A — one on either side of the larger branches — and then posi-tioned the frame so when the top of the A was pulled upright, the chain running down to the underside of the tractor would gradually pull the whole vehicle over onto its tracks. At least, JayCee thought, that was the theory.

He saw the cannoneers were standing ready on the rope running over to the huge gun. It was time to throw the dice and pray.

"Okay...now!" JayCee yelled, bringing his arm down sharply.

Hooley gunned the motor of his three-quarter-ton and the

winch-cable began to tighten.

"Pull, you puny bastards," Vince yelled at the straining can-noneers, as he himself pulled till sweat burst out on his fore-head.

The slack was pulled out of the winch-cable and the A-frame began to quiver as the strain was transferred to it. One leg of the A-frame began to slip a little—then slid into the hole provided for it. Hooley was watching the frame and tractor carefully as he let the cable continue to tighten around the winch.

Meanwhile the cannoneers had already pulled so the gun was beginning to turn upright.

"Ease up a little Vince," JayCee shouted. "Let the winch catch up to you."

"Hold it steady, you ninety-seven pound weaklings," Vince shouted. "Wait till all the horses in that machine catch up."

The winch cable was now taut, and the top of the A-frame was a foot off the ground. It moved up another foot, then an-other. Then the chain running down to the tractor was pulled tight and for a moment everything stood still.

Then slowly, quivering all the way, the frame rose higher. The chain, stretched tight, pulled against the tractor. For a moment everything seemed suspended. Hooley gently in-creased the power to the winch...the tractor shuddered...then slowly began to tilt upright.

"More power on the rope, Vince," JayCee shouted. "Hurry! The damn thing's going to make it."

"Get your backs in it, you black bastards," Vince shouted, as he strained along with the cannoneers.

Then suddenly some point of gravity was passed, and trac-tor and gun came upright together, with the gun bouncing slightly as it landed on its huge rubber tires.

"Hold it, everybody!" JayCee yelled joyfully. "Stop the winch, Hooley. Hold the rope steady, Vince. See if she'll stay up."

The noise of the motor pulling the winch cut to a steady drone and the taut rope from the cannoneers to the gun slackened. The tractor shifted slightly — but stayed upright.

"We got it!" JayCee yelled. "She's going to stay up."

"Okay," Sergeant Hooley Jenkins bellowed. "God-damn, I knew we could. Now...we just gotta pull it outa there."

JayCee walked up to join Hooley by the tractor.

"How we gonna do that, Hooley?" JayCee asked. "You gonna take your winch off and try to use that? That's a lotta weight, straight up that twenty, twenty-five feet."

"I got to leave my cable on where it is — so she don't tip over again," Hooley said. "Here's what we're going to do. Vince, can you get in that thing and start it up again?"

"Hell, yes," Vince said confidently. "I don't think she damaged anything — just slid back and over easy."

"Give 'er a try," Hooley said. "Careful where you put your weight when you get in—so she don't tip again."

They watched as Vince clambered over the side held up by the A-frame. Next he slid into the driver's seat, and a moment later they heard the starter grind...and then the motor roared to life.

"She's good as new," Vince yelled. "What next?"

"Here's the story," Hooley shouted over the roar of the motor. "I want you to let your winch-cable out a little. Then when I get aholt of it you pay it out as I carry it up the slope."

"Right," Vince said. "You gonna let it pull itself out?"

"That's how we're gonna do it. While my winch holds it from the side to keep it from tipping again. And JayCee, you keep the cannoneers on the rope so that gun don't tip — and then the whole god-damn contraption's going to pull right out of there in one piece. We got the hardest part done, fellers. Just trust me."

JayCee only then became aware of the glowing sensation he must have been feeling for some minutes. Jesus — this was the way it was supposed to be. Why did they have to be stuck with "leaders" like that horse's ass Ransom?

Then suddenly he noticed how quiet it was up on the road. The steady traffic that had been rushing past had thinned — until now the road stretched past them, quiet and empty.

There it was, finally. Just a clump of lumpy old stone buildings clustered together on a low ridge just ahead. So this, Colonel Berrigan thought grimly, is to be the scene of my indoctrination to the real thing. My Saratoga, my Gettysburg, my...Waterloo, maybe?

Something about the setting — the drab ugliness of the buildings, the forlorn-looking landscape lying barren and lifeless under the dull gray December sky — struck him as a fitting scene for a hopeless, destructive "final battle." Now I know how King Arthur must have felt, he thought, when the final day of battle dawned, and he knew Camelot was already a vision of the past.

The little town was only a half-mile ahead. And he could see, even at that distance, the plodding little figures of infantrymen scattered along the half-mile of road to the town. They didn't look like organized units — just a sparse scattering of individual figures, looking neither right nor left, heads down and eyes fixed on the ground a few feet in front of them. Was this to be the stuff of his command — men he was supposed to weld into a solid unit, confident and capable enough to hold back hordes of German tanks and infantry rushing forward in an irresistible blitzkrieg?

Well, no time for such speculations now. Wallowing in the futility of it all was a luxury he couldn't afford. It was a hell of a mess — but it was his mess, and he'd better get busy seeing what to do with it.

It was fortunate the platoon of light tanks the general had sent up had stopped short of the town. Colonel Berrigan had gathered them up as he went past, and all five were now in line directly behind him.

"Hold up, Sergeant," he said to his driver, jumping out of the jeep the moment it stopped. He walked quickly to the first tall Stuart tank behind him and shouted up to the tank commander, who was riding with the hatch unbuttoned, his head sticking out of the turret.

"Who's commanding your platoon now, Sergeant?"

"I am., sir. Lieutenant Bartlet's been gone on sick leave."

"Okay, here's what I want you to do. Detach one tank under a trustworthy non-com to stay behind while you take the rest of your platoon with me into town. The moment we get there, here's what you do. Proceed through town and set up a block at the bridge over the river on the far side of town. Never mind for now about the enemy. It's the friendlies we've got to stop first. Have you got that?"

"Wilco, sir."

"Fine. Now, you're to stop *everything* crossing that goddamn river. It should be easy — all the traffic will be funneled across that one small bridge, and you'll have four tanks they have to get past. You're to hold everything, vehicles and men, right on the main street by the bridge. If there are any officers still in charge, tell them Lone Bandit Six has a blanket order to attach *all* units passing through this area to his command. And he expects immediate compliance from *all* personnel. And the tanks are there to see he gets it. Is all that clear?"

"All clear, sir. What do you want my other tank to do?"

"He's going to sweep up all the stray pieces he can of those who have already crossed the bridge and are coming down this road. Tell them they're to go back to the village — where they'll get some hot food and dry socks before they do anything else. It's going to be a tough job — it looks as if a lot of these men are just strays without anyone in command. The tank commander can use whatever baits and threats he needs to herd them back into town. I'll have things ready to handle them there. Then he can report back to you at the bridge. Any questions on all that?"

"No questions, sir. I'll leave Sergeant Judkins here. He's a good man."

"Excellent, Sergeant. Carry on."

The colonel wondered if the Sergeant Judkins would succeed in shepherding many of the retreating infantrymen back into town. He didn't expect much — but he had to try for all he could get. The big thing was to get that block at the bridge in just as fast as possible. With everything funneled across the one small bridge — and four tanks to block the way — there was a good chance of salvaging a high percentage of whatever came by. He just had to hope there were still a lot of sweepings left up ahead.

But that's the trouble, he thought grimly. Sweepings — that's all they are. And how in hell can I make a functioning unit out of beaten, discouraged "sweepings" with their morale down around their ankles?

That, ol' buddy, he told himself, is why they gave you a commission and called you a "leader of men."

"Let's go, Sergeant," he said to his driver. "I want a quick look-see at our future battleground."

A few minutes later the colonel was driving past the first few buildings of the town. It looked deserted — except for the few soldiers plodding doggedly down the main street. At the near end all traffic seemed to be funneled toward the main street which ran through the center of the town. Further down the street he saw the town widened so at the mid-point it was three or four blocks across. The old stone buildings he passed, hunched down over the narrow main street, caused a perpetual twilight even at mid-day.

It wasn't much of a town — scarcely three hundred yards long. And this was "Monville" — or so the sign outside the town had stated. Not a very impressive name for a place of heroic deeds. But then again, he thought grimly, the military force defending it is not exactly impressive either.

He glanced back at the strange assortment of vehicles following him in a straggling column. First came the four awkward, high-silhouetted Stuart tanks, with the ridiculously skinny barrels of their thirty-sevens jutting forward pugnaciously as if they were capable of real armored combat. Then came the formidable M18 Tank Destroyers. With their seventy-six-millimeter high-velocity weapons, there was hope for them. Except for their not-so-formidable leader, he thought, as the image of the baby-faced, blond-headed lieutenant, bearing his entrenching tool and roll of toilet paper, reappeared etched in his memory. How could men with no more leadership than that ever be made to stand and slug it out with Panthers and Tigers?

Far back he saw the bulky kitchen and supply trucks round a corner and follow the column like two giant waddling ducks — thin-skinned, vulnerable, hopelessly out of place here in line of battle.

And then came the piece de resistance, chugging along at the end — Sergeant MacKay's tarpaulin-wrapped, pregnant-looking "circus wagons." "Experimental models" indeed, manned by their rear-echelon ordnance crews — men without a minute of combat duty between them.

And this was the "crack outfit" he had hoped to build his combat record on. Jesus — what a laugh.

But "you don't fight a war by waiting for the right circumstances to come along," he'd always told his students. "You take the circumstances you get the first time around, and fight 'em like they're the last you'll ever get – which they well may be." The words seemed vapid and pretentious to him now. How had he had the gall to stand up there and pretend to tell them what "combat command" was all about?

Well, pretentious or not, those words had their element of truth. And he would have to live up to them now — not just strike poses in a lecture hall.

"Pull over here," Colonel Berrigan said sharply to Sergeant McClanahan. "We'll put our C.P. in that building there," he pointed to a large, solid structure of rock and cement — obviously some kind of public room, perhaps a tavern.

"Now," he continued quickly, "I'm going to climb up in that church tower over there for a quick look around. I want you to take charge of getting this column off the road and into temporary positions. Here's the way I want it.

"The light tanks are taken care of — their block will be right here by the bridge. Tell the T.D.'s to pull off the road and in among the buildings — but not far in. And those two big circus wagons should stop outside of town where it's high enough to cover the open area across the river. That leaves the trucks. You tell the sergeant in charge of the kitchen truck to immediately — *immediately*, that is — find a building near the backend of town that's big enough for feeding a large group of men. He can cook inside or outside — but I want those men to do their eating *inside*. And I want it warm inside there — tell him he can use fireplaces, stoves, whatever he can find. And if he can't find anything he'll just have to unload his cooking stoves and do his cooking inside. That'll provide heat enough to take some of the cold misery out of these pitiful-looking foot-sloggers

"Then as soon as he's set up he's to start cooking. Something good and hot and lots of it. Better tell him to make it pancakes. Lots of 'em with plenty of butter and that thick Karo syrup. Everybody gets all the hot coffee they want. Too bad we can't throw in some sausages too. Hell — maybe he can fry up a lot of spam. Spam they've always got lots of, and hot-fried with pancakes, even that's edible. Tell him this is no one meal and out. He's going to have men coming by here for hours — and every man that passes through is entitled to hot food, and plenty of it. They're going to be cold and hungry and tired, and he's going to be the warm little haven for them all.

"And we're going to see they work the bill off afterward?" Sergeant McClanahan asked with a grin.

"They'll pay the bill all right," Berrigan said grimly. "But that's not his concern. He stops 'em, feeds 'em, gets 'em nice and warm and sleepy. We'll take it from there."

"Yes, sir," the sergeant answered crisply. "After I finish, you want me to find you in the church?"

"No. Start setting me up a C.P. in that building I showed you. I'll join you there after I get a look-see at what the terrain is like for this little battle coming up."

"Roger, sir."

The colonel picked up his map and field-glasses and strode toward the church across the street.

He quickly climbed the steps that led to the church tower. Judging by the number of infantrymen straggling back he still had some time left — but there was no telling how much. He might be hit by the first German recon elements within an hour. That would be really tough. Two or three hours would be better.

Inside the tower he found small openings for observation on all four sides. He saw the view across the river to the east was especially clear and unobstructed.

The church was the last building on the eastern edge of town, and a hundred yards past it was a bridge, under which flowed a small srtream -- little more than a creek, really, but apparently swollen with recent rains and bordered by banks a little too steep for tanks to ford. By God, he thought, I have that much luck anyway. He would have to stake a lot on that little bit of water and those steep banks.

The terrain to the east past the bridge was generally open and nearly flat—as far as a ridge at least a half mile away. And the road from the bridge ran straight across the open space and up the low ridge. The terrain beyond the ridge was hidden from view, except for a further ridge which jutted up behind it. Just a small ribbon of road was visible as it passed over the further ridge. He glanced at his map and estimated the valley between the two ridges must be a thousand yards across. Not too bad, he thought — at least so far.

Next he turned his attention to his flanks. For about a quarter-mile on either side of the village the land was open and gently rolling. Beyond the open space on both flanks evergreens stood darkly watching against the lead-colored sky. Not much chance for tanks there, unless there was a road through the forest. The map showed none — and he could only pray the map was right. No time to check now. The creek fortunately went all the way across the open land, perpendicular to the main street of the village. A small dirt road paralleled the near side of the stream. This "creek road" turned back toward the rear at the edge of the forest on the left. But on the right the map showed it crossing the stream and angling off toward the southeast. That was a danger point. He couldn't see the spot from where he was observing, so he wasn't sure if there was a bridge — but there was obviously a crossing of some sort. That and the main bridge east of town had to be covered right away. That's where the German tanks would come. They'd try the main bridge east of town first — then, if he could stop them there, they'd try around by that other crossing to the south. If it was only tanks, his little force might hold out for quite a spell. But the Krauts had been playing this game for a long time, and they'd almost certainly have infantry there soon. And there was more than a half-mile of open country to cover — at any point of which infantry could walk across that creek.

From where the forest began, a quarter-mile away on either flank, he could see nothing but trees covering hilly terrain. He studied his map carefully, looking for all possible avenues by which tanks could work around his position. Judging by the often close-together contour lines and the lack of any roads through the trees, there was not much chance tanks would try to outflank him. The nearest good parallel road on the left was at least four miles away, and the one on the right looked to be at least three.

Well, he thought, you've had the good news. Now let's get busy with the dirty work.

6

JayCee Washington was feeling great. He knew it was crazy, but that was just the way he felt. Here they were, with probably nothing left between them and the German panzers — who might in fact be about three minutes down the road — and it was the first time since he had joined the army that he felt he wouldn't mind his great-grandfather looking down and seeing what he was doing.

Staying behind to save that howitzer had been the best thing in the world for all of them. Before, the cannoneers had been so nervous and worried about getting out in time they'd lost all sense of pride in their outfit, in themselves even. And now here they were with four perfectly good one-five-five howitzers the battalion had abandoned — all pulled out and sitting by the road, ready to be towed away.

He didn't know whether Hooley or he had first suggested trying to pull it off. But when they had finished pulling their own gun up to the highway he and Hooley had paused a moment, looking down on their previous position.

"Jesus — look at them two A Battery guns," Hooley had

said disgustedly. "I bet they didn't even half try to get them out."

"A Battery commander's a real gutless wonder," JayCee said. "I heard he once tried to crawl up to the forward OP — just to say he'd been there, I guess. I know two of the guys on the OP crew. They said he got within fifty yards — crawling on his belly, even though everyone else was walking around like it was summertime at the beach. Then a shell came in about three hundred yards away — and ol' Captain Barstow, he sorta spun 'round on his belly without even getting up and just scuttled off like a damn crab. They said he must've set a new record for belly-crawlin' the hundred meters. And the OP never saw him again. He wouldn't care how many guns they left behind — long's he got his ass out fast enough.

"There's that one Charlie left behind, too," Hooley said, pointing down at a howitzer whose trails were sunk in a muddy ooze.

"Hell, they coulda put a counter-weight on the end of the tube and it woulda raised those trails right up," JayCee said, spitting contemptuously.

They had been silent a minute. He remembered that.

Then they had suddenly turned to each other and burst out together: "God-damn, how about we—"

They had stopped, stared at each other a moment — and then their excited laughter had spilled forth.

"You think we got time?" JayCee had asked.

"Shit, I don't see no panzers yet. We could leave one man here for a look-out — he could see back there more 'n a quarter mile. We could still have time to shag ass."

"If we could get them out," JayCee said, hearing the joyful excitement in his own voice, "we could pull one with your three-quarter-ton — and Vince can pull ours with his tractor. What would we do about the other two?"

"Who knows?" Hooley said. "Maybe — like my ol' mammy always said — maybe the Lord will provide. They might be anything could come by here yet. Even a god-damned jeep would do in a pinch."

"God-damn it then," JayCee said decisively, "let's give it a try!"

"You just convinced me," Hooley had said. "So what're we waitin' on?"

Just like that. And their what-the-hell spirit must have been infectious — because not one of the cannoneers had objected. In fact, they had turned to with more spirit than JayCee had ever seen them display.

It had been a snap. The C Battery gun had come right out with the tractor's first try. And A Battery's first one had come out after they'd pulled its trails loose with the tractor. Only the last one had held them up. That had been a bitch and they were thinking they would have to leave it. They couldn't get a vehicle in where they could hook it up. They were thinking of trying the winch — when one of the cannoneers said, "Shit! Everybody grab aholt and we'll manhandle the god-damn thing out."

And that's the way they did it. So now they had all four guns up by the road — and only two vehicles to tow them with. And none of them had been seriously disabled — JayCee was sure he could have them in firing condition in less than fifteen minutes.

"Jeez — I sure hate to leave any of 'em," Hooley said. "After we brought them this far."

"Too bad we couldn't tow two with one vehicle," JayCee said. "That tractor would pull 'em. But I can't figure any way to hook the second one on."

They were all silent a moment. JayCee knew they would have to do something soon — or they'd lose them all. They couldn't have much more time left. If worst came to worst they'd have to dump a thermal grenade down the tubes of the two extra guns — that would keep the Krauts from using them, anyway.

"Hey, here comes something."

It was Eustis Crump, JayCee's gunner corporal, who had shouted. They all turned and looked where he was pointing. There just emerging from the trees a quarter-mile away was a small cluster of soldiers — and in their midst were not one but two vehicles.

"My eyes ain't so good," Hooley said. "What are they?"

JayCee peered at them closely.

"Both jeeps," he said.

"Hell, jeeps is good enough," Eustis said.

"Only trouble is," JayCee said, "one of them jeeps is already pulling a gun. And looks to me like they're a roadblock that decided to take off. The damn Kraut tanks probably aren't far behind them."

"Well," Hooley said, "let's get everything out on the road ready to go — and we'll see what kinda deal we can strike."

In two minutes they had everything loaded and ready— except for the two guns without vehicles, which they had dragged into the road just in case they could work something out.

The jeeps were moving at the speed of the walking men, and it seemed to JayCee to take forever for them to arrive. Because the soldiers were plodding along with their heads down, most of them didn't even see the waiting artillerymen until they were a few yards away.

When they did see them, it created quite a sensation.

The leading soldier, an infantry private, lifted his eyes, looked — and stopped dead still. The words that came from his surprised lips seemed pulled out by some external force.

"Jesus — they hadda bring up the boogies! Things must really be shot t' hell."

Anger flared up in JayCee. Hell, he told himself savagely, forget it. He's no worse than all the others. He doesn't know we're even hearing him. He probably doesn't think we understand English.

JayCee searched through the other soldiers quickly and saw what he was looking for sitting beside the driver in the first jeep. Though he was a very disconsolate-looking leader at the moment, he wore a single silver bar on his shirt collar. Clearly he was in command.

JayCee stepped up to the jeep and saluted smartly.

"Excuse me, sir. We're trying to save some one-five-five howitzers that were left behind. We got them all out — but haven't any vehicles to tow two of them with. We were hoping you could help us out. Just back far enough so we can get word to our outfit to send some tractors up for them."

The lieutenant, who had been riding along with his eyes closed and his head nodding, looked up at him, startled. He obviously didn't know what to make of these black faces in a forward combat zone. JayCee didn't like the distressed look that came over the officer's features. It was almost, JayCee thought, as if he was *annoyed* by this interruption of his despondent thoughts.

"Well, we can't — we have to — "

The lieutenant finally pulled himself together enough to get an answer out.

"Hell, we can't fool around with this rear echelon stuff. There's five panzers right behind us. We got to set up another roadblock. You'll have to leave them. Throw a couple grenades down their barrels. We gotta get outa here."

JayCee felt his former excitement turn to sick disappointment. Then a thin flame of anger flashed through him.

"Sir, these are very valuable weapons. These men all stayed behind to get them out. And we can save them with just a little effort from you — "

"Sergeant," the lieutenant flared up, hearing the anger in JayCee's voice and apparently not liking it, "we've got orders to carry out and we can't fool around with your god-damn guns. Now get — "

"Just a minute, Lieutenant. I think I can help out here."

JayCee looked around to see who had spoken. It was another lieutenant — this one much taller and more self-assured. He wasn't like any lieutenant JayCee had ever seen. He looked more like a studious college student. It must have been the heavy-rimmed glasses he wore. But there was something about him that JayCee liked. Maybe it was the direct, interested way he looked at you when he spoke. This one, JayCee thought, is not always busy trying to convince everyone he really deserves those bars. It was more like the bars and the rank didn't matter that much, either.

JayCee turned to him hopefully.

"If we could just get two guns towed even a short way — we can handle it all right then. Maybe two or three miles will be enough."

"Hell, can't you see," the first lieutenant spoke up quickly, obviously not liking anyone questioning his decision. "Can't you jokers see I already got a gun on back here? You want us to throw ours away and tow yours?"

"That won't be necessary, Lieutenant," the officer with the owl-eyed glasses said quickly, his voice soothingly polite. "I have a hitch on my jeep — and I'm not towing anything." Turning back to JayCee he added encouragingly, "You can hitch one of them to my jeep. I'm from a one-five-five outfit too. It's a long war, and we're all in it together."

JayCee didn't wait for the first officer to queer the offer.

"Thank you sir. Eustis, have the men hitch one of the guns up to this officer's jeep."

"Just raise it up and my driver will back up to it," the owl-eyed lieutenant said.

"Well — you can do what you want with your jeep," the first lieutenant grumbled. "I got to get on with this gun. That's my responsibility."

"We ought to do anything we can to save these guns," the second lieutenant said, his voice pleasantly polite. He knows he has to baby this other one, JayCee thought. Why in hell do so many officers have to be such god-damned little pricks?

"Well — god-damn it, I'm responsible for this gun of mine."

"You're right there, of course," the owl-eyed lieutenant agreed. "No question, your gun is your first responsibility. I was just thinking if there was some way we could save *both* guns."

The first lieutenant looked back at him blankly. After a moment he muttered defensively, "Hell, there's only one hitch on this jeep. So there's no god-damn way we can put two guns on it."

"I know what we could do," a hesitant voice spoke up. JayCee turned and to his surprise saw it was one of his youngest cannoneers — a new replacement barely five feet tall with open, babyish features. He looked embarrassed now as everyone turned to stare at him.

"Go ahead, Wally," JayCee said encouragingly. "Give us your idea."

The baby-faced Wally swallowed down his embarrassment and spoke up with a voice that quivered only slightly.

"We could hitch the big howitzer to the lieutenant's jeep and — "

"I told you I got to haul my own god-damn gun!" the lieutenant flared up immediately. "And we can't afford to fart away any more time here. Let's go!"

"But we could take them both!" little Wally fairly shouted in desperation. "The jeep could tow the big gun — and that little fifty-seven...why, a few of us could manhandle it well enough to keep up with a walking speed."

JayCee and Hooley looked at each other in surprise. Of course! It was damned hard work — but if the cannoneers were game to try it....

"By God, we could do it at that," JayCee said. "Good thinking, Wally. I don't know why we didn't think of it before. We got enough manpower to relieve the manhandlers every few hundred yards."

"That little pipsqueak don't look big enough to manhandle a pea-shooter," the first lieutenant said contemptuously. "To say nothing about a fifty-seven."

"We got plenty to handle it," Billy Bascomb, the tallest and strongest of the cannoneers, said confidently.

"That gives me an idea," the owl-eyed lieutenant broke in quickly. "You got lots of power in that heavy tractor there. But it's already towing a big gun. So you just tie a rope to the big gun, run it back to the little fifty-seven. Then you fix a cross piece so four men can hold the trail-end up off the ground—and let the rope pull the little gun along. All the men have to do is hold the trails up."

"That's it!" JayCee burst out. "And if it doesn't balance easy, we'll just put little Wally part-way back on the barrel until the trails lift up by themselves. The men on front will just have to keep it balanced."

"No sweat, by God!" Hooley said, slapping his thigh

loudly. "All right, you strong-backed, weak-brained cannon-eers. Heave to just like the lieutenant said."

A few minutes later they were proceeding down the road, the vehicles going just fast enough to stay ahead of the men on foot. The little fifty-seven cannon, the diminutive Wally astride its barrel and two cannoneers holding up its trail-end, was bobbing along behind the huge one-five-five howitzer like a tiny duckling following its proud mother.

Colonel Berrigan watched from the window of the C.P. as the sad-looking column of infantry straggled into town and halted at the square. They hadn't come back on the main road — otherwise the Stuart tanks would have stopped them at the bridge. They somehow must have come in from the west end of town. Then he realized they'd probably been on the main road two miles to their rear — but when they'd come to the junction with the road leading to Monville, the leader must have turned east rather than west. A sorry-looking crew like that had to be trying to retreat from whatever "front" was left. But the leader had taken the wrong turn — the one leading back toward the enemy —and ended up at Monville.

"Go find the commander of that bunch of infantry that just came into town," Colonel Berrigan said to Sergeant McClanahan. "Tell him the 'local commander' wants to talk with him for a minute."

"Yes, sir," the sergeant said, grinning appreciatively. "He must be a dumb son-of-a-bitch — to take the wrong turn back there, and then to keep on coming against the flow of what-ever stragglers got by us. And then to call a rest halt right out-side our C.P. Someone ought to file suit against the Army for putting a dumb klutz like that in charge of men 'fighting for the glory of their country.' "

"I don't see much over there that looks like 'fighting men' — for glory or anything else," Berrigan said.

"Excuse me, sir," the sergeant corrected, his grin widening. "I mean 'men about to die for their country.' They look like they might just barely be capable of that."

"Don't look a gift horse in the mouth, Sergeant," the colonel said, wondering just how much this highly-recommended non-com could be depended on. "And we better hope for a few more dumb klutzes to come by and turn the wrong way. Otherwise you and I are going to have a hell of a time holding off those Panthers and Tigers, all by our lonesome."

"Yes, *sir*. Reprimmand duly noted." The sergeant strode quickly toward the door. adding as he did, "Praise the Lord for dumb klutzes — and please send a bunch more this way."

The colonel watched through the window as the sergeant approached a dejected-looking lieutenant seated on the sidewalk and staring intently at his map. The sergeant stepped up to the lieutenant, snapped a quick salute, then spoke briefly, motioning toward the C.P. across the street.

The lieutenant, with the delayed responses of a man moving underwater, was still trying to return the sergeant's salute when McClanahan had already finished speaking. The lieutenant looked up at him dazedly, raised one hand to scratch a high, balding forehead, then folded his map and climbed wearily to his feet. Sergeant McClanahan turned smartly and walked back across the street to the C.P. The lieutenant, still moving with those same slow underwater motions, rose and followed him.

Colonel Berrigan remained staring out the window until he heard the door open. He turned immediately and spoke before the lieutenant could assemble his slow-moving joints into an approximation of attention.

"Welcome to Monville, Lieutenant," the colonel said, his voice brisk and friendly. "Your troops have been assigned to me. We've got a little problem here, and I want your help in solving it."

Private Lucas Hatfield had watched the back of the lieutenant walk across the street and into the building. So what happens next, he wondered. He'd long ago given up interest in what the people who gave the orders decided. Whether it was good or bad, wise or stupid, it wasn't the deciders who had to carry it out. It was him and the other footsoldiers sitting lifelessly now on the sidewalk or spilling over onto the street — they were the ones who would have to carry out the orders. And wise or stupid, when the orders were carried out some more men would get killed. Like Sergeant Forte got it this morning. And after you found out whether you were among the killed or the living, they lined you up and marched you somewhere else and it began all over again.

Somehow he had never felt so lost when his own sergeant was there. Sergeant Forte had never worried about whether the higher-ups' orders were wise or stupid. "Just assume all them bastards are stupid," he'd once told Hatfield when they had been resting between stints on the line. "Then you may be wrong once in awhile, but you'll damn sure be right ninety-five percent of the time. Wise or stupid don't matter to grunts like you 'n me, Hatfield. Our job's to follow their god-damned orders and try to stay alive in the process. Just remember, it don't matter much to them whether you're alive or dead. With them it's all percentages. 'We gotta take that town, captain — we figure ten percent casualties, maybe fifteen. If it takes twenty, maybe even twenty-five — hell, Corps won't like it but tough shit, captain, we gotta take that town.' We're all percentages down here below field-grade, Hatfield. You got no choice. You gotta follow orders. You can't get around that. But what they can't stop you from doing is trying like hell to stay alive while you do it.

And this morning Sergeant Forte hadn't been able to do it. This morning he had become one of the percentages. Hatfield realized it didn't change much of anything. But it sure made all the difference in how he felt about it. Combat had always been a confused, frightening blur to him — but always before there had been the calm, slightly amused presence of his friend the sergeant to give a glow of warmth to it all, however bad the situation. Now it was not only a confused blur, but cold and lonely as well.

He suddenly heard a sound that didn't fit into his surroundings. At first he didn't even recognize what it was. Then he heard it again and this time he knew.

He turned to his left and saw a soldier sitting apart from the others. It was the tow-headed new replacement who had fallen beside him earlier when they'd had the scare as the tanks went by. And the sound had been that of a scared kid trying to keep his weeping silent so no one would hear. Hatfield knew all about that. He had broken down like that after his first day in action. But he'd been in a foxhole by himself and it had been easier to keep everyone from knowing. That was before Sergeant Forte had latched onto him. Maybe...maybe Sergeant Forte had heard him that night. Maybe that was what made the sergeant look out for him. Before, he would have been disturbed to think the sergeant had seen him so weak and blubbery. Now things like that didn't seem to matter at all — when you put them beside the terrible loss of Sergeant Forte himself.

He could see some of the other men were aware of the young replacement's silent weeping. But they were all carefully ignoring it. He knew some of them would be screening it out as just another cruel detail they didn't want to have forced upon them. But maybe a few were pretending not to notice because they saw the boy was trying to hide it, and if his fears left him that much courage, he deserved that much help from them.

Hatfield didn't want to make things harder for the boy. But maybe he could do something. Not much — but whatever little he could.

He got up and walked over to sit down beside the boy.

"You got any rations on you?" Lucas asked. "I ain't had a thing to eat all day."

The boy shook his head no and turned slightly away. Hatfield could see him wipe at his eyes once furtively.

"That's what I thought," Hatfield went on pleasantly. "I had one of them K-ration chocolate bars I didn't eat last night. Here, I'll split it with you."

He took the small ration bar from his pocket, carefully broke it in two, and reached out one segment to the boy, who seemed uncertain what to do.

"Go on, take it," Hatfield said encouragingly. "You'll be surprised how much better a little piece of chocolate can make you feel, sometimes. Sergeant Forte used to say the Army teaches you to make the most of little things. You let things get bad enough and even a little candy bar looks mighty good."

After a moment's hesitation the boy reached out and took the piece of chocolate. Hatfield was glad to see there were no fresh tears welling from his eyes. The smears on his face were from the boy's wiping the old ones away.

"Well, here comes that sergeant back again," Hatfield said as he saw the non-com come out of the building and walk across the street. "I wonder what good news he's bringing." He suddenly realized his voice had had a little of that amused cynicism Sergeant Forte's had so often had in the past.

"Okay," the sergeant shouted. "All you First Battalion men

come with me." His cheerful voice rode right over the low groan that greeted his announcement. "Take it easy. You're just going down the street for some hot rations. Never say the 'Lone Bandit' doesn't look after its own."

Colonel Berrigan was beginning to become more that a little anxious about what was supposed to have been the main element in his task force — the remnants of "Task Force Doyle." Here he was an armored commander, preparing for an important armored battle, and where in hell was his armor? Not one medium tank had appeared. And that "Doyle" remnant should have been in Monville when he arrived. He had been told they still had a number of Shermans left. And although his close study of the armored battles so far in the war had led him to be highly critical of the Shermans, they were still the only American medium tank.

Just two months before he had written a long report on the inadequacy of the Shermans for fighting German armor. The report had been forwarded to the weapons procurement people in Washington. He felt he had proven beyond a shadow of a doubt how completely inadequate the American mediums were for going head-to-head with either the German Panthers or Tigers. Not only did the enemy have the advantage of heavier armor — especially in front where it counted most — but the American short-barreled seventy-fives were no match for German eighty-eights

He knew others before him had leveled similar charges at the Shermans, but most armored commanders had accepted the tanks without protest. There were two good reasons for that. First, the basic mistakes had been made so long ago, by ignorant or incompetent generals in charge of procurement, that it was impossible to correct them now. The factories were already turning out the Shermans by the tens of thousands. You couldn't put the war on hold for a year or two while a new tank was developed and produced.

But he felt sure the second reason was perhaps even more important. The people who were being given high command positions in the armored force knew where their bread was buttered. If they kept their mouths shut and "carried on," they got their commands and promotions. But if they made a lot of noise about the inadequacy of their basic weapon, they got a thank you for your criticism and a quick transfer to a rear-echelon position.

He'd often wondered if his strongly critical report had affected his own status. Some higher-corporate management personnel had been sent out to "confer" with him about his criticisms. Some "conferring." They'd tried the soft-soap and then the hard-sell techniques on him. But when they saw he really knew what the hell he was talking about, had the facts to back up his position, and wasn't afraid of where the waves he was making might splatter — they'd gone back to Washington pretty fast. Probably with a report saying he was a hopeless case.

By God, he thought, maybe it hadn't been his "string-pulling" that had finally got him a combat command. Star-grade officers who wouldn't go along without criticism weren't wanted for major command positions. But lieutenant colonels of armor were a different matter. Their complaints wouldn't get much attention — and there was a pretty good chance that an energetic, "follow me" kind of lieutenant colonel wouldn't be around long enough in combat to make any more waves.

But for now, Shermans were all there was in this game, and where the hell were his?

He'd been successful at collecting a fair amount of stragglers — perhaps the equivalent of a reinforced company of infantry out there ready to put into position. But without good medium tank support, what the hell good would they be when the Tigers or Panthers showed up?

His eye suddenly caught something approaching the bridge from the east. The road had been yielding a regular stream of infantry and occasional vehicles — but the stream was becoming a trickle. And it was one of the "trickles" that had caught his attention.

First came a jeep towing a gun that dwarfed the vehicle pulling it. He knew it must be an M-1 medium artillery piece. Following that came a three-quarter-ton vehicle towing a similar gun — then another jeep with a third gun. On both sides of the vehicles something less than a platoon of infantry plodded along doggedly. And then right at the end came the real eye-stopper — a regular artillery tractor pulling another one-five-five...and dragging in its wake a second, much smaller gun, with two men holding up the trail-end and a third, small enough to look like a mascot, riding proudly on the barrel.

Colonel Berrigan felt he had to see this group a little closer. They might be what Sergeant McClanahan called "battle garbage" — but garbage with enough morale to put out such an effort to save their weapons was "garbage" he'd happily accept and beg for more.

Then he saw he wouldn't have to go out for a closer look. After the vehicles had been stopped by the Stuarts at the roadblock, the second jeep pulled out of the little column and headed straight for the C.P. It stopped right outside the headquarters and a tall lieutenant seated beside the driver jumped out and walked quickly to the door.

Lieutenant Clarence Huntington Stallingsworth had been pleased with the sense of activity he'd seen as he entered the town of Monville. Not only did there seem to be a lot of infantry about the main street, but the few glimpses of armor he'd had were encouraging. It wasn't just those four tanks by the bridge. He knew they were only light tanks and not worth much against a real armored unit. But he'd seen down the street three gun barrels peeping out from between buildings. And he knew those babies must be at least seventy-fives. Which meant they were Shermans — or possibly some of the even larger guns the tank destroyer units had now. Maybe they had something in this town that intended to stay and put up a fight. Now, he thought, if there's just somebody here with communications open to rank high enough to make that chicken-livered colonel of mine stop filling his pants and start doing his job, we can go into business right here.

After jumping from the jeep he strode purposefully to the entrance which bore a fresh-painted cardboard sign announcing "Lone Bandit C.P." Judging by the collection of personnel in the square he had just driven through, this seemed to be the choke-point for every outfit trying to get out ahead of the panzers.

"Who's in command here?" he asked brusquely of the sergeant sitting by a table near the door as he entered.

Before the sergeant could answer, a man who had been standing by the front window turned to look at him. Lieutenant Stallingsworth noted the silver leaf on the shirt collar. He looked awfully young for that much rank. For just a moment the lieutenant wondered if he'd been a bit too abrupt. To hell with it, he thought. It's time somebody said screw the military etiquette and let's start fighting the god-damned war. So he plunged on recklessly.

"Are you going to hold this position, sir?" he asked.

"We are indeed," the young field-grade officer said flatly.

"And you're going to help us. Now — what have you got?"

The lieutenant liked the direct answer. "I've got a battalion of one-five-fives with a full load of ammo," he said just as flatly. "That is — I've got radio contact with them right now, and their maximum range can reach here. But they're liable to march order any time. And I've got a commander who gets antsy every time he hears a rumor of a tank. Now each time those guns fire, over half a ton of high explosive will land anywhere you need it most. Battalion ten volleys will pack one hundred and twenty hundred-pound shells into any square a hundred by a hundred yards you designate. And I can put them there on request. It's not direct fire — but with those odds you've got a good chance of disrupting any tank attack...and just devastating any infantry formation. It's all yours — if you've got contact with rank high enough to tell that bastard to stay in position until they let him loose."

He watched the colonel's face to see how he was taking this breach of military decorum. The officer's eyes bore into his for a moment — then the jaws relaxed into a smile.

"Lieutenant, you're just what I've been waiting for. Sergeant, see if you can get a message relayed to the General through the radio in one of the light tanks. Just say we *must* have priority fire support from this lieutenant's battalion, and under *no* condition should they be allowed to take their guns out of firing position. I think he's just the man to put some cement into the bowels of any commander with the runs. I'll guarantee 'that bastard' won't need a latrine for a week."

Lieutenant Stallingsworth's tense face relaxed into a grin. By God, he thought, here was somebody who knew how to fight a god-damn war.

Private Hatfield sat on the floor of the crowded room, his back against the stone wall, sipping slowly from the hot coffee in the tin cup. The moment of warmth and rest, he knew, would have to be paid for soon. Right now he didn't care. It was the first time in days he had been warm and could feel dry socks on his feet. Whoever was running this outfit was all right. "Get these men inside and give them some hot coffee," the sergeant had shouted when they had arrived at the kitchen truck parked outside the busy-looking building.

All this was going to cost them, Hatfield was sure. The Army never did anybody any favors. But what the hell — with your body warm and hot coffee slowly circling down inside your gut, it made you feel almost human again. And with the town filling up outside with all sorts of straggling units, you could almost feel you were part of an army once more. And there were men from all three battalions of the regiment.

"Okay, you chow hounds," a sergeant he had not seen before shouted. "We know you're anxious to show your gratitude for all this hot food. You got fifteen more minutes to relax and get warm. Then we'll take you to your new home — where you can show your gratitude for all the goodies we've given you."

"That's the mother-lovin' army," a soldier beside him muttered. "Feed ya before they bleed ya."

"Better than the other way 'round," a man near him replied. "This way you at least get your meal while you can still eat it."

7

Sergeant Bradovitch was pissed off. He knew he was overdue to arrive at that town of "Monville" — but he couldn't help it if one of his tanks had run over some damn sharp projection in the road that had caused it to throw a track. And as if that wasn't enough, the damn ledge or hole or whatever had caused it had damaged the tread so a new section had to be put in its place. Then they'd discovered another tank was low on fuel. So they'd pulled over again to check it out. Sure enough, there had been a leak in the fuel line. Fortunately one of the tank commanders was a whiz at emergency tank repairs, and he had managed to patch it with ordinary black electrician's tape. It seemed to be okay — though Bradovitch would be damned if he'd be happy to ride in a tank patched that way. These damned Shermans were too easy to "brew up," as the British called it, even under normal conditions. But happy or no, he knew he'd have to ride it any which way it ran, if it came to that. When you had panzers pouring through like they were doing here, you damned well threw everything that would run *and* the kitchen sink at them — and prayed it was enough.

But now this was too god-damned much. They had just got back on the road, with Monville still at least fifteen minutes away, and here they had to run into this damned inquisitive MP roadblock.

"We don't have any officer with us," Bradovitch answered irritably.

"This many tanks and you don't even have one officer?" asked the non-com, who wore an MP armband below his five stripes.

"Hell, we had a lieutenant, and we even had a god-damned colonel — but we left them back there a ways...*sir*!"

He added the final word more as an indication of his boiling frustration than a sign of respect for the lieutenant who had now walked up and stood behind the tech sergeant.

"What do you mean you 'left them back there'?" the MP lieutenant asked suspiciously. The bastard acted like he'd caught them heading for town without a weekend pass, Bradovitch thought.

"I mean I left them resting easy — inside their tanks, which were burning already, and with their ammunition about to go up like a Fourth of July grand finale. And we're overdue at another little party we're on our way to right now. So if it's all the same to you, it's been great stopping in on you, but I'm going to have to take off — *sir*!"

Bradovitch saw the red flush creeping up the MP officer's face.

"You'll 'take off' *if* and *when* the Lieutenant says you can take off," the tech sergeant said gruffly. "You want us to unload them and search them, Lieutenant?"

The lieutenant hesitated a minute.

"You mean there isn't a single officer with an identification card in all these tanks?" he asked.

He just can't make up his mind if we're for real, Sergeant Bradovitch thought disgustedly. What the hell does he think we are, anyway?

"*Sir...*" Bradovitch began again, putting the term of respect loud and clear right at the beginning, "*All* these tanks is only five, sir, and five god-damn tanks is only a platoon — and a god-damned platoon's only *entitled* to one god-damned officer — and as I already told you, he's delayed back there a ways getting fried for breakfast. *sir!* "

"Let me handle this joker, sir," the tech sergeant said to his lieutenant. "And now, wise guy, if *five* is a platoon, and your god-damned platoon commander's back there in another tank burning up, that's *your five*—and his makes *six*! How do you account for that?"

The tech sergeant glared at him triumphantly — as if he was Sherlock Holmes catching the butler in a guilty admission.

Bradovitch glared back at the tech sergeant with equal ferocity.

"How do I account for WHAT, god-damnit?"

"Your god-damn arithmetic, smart-ass. *Five* is *five*, and one more makes *six* — and you said a platoon only has *five*. "

Bradovtich stared at him in angry disbelief.

"Yes, I said a *platoon* only has *five*, god-damnit. Only we had a whole god-damned *company* when we started out. And the arithmetic may be a little too complicated for you, but let's try and see. There's *five* here...and *twelve* more — plus Colonel Doyle's tank — back there a ways. That makes *eighteen* all together. You think you can add and subtract that high, smart-ass?"

"Excuse me, sir, but I think I can help out here."

The words came from a quiet-spoken T/5 who had been observing the altercation without comment.

"What state do you come from, Sergeant?" he asked Bradovitch politely.

Sergeant Bradovitch stared at him with increased disbelief.

"What *state*?"

"Yes, Sergeant. I know it sounds kind of silly — but I have a reason for asking."

"Well — Missouri. Is that the right answer?"

"We're getting there. What's the biggest city in your home state?"

"St. Louis, I guess. Yeah, St. Louis."

"Fine. Now — what's the name of the St. Louis baseball team?"

"The Cards, unless they god-damn changed it."

"No, it's still the Cards. Now, can you name a man who pitched for the Cards — and give us his brother's name too?"

This guy may be psycho, Bradovitch thought, but at least he's better than that horse's ass with all the stripes on his arm.

"Shit. Dizzy Dean — and his brother Daffy. Any horse's ass," he added, looking meaningfully at the tech sergeant "knows that."

"I think he's all right, sir," the T/5 said to the lieutenant. "Not many Germans would know all that."

The lieutenant appeared relieved to let it go at that. But not so the tech sergeant.

"So maybe they're not Krauts, sir," he said grudgingly. "But here they're a whole bunch of perfectly good tanks — barrel-assing to the rear. And we also got orders to be on the lookout for deserters and stragglers trying to take off."

Bradovitch felt the anger inside him really boil over.

"Why, you piss-ant, yellow-bellied, rear-echelon ball of slime — who the hell are you to talk about heading for the rear? You probably spent most of the god-damned war checking weekend passes in London, England, for Chrissake. We got orders to join a task force that's blocking a main road near here, and we're already late getting there, and if we don't get there pretty god-damned soon there's going to be a shitload of Panthers and Tigers sending you rear-echelon bastards back to Brussels with an eighty-eight up your ass!"

The tech sergeant, his face livid, started to pull his forty-five from his holster.

"You want me to put this wise-ass under arrest, sir?"

"What's the town you're headed for to set up the road-block, Sergeant?" the T/5 asked, his voice still remarkably calm.

Bradovitch couldn't think of the town for a moment, he was so mad. Then it came to him.

"What town? Monville. Yeah, that's it. Monville, for Chrissake."

The T/5 looked at a map he was holding, then pointed to a spot on it for the lieutenant.

"That checks out all right, sir. They'll probably be needing them up there pretty bad about now."

The lieutenant again appeared relieved.

"Very well, Sergeant. You may proceed."

"Let's get the hell out of here, Bugsy," Bradovitch said into his intercom.

"And you better watch your god-damned mouth when you speak to a superior officer," the tech sergeant said as the tank started to pull back onto the road.

Bradovitch snapped and held a stiff salute for the lieutenant, who returned it quickly and turned away. As soon as the lieutenant's eyes were averted and Bradovitch faced only the tech sergeant and the T/5, he let three fingers of the stiffly-held hand curl inward. Then as he brought the salute down he winked at the T/5 and, with elaborate formality, gave the tech sergeant the finger.

Sergeant JayCee Washington knew he had to do something soon. He had been able to stall making a decision by letting the men stop at the "dining hall" for a hot meal. But in a few minutes he would have to be getting on the road back to his battalion. *If* he intended to go there, that is.

He was enjoying the warmth of the improvised dining room, seated with the motor sergeant at a "table" the mess personnel had hurriedly constructed by taking a door off its hinges and placing it across two sawhorses. He was wondering if Hooley had been having any of the thoughts that had been bothering him.

"You know they really figure on putting a fight up here, Hooley," JayCee said tentatively.

Hooley looked at him suspiciously. "I guess that's what we're all here for," Hooley said without expression.

"I suppose so," JayCee agreed, "though sometimes it hardly looks that way — for some of us, anyway."

Hooley's eyes were watching him noncommittally.

"Which ones of us would you be talking about, JayCee?"

"Hell, Hooley, you know damn well what's going to happen when we get back to battalion. They're going to take these guns and pretend they're glad to get them back — even that bald-headed son-of-a-bitch they put in command. Hell, we probably got him because we was only 'niggers' and everybody knows niggers won't fight, so why waste a competent commander on us? But that old bastard's really going to be plain pissed off we brought his guns back. Without the guns he probably figured they wouldn't put him into action again. Hell, the bastard may be halfway back to the beaches by now."

"So what're you saying, JayCee?"

Sergeant Washington took a deep breath and plunged ahead.

"I'm saying how about...how about we don't go back to the outfit? Not yet."

"You talking desertion, JayCee?"

"Shit, you know better'n that. But we got one third the firepower of the whole god-damn battalion right here — right in our own god-damn hands. You ever think of that, Hooley?"

Hooley looked at him with those same noncommital eyes without speaking.

"God-damnit, Hooley, stop shittin' me. You know god-damn well what I mean. We could — we could get that lieutenant who helped us bring the guns here. *He's* staying here. I bet he'd go with us to see that officer who's running the show. And you think he wouldn't be damn glad for a little more help?"

"Nigger help, JayCee?"

"Shit! Nigger-help, chigger-help. They're gonna need every god-damn bit of help they can get."

"I'm just a god-damn motor sergeant, JayCee. What business I got risking my neck and the guardhouse just so your great-granpappy can be proud of the fightin' stock he produced?"

The hot angry reply was almost out of JayCee's throat when he saw the glint in Hooley's eyes. The bastard! JayCee saw in a moment what Hooley was doing.

"You cheap son of a bitch, Hooley. I'm serious. Stop putting me on."

Hooley must have felt he'd carried his put-on far enough. For he broke into a long suppressed laugh.

"What'd you think, JayCee — I'd gone chicken on you? You know me better'n that. Hell, it's true I'm not so sure what good we're gonna be up here. Or how happy they'll be to have medium artillery in the frontline — and nigger artillery at that. But I'm game to try. How you wanta go about it?"

JayCee could feel his spirits rising as he talked.

"First we'll check with the cannoneers. We're not exactly in position to order them. But if they'll go along, I figure we should talk first to that artillery lieutenant. He's still around because I saw him bringing his men down here for some chow. Then if he'll go with us, we'll go see the head honcho himself."

"JayCee, you're a trouble-making, uppity god-damned nigger. So what are we waiting on?"

Colonel Berrigan wished he at least had a skeleton staff. Even an executive officer would have been something. But all he had to call his own was Sergeant McClanahan — who didn't act too thrilled about being here. There was not one solid officer he could depend on. And he knew damn well he ought to stop trying to carry everything around in his own head. That was the way to foul it all up.

Of course there was that little blond-headed pip-squeak who "commanded" the T.D.s. He could imagine what his men would say about him as a "commander." "*Him* command? Wouldn't trust him t' command a third-class shithouse. Prob'ly get himself flushed down by mistake."

That ordnance sergeant MacKay, now...he had impressed the colonel as highly competent. But he was only a non-com — and he was completely without experience or training for combat. The artillery observer might be okay. But he was just an observer, with no real command function. And the infantry...there'd been no senior officers with the men his Stuart tanks had stopped. The bad ones had taken off while they had transportation. The good ones were no doubt up there still —

their lifeless bodies a frozen testimony to their dedication to duty.

There were a few lieutenants and one captain among the infantry. But none of them looked too promising. He hadn't had a chance to talk to the captain yet, though he didn't have any high hopes. And the lieutenants...take the one that had turned the wrong way and got back up here in the combat zone by mistake — most likely he was typical. God, he hoped not. He could still see him, slow of motion and speech, scratching that long, balding forehead while he searched for words to express a simple idea. God, what a bunch.

Yet he knew he had to do something about getting his hodge-podge of a force into fighting positions. So far he had concentrated almost exclusively on trying to raise the morale of these bits of flotsam and jetsam. Battered and discouraged as they were, he was afraid he'd lose most of them before the enemy even got close — and the rest of them at the first shot fired in anger.

He was glad he'd taken the time to get that kitchen truck. That was the most helpful sign of all. The cooks had been serving food steadily — and when he had checked in to see how it was going, it hadn't seemed bad. In fact, the mood in the warm room filled with men hungrily gulping their hot chow was almost lively.

Earlier he had sent out a small patrol in a jeep. He had told them to go up no more than three miles — and to make damn sure they could get away to give plenty of warning of approaching enemy units. The fact that they had not come back yet indicated he still had a little time. But he had to be getting the men into position — and he wanted those Shermans here to build his position around. Yet it was beginning to look as if he would have to do without them.

His thoughts were interrupted by the sound of a jeep driving up outside. Then boots clattered outside the C.P. door.

Three figures came trooping in — the artillery lieutenant,

followed by two of the black soldiers he had seen coming back with their guns. Considering the vehicles they'd had to use to save their guns, they must be pretty good men. For just a moment he had considered adding them to his collection of cast-offs. But since they had gone to such trouble to save their guns, he couldn't bring himself to tell them to abandon them now to join him as mere infantry soldiers. And up here was no place for their large artillery pieces — so he'd let them pass on through.

Now the bespectacled lieutenant approached him and saluted smartly.

"The sergeants asked me to put a proposal before you, sir," the lieutenant said.

"By all means, Lieutenant," the colonel answered. "Let's have it."

"They had been ordered to abandon their guns, but they stayed behind on their own to save them. So they don't know where their unit is now. But given the importance of holding this position — and the desperate need for personnel here — they wanted to suggest they stay here and help in defense of this position. While I have never known them before today, I have seen first-hand evidence of their resourcefulness. If I could be permitted an opinion, sir, I think they would be a welcome addition to our force here."

The colonel noted how naturally the lieutenant had made himself a part of "our force here." By God, that was the kind of unit spirit he would have tried to build — if he had had time to do it. But he hesitated before answering. He knew the danger of men making combat decisions for "sentimental" reasons.

"You mean they want to abandon their guns and serve as infantry?" he finally asked.

"No, sir," the taller, leaner sergeant answered quickly. "Not abandon our guns. We're trained artillery men. That's what we can do best. We mean *use* our guns. We've got one-third the firepower of a whole medium artillery battalion here. But if we just take the guns on back to the battalion, it'll probably be a long time before they get into action — if ever. But right here they're Johnny-on-the-spot. You can have their firepower, sir, any time you need it — for any target you want it on. *Direct-support* artillery, sir. No need to go through five or six layers of command — and hope nobody else wants them when you do."

The colonel looked at him, trying to keep his face expressionless. It wouldn't be fair to let them see the way his spirits had risen at the sergeant's words.

"I certainly appreciate your offer, Sergeant. And there's no denying we need all the help we can get here. But medium artillery up here? Your weapons are excellent for indirect fire, but they're not exactly the kind you can direct-lay on a column of attacking panzers. One-five-five howitzers weren't designed to slug it out toe-to-toe with German tanks."

"No, sir," the sergeant answered quickly. "We know they're not eighty-eights. But they're better than eighty-eights, when it comes to stopping, say, an infantry attack across a river."

"And if you can hold up the tanks at the river," the artillery lieutenant burst in excitedly, "the Germans are going to have panzergrenediers here fast to help out the tanks. I feel sure these weapons can be a big help."

It was appealing all right. But there were some practical matters to be considered.

"What you say is very true," the colonel agreed. "But if they're going to fire indirectly, like regular artillery, they've got to have defilade positions where they can't be seen. Then they'll have to have an observation team and communications. And they'll need more ammo than I could see in those little vehicles pulling the guns."

"We've gone over all that, sir," the lieutenant hastened to

add. "There's a good position less than a half-mile back from town — in a depression just behind a stand of trees on a reverse slope. It's ideal. And I'm a trained observer. That's my job. I can direct their fire in addition to my own battalion's."

"How will you communicate your commands back to them, Lieutenant?"

"All taken care of, sir. I communicate with my own Fire Direction by the radio in my jeep. But we also have two walkie-talkies for close-in communication, in case I have to leave the jeep and the radio behind. I'll keep one of the walkie-talkies and give one to the sergeant to use at the guns."

Talk about resourceful, Berrigan thought — what won't these guys be able to work out?

"Very ingenious," he admitted. "Now if you could only solve the one remaining problem as easily. How many rounds do you have with you, Sergeant?"

At this the sergeant's face took on a crestfallen look. They do have a problem they couldn't solve then, the colonel thought. Too bad — with their spirit they would have been a big addition.

"We've got lots of primers and fuses," the sergeant said. "And I'm carrying twenty-three regular H.E.shells and twenty-seven powder charges. That's a start. Then I thought we might send some vehicles back to look for an ammo dump — if we only knew where to look I'm sure we'd find some ammo available."

"Ordinarily maybe, Sergeant. But considering the messed-up state everything is in, and the limited time we have — the odds don't look too good."

"I've been puzzling this one out," the lieutenant said. "And I think we may have at least a chance of a solution. My own battalion has displaced a number of times in the last couple of days. And I know damn well when our colonel gets panicky, a lot of things get left behind. I got word from my battery they've left a lot of ammunition in the positions they had to vacate hurriedly. Now, I have the coordinates of a position they were in just a little over two miles east of here. It's off to the right of the road a mile or so on a side road. I propose we take every vehicle that can carry shells, run them out there, load up, and run on back. If we're lucky we can get up there, load up, and get out before the panzers get there."

The colonel made a quick decision. It was risky as hell — what would happen if they got up there on the side road, and while they were loading, the panzers came down the main road and cut them off? Well, he was in no position to ask for sure things.

"All right," the colonel said decisively, "you sold me. Now here's what you do. Take every vehicle you can dig up bigger than a jeep. Take the supply truck down at the kitchen. I already had them unload it. Tell the mess sergeant I said unload whatever's left in the kitchen truck. And take any of those trailers that can be emptied quickly. With your tractor and three-quarter-ton, you'll have quite a little ammo train. Then add anything else you can find that has wheels and runs. If anybody objects, tell them I gave the order. Just don't bother with anything that's going to take more than a few minutes to unload. Time's too valuable."

"And Lieutenant," he added after a brief pause, "while the sergeant's getting the ammo train ready, I want you to take your jeep and find that place your battalion was in position — see if there really is any ammo left there. If there is, you shoot back to the main road and meet the vehicles coming up to collect it. Send one of your men with them to show them where the ammo is. Give him one of your walkie-talkies. Keep the other one yourself and go on down the main road past where they turn off. I have a patrol out there in a jeep keeping a lookout for the panzers. If you see them coming back to warn us the German tanks are on their tail, radio your man to have all the vehicles pull out *immediately* and hightail it back here. Remember, if they don't get to the main road junction before the German tanks do — we'll have lost nearly all our transportation. So this is going to be a squeaker. It's a gamble — but it's worth it, if you play it just as I've told you. Have you got it?"

"Yes, sir!" the lieutenant shouted, already halfway to the door. "Come on, you two. I'll run you back to the kitchen. Thank you, sir."

The last three words were hurled back as an afterthought. By God, Colonel Berrigan thought, I'll bet they do it, too.

8

Immediately after the artillerymen had left, Colonel Berrigan decided he could put off making his final dispositions no longer. Shermans or no Shermans, he would have to be ready to put up his fight when the panzers came over that eastern ridge and started across the open half-mile of terrain leading to the town. He'd lectured often enough about coping with an apparently "hopeless" situation. The message was simple: forget the belly-aching and get on with it; do the best you can with what you have. You never know when hanging on a little longer in a "hopeless situation" may be the one little factor to turn the tide in a whole battle.

"Sergeant McClanahan," he had said when the nom-com had come back from taking a last group of stragglers down to the "dining room" for dry socks and a hot meal, "I'm ready to see all the unit leaders on that list I gave you. Tell them to be here in...just ten minutes from now. Do you know where to find them all?"

"Yes, sir," the sergeant said. "They're all within a couple

hundred yards of the C.P. No problem."

Then, only shortly after the sergeant had gone out to perform his duty, Berrigan's pulse quickened at what he thought might be the sound of a tank motor. He held his breath, listening carefully. Could it be only one of the T.D.'s changing position?

No. It was too steady and too loud for that. This had to be a number of heavy, tracked vehicles in column — it was too steady a sound for anything else.

The colonel strode quickly to open the door and stand outside, peering back up the street. Yes, by God, it had to be them. The head of the column came around a curve in the road and he saw the square body and rounded turret of the first vehicle was indeed a Sherman. Then, one by one, the others came sliding around the curve and headed down the main street. Even with all the defects he had pointed out again and again to his superiors, the Shermans were a welcome sight now.

They came down the main street at full speed and in a moment were sliding to a stop before the C.P.

A tough-looking sergeant jumped down from the turret of the leading tank and walked briskly to stand at attention before the colonel. He saluted and spoke like a man in a hurry.

"Sergeant Bradovitch, sir, reporting with the remnants of Task Force Doyle."

"You're a welcome sight, Sergeant. Have trouble getting here?"

"No, sir. That is — a little mechanical trouble, then a bunch of M.P.'s thought we were either Nazi stormtroopers or deserting G.I.s. They held us up a little. We got here as soon as we could."

"And that's soon enough, Sergeant. We're just about to have a quick meeting of all commanders. You can tell your men they've got a few minutes to go back to the kitchen for some hot chow. But I'll want you to stay here for the meeting. I take it you're commanding this unit now?"

"Yes, sir. By elimination. We lost all our remaining officers in the last little fire-fight we had."

"Well, I'm glad you made it. See to your men — we'll be meeting in about five minutes."

Five minutes later they were all assembled in the large "public room" of the C.P. In addition to the recently arrived tank commander, there was the slight, blond-headed tank destroyer lieutenant, the sergeant acting as commander of the five Stuart tanks, Sergeant MacKay of the two "circus wagons," a combat engineer sergeant who, with a dozen of his men, had become detached from their unit and caught up in the net at the bridge, and a captain and three lieutenants — all from different units of the infantry division that was breaking up in front of them. He couldn't tell much about the infantry officers — except it was obvious none of them was in a very high state of morale. The understatement of the year, he thought. The captain claimed to have been a staff officer and had never commanded a line company. The three lieutenants had all been platoon commanders. Two were quite young and struck him as very jumpy. The third was the somewhat older officer with the long balding forehead and the calculated slowness of speech and action. No ball of fire, obviously — any of them. But which one of them was least likely to panic and cop out under pressure? He'd be damned if he could tell from what he could see. They all looked, frankly, shaky as hell and a sorry lot.

Well, he thought, their opinion of me probably runs along similar lines. He could imagine what they were thinking. "No combat experience, too much damn rank for his years, probably got it by climbing over the competition state-side, now shoved out here, doesn't know his ass from a hole in the ground, and quite willing to get his next promotion over our dead bodies."

And could they be right, he asked himself. So far as evidence is needed to disprove the judgment — there isn't any yet. Despite all I've learned through study, all my impressive performances in training, and all my high evaluations in noncombat jobs — how I'll pan out when the pressure is on is anybody's guess. They know perfectly well why my face doesn't have the slack despair you can see in theirs. They've been through a lot and maybe had some successes along with their failures — but I'm simply untested and therefore no one knows how quickly I'll crack. And they'll assume the worst.

But enough introspection, he told himself — you're their commander now, and from this moment on it's all your baby.

"Gentlemen," he began, "I'm Lieutenant Colonel Berrigan, commander of Task Force Lone Bandit. I've been authorized to assume command over all military personnel in this area. You all know why that is. A very powerful German attack has hit us where we were least ready for it and has caused a real crisis for the whole European theater. And we have to face up to just how bad the situation is. But remember: it's not a hopeless situation — in fact, it may turn out to be very much to our advantage.

"Hitler realized he was losing the war and we were winning it — but by slow, costly means for both of us. So he's chosen to throw all the chips into one big gamble. His hope is to cause a deep penetration and resulting panic in one area of the Allied line. He plans to throw irresistible power against one section of our line until that section collapses and the resulting panic allows his troops to 'roll up' the rest of the Allied line in the same way he rolled up the French at the start of this war — and then almost did the same with the Russians.

"Now he doesn't have a great deal of strength compared with us, over all   but he's done what a commander of even an inferior army can always do. He's *concentrated* his power in one spot, so that he *does* have tremendous superiority in this one area. His gamble comes down to this — can he throw such panic into our forces here that we will collapse, let his blitzkrieging armor push on through us and run loose in the Allied rear? That is what he has to do to have any chance of achieving his objective."

Colonel Berrigan could see they were all listening attentively to every word. Their faces didn't show much emotion. Well, this was no pep-talk; he had determined to give it to them straight. And when you do that it's always a risk. He just had to hope that the "quality of personnel" of this hodge-podge assembly of American soldiers was equal to facing the truth head-on and not be frozen up by it.

"Now," he continued, "that's his hope, that's why he's taken this big gamble. And we have to realize there's always a chance his gamble could pay off. But whether it pays off or not, gentlemen, comes down to whether his judgment about you and me is correct. He's trusting in his belief that Americans, if confronted with a sudden crisis, will collapse. He's convinced himself that while we may have superior numbers and more weapons, as human beings we won't have the internal strength he's convinced his troops have.

"And whether he's right or wrong, gentlemen, depends on you and me. Because our leaders know perfectly well how to counter his ploy. He hit us where we had few troops; therefore all we have to do is shift a lot of our troops down from the Ninth Army and up from Patton's Third Army to surround the penetration he's punched into our line — and then to counterattack with our superior forces.

"But the problem is — shifting those forces takes time. And the big question is this: can a small number of American troops in this area, troops that have already been hit very hard — in other words can you, gentlemen, hang on until enough reinforcements have been shifted to defeat his plan? If troops in just a few key areas panic and run, Hitler's forces have a chance to win their big gamble. But if you and I and the men under us do not panic, do not run when it looks as if the full weight of the Nazi army is directed right at us — he will have lost his gamble. It's as simple as that. Simple — but not easy. Because we *are* going to be terribly over-matched for a short while. They're going to have many times the power we have. We have to face that. But we have a simple task. *We just have to hang on.*

"There is a full American division coming up behind us to plug this particular hole. They're coming as fast as they can. What we somehow have to do is hold together and keep fighting, keep the enemy from punching a way through us before that division is here to handle them. So it turns out that one American soldier where you are today is potentially worth more than a hundred in another part of the line. I say 'potentially' because it all depends on how we behave under pressure. For the pressure is going to be immense. There will be times when any normal human being will begin to wonder if it's 'worth it' — will begin to resent the fact that *we're* the ones who have to take it.

"We may grumble 'why us?' Well, gentlemen, it's the luck of the draw. Many Americans will go through this war and never face the stark fact that victory or defeat depended on *what they did*. But we have to face it. Call it good luck or bad, but it's our luck to be stuck right where what we do in the next few hours will make a big difference."

He had kept his voice from rising all during his speech. But he hoped they had been able to read the genuine concern in all that he had said.

"Now," he resumed, "I wanted to tell you the straight facts because I feel you and your men have a right to know the truth — to realize just how much depends on all of us today, tonight, and tomorrow. But it's not speeches that will make the difference. We've got to have a good plan of action, we've got to be prepared to put it into effect — and most of all we've got to be ready to do whatever we have to do, when the plan seems to have gone all askew, to keep our men in the action, to refuse to let the enemy punch a hole through us. No matter what is necessary to prevent it.

"So that's our next job — to distribute our forces so they can best stop this powerful onslaught when it hits us. Now, our position has some disadvantages, as well as some big advantages. I don't have to dwell on the disadvantages. They're obvious — the most important one being our need to cover so much space with so little strength, especially armored strength. But look at the advantages.

"While we have perhaps four or five miles of possible front to cover, the terrain is quite a bit in our favor. First, to accomplish their objective, the enemy has to move fast with heavy armored forces. Which means he is pretty much bound to the road network. And it just so happens that there is *only one* good road through our position. The enemy has to come at us on that road. And he is pretty much restricted to crossing the river on this one bridge — at least until he constructs another one.

"Now if he finds he can't just barrel through on the road, of course he can deploy infantry on either flank to attack across the river and into our rear. But even here he has a problem. The area on either side of the river is open terrain. And before they get to us, his infantry will have to cross considerable open terrain and then the river itself — all the way under all the defensive fire we can put out..

"So here's my plan. Our tank destroyer power is going to be concentrated in the town and near the main road. That's where we have to expect the panzers. Lieutenant Hood," he said, addressing the baby-faced, blond-headed young lieutenant, "immediately after this meeting I want you to put your

T.D.s where they can cover the bridge, the road through town, and the open space around it."

The young lieutenant, who had started when the colonel mentioned his name, gulped and stammered a reply.

"Ye — yes, sir." He didn't seem to trust himself to say more.

"Sergeant MacKay," the colonel went on quickly, "I want your two secret weapons kept in reserve until we have to use them. Yours are the only weapons we have that can be sure of taking out a Panther or Tiger head-to-head. So I want you to find two positions, back west of town, where you can cover the open space across the river, the main road through town, and the open spaces on either flank — in case any heavy panzers find a way to skirt around the town.

"But make sure you're located where you can pull out quickly and go back to the major crossroad in our rear. We have to consider the possibility of German tank columns breaking through on either of our flanks and sending units racing down that major highway two miles in our rear. If they should do that, we've got to have something that can stop the German heavies until we can shift our forces. Against heavy armor, you're our only reserve — so don't waste your shots or give your positions away unnecessarily."

"Yes, sir!" the tall, dirty-coverall-clad figure snapped back.

"Now the infantry," Colonel Berrigan continued, "is going to have a tough job — as usual. Because there's more than a half-mile of open frontage out there, plus a helluva lot more undefended forest terrain. There's just a lot of god-damned space where they can come at us. They won't hit with the infantry first — but after we stop their panzers your turn will come. The Germans are very good at bringing armored infantry into action quickly. As soon as they can see they've hit a major defensive position their tanks can't take out, they'll move their infantry up. And they can muster a ground attack that can hit at any number of specific points all at once.

"Our main advantages are two: the river they'll have to cross to get at us; and the fact that they're not going to be able to end-run around either of our flanks — at least not easily. Of course if we succeed in stopping their first few attempts to get at us along the half-mile of open space, they'll probably try to work through the forest on either flank — particularly after dark. And the dark now comes early and stays late. They'll surely work some troops around us tonight. It's something we have to expect and be ready for.

"But they can't work any kind of armor through either of those forests — except for one spot just at the edge of the woods on our right flank. There's a ford there — but you're going to have help at that spot. And I think we can make it very tough on any armor coming at you that way. Besides, any panzers crossing there are going to have to approach single file — the hardest way for them to throw in a full panzerblitz on us."

"Now, Captain Bergoff — " He hoped he'd remembered the name of the former infantry staff officer correctly. "I asked you to get me a quick estimate of our infantry strength in both personnel and weapons. Do you have it?"

"Yes, sir," the infantry captain said promptly. Colonel Berrigan still didn't know how to evaluate this smooth-faced, slightly stout, former staff officer. He obviously hadn't had any line-company combat experience. And as a member of the division the Germans had just chewed up in the last few days, his confidence would probably be at rock bottom. And he might very well be one of those pampered souls with friends in high places — who made sure he got his soft staff positon. But how would he react when he realized the soft touch was over for him — maybe permanently? There was no predicting the answer to that.

There's no predicting the answer for you either, a small voice within him echoed — now that your own soft touch is gone.

"Captain Bergoff," he went on, "what's the breakdown on the infantry?"

"The only thing like an organized unit is a rifle platoon from Third Battalion. They were in reserve and didn't get thrown in until the line had pretty well gone. So they've got forty men still present — under command of their regular officer, Lieutenant Kolinski. Next, we have a platoon made up of all the other Third Battlion units — twenty-nine men, all told — under Lieutenant Brownell.

"The First Battalion had been in line pretty far forward, and not many of them made it back. Out of their three line-companies, plus the weapons company, I found only nineteen men. A lot of them, including their battalion staff officers, were probably captured in the first armored attack. Lieutenant Magruder, a platoon commander from the weapons company, is now in command of them.

"Finally, there's a collection of about twenty-two men from all other sources—Second Battalion, plus part of an I and R platoon from regimental headquarters, and five or six from the adjoining division. I put them together as another platoon which I will command. That gives us a total of, say, a short infantry company, organized into four platoons as you suggested."

He's efficient at the staff work anyway, Berrigan thought. Though God knows how he'll be when the first bullet whizzes past his head.

"Excellent," the colonel said. "Now, here's how we're going to deploy them. We'll take the strongest platoon, Lieutenant Kolinski's, and place it in the center. They'll be defending the eastern edge of town, where the first and biggest assaults will obviously come. Lieutenant Kolinski, you can put some of your men in the buildings that overlook the river. And you'll have to have one squad on each flank — in houses or along the riverbank, whichever way you can cover the area best — for you'll be responsible for the nearly quarter-mile of terrain in our center, including the bridge.

"Lieutenant Brownell, yours is the next strongest platoon, so I'm going to assign you the right flank. You'll have almost a quarter-mile to cover — and you'll have responsibility for a ford where tanks and vehicles can probably cross. You also have to be aware that, after the initial assaults fail, the enemy may send infantry deeper in the woods and around your flank. You're going to have some anti-tank support for that river crossing. I personally doubt they're going to send their heaviest tanks through that difficult terrain. But they might. And there's a very good chance they'll send Mark IV's and panzergrenadier tracks. Whatever they send, you and your support will have to handle for just as long as you can.

"Now, Lieutenant Magruder, you've got a tough assignment."

The tall, slow-moving officer with the long forehead looked at him apprehensively. I hate to entrust men to him until I have a better reading on just how capable he is, Colonel Berrigan thought. But what other choice have I got?

"You have only nineteen men, but you're going to have to take responsibility for the whole quarter-mile of the left flank, plus the forest beyond. That's a helluva lot, but your advantage is that it's highly unlikely you'll have to face any direct attack from tanks or tracks. There's just no way for them to cross without constructing a bridge — and there's no way for them to do that secretly. And if you find they're doing that, we'll try to get some anti-tank support to you."

Lieutenant Magruder looked as if he was getting too much to absorb too fast. But either he finally understood it all, or he had become so confused he had given up trying — it was a little hard to tell which. I'll just have to send him out and try to make some kind of check on him, Berrigan thought.

"That will leave us your twenty-two men, Captain Bergoff," the colonel continued. "That's our reserve. I want your men kept in the town itself — but not on the eastern edge where Lieutenant Kolinski's men will be.

"Now — what about automatic weapons?"

"Kolinski's in the best position for machine guns," Captain Bergoff replied. "He's got two light machine guns and a water-cooled 30-caliber. The other three platoons each have a light machine gun. In addition, there are some BAR's in each platoon."

He's really done his homework, the colonel thought.

"How about ammo?" Berrigan asked.

"Skimpy," the captain replied. "I'd estimate only about a couple hundred rounds per gun. We could be hurting pretty quick if we get hit by a couple of determined infantry attacks."

"Fortunately we're covered there," Colonel Berrigan said. "Before I left division I had them throw in a few boxes — both machine-gun ammo and clips. Each platoon leader, before you move out, be sure you have your men load up with ammo."

He paused for a moment. That was just enough for the sergeant in charge of the Stuart tank platoon to speak up.

"What about the light tanks, sir? Where do you want us?"

"Just coming to you, Sergeant. Now, we don't want you bouncing your little thirty-seven shells off any tanks. In fact, you may not use your cannons at all. You have two weapons we do want very much to use, however — your machine guns and your radios. One problem with a hastily assembled task force like this is lack of communications. But the Stuarts all have radios that can talk with each other. So here's what we're going to do. Sergeant, your tank will stay behind the C.P. and keep contact with your other tanks. One will be with each of the flank forces. The other two are our insurance policy on that main highway behind us. I know they don't have much fire power, but they're going to be our trip-wire. They should go back to the main highway behind us and then move out about three or four miles — one to the north and one to the south. If they get any indication German forces are on their way down that road, they should radio an immediate warning. And be sure that waning gets to me without delay. Any questions?"

"No, sir," the tank platoon commander said. "All clear."

"Fine. Now I want the infantry to get into position immediately — so your men can start digging in. Key to our defense is having our infantry positioned so they can take a heavy toll of attacking infantry. We'll keep the tanks off you — if you can keep the enemy infantry from establishing a bridgehead along the half-mile of open terrain. I want the engineer sergeant and the commander of the Sherman tanks to stay behind for further instructions. The rest of you, go back to your units and start your movements into position immediately."

9

"Did they give you those coordinates?" Lieutenant Stallingsworth asked his jeep driver as they sped along the deserted road that led eastward from the town.

"I had to pry a little," Corporal McGonigal said, his short, slight body hunched over the steering wheel. "The bastards wanted to clear it with Corps Intelligence or some damn rear-echelon bureaucrat. Did they think the Krauts would shell our *former* positions, for Christ's sake?"

"Anyhow," Corporal McGonigal went on, "while Battalion staff was trying to clear it with somebody at Corps, Sergeant Hooker checked around quick and gave me the rough coordinates. Here they are, sir. I circled the areas on the map."

Lieutenant Stallingsworth took the map the corporal handed him. A quick glance showed him it was going to be easy enough to find the place. The batteries had been lined up on the north-south side road — Able and Charlie Batteries behind it and Baker Battery in front. Able Battery's position had been only about three-quarters of a mile in on the side road, and the battery positions extended a mere half-mile along the road."

"What's this other circle here?" the lieutenant asked.

"Service Battery. I had half the non-coms in our battery searching out the information and when Sergeant Dooley, in charge of the fifth-section ammo supply, found out what we wanted to know for, he said check service battery area. He was sure Battalion had really screwed up on the ammo supply. The ammo train had just got back to Battalion with a full load of shells, and the colonel had been so anxious to get them out for another load he had them dump the whole lot at Service Battery and take off for another load. He was going to have each firing battery haul their own shells back to their batteries."

Lieutenant Stallingsworth slapped his thigh and burst out laughing.

"Then they had a quick march order and left it all sitting there?" he asked.

"Damn right," Corporal McGonigal said with a knowing smile. "The Colonel suddenly thought they were being cut off — so he gives 'march order' and leads the way out. Hooker said the Colonel was gone in thirty seconds flat. And he wasn't giving a damn what they left behind. So here's all these piles of shells —a whole ammo train load of them — sittin' there on the god-damn ground. And Service battery without one ammo carrying truck available. Nobody at Battalion even thought about it until half an hour later, when they were five miles away. Then Hooker said Battalion was trying to monkey with the records to cover it up. But one thing was sure — nobody was going back there after those shells."

"Hell," the lieutenant said, "we'll have more shells than we have space to carry — from that one spot alone. If we can find it."

Corporal McGonigal snorted contemptuously. "We won't

have any trouble finding it, sir. Hooker says those shells were piled up in full view of the road — stacked up like a load of cord wood."

"Great. Now here's what we'll do. We'll shoot up that road, find the shells, then leave Cordova there to direct the vehicles to them. Coming back we'll drop Smitty off as a marker at the junction to the main road. Then we'll push on to find that patrol — or maybe the Germans, if the patrol's had some bad luck. Cordova," he added to the T/5 radio operator riding in the jeep's back seat, "we'll leave you a walkie-talkie and warn you if it looks like you should pull out in a hurry. Remember, if I yell simply 'May-day, May-day,' that means clear the hell out, pronto. Tell all the trucks to stop loading immediately and try to beat the Germans to the junction at the main highway. If I'm not there with the jeep, you just ride back with one of the ammo carriers. Got it?"

"Sure," the radio corporal with steel-rimmed glasses said. "No sweat."

It had been so damned easy, Lieutenant Stallingsworth thought ten minutes later as he approached the main road again. Their informant had been right. Shells piled up four and five feet high. Hundreds of them, probably. He hadn't even bothered to count. At a hundred pounds a shell, the problem was they had more than their vehicles could carry. A whole ammo train full. He knew Sergeant Washington would ignore the prescribed weights-loads and put in all the trucks could carry, since it was all on a good road and they didn't have far to go.

"Okay, Smitty," he said to the remaining soldier in the jeep's rear seat as they reached the junction. "You jump out here and make sure the vehicles turn down the side road. You can go with them to help load. And if we're not here by the time you return with the trucks, ride back with them.

Smitty, a tall soldier with an athlete's build, jumped out as McGonigal pulled the jeep on to the main road.

"Now," the lieutenant said, his voice sounding eager and slightly breathless to his own ears, "let's step on it and see if we can find that patrol."

It didn't take long. In little more than a mile they saw the patrol's jeep pulled off to the right side of the road and partially hidden by a clump of bushes. It was on the back slope of a slight rise, and Stallingsworth knew the men would be at the crest.

"Stop here," he said when they were opposite the other jeep. "You can come for a look if you want — but keep low and out of sight."

He walked up the rise until he was near the top, then dropped to his knees and crawled the rest of the way. At the top he saw them, three men lying prone and looking toward the east. Two of them had field glasses and were examining the far terrain carefully.

"See anything?" the lieutenant asked.

"Maybe," one man answered. "It's kind of hazy but I think I saw something go over a ridge — the second one back."

"Hey!" a second soldier said. "God-damn — there they come."

Quickly the lieutenant raised his field glasses and scanned the distant ridges carefully. At first he saw nothing — then as his glasses shifted to cover the top of the nearest ridge, perhaps half a mile away, he saw it. Through the eight-power glasses it struck him suddenly as huge — even monstrous. The body had a peculiarly "squat" appearance with its wide tracks waddling its heavy body forward as if it were some gigantic alligator with impervious, armored hide. He wasn't sure whether it was a Panther or Tiger — but the extreme length of the gun's barrel and the heavy knot at the end meant the gun was one of the dreaded high-velocity cannon that would have no trouble taking on any Sherman head-on. Though he had been earnestly seeking out this monster now for days, he knew the sudden twist to his insides was not caused by eagerness alone. He might as well admit it — there was a hell of a lot of fear there too.

He hadn't expected that. He had written off the chance that he might be killed, admitted the intellectual possibility when he had enlisted. He thought, having done so, he could concentrate on performing his duty with the greatest effectiveness. And now he had to realize the feelings that squat monster had brought to life in him could never be "written off" by any intellectual process. That immediate, freezing fear would probably be with him always.

Well, if that's the way it was, he'd just have to accept it and go on from there. So he didn't have the internal wiring for a hero — so he'd just have to make do with whatever equipment he did have. And "bravery" for him could never be the joyous experience of a John Wayne movie hero. So be it. That didn't mean he had to choose the coward's way.

"There comes a second one over the ridge," one of the patrol said.

"Looks like that's only a Mark IV," the man beside him commented. "They're not coming so fast, either."

"I don't blame them," Lieutenant Stallingsworth said, trying to make his voice flat and noncommittal. "They know there's nothing in front of them but enemies — and right now they feel like the number one target of the American Army. How in hell are we going to slow them down?"

"Famous last words," one of the patrol members said. "What you going to hit them with — your good ol' Colt forty-five?"

"We ain't supposed to stop them," a second one added. "We ain't a roadblock. We're only a god-damned tripwire. The Colonel said just be sure to get back with plenty of warning time. But we better get back to the next ridge before they spot us."

"I know," the lieutenant said. "But we've got a little more difficult problem. We have a bunch of trucks back there on a side road trying to load up all the ammo they can and still get it back to Monville in time. Those shells can help out a hell of a lot when the attack on the town comes. So we got to figure some way to get maybe ten, fifteen minutes more for them to load the shells on the trucks. That could make all the difference," he added hopefully.

"It could make the difference," one of the patrol said resentfully, "of us being alive or dead. Did you ever think of that?"

"Hell yes — I think of it all the time," the lieutenant said. "But that doesn't change what we have to do."

"What *you* have to do, maybe," the soldier answered decisively, pushing himself backward until he could stand erect without being seen from the road to the east. "What *we* have to do's altogether different. Let's go, you guys. Let the heroes stay if they want."

A second man slid back and rose to his feet. The third man began to slide backward more slowly — then stopped.

"C'mon, Jonesey. No time to drag ass," the first man said quickly.

The man who had paused started again to slide backward — then stopped.

"You guys go ahead," he said. "I b'lieve I'll stay just a bit an' see if I can give these fellers a hand."

"You 'stay just a bit' and you'll give 'em more than a hand. It'll be both hands and both feet — right up to your god-damn asshole. But like the feller says — it's your asshole. We're goin' on back like the Colonel told us. You want to come with us, it's now or never."

"I b'lieve I'll jus' stay a bit with these fellers."

"Okay, asshole. A man don't look after his own, I always say he's gonna end up bein' one for somebody else. Good luck."

The two men ran quickly down the slope to the jeep. In a moment the driver had swung it around and was becoming a diminishing spot in the distance. Lieutenant Stallingsworth found himself torn between two emotions — a terrifying aloneness and a sense of pure excitement.

"What you fellers figure on tryin' now?" Jonesey asked as he stood up and faced them.

McGonigal looked up at the lieutenant inquiringly.

"Yeah — what we gonna do, Lieutenant?"

"I don't know yet," the lieutenant said. "We've just got to find some way to make those tanks slow down, at least for a few minutes — make them *think* there's something here to be cautious about."

"How about our own battalion's artillery?" McGonigal asked. "Do you think there's any chance they could reach this far?"

"Not a chance," the Lieutenant answered. "I checked on the map. By shooting charge seven at maximum range they *might* be able to reach the junction where we had our convoy turn off. But nowhere near this far."

Lieutenant Stallingsworth racked his brain for some tactic or trick he might have been taught and forgotten. There were indeed ways to stop tanks — but they all required at least some weapon, some explosive, something to work with. He remembered one lecture where they'd been given a number of suggestions — and yet not one of them seemed feasible here.

Take that one about the blanket. Just string a rope across the road and hang a blanket on it, the lecturer had said. Tankers are nervous — they'll be afraid about what might be behind it. But hell, what good would that do by itself? They'd just put one round of H.E. in to disintegrate the blanket and show there's nothing behind it to worry about. There had to be some explosive worked into it somehow.

"What have you got for explosive on board?" he asked the driver. "Anything at all?"

"Just three thermal grenades — in case we need them to destroy the radio or the jeep. Nothing else. What were you hoping for?"

"I don't know," the lieutenant said hopelessly. "Anything to make a bang, I guess."

"Too bad we didn't know sooner," Jonsesey said. "We had a bunch of TNT blocks in our jeep. We're engineers, and we were sent up to blow down trees to block a highway. Only before we got to the place we were supposed to block, the Kraut tanks were already through it."

Lieutenant Stallingsworth looked back down the highway behind them. The jeep had already passed around a curve and was out of sight.

He turned to look the other way and saw the leading tank had paused momentarily at a crossroad at the bottom of a slight valley. Probably checking their maps and deciding just where they are and where to go next, he thought. Was it possible they'd turn off down the other road? No such luck, he thought.

He raised his glasses and saw another tank had pulled abreast of the first. Then a third tank joined the first two. He peered anxiously through the glasses to see what they were doing. He saw the hatches open and the commanders of the second and third tank emerge and begin to confer — each with a map in his hand.

"Jonesey," he said. "Do you think your buddies are going all the way back to town? Or will they stop along the way to keep tabs on the enemy column?"

"I b'lieve they'd stop every so often. Maybe that ridge back there," he said, motioning toward a sharper rise a half mile behind them. "Though the way they took off outa here, I couldn't rightly say."

"McGonigal," the lieutenant said decisively, "leave those thermal grenades with me. Then take Jonsesy and head back to that next ridge as fast as you can. Jonesey, have they got many of those TNT blocks?

"Yassuh. We had a near-full box."

"Good. I remember there was one spot back maybe three-quarters of a mile where there are some big trees lining the road. Tell them we're going to try to hold the tanks here for a bit — and ask if they'll put some TNT blocks on those trees — ready to blow them so they'll fall across the road. Tell them not to blow them yet, for God's sake. We've still got to get our jeep through. They should have time enough to prepare quite a few for blowing before the tanks are anywhere near them. Especially if we have any luck up here."

The lieutenant thought a minute. He still didn't know for sure what he would do. But he'd have to figure something. Could he get back without the jeep? On the north side of the road there was just open slope, but on the south side, beginning about twenty yards from where they were, there was an area of recently planted trees. Most of them were eight to ten feet tall and the foliage was fairly thick. If he could make it that far without being seen, he should be able to pass through the trees quickly. And the road curved to the right that way —

so going straight through them the distance back to the road was less. Once back to the road he would be out of sight from this rise all the rest of the way — except for a few yards at the end. *If* he could make those tanks hold up a few minutes.

He still had only a vague idea about what he might do — but he had to get the jeep out of there fast.

"Okay, McGonigal — leave me your five-gallon gas can. Is it full?"

"Full, sir — and I got plenty in the gas tank."

"Right. Now, if I can figure out some way to hold them up, I'll try to make it back through those woods there and then up the road. But one thing you have to understand —I don't want you to come back here with the jeep. If I can't delay those tanks long enough to get back to the jeep — you've got to take off for the junction without me and contact the convoy. Tell them to pull out immediately. Remember, our first priority is to get those vehicles with the ammo — plus our own jeep with the radio — back to town. You got that?"

"Okay, Lieutenant, if you say so. It's your ass."

"Right. And I intend to take care of it — and bring it back to fire those damn guns once at a real target. Remember what I told you. Now take off."

"McGonigal can tell them about the TNT blocks," Jonesey said quickly. "I b'lieve I better stay back here with you, Lieutenant."

Lieutenant Stallingsworth felt again that sudden lift of spirit. Old slow-talking, "b'lieve-I-better" Jonesey, he thought. He's turning out to be quite an inspiration.

"Okay, if you want to — though I'm damned if I know for sure what we can do here."

"I b'lieve I better," Jonesey said, his eyes downcast and his voice noncommittal.

"All right. I sure can use you."

McGonigal had been unstrapping the extra gas can as they were talking. He raised it off its mount on the back of the jeep and placed it by the thermal grenades he had already set out by the roadside. Then he jumped in the jeep, quickly turned it around and sped back down the road.

The lieutenant crawled back to the top of the rise and looked again through his field glasses.

There seemed to be some argument going on down there between the conferring men in the tank turrets. Keep it up, he thought. Have a real strategy session — anything to use up time.

But he had to start preparing something for when those tanks started up the slope. He had only a vague idea — but something was better than nothing.

"Jonesey," he said, turning his head to look back at him, "are you a good shot with that Ml.?"

"Yassuh. I always did a lotta huntin'. An' I got the marksmanship medal — it was downright easy."

"Did you ever elevate that sight for shooting at a long range?"

"I fooled aroun' with it some, yassuh. It's a right fine gun, shoots real true, if you can figure the range and elevation right."

"Well, here's what I'd like you to try. Those tanks down there — they're probably over six hundred yards away. Can you get over to the side there, where there's some bushes to cover you, and put a shot in close to those guys half out of their turrets? Maybe two or three shots — if you can do it without them spotting your position. That's too far to hit them — but I want them to know somebody's shooting at them. And if you can come close, all the better. Could you do that?"

"I b'lieve I could, suh. If I get there under one of them

bushes, I b'lieve I could give them a full clip without them spotting me exactly."

"Great. But remember, if they spot you they'll cut down on you with an eighty-eight —and they don't have to come too close to get you with that."

"I can handle it, suh. You want I should try it now?"

"Just as soon as you can. Then come back here. But keep down below the ridge line. They'll probably plaster the whole area with cannon fire — just to scare us out."

Jonesey slipped back, picked up his Ml rifle, and ran crouching off to the right of the road — then crawled until he was at a point where he could look down into the long valley. He had ended directly under a large bush which the lieutenant thought would effectively screen him from view of someone six hundred yards away — at least for a few seconds.

While Jonesey was elevating his sight and estimating the distance, the lieutenant glanced along the side of the road for the usual tangle of wires. Good — from where he was he could see two. So far, so —

"Crack!"

The first shot rang out — followed in quick succession by a number of others.

He glanced quickly back at the tanks in time to see the hatch on one turret closing. The other was already closed. Then he saw the monstrous barrel of one of the guns traverse until it appeared to be pointed directly at the lieutenant. Quickly he pushed himself backward — then rose to a crouching run and scrambled back from the ridgetop. Ten yards back he threw himself flat at the side of the road.

He heard the whish of the approaching shell a fraction of a second before the shattering explosion just the other side of the ridge. The blast was like the stroke of doom — but he told himself he and Jonesey were protected so long as they stayed down below the ridge level.

Jonesey flopped down beside him. His usually placid face wore something like a satisfied grin.

"I bounced a few off their tank-metal," he said. "And I b'lieve I winged one of 'em a little."

"Great," Lieutenant Stallingsworth said. "Now they're going to spray the landscape for awhile. So stay down. I see you have a pair of pliers on your belt."

"Yassuh. Combat engineers have to use them for wire and fuses and things like that."

"Good. What I need now is about forty yards of wire. Cut it out of those wires along the road. And let me have your entrenching tool."

Jonesey handed him the entrenching tool and then hurried off to get the wire. The lieutenant carefully examined the road on the near side of the ridge crest. There was a slight dip down, then a level spot for a few feet, after which the road started a gradual downward slope. If he could just scoop out a shallow depression there....

More sharp cracks could be heard from the far side of the crest. He had been right. Those tankers sure wanted to intimidate whatever had shot at them.

They don't have to try so hard on me, he thought wryly. You might say they've done the job already.

He crawled back up the slope to the flatter section of the road, locked the head of the entrenching tool into the 'pick' position and scratched at the road surface. It was hard, but a small amount of the surface scraped away. Desperately he applied more power to his efforts and felt a growing amount of surface debris coming away.

What he had in mind would have been impossible — except for there already being something of a natural hollow there already. Seeing that, he concentrated his efforts on building a slight retaining wall an inch or two high around the hollow area. Despairing of ever getting enough road surface scratched away, he finally crawled to the side of the road and shoveled some sand onto the area where he'd been working. Quickly he scooped this into a now fairly definite retaining wall more than two inches high.

Looking up he saw Jonesey coming back dragging a long strand of wire behind him.

"Good," the lieutenant said. "Now tie the wire to something solid on that side of the road there and bring it out here."

While Jonesey was doing it the lieutenant slipped back down the slope to pick up one of the thermal grenades and the gas can. Crouching and feeling his pulse pounding in his head, he ran up the slope with them. Jonesey had already tied the wire to a small tree and was scampering back to the hollowed-out area.

The lieutenant seized the wire and tugged at it as hard as he could. It held.

"Okay, Jonesey," he said. "Here's what we're going to do. You tie the thermal grenade firmly to the wire — so it can't move when we pull the pin. Tie it so when the wire's pulled tight the grenade'll be in the middle of this hollow. Give me the other end of the wire — I want to run it over to those little trees. They're going to save our lives — I hope."

Jonesey handed him the end of the wire, then went to work tying the wire to the grenade. The lieutenant scurried across the road and the twenty yards of open ground to the newly planted evergreens. He saw there was plenty of wire. He ran it into the trees about ten yards — taking care there was nothing in its path for the wire to catch on and prevent its being pulled freely. Leaving the wire lying there he returned to the road, where Jonesey had just finished tying the wire to the grenade.

The lieutenant examined the grenade carefully and saw Jonesey had tied it so it would be impossible for it to be pulled out of the hollow.

"Good job, Jonesey," he said. "Just what I had it mind."

"Now you want me to tie that other wire to the pin?"

"Right. Then take that tape off — and be damned careful not to move that wire once it's tied to the pin. Just be sure the grenade's lying so the pin will slide out easy with one tug."

Once more the lieutenant crawled up to the top of the ridge. All the while they had been working, the tanks had been firing their big guns, covering the other side of the slope with random explosions. Raising his head cautiously just enough to peer over the ridge, he saw with a constriction in his chest that the first tank was much closer —probably a mere hundred yards away. Momentarily frozen, he saw the flash as the gun fired and felt a sudden blast of air rush past, just to the right of his head. This time there was no instantaneous explosion — then it came, muffled by distance far behind him.

He knew they would be shooting for the ridge crest now— a few inches lower and that shell could have taken care of both Jonesey and him.

He scrambled back down from the crest, taking care not to disturb the wire. One twitch of that wire and they would have saved the Germans the trouble of wasting a shell on them.

"Got it, Jonesey?" he asked anxiously.

"Yassuh. It's all set now."

"Good. Now follow the wire back to the trees."

Jonesey slung his rifle over his shoulder and hurried toward the trees.

Now if I can just handle the rest of this properly, the lieutenant thought. He picked up the gas can, carried it to the hollow containing the grenade, and unscrewed the cap. For a moment he was afraid it was going to stick — then it turned freely and came off, to dangle by its chain.

Swallowing back his panic at the thought of how close to the crest that first tank might be now, he spilled some of the gas out over the hollowed out area—then overturned the can so the gas would continue to pour out. The gasoline quickly began to fill the hollow. He readjusted the can slightly so the gas would not pour out so fast. He wanted that can about half full when the moment came to pull the pin.

He could hear the first tank's approaching motor filling the void between gun explosions. One more check of the grenade's position, the wire — then up and scramble desperately for the tree line.

He could hear the tank nearly at the top now. He expected to feel something big and huge and explosive blasting into his back. He ran the last few steps...and with a flooding sense of relief was at last in among the trees.

He turned and looked back behind him. Still no tank visible on the ridge. Then he heard why.

The tank was blasting at the road area with its big gun — and in between the loud shellbursts the lieutenant could now hear the chatter of machine-gun fire.

"I guess we scared them enough," the lieutenant said to Jonesey, who was kneeling, the wire to the grenade in his hands. "They figure on taking no chances here. They're afraid to cross over the ridge until they shoot up a storm."

The explosions and slicing bullets continued a few moments longer. Then suddenly they ceased.

"Here they come," the lieutenant said. "Wait until I tell you. Then give it a good tug."

"You think they'll see the gas can?" Jonesey asked.

"I don't think so," the lieutenant answered breathlessly.

"When they first come over the crest they'll be tilted back — they won't see the road at all for a second. I hope that second's enough. If they keep on moving, then they'll be right on top of it before they have time to think about it."

They heard the tank motor roar loudly, then the muzzle of the big gun and finally the top of the turret came into view.

"Easy now," the lieutenant cautioned. "Let him come a little further."

The tracks of the tank pushed it higher...it was now almost halfway over the crest. Then with a jounce the center balance-point of the tank passed over the ridge and the gun's barrel moved sharply downward. The tracks were just short of the hollowed-out area, where the overturned gas can sat quietly, a trickle of gas still spilling from it. It should be half-empty by now, he thought.

"Now!" he hissed.

Jonesey gave a tremendous yank and the lieutenant saw a glint of metal as the pin came flying out of the grenade.

For a moment nothing happened. What could be wrong? But then he remembered there would be a slight delay before the grenade exploded. Would it take too long? The tank was now completely over the hollow area so the gas tank was obscured from the lieutenant's view by the near track and boogie wheels. What was wrong with that damn grenade?

Suddenly a great flowering of orange flame came from under the tank, instantaneously surrounding it and roaring skyward with a tremendous blast. That half-empty gas can must have acted like a compression chamber, the lieutenant thought. It was more an explosion than a flame.

Now flames were eating at the tank from all sides, roaring up to flare high above it.

The tank jerked to the side and stopped. The turret flew open and a head started to come out, ducked back in as flames

leaped into the opening — then reappeard as the tank commander desperately tried to get through that wall of flame.

He scrambled out, flames licking all around his body.
He jumped wildly to the ground on the near side of the tank,
fell and rolled over once, leaped up, flames still licking down
his back. Then he turned and ran screaming back up the slope
and over it.

"Let's go!" the lieutenant yelled.

The two of them rose and ran deeper into the trees and then
down the slope. Behind them they could hear the crackle of
flame, punctuated by more tank-gun explosions and rattling
machine-gun fire

10

Colonel Berrigan gazed at the two men in front of him and thought how different they were. Both had in their control a large part of his armored power — yet there the similarity ended. Sergeant Bradovitch was a Hollywood-movie-director's model of the tough, cynical, experienced non-com. His face, covered with at least three-day's growth of beard, gazed stonily out at a world that had long ago ceased to surprise him with its indifference and cruelty. But Lieutenant Hood — what could one say of him? Or more important — what could one expect of him in a crisis? Curly blond hair above the soft, innocent baby face, the small gold-wire spectacles that gave him a curiously squinting look, the slight body that seemed lost among the folds of the officer's all-weather long coat — he should be...a boy scout patrol leader, perhaps?

And yet there was something — mingled with his obvious fear and uncertainty at being thrown so suddenly into combat — there was something almost eager about him. But it was the eagerness of a young puppy running wildly about and sniffing curiously at a world that fascinated him even as it terrified him. How could the colonel expect cool, level-headed leadership from a youth so obviously overmatched by the realities about to engulf him?

Of course the colonel had first seen him at a bad time. Even a toughened soldier can appear weakened during a bout with dysentery. But he recalled again how the lieutenant had walked out of the trees carrying the roll of toilet paper and dragging the entrenching tool behind him — a wretched, hopeless boy lost in a man's world.

Well, he thought, it's time to decide what to do with this "fighting material." He had his ridiculously small group of Shermans and Lieutenant Hood's T.D.'s. Then he had Sergeant MacKay's two "experimental models," manned by their garage-mechanics-turned-warriors, and those grotesquely awkward-looking Stuart tanks with a main cannon good enough to crack walnuts fifty percent of the time — maybe.

So for armor he had one platoon-size group of Shermans he could depend on, and for the rest — who the hell could tell? But he would have to get some real use out of those five T.D.'s, regardless of how much he could trust their officer.

"Gentlemen," the colonel began, as Sergeant Bradovitch and Lieutenant Hood faced him, "we're going to have to fight an armored battle here very shortly. And when the Germans come over the crest of the ridge and head for the river, we have to anticipate what they'll have and not be intimidated by it.

"They'll have perhaps a company of tanks immediately available to them — and they'll no doubt have support tanks stacked up for miles. It won't be just one push we have to stop. It'll be one attack after another — and no matter how many of their tanks we knock out, they're going to have plenty more to send up in their place. And don't kid yourself —

they'll be willing to expend them. This is a gamble their high command has decided to take, and they know that if they can't push it for a big, immediate advantage — they'll probably have lost the war.

"So our problem is not just to stop an attack or two — but to stop them again and again. And there's the problem, given the limited number of tanks and tank destroyers we have.

"We've not only got to use our forces effectively — we've got to use them economically, too. We somehow must preserve enough armored power to stop their follow-up attacks. Which means that we don't want simple stand-up, one-on-one, slug-it-out match-ups. We can't afford to accept one-for-one losses — or we'll be all through in a few minutes and they will have broken through. So in our tactical decisions we always have to keep in mind — how can we best stop this guy *and* not lose a Sherman or a T.D. in the process?"

"That's easy to say, sir," the hard-faced Sergeant Bradovitch said, his voice respectful but unyielding. "But we can't kid ourselves. They've got Panthers and Tigers — and plenty of them. I'd go against a Mark IV any day, and still bet I'd get him before he got me. But our guns won't penetrate those Panthers or Tigers. Not head on. The standard instructions for engaging these heavy tanks say we have to have three or four tanks to their one, so at least one or two of ours can get in a shot from the flank or rear, where their armor is thinner and we can penetrate. So what do we do to change those odds?"

"You *can't* do it yourself," Colonel Berrigan shot back immediately. "Our only hope is to use *all* our forces in the most effective way. We'll have artillery — maybe some of it very close-support, if our vehicles get back with those shells."

"Artillery's not the recommended weapon to fight tanks," Sergeant Bradovitch said. "Their dispersion's too great for pinpoint accuracy — and you practically have to get a direct hit on each tank you want to stop."

The colonel knew Bradovitch was perfectly right in his argument.

"So we've been told," the colonel agreed. "And I'm not saying we've been misinformed. But artillery *can* be potentially effective — if we can use it properly. And I think we have an artillery observer with us who can go beyond the standard operating procedure and use it with ingenuity and intelligence.

"Then there are the terrain advantages. If we plan and execute well, gentlemen, that little river with its steep banks is going to make it possible for us to stop the first few assaults without any loss of our armor. *If* we react properly.

"What I'm saying, gentlemen, is I don't want your guns to shoot until they are really needed. If it looks like someone else can do the job — let them. *Don't give.your position away unnecessarily.* That is crucial.

"In the first asaults, if we're lucky your people should be able to stay out of it. Tanks the other side of the river are someone else's job. And when they get to the bridge — leave that to the engineers. But once they're *across* the river, then, gentleman, you're going to have to carry the big load.

"But even then it can't be a one-for-one game. Spell this out to all your men — when it's your turn to fire, try for the good flank shot if you can get one. But after you fire, *change position immediately*. Tell each of your tank commanders they've got to have a number of positions already reconnoitered. Ideally, take position just behind a ridge, or between two buildings. Poke your nose out just long enough to get a kill — then get it the hell back in again. Fast!

"I know," he continued, "once they have a large number of tanks across the river, all fancy instructions go out the window. Then you'll have to fight as hard as you can with whatever odds you've been given. But we'll try to put that moment off as long as possible. The longer we can put it off, the greater our chances to pull off the kind of miracle they wanted when they sent us up here."

"Just how do you want us deployed?" Sergeant Bradovitch asked.

"I was just coming to that," the colonel said. "At the start we'll have two main avenues of attack to cover. So that's what we'll concentrate on first. They're sure try the bridge first. The engineers will have that wired and ready to blow. But the Germans will probably try to put in some kind of temporary crossing at about the same place. Lieutenant Hood, I want your T.D.'s placed so they can cover the bridge and the area around it. Position your T.D.'s so they can fire on it from many angles — and remember the need to keep maneuverability."

"Yes, sir," the young lieutenant said, his voice striving — with only partial success — for a calm and confident note.

"Now for the other route," the colonel went on. "Sergeant Bradovitch, that's going to be your first responsibility. The danger point is the spot where the dirt road fords the river about a quarter-mile off to our right flank. You'll find it's where the trees begin also. That's probably both good and bad. The trees can give you some cover — though they'll give even better cover to their panzergrenadiers, when they move them in. But you'll have some help there. Lieutenant Brownell's platoon of infantry has been assigned to defend that right flank area. Let him know just where you are and what sort of protection you want from him. Your communications with me will have to come through the Stuart tank stationed on that flank. He can communicate with the light tank I'll have right outside my C.P."

Colonel Berrigan hoped he was making the right choice in positioning these officers. He knew he was bound to be hit first and hardest over the bridge in town — and his one experienced tank leader would be far away from it. But this way he would have Lieutenant Hood right near the Task Force headquarters. He couldn't take the chance of losing those T.D.'s by some panicky move on the young lieutenant's part.

"All right," the colonel said, "we've got probably a half-hour yet — maybe a little more. Get your positions chosen and your men briefed. Good luck."

The veteran sergeant saluted and strode out of the C.P., the baby-faced lieutenant right behind him. The colonel noted how the lieutenant tried to ape the confident, almost swaggering walk of the veteran. Well, he thought, let him have whatever confidence his little pose can give him. He'll need all the help he can get.

Fifteen minutes later the colonel drove back along the road out of town looking for Sergeant MacKay's positions. Because he had thought it best to leave Sergeant McClanahan back at the C.P. while he was gone, he was now driving the jeep himself. He had driven first along the dirt road by the river to the infantry platoon digging in on the left flank. He'd been anxious to see how that tall, slow-talking and slow-thinking lieutenant was getting his men into position.

He had found the men all working hard enough. There was never much trouble getting even company goldbricks to make the dirt fly when they were facing an imminent attack without a hole to "cover their ass."

And slow-moving Lieutenant Magruder was living up to expectations. He had established his C.P. in the edge of the woods, about a hundred yards back from the river, and was digging with his customary deliberateness — thinking carefully before throwing each shovelful onto the parapet surrounding the hole. Yet the colonel saw his dispositions were actually quite acceptable — though that may have been because of the soldiers' own choices.

"Tell me your plan of action, Lieutenant," the colonel had said without introduction.

"Well," Magruder said cautiously, "we're going to put most of the men — we only have nineteen — in the edge of the forest. I didn't want them strung out all over the open field for a quarter-mile. If the enemy attack across the river, anywhere in that open space between here and town, we can put fire on them from here pretty well. If they go straight through we'll be firing on them from the flank. And if they turn toward town we'll be in their rear. I think they're going to have to come right at us to take us out. Then I hope the captain's men in town remember we're over here — because then his men can fire on their rear."

"I'll be sure to remind him," the colonel said. He knew the tactics were sound — but it would be a hell of a lot more complicated to carry out when there were a hundred or more panzergrenadiers attacking this pitiful group of nineteen men.

"What are your plans for after dark?" the colonel asked. "We're going to have a long night to get through."

"Yes, sir. I realize that. It's going to be...right difficult. I guess we'll just have to keep half the men awake as guards all the time. One thing — I wish we had some flares. It's going to be right hard to stop anybody infiltrating across that open space in the dark."

"That's one thing we've got plenty of," the colonel said. "When we picked up the small arms ammo from division, I had them throw in quite a few boxes. I'll get a box out to you before dark."

"Thank you, sir."

"Where's your tank support?"

"Our one Stuart's back there fifty yards, just inside the trees.

He claims he wouldn't last thirty seconds if he was out in the open."

He's probably right, the colonel thought. But just how many seconds does he think any of these foot soldiers are going to last out here?

"He has two reasons for being here," Berrigan said. "First, he's your communication with me. And then if you get a heavy panzergrenadier attack, his machine gun's going to come in very useful. Besides that, the tank should give you a good rallying point during the night if your position starts to crack. You and he have to depend on each other out here."

Before leaving the area the colonel had talked briefly with the tank commander. He was a surprisingly young sergeant who clearly had little in common with the veteran Bradovitch. When the colonel had reminded him of his responsibilities to the undersized platoon of infantry, he had seemed quite defensive.

"Sir," he had said, his voice trembling slightly, "we'll do our best, naturally. But light tanks are reconnaissance vehicles — we can't stand up and slug it out with even a Mark IV. To say nothing of a Tiger. Our shells would just bounce off them like ping-pong balls. Then one shot from their tank gun and we'd be nothing but fried meat."

"A lot of people are doing things that were never expected of them," the colonel said, keeping his voice calm and fatherly. Some father, he told himself wryly — he may be young, but you probably haven't got more than four or five years on him yourself.

"Battle doesn't go by regular rules," he continued. "Every situation is different — and you use whatever you've got in the best way you can. What you've got is a machine gun with a rapid rate of fire. And you can shoot it from inside your own metal foxhole. You can be a big help to these foot soldiers —

especially after dark. You can imagine how lonely they're going to be feeling out there.

"Now, you're right about keeping back here in the trees during daylight hours. I don't want your tank knocked out, either. If it goes I've lost all contact with my left flank. You're vital to me for keeping this battle in control."

"Yes, sir," the young sergeant answered respectfully. He appeared to appreciate being told of his importance in the battle. He's a good kid, the colonel thought — but he's also an intelligent kid and knows the odds against him.

"And I want you to realize," the colonel went on, "that you've got a few more things on your side than you realize. You don't want to take on any Panther or Tiger. Well, I don't want you to, either. That would be a waste of a tank and some good tankmen. And I can't afford to waste you. But remember, the chances of your getting a heavy tank on this flank are damned small — that's why I put you here. To get at you directly, a heavy tank has to come over here— more than a quarter-mile from the road. Then he has to get across that river. And the enemy's not going to come way over here to put a bridge in. The fact is they won't care about you. They want the road — and a chance to press on in a hurry. If they have to come way over here to attack the town, it's a plus for us. Because that would take a lot of time — and time is what this battle's all about.

"So keep back in the trees, and keep your communications with me open. But when the panzergrenadiers attack — get your machine gun into action fast and give those poor lonely guys out there a feeling they've got some support."

"Yes, sir," the young man said again — this time, Colonel Berrigan thought, with greater determination.

He was glad he had gone over there. That was going to be a helluva place tonight — if not before. But now he wanted to see what shape Sergeant MacKay was in. He hoped the eager mechanic-turned-armored-commander had some of his former positive spirit left. I could use a little positive spirit right about now, the colonel told himself grimly.

Sergeant MacKay turned out to be just what he needed. The sergeant's choice of positions had been ideal — and so well concealed by clever camouflaging that the colonel didn't notice them until he was almost on top of them. They were about a quarter-mile behind the town, just past the high point of a ridge that gave good observation on the town, and especially on the road through it. Both T.D.'s were hull-down, with only their guns and parts of their turrets visible. And these had been so well camouflaged by a few of the bushes that dotted the field that it was going to be damned difficult for a tank gunner to spot them.

"I like your positions, Sergeant," he said when the gangling mechanic in his grease-spattered coveralls jumped down to stand beside the jeep. "It looks like you can get excellent observation from here."

"We can cover the road all the way into and through the town," Sergeant MacKay said confidently, "except for one little bend in the town itself. And we've got observation across the river — as far as the first ridge, and even beyond in some places. We can do us some right smart damage on any tanks that come up that road — long before they get to the bridge."

"That's one reason I wanted to talk to you," Colonel Berrigan said. "Remember, your 'secret weapons' are our only defense in head-to-head battles with Panthers or Tigers. We don't want you doing anything that might give your positions away so you could be taken out early by a lucky shot. Because when their heavies make it across that river, you're all we have to depend on for a sure kill. The Shermans and the T.D.'s may be lucky enough to get a Panther or a Tiger — but with them it has to depend on luck. If the German tanks come at them the wrong way, they've pretty much had it. That's why you're so important — and we can't take a chance on losing you. Under no conditions do I want either of your big guns to fire at a target until it has definitely crossed the river."

The sergeant appeared disappointed by the colonel's words.

"How about if we go up to that knoll, sir?" the sergeant asked, pointing to a commanding rise of ground across the road another quarter-mile behind them. "We could shoot a round and duck down — then try it again from a different spot. And we'd have plenty of time and cover to get back here for our main job before the Krauts make it across the river."

The colonel had to think for a moment. This mechanic was no slouch as a tactician.

"All right, Sergeant," he finally answered. "There's some risk — but it's minimal that way. And the pay-off may be worth it. But only under these conditions. During daylight hours you keep your T.D.'s out of sight behind the high ground. Do your observation without them. Do you have any field glasses?"

"Yes, sir," the sergeant answered quickly.

If he found he needed one, the colonel thought, I bet he'd have a kitchen sink stored on that thing somewhere.

"Okay. When you spot them — say on one of those distant ridges — you're authorized to fire. One shot per tank. Then duck down again."

"Yes, sir. Then can we try again?"

"After at least a one-minute wait. And never move up higher than just enough to stick your gun out. But know where your target is *before* you pop up. Then a quick shot and down — immediately. And the minute you take a return shot that lands anywhere on your ridge — that's it. You beat it the hell back to your positions here. And once *any* tanks have got past the top of that last ridge, about a half-mile from the river — that's when you get back here. Whether they've spotted you or not.

Can you keep all that in mind?"

"Yes, sir!"

Suddenly, as he stood looking out over the town and the terrain beyond, his eye was caught by a slight motion on a ridge in the distance. He raised his glasses quickly to look at the spot.

There on the second ridge he saw vehicles passing over the crest and down out of sight. It looked like a three-quarter-ton, followed by another, then the supply truck and the kitchen truck. He could see them well enough to make out they were heavily loaded.

"It looks like our ammo train is coming back," he said abruptly. "Loaded so heavy they're practically riding on the rims. Carry on, Sergeant. I've got to get back.

11

Sergeant JayCee Washington was getting a kick out of leading the column with Hooley's three-quarter-ton. Some picture to send back to, say, Mississippi, he thought: a convoy of pure-whites led into battle by an uppity nigger.

And it was a pure pleasure to see all those hundreds of shells stacked up by the roadside — shells those nice white-skinned American boys had run off and left. JayCee had loaded the vehicles like they'd probably never been loaded before. It was only a short distance to go on good roads, and he was sure the tires could take the weight that far.

It had all gone like clockwork. The message to pull out had come over the radio just as JayCee was trying to decide whether to add a few more shells to the two-and-a-half-ton truck Hooley was driving. So he hadn't added the extra shells — which was probably just as well, considering how low Hooley's truck was already riding.

They'd got back to the junction to find the artillery

lieutenant's jeep hadn't returned. So they'd gone on through as agreed, and JayCee was still leading the column when they neared the bridge leading into town.

He wondered what had been happening further forward. At the road junction he'd seen a column of black smoke rising from behind a ridge not far to the east. That artillery lieutenant was up there somewhere. He seemed like a reasonable-enough fellow, for a white man and an officer. JayCee hoped that smoke wasn't from his jeep. JayCee's "battery" was going to need that officer for both his observation skills and his radio.

Now he wove his way through the carefully marked passage that avoided the mines the engineers had laid before the bridge. He saw the engineers were still working on the bridge. Probably going to blow it sky-high when the Krauts try to cross it, he thought.

As he drove off the bridge he saw a jeep approaching from the west end of town. The colonel himself was driving it, and he braked to a screeching stop as he came abreast of JayCee.

The colonel vaulted from the jeep and ran up to the three-quarter-ton as JayCee pulled off to the right and waved Hooley and the rest of the column on past.

"I see you struck a big haul," the colonel said. "Did you get everything you need?"

"Yes, sir. Plenty of shells — H.E. shells, a few white phosphorus, plenty of powder bags and fuses. Even some extra proximity fuses. We'll be ready to give you some real close support, sir — just as soon as we get unloaded. And as soon as the artillery observer gets back."

"Isn't he with the column?"

"No, sir. He left us where we turned off. He went on ahead..

The colonel appeared slightly concerned.

"Did you hear any firing?"

"Yes, sir. Quite a lot of tank guns, I guess — nowhere near us, though."

"I saw where you've placed your guns, Sergeant. They look like good positions. But I noticed you're close up to the hill in front of you. Won't you have to elevate your guns so high to clear the hill you won't be able to fire the close-in support we'll need?"

"I figured that out, sir. I have the men digging deep recoil pits. We'll use high-angle fire. We tilt the guns way back, the shell clears the ridge by plenty, goes nearly straight up a few miles. Lots of height instead of distance. Comes down as close as we want.it to. Just like a mortar."

"Can you adjust accurately that way?"

"Yes, sir. I think it may even be more accurate. I just have to remember to reverse the elevations for range-changes. To increase the range we have to *decrease* the elevation — instead of the opposite. It'll work out fine — as long as they've dug those recoil pits deep enough while I was gone."

"All right, Sergeant. I see you know what you're doing. Get ready to fire as quickly as you can. We're going to need all your tricks — in just a few minutes now."

"Yes, sir," JayCee sang out as he shoved the vehicle into gear and followed the convoy down the main street.

The colonel was partly reassured after his brief talk with the black sergeant. That was one soldier who knew his weapon and how to use it. High-angle fire — what a great idea. The colonel had forgotten all about that capability of the shorter-tubed howitzers.

But he was still concerned about the artillery lieutenant. He hoped he wasn't trying some heroic stunt. The colonel had developed a plan that was going to make heavy use of his one advantage in this little battle — his close artillery support. And it wasn't even armored artillery — that was the irony of it. Just some regular old field howitzers. This battle was really going to be one for the books. Five medium tanks, a platoon of T.D.'s led by a boy scout, and a couple of anti-aircraft guns commanded by a garage mechanic. With that and some old-fashioned field artillery he was going to take on what probably would soon look like half the German army.

And damn it, he'd do it too — if that artillery lieutenant hadn't gone off and got himself killed or something.

He felt a surge of hope well up within him as he saw a jeep crest the ridge to the east and speed down the road toward the town. This must be the lieutenant. He found himself holding his breath as it approached rapidly. In a moment he could make out the man in the seat by the driver.

Damn! It was just the patrol he had sent out to give an early warning of the enemy approaching. This could be real bad news. He had expected the patrol to be the last vehicle in before they completed wiring the explosives on the bridge. Did it mean the lieutenant had really had it?

He ran to the near side of the bridge and flagged the jeep down as it sped through the cleared passage and onto the bridge.

"Tanks coming?" he shouted at the non-com driving the jeep.

"Damn right, sir. They're on our tail."

"How close?"

"Depends on what that crazy lieutenant and Jonesey do next. If they ain't dead yet already."

This was what the colonel had been afraid of hearing.

"What exactly have they done?" he asked.

"Well, when the Kraut tank column showed up at the cross-road about four miles east of here, we had to take off to get back here to warn you. But the lieutenant said we had to hold them up a little longer so his ammo train would have time to get out. We told him hell no, your orders were for us to stay alive and get back here. So he said he would stay and slow them down. He didn't even know how he was going to do it. So that crazy bastard Jonesey stayed with him."

"And you haven't seen them since?"

"Hell yes, we saw 'em all right. I don't know how the hell they got out — but they told us they did slow 'em down. Used a thermal grenade and a can of gas, they said. And we saw a big column of black smoke back that way — so I guess they weren't shittin' us. But that wasn't enough for them. They wanted us to put TNT blocks on a bunch of trees along the road. They finally come back just as we were getting ready to blow those trees and clear out — even if their jeep was still on the wrong god-damn side. When you got Tigers crawlin' up your ass there's no time to hang around. But they finally made it back, so we blew those trees good. Bastards fell just right — across the road from both sides. Really jammed the road up.

"And you know," he continued, "that still wasn't enough for that god-damn lieutenant. He wanted to play some more games with my spare gas can and some TNT blocks we still had left over. The lieutenant said if we didn't pull some other tricks on them they'd get past those downed trees too fast. Hell, a hillside of trees on one side of the road and a steep drop-off on the other — and we left those tree stumps about three or four feet high on both sides of the road. But that wasn't good enough for him."

"So he stayed behind there?"

"That's where they stayed. Him and his driver and that crazy

Georgia cracker Jonesey. We did run a wire back for them so they could blow the rest of those TNT blocks without having to let the Kraut tanks get too close. The lieutenant said he would wait till they worked a tank up that far. He figured the road was so narrow there, if they could blow a tank right at that spot they'd have a helluva time gettin' around it."

"So did it work?"

"Damned if I know. We hauled ass outa there. They took a big chance once and got away with it. If it was me I wouldn't be about to shoot the dice again on those odds. We didn't hear any big explosion, though. And with all the TNT we left them — I bet you could hear it half way to Paris."

Damn, the colonel thought, I just hope the hell he hasn't got himself killed. But as bad as the situation would be if the lieutenant was knocked out — with the only communication channel to the guns in the rear — he knew what he really felt was a sense of wonder at the man's dedication. That crazy Stallingsworth. Even his name — it sounded like some rich prep-school kid's. He knew the mess everything was in, and he was taking it on his own shoulders to do whatever had to be done to get those ammunition trucks back. If I only had a command with men like that, the colonel thought — no matter if they were experienced veterans, gung ho heroes or damn fool novices — I'd match them against any force. But I never expected to find men like that in a patched-together outfit like this.

Suddenly, coming from the east, a low, rumbling blast reverberated through the air.

"By God, I believe they lived long enough to blow it," the leader of the patrol marveled, his voice quiet with awe. "Those stupid, lucky bastards. 'Course that's probably the end of them, too."

"Okay," the colonel said. "You can get back to your post now. One way or another, we're going to have callers pretty soon."

But I bet you're right, he thought. I bet those bastards really did do it. Now if they could only make it back here somehow...

He suddenly realized he was saying it to himself almost like a prayer.Trying to shake off the feeling, he turned to walk swiftly into the C.P. Inside he found Sergeant McClanahan taping a homemade map on one wall.

"Thought you'd like to see your situation at a glance, sir," the sergeant said. Colored thumb tacks showed where all the tanks and T.D.s had been positioned. It really was a big help. He saw the concentration of five yellow tacks for the Shermans over on the right wing. Three were up fairly close to the river, while two were further back behind two swells of ground. Two of those up close appeared to be back in the trees on the right, while the other was nearly up to the river. Probably has some scattered tree cover, he thought — or maybe a hump in the river bank. But whatever he's got, it's a good spot — because he has a perfect flank shot at anything crossing at the ford. So Bradovitch had done well in placing his Shermans. But what about the boy scout and his T.D.s?

They were in a very obvious formation: three north of the town's main street, two on the south. He was glad to see they were all on the very edge of town. That way they would be able to cover the vast open area on both sides of the clustered buildings. And with only slight changes of position they could fire at the bridge area.

So the boy scout hadn't done too badly. Nothing fancy — but the points that had to be covered were covered.

Of course one of the boy's non-coms might be responsible for it. All the enlisted men had seemed to treat the little blond four-eyed officer with a certain humorous condescension.

"Is this the lieutenant's T.D. here?" the colonel asked, pointing to the green thumb tack nearest the bridge on the north side of town.

"Yes, sir. He's just a couple of buildings over."

"Have all the infantry reported in ready yet?"

"The two groups in the center have — they could use the buildings for protection. The small group on the left are still digging in. Same with the platoon on the right. But the lieutenant there claims they'll be set in another fifteen minutes."

"Good. Then I guess we're about ready — if I just had my artillery lieutenant back again. Have you checked all the communications?"

"All checked, sir. Our light tank with the radio is right against the rear wall — you can practically yell out the window to him. The two Stuarts out on flanks come in loud and clear. The two you have back on the road behind us sound a little fuzzy — the distance is a lot greater. But when I checked ten minutes ago, I could make them out okay."

Colonel Berrigan sat down at the table he had been using as a desk. He suddenly became aware of how pleasant it would be to relax for a moment — maybe even drift off for a few minute's sleep. He'd been traveling steadily, night and day, for the last forty-eight hours. Then he had arrived at the armored division headquarters. And since then he had not had a moment to think of anything except the immediate crisis. But you shouldn't even be relaxing here like this, he told himself. It was about to begin — and when it did, the horrifying shocks and crises of combat were going to pile on top of each other, and he would somehow have to ride with it all. And control it? Like hell, he thought. Maybe work like hell to influence it slightly.

Suddenly he realized he was very hungry. When had he last eaten? No time for breakfast. No dinner the night before while he was flying in from Iceland. Jesus — he was really hungry and he hadn't even known it. That's what living way out on your nerve-ends can do for you.

Maybe there would be time for him to duck into the dining hall? He'd told the kitchen sergeant to keep the hot food ready right up until they saw an eighty-eight poked through the window. The mess sergeant had looked at him a little strangely. "Only half joking, Sergeant," he had said. "You can load your stoves back up when your kitchen truck gets back. And when things get hot in town you can pull back — but only a mile or so. Then set up and get your stoves going again. I want you to remember, you're a key part of this task force. Nothing like what a cup of hot coffee can do for a tired, discouraged foot soldier at three o'clock in the morning."

"Yes, sir," the sergeant had snapped back — and his voice sounded as if he had suddenly felt appreciated for the first time.

A bite to eat sounded like a terrific idea, he thought. Could he afford that much time? Hell, there was not much else he could do, was there?

That's a lot of crap, he thought. There's a million things you haven't done. He hadn't inspected all the infantry positions. Yet maybe he'd have time for a cup of coffee and a sandwich to take with him.

He rose abruptly to his feet. "I'm going back to the kitchen truck," he said. "If anything starts I'll be right back."

He went out the door and had started to climb into the jeep when he heard it.

A motor, coming fast from the east. He looked up in time to see the jeep come bouncing over the eastern ridge.

Was it...? It would have to be. It was the only one left out there.

As the jeep wove through the marked path to the bridge he recognized the tall, scholarly-looking officer sitting beside the driver.

By God, he thought, now we've got it all together. The pathetic little task force was now complete — a juggernaut of combined arms, no less. And wait till you see what we can do, he thought, before you laugh your fool heads off at us.

Lieutenant Stallingsworth clung to the windshield post as his driver swerved the jeep through the marked minefield and across the bridge without even slowing down.

"Hold it up here!" he shouted at his driver as they left the bridge and started down the main street. He wanted desperately to get back to his O.P. and prepare for the first real fire mission he had ever directed. But his eye had caught a glimpse of the colonel coming out of the C.P. and running down toward the bridge. The task force commander would want a report on what was coming — and the lieutenant could sure give him an earful on that subject.

The jeep skidded to a stop and the lieutenant leaped out just as the colonel ran up.

"Jesus, I'm sure glad to see you," the colonel said. "What have you got behind you? And how close — "

The lieutenant could see it was no time for a full report. The colonel's face and tone said it all: give me what's most important and don't shit around.

"Full armored column, sir. Tanks stacked up back as far as we could see. All kinds — but plenty of heavies. Just tanks up front. But I got one glimpse of their follow-up force when it passed over a ridgetop a long way back. And there it was all panzergrenadier tracks. So it's pretty sure they've got it all — tanks, infantry, maybe even artillery, though they haven't needed to use it yet."

"How much time do we have before they get here?"

"Hard to say. Depends on how good our last little ploy

works. I'd say minimum — ten minutes. Maybe even a half-hour. No more."

The lieutenant saw the colonel's tight features relax slightly.

"Okay. That's good enough. Are you going to keep your O.P. in that church tower?"

"Yes, sir. It's the best observation spot in the area. I figure I can use it for the first assault. Or part of it. They're going to wise up soon enough and turn an eighty-eight on it. But I intend to clear out before they start to zero in."

"Be sure you do, Lieutenant. We've got a long battle here — and I'm going to need you for all of it. Tell me what's still holding them up — then get up to your O.P. and have your guns ready."

"We stopped them once by knocking out a tank on a ridgetop. That gave us time to get back to where the engineers had prepared some trees to blow down. They did a fine job of it, too. Then I found a spot where the road was narrow with no easy way around. My men and I prepared some trees for blowing there, too. The trees fell across the road from both sides. It made a beautiful mess.

"We were watching them from a ridge just a little over a quarter-mile away. They were pretty mixed up for a few minutes. But they recovered fast. They started using some of their tanks as bulldozers to push the trees off the road. But with so many trees down and all tangled up with those three-foot high tree stumps — it wasn't easy. It was going to take them quite a long time — and they might have to wait for some real tank-dozers or engineers. But they sent a small patrol up the wooded hillside and damned if they didn't find a way through. There must have been an old road through there or something. I was kicking myself for not thinking about it earlier. I could have figured out something to block a small trail easy enough.

"But it was too late when we realized what they were doing. They had some Mark IV's almost through before we realized it and had to take off. I don't think they'd dare send Panthers or Tigers up through that logging trail though. Tanks that heavy would probably bog down and jam up the trail.

"Anyway, we had to take off when we saw what was coming. That was all we could do until a place about a mile out. There we found a spot where the road was dug out of the side of a steep hill to go around a corner. It was a perfect spot. Real steep slope up on one side and down on the other. Where it sloped up it was almost overhanging the road. So we took all the TNT blocks we had left and blew the damn overhanging part down onto the road. It was beautiful. No road left there — just a pile of rocks and dirt and blasted trees. And I don't think there's any easy detour they can take there."

"Are they going to have to go back and find some secondary roads to get around?"

"I don't think so, sir. They may have to bring up some engineers with bulldozers — but they probably have some riding not far back in the column. Then they'll dig or blast a way through. But it ought to take them quite a few minutes for sure. That's why I think we may have close to half an hour."

"Sounds good, lieutenant. I got word you were taking quite a few risks out there — knocking out that first tank with nothing but a thermal grenade and a can of gas. It sounded like you had forgotten what I said about not taking unnecessary risks. I thought if you ever made it back here I was going to have to kick your ass for disobeying orders."

"We didn't take any unnecessary risks, sir. If we hadn't stopped them for at least a few minutes our ammo train would have been caught. And we'd have lost all our transport — and our artillery personnel. The Tigers would been blasting through here an hour ago. We *had* to have some time, sir."

The lieutenant seemed genuinely disturbed at the colonel's

157

criticism. Here he does something good enough to win him a medal, the colonel thought, and he thinks I was really criticizing him for it.

"Don't take that 'criticism' too seriously, lieutenant. I know what kind of a bind we'd have been in if you hadn't taken the risk. And don't think I don't appreciate it. Now get over to your O.P. and I'll join you there after a bit."

"Yes, sir. Thank you, sir."

Fifteen minutes later Colonel Berrigan figured he was as ready as he was going to get. He had told the commander of the light tank behind his C.P. to radio a warning of the approaching column. Then he had taken the mike and talked with the infantry lieutenants commanding both of his flank forces. Lieutenant Brownell on the right said he was ready. And on the left old slow-motion Lieutenant Magruder said he was far enough along in his preparations so his men could fight in a pinch. "The men's holes are still pretty shallow," he had said in his slow, cautious voice. "I hope we're going to be allowed time to deepen them before we have to fight off an attack."

"Well, Lieutenant, *I'm* going to allow you time. But we just got word the tanks are arriving in maybe ten-twenty minutes. So I don't know just how many minutes the Germans are going to allow you. Just keep your men hard at it — until they have to jump in and start shooting."

"Yes, sir," the lugubrious voice replied. "But we really do need some extra time. I hope you...er...*they* allow it."

What a character, the colonel had thought. But was he going to be as bad under fire with everything collapsing around him? Probably — except for a miracle. And in a battle it's not exactly a wise decision to count on miracles.

Next he had sent a messenger back to the garage-mechanic with the two ninety-millimeters, telling him not to open fire until someone else did. He wanted those 'secret weapons' as a reserve he could count on. And if they fired first, there was a fair chance they would be spotted and picked off. That left him just one more task. He jumped into his jeep and drove the short distance to where the young lieutenant's T.D. was parked close to the last house before the quarter-mile of open field began.

"Get in," he said as the lieutenant jumped down from the squat, topless turret that crowned the destroyer's tracked, solid-looking body. "Let's take a run around the town once to look at your dispositions."

"Yes, sir," the diminutive officer snapped in his high, almost adolescent voice. The colonel drove along the river, passed the bridge, and turned right to skirt the buildings on the south edge of town. The lieutenant pointed out each T.D. as they passed it, and in a tight but proud voice gave a rather lengthy explanation of each position — with its field of fire, concealment, and possibilities for maneuver.

"Have any of your men been in action before, Lieutenant?"

That stopped the young officer's lecture on tactics fast enough.

He started to answer, apparently choked up on his first word, swallowed hard and tried again.

"Nuh-no, sir. That is, my platoon sergeant was with an outfit that saw a little action in Normandy. Before he was transferred out to my platoon. He's — he's a very good man, sir."

"Weren't you in position up ahead earlier?"

"Yes, sir. That is, we never got to go into action."

"Did you see any enemy tanks?

"Yes, sir — a whole column of Tigers. That is — I didn't

see them myself, sir. Sergeant Whipple — he's the sergeant who saw action in Normandy — he was in position ahead and he saw them. In fact, if he hadn't helped me make the right decision quick, we'd have been wiped out."

"He made your decision to run without firing a shot?"

"Well...he...*we* decided our position was hopeless and we'd better get our T.D.s out while there was still a retreat route...."

The young lieutenant stopped, as if suddenly realizing how his words must sound.

The colonel didn't say anything for a few seconds, merely observing quietly the young man's face begin to redden with discomfort.

"I...uh...I've had to rely on Sergeant Whipple quite a lot. I...I just got out of O.C.S. two weeks ago and they shipped me right over. So I was glad to have a sergeant who...I mean, really knew the score. Because...I was...sort of all confused when things began to happen fast. I thought we had to stay there, but I really wasn't sure how to...handle the situation. But Sergeant Whipple stepped in and gave...helped me make the right decision. I learned a lot from him. He explained to me, after we had got out, why it was a tactical necessity for us to change positions there fast. That way we saved all five destroyers."

The colonel still didn't say anything as the lieutenant finally wound down like a top running out of spin. After a moment the colonel thought he had given the young man the brutal silent treatment long enough.

"Lieutenant...Hood, is it?"

"Yes, sir. Hood — Lee Beauregard Hood."

Jesus Christ, the colonel thought, barely able to stop himself from bursting out laughing. What a string of Southern heroes to hang onto an undersized young boy scout. Probably they've still got the old Confederate uniforms hanging upstairs in the attic — with all the medals carefully put away in little boxes.

"You're from Texas, Lieutenant?"

"Yes, sir."

The young man seemed caught somewhere between shame and pride.

"Any relation to the famous Confederate General Hood from Texas?"

"Yes, sir. I've always known all about him. He's...uh...was my great-great-uncle. On my father's side. Our family always paid a lot of attention to family history. We...we were lucky, I guess you'd say, in our ancestors."

"Your mother was a...Lee?"

"No, sir. She was a Beauregard. The General that beat the Yankees at First Manassas. A direct descendent on that side. They just decided on Lee as a...an appropriate first name."

How right they were, the colonel thought grimly. With a string of monikers like that, it's a wonder your joints could bend enough to walk around like a human being's.

"Well, Lieutenant Hood, you certainly have a very proud tradition to live up to. But in battle, we all start out alike — scared shitless and our thinking capacity blown clear out of our minds. It's only later on, when other people get ahold of what happened and twist it into a neat little tale to make everybody feel good — only then does war get romantic. But out here we have to live in the first phase — scared shitless and scatterbrained. Yet if we hang on we can all do it somehow. And you can too. Then your relatives can make up some good stories to go with the family tradition.

"But you and I don't have to worry about all that. We only have to worry about how to get through today and tonight, and maybe tomorrow. Doing our job the best way we can. And never mind about heroes or family legends.

"Now," he went on more crisply, "your positions look fine. And your weapons are about the best we've got. Your job is to use them as effectively as you can. Not like a tactical genius. None of us are tactical geniuses any more. Our weapons are too advanced now, too deadly to leave much room for tactical genius. I'm afraid we have to use our guts and our bodies instead — and as much common sense as we can muster with all the pressure on us.

"So don't worry too much about your lack of experience. Or how young you are. And don't trust too much in what Sergeant Whipple may tell you. It's *you* who have to make the decisions and give the commands. I don't know Sergeant Whipple from Adam, and I might be all wrong about him. But frankly, from what you tell me, I'd be willing to bet Sergeant Whipple was transferred out of his old outfit because they thought he had fouled up somehow. Maybe even then he was a little too fast to 'pull back in time to save the whole platoon.' People don't get transferred out because they're such balls of fire. In the army everyone knows when you get an order to 'transfer out' so many enlisted men, that's when every commander goes down his roster and gets rid of every goldbrick, blowhard and incompetent he can.

"So *you're* running this outfit, Lieutenant. Not Sergeant Whipple or your family tradition or your own ideas of what you ought to be in combat. You'll be just all like the rest of us — scared shitless and muddle-minded. But you can hang on and do it anyhow — just like the rest of us."

The colonel paused a moment, wondering if he had said the right thing or simply made matters worse. The boy was looking at him with wide-staring eyes. Was that only horror he saw in them? Or was it horror mixed with the beginnings of a desperate knowledge?

Well, he thought, it's the best I can do. Because who the hell am I to give lectures on what real combat is like? Me —

who's never heard a shot fired in anger.

"Now," he continued," I don't want your men to fire on this first attack unless a tank makes it across the bridge. When it does, you'll have an angle partly from the flank — so with those high-velocity seventy-sixes of yours, you've got a damn good chance to penetrate on the first shot. If it doesn't, get the second one in fast. Then move. That doesn't mean to take off to save your destroyer. That's just to make you a harder target. Is that clear?"

"Yes, sir."

He wondered if he did have it. Were those wide eyes comprehending or merely desperately lost?

"Good luck, lieutenant," he said as he stopped the jeep by the lieutenant's destroyer and watched him climb out, tripping slightly on his oversized all-weather coat. Then he pulled the jeep around and headed across the main street toward the church, which stood dark against the gray sky on the edge of town nearest the approaching enemy.

12

Lieutenant Stallingsworth stood with his eyes glued to the tall tripod-mounted B.C. scope and stared at the tank approaching in the distance. The roof timbers of the church-tower were just above his head. He knew the Krauts were sure to blast this church tower when they discovered they were up against observed artillery fire. But it gave just too perfect a view of the bridge and the terrain beyond not to use it initially. And from this height the radio could reach battalion with no difficulty. He just had to remember not to stay too long.

Corporal Cordova, the radio operator, glanced down the narrow stairwell at the sound of approaching footsteps. He quickly turned to the lieutenant and uttered an urgent, quiet-voiced warning.

"Chicken junior crawlin' in the nest."

The lieutenant shifted his gaze to the opening in the floor and saw the lieutenant colonel climbing through.

"Easy, Corporal," he said in a half-whisper. "This one's OK." He put his eyes back to the B.C. scope and raised his voice. "We poked another hole in the roof just ahead of you sir, if you want to use glasses."

"Thanks, Lieutenant," the entering officer said, taking out his field glasses and stepping forward. "What do you figure is the best way to play this? You want to put a concentration on them just short of the bridge — or way back as they come over the ridge?"

"The way they've been coming over that second ridge line back there, sir, we have a real chance to start out with a big kill."

"How do you mean, Lieutenant?"

"I've just come back over that road, sir, and I checked direction, distance, everything. Between the two ridges, the part we can't see from here comes straight as a die, and the map distance is correct to within a few yards. The enemy are going to know they're under observation from town when they go over that near ridge. Then they'll probably be moving with a lot of distance between tanks. But back behind that first ridge we can't see anything — except for those few yards right at the crest of the second ridge. And they've been coming over that second ridge really jammed up."

"And you want to put a concentration on that second ridge-top?"

"No, sir. We can do even better. I think we can bet they're going to stay jammed up all the way on that road between the two ridges. Then when they pass the near ridge they'll stretch out to their proper intervals. The time to hit them is *before* they get spread out."

"But you can't see to adjust the fire there, can you?"

"No, sir. But we won't *have* to! The battalion has already got a good adjustment on a map point in the general area. And since we know the road is correct on the map — running straight between the two ridges — my battalion should be able to put a concentration down right where the road's getting all jammed up with tanks. We won't *need* observation, sir. Fire Direction can plot it right off the map. A TOT — Time On Target. That's what we should have. Start with battalion ten volleys — one hundred and twenty of our hundred-pound shells – without any adjustment rounds to warn them. That road'll look like a tank graveyard, sir!"

"Aren't you forgetting the big dispersion you'll be getting with those big howitzers? What is it —a hundred yards?"

"That's only in *range* — in distance, sir. The new one-five-fives get very little dispersion in deflection. And —" here the lieutenant's voice took on the excited note of an enthusiastic player seeing a clear opening for a score – "and that god-damned road runs practically smack-dab on our gun-target line. Hell — the guns will be firing almost zero deflection. Those shells won't vary more than five or ten yards from that god-damned road! Let the shells disperse all they god-damn want to in range! We'll just be hitting another chunk of road — a road jammed up with Tigers or Panthers! Jesus, sir – it's a god-damned godsend!"

The lieutenant's exuberance was sucking the colonel into its pull.

"It sounds great, Lieutenant. What are you waiting on?"

"The tanks are almost where I want them, sir. Another three or four minutes and I figure they should have that road lined up practically bumper-to-bumper. But that damned colonel of mine — he can't bring himself to take the plunge! He's 'checking it out.' Which means he and Major Grampton, his executive officer, are humph-humphing each other around the C.P. tent while they try to decide if they should spend a hundred and twenty shells on a god-damned second lieutenant's judgment. And if they don't build up enough guts to make the right decision — they're going to shoot the chance of a lifetime down a rat-hole!"

There was a desperate plea in the lieutenant's voice.

The colonel turned to the radio operator.

"Can you get me your C.O. on that thing?"

"Yes, sir!" Corporal Cordova said   promptly. He pressed the button on the microphone and spoke urgently.

"This is Charlie Three. The Six of the whole damn task force here wants to speak to our Six. Immediately! Over."

A long pause followed. There were two or three sudden squawks as if the microphone button was being struck as the mike was passed from hand to hand. Finally a tremulous voice was heard.

"Er...this is Valiant Six here...er.. .go ahead, Lone Bandit Six."

Corporal Cordova handed the mike to the colonel, who grasped it and spoke into it firmly as he pushed the send button.

"Valiant Six, I'm the Six of that important mission I believe my double-star talked to you about just a little while ago. This mission is crucial — and I intend to be sure the General gives full credit to those who make it succeed. Or fail. Are you receiving me?"

There was another pause. Then the same hesitant voice replied.

"Roger. We'll do everything possible to help. We've been trying to advise our observer what will be most helpful."

"That's fine. Now we've got a unique situation here. Too complex to explain. But the observer here has figured this problem out just fine. It's important his request be carried out exactly as he made it. Now how many volleys had you intended to give him?

"Fi—the full ten requested, sir."

"Excellent. I intend to notify my Six of the fine cooperation you are giving us in this crisis. Are there any other decisions to be made on this? Over."

After a moment the tremulous voice again came through the speaker.

"Er...nuh—that is, the lieutenant is requesting the concentration on a twenty-five yard front. That must be in error. One-five-fives shoot a minimum of a hundred-yard front. A twenty-five yard front would be unprecedented...and we'd have a tough job justifying that to Corps when it was questioned...as it surely would be. I trust you agree on that, Lone Bandit Six. Over."

"Valiant Six," the colonel said in a loud, firm voice, "I trust you will understand we are dealing with a *completely unprecedented* situation here. A hundred-yard front would be shooting eighty-percent of your rounds down a rat-hole. Twenty-five yard front — that's the absolute maximum we can tolerate here. Then your battalion can take credit for a real coup. Your observer has set this up to give your battalion a unit citation if you can deliver on this one. Tell your gunners to align their stakes and level their bubbles well and it'll be one for the books. Only they must be ready to fire on the observer's command in the next two minutes! That is urgent. No further delay! Over."

There was another pause of a few seconds before the same tremulous voice came again from the speaker.

"Er...wilco, sir...er...firing commands going down now...we'll be ready to fire in ...er...sixty seconds. Over."

"Excellent, sir. Rest assured your immediate recognition of the need for unprecedented action will not go unnoticed. Have the guns fire at your observer's command."

"Wilco, sir."

Lieutenant Stallingsworth suddenly felt as if a shaft of sunlight had burst through the gray December sky. He turned quickly back to the B.C. scope. By God, once in a while you met a field grade who knew how the hell to fight a war.

Private Hatfield paused a moment in his digging and glanced around. Everyone else was digging seriously. He was in the hastily organized "first squad" of six men, including himself and the young soldier who had tried to hide his sobbing back in town. The squad leader was a sergeant he'd never seen before. The lieutenant had scratched his balding forehead while he thought about it a rather long time — then told them to dig in on the edge of the trees, about a hundred yards back from the river. The sergeant hadn't given them any further instructions, so Hatfield had motioned to his new friend to come and dig beside him, and they had been digging ever since. They now each had a hole about a foot deep — which would give some protection, but not nearly enough.

"Deep," Sergeant Forte had always told him. "That's the secret. Deep! Remember — another few inches down can mean you're still alive after a close shellburst. And if there's a chance of enemy tanks — then the word is 'deeper still.' And keep the sides straight so the tank treads can't crumble 'em.

For a moment Hatfield felt the horrible loneliness of knowing Sergeant Forte would never be there again for him. Would he have had some little tip about how to dig into dirt frozen as hard as this?

Well, there was nothing to do about it. Except to try and remember the things the sergeant had told him – and to use his own common sense for the rest. It was a long war, and the only way out was going the way Sergeant Forte had gone. Unless a shell or mine or something chewed you up so much you weren't worth a damn — then they might send you home. If anybody still wanted you around after that. All in all, it was a pretty grim outlook.

Still, when he glanced over and saw the innocent-faced young kid digging dutifully in the hole beside him, it gave him a little comfort. Of course it couldn't be like it was with Sergeant Forte. This kid beside him was more lost than he was. Yet it was kind of good to know he was right there. The boy was actually coming to depend on him a little. That was a laugh. He felt as green as he had on the day he arrived at the front. Yet by the way that new young soldier looked at him, he could tell the boy was thinking of him as some kind of veteran. And that was kind of pathetic.

But kind of nice, too.

"Say, look over there — between those two ridges.!"

Another soldier a few yards away had stopped digging and was pointing across the river and off to the right.

Private Hatfield followed his pointing finger and saw something to make his heart freeze. There on the road were what looked like more tanks than he had ever seen that close together.

"Jesus!" another soldier breathed. "Are we supposed to stop that? Why'n hell don't those tanks of ours fire?"

"They can't see 'em yet in town," the corporal said. "That first ridge is in the way. We can see 'em from here because the ridge peters out on this side."

"Well somebody better do somethin'. Or we ain't doin' no good diggin' over here."

A sudden rush of incoming shells, followed by the distant thumps of artillery firing, sent them all full length into their partly dug holes.

Hatfield waited for the bursts, praying they would miss him. Then they landed with a rapid series of whump-whumps. They weren't even close. He raised his head and looked.

"Hey," he yelled, "they're ours! Look at 'em land!"

Timidly at first, others joined him — standing and watching in fascination. The rounds kept coming in, each erupting with a red-orange flash and a tower of smoke and dirt. They seemed to be striking all around the tanks and vehicles. And some obviously were hitting, leaving tanks burning a deep red in the gathering dusk. Still the rounds came crashing in, leaving more burning hulks lined along the road.

The men were left speechless as they watched. It must have gone on for nearly five minutes. Then it was over, and the road was lined with burning shapes in the dusk. Little figures could be barely seen spilling from them.

"Wow," someone finally said, breaking the new-fallen silence. Then without thinking they all burst out in a spontaneous cheer.

"Did you ever see anything like that?" one soldier asked in disbelief. "Hell, we might even win this goddamn war, ya know?"

Back at the church-tower Lieutenant Stallingsworth knew the rounds were hitting home when he saw the columns of smoke rising from behind the first ridge.

He stepped quickly to where Corporal Cordova sat holding the radio microphone. Seizing it the lieutenant spoke into it urgently.

"This is Charlie Three. Fire very effective. Repeat — fire very effective! We can see many columns of smoke rising from between the two ridges. We've caught them all jammed up! Now — aim another concentration, say battalion five volleys, at the section of the road immediately beyond the one we've just hit. Read it right off the map. I've checked — the map's highly accurate about that part of the road. Then when you've finished there, come a couple hundred yards short of your first volley and give another battalion five volleys there. Hurry — or they'll be trying to get off the road. Over."

This time the response was immediate.

"This is Major Schwartz. We'll have your second mission on the way in just a just few seconds. Five volleys. Then the same at the shorter range. Good work, Charlie Three. See if you can give us any definite results — so we can tell the cannoneers something to boost their morale. Over."

"Major Schwartz is okay," the lieutenant said to Colonel Berrigan. "He's head of Fire Direction Center. He'll do the right thing if the colonel will let him alone. I bet he'll — "

He broke off as a "whissst" suddenly increased in volume until it slammed into the roof of the church tower, tearing a section of it loose and scattering pieces down on them.

"Take off, everybody!" the lieutenant shouted, clapping the legs of the B.C.scope together in one motion and hoisting it on his shoulder. "They figured out where we are and they're shooting from the far ridge."

Corporal Cordova unlatched the radio from the battery pack. The colonel, seeing what he was doing, seized the handle of the battery pack while Cordova picked up the radio. Then they all scampered together down the narrow, steep stairway to the upper story of the church. Without pausing they hurried on down the wider stairs to the main floor. There they all fell flat as they heard a whole series of "whisssts," followed by three explosions, one after another, above their heads. The lieutenant lay for a moment with his heart pounding against the rough wooden church floor. Then he looked up and saw debris falling into the main section of the church. Another round came in to strike directly overhead. He looked straight above him and saw a huge opening appear suddenly in the ceiling.

"Come on!" Cordova shouted. "The god-damn walls are caving in."

The corporal jumped to his feet, seized the radio by the handle and fled through the door. The colonel was right behind him, and the lieutenant followed with the awkward B.C.scope now under one arm. They ran the twenty yards that took them behind a solidly built structure and sprawled there to catch their breath.

Looking back the lieutenant saw more rounds hitting the church.

"They're firing high explosive shells now," Stallingsworth shouted. "Lucky that first one was armor piercing. If it had been H.E. they might have got us all."

"Where are you going now?" the colonel asked.

"We've got an alternate O.P. already picked out," the lieutenant said. "That tall house behind your C.P. We'll go there and set up."

"Right," the colonel said. "I'll be at the C.P. Keep me informed of what you see and what you're doing."

Nearly a half-mile behind the town Sergeant MacKay had been waiting anxiously for the firing to begin. He had taken his two "secret weapons" to the ridge he had told the colonel about. There he had seen the approach of the German tanks. From his new position, considerably higher than the town, he could see the two ridges across the river clearly — and even a small stretch of the road as it gradually descended from the further ridge into the valley.

He had left both his destroyers completely below the ridgeline and was now lying on his belly in the grass, gazing at the distant ridge intently through field glasses. Sergeant Kowalsky, his top mechanic and now temporary commander of the other "experimental weapon," lay at his side. He was sure they could not be seen in the long grass, even though they were right at the crest of the ridge.

Sergeant MacKay had been impatiently waiting to try out his new "baby." He had been sure the ninety-millimeter anti-aircraft gun could penetrate as well as the famed German "eighty-eight." Once he had begun to read the reports of how the Shermans were faring against the German heavies, he had been trying to convince every officer he talked to of the folly of playing around with seventy-fives — or even the newer "high-velocity" seventy-sixes. They should, he argued, go straight to the ninety-millimeter. Then the American tanks could have an equal chance against the enemy's biggest and toughest. Sending American tankmen into action with those popguns was just telling them the leadership was perfectly willing to sacrifice four or five of our tanks — and their crews — to destroy one of the enemy's.

But mere sergeants — even top-ranking technical experts with three stripes up and three down under — didn't stand a chance to get the ear of a general high enough to challenge the system.

But by God he was in a position to show them now. He'd been playing around with these babies ever since the middle of October — and when this new offensive hit, the generals had been desperate to throw in anything that was available. He knew they didn't have a lot of faith in his idea. Which was all right with him. He had enough faith for all of them. And now was the time to show them.

"Ain't we gonna pull up to the ridgetop now and blast hell outa them?" Kowalsky asked eagerly. Sergeant MacKay knew his fellow mechanic was as anxious as he to put their "babies" to a real test.

"Not yet," MacKay answered. "I promised the colonel I wouldn't fire first. Besides, if we're going to show the big brass we got the right system here, we don't want to take a chance the Krauts might get a lucky shot in before we blast a bunch of them. So we're not going to let them have even a little peek at the top of a turret until we're ready to pull up and shoot. No delay — just line up the sight and let 'er go. We got to have the range and everything set. We'll try to fire at something on that second ridge. The map shows it's about 2900 yards from here — which looks about right to me. And at that distance the deflection ain't gonna vary worth shit. Elevate for 2900 yards — practically nothing for the high-velocity we're shooting — and aim dead center at where you want to hit. We'll probably have to go for the turret head-on, because they're going to be pointing this way."

"Hell, all the better," Kowalsky said, his square, pugnacious face scowling fiercely. "That's what we always told them, wasn't it? We could take a Panther or even a Tiger head-on, right through their thickest god-damned armor. Ain't that what we told 'em?"

"We told 'em, all right. And now we have to show 'em we weren't just whistling Dixie."

"How the hell long are they gonna hold back?" Kowalsky muttered, looking through his own field glasses. "They'll be coming over that first ridge in a couple minutes."

"The colonel said not to fire first. And I said we wouldn't."

"Hell, maybe down there in town they can't see the second ridge, and they don't even know what's comin' at 'em."

"They can see the top of it where the road goes over. So the colonel must be planning something special for them. We'll give him his chance first. Don't worry — considering how many tanks we already seen go over the ridge, there's gonna be plenty to go round."

A sudden series of dull thumps came from far to their rear — followed by a rush of air overhead. Then down in the valley, between the two ridges and just out of their view, a number of explosions erupted. After a moment smoke began to rise high enough into the sky for them to see it. A few seconds later more shells landed — then the shelling continued without interruption for what seemed like a long time.

"That's what the colonel was waiting on," MacKay said. "Artillery. Caught 'em all on the road."

"Artillery can't hurt 'em that much," Kowalsky said. "They think a shell fragment's gonna punch through the armor on a Tiger?"

"Hell, no," MacKay said. "Them things are the big ones — one-five-fives. And they're throwing so damn many of them in — look, see how they're all concentrated on the road? They're going for direct hits."

"They got no muzzle velocity like we do," Kowalsky muttered defensively. "I bet they can't penetrate any better than us."

"They don't shoot for penetration, like we have to," MacKay said. "Anybody gets hit by a hundred pounds of high explosive — they're not going to just drive away and forget it. Look at those smoke columns coming up. I bet there's a whole lot of them down there where we can't see — burning to beat hell."

"So now somebody's shot first — so now we can shoot, right?"

"I think the colonel meant direct-fire shooting — not artillery. Don't worry. We'll get our chance soon enough."

MacKay heard Kowalsky grumbling under his breath. He's really anxious to blast away at something, MacKay thought. Well, so am I. But we better go by the colonel's plan.

Then he saw two tanks near the top of the second ridge pull

off to the right of the road. In a moment two more pulled to the left.

"Here we go!" he shouted. "See those four tanks on the ridge? They're about to let fly. When they do — you an' me are up at bat. There! The bastards are shooting. Trying to knock down the damn church steeple, I guess. Now do like I said. Pull up just enough, have the range all set, and you take two tanks to the left — I'll take the ones on the right. And remember — one shot and then down. And wait a minute before you come up — in another place. You got it?"

"Hell, yes!" Kowalsky shouted, squirming backward through the grass. "Let's stop this fartin' around and do it!"

MacKay grinned at his friend's impatience as he too worked his way back over the ridgetop. Kowalsky might be impatient — but he was a good man and he'd follow directions.

Now, Sergeant MacKay muttered to himself, let's see what we can do.

He climbed into the open turret and shouted down to Corporal Hawkins, his driver.

"Okay, Hawk! Here we go. Up slow and easy — and stop the second I tell you."

"Right, Sarge. Easy does it."

Sergeant MacKay set the range as they were moving forward. Then he glanced through the sight. Still nothing but the grass of his own ridgetop. Then they were over the top and he saw gray clouds — and as they rose a little higher, the second ridgeline appeared in his gunsight

"Hold it, Hawk!" he shouted down at his driver. Hawkins obediently stopped the vehicle. Quickly Sergeant MacKay traversed until the tank on the extreme right came into his view. He centered the tank in his sight, elevated just a little until the tank's turret was in the center of the cross hairs.

The crash of the gun blasted his eardrums as he fired.

"Back down, Hawk!" he shouted.

Hawkins must have had it in reverse waiting , for immediately the tracks spun backward and they were again below the ridgeline.

But not before Sergeant Makay had seen the high-velocity shell strike just to the left of the huge gun protruding from the German tank's turret. He knew that one hadn't bounced off. It had gone right on through.

He heard Kowalsky's ninety-millimeter cannon blast away just a moment later.

"I got the bastard," Kowalsky's voice shouted from the radio. "Dead center. How'd you do, Sarge?"

"Ditto. No bouncey. Straight penetration."

"Let's go back for the other two. Jesus, we can win the god-damn war with these babies."

"Wait the full minute now. And come up in a different place. Remember, it's a long war. And we got a lot more tanks to plug."

Sergeant MacKay directed his driver to pull about twenty yards to the right before trying again. He waited the full sixty seconds, then shouted down, "Okay, Hawk. Here we go again. Nice and easy now."

Once again he checked the range setting, then glued his eye to the sight as they popped up over the ridge. For a moment he didn't see the tanks. Then he realized his gun was too far to the right. He traversed left, past the smoking tank he had just blasted, to the second tank on the right. It was all so easy. Center the target on the cross hairs, move the elevation just slightly, and fire!

"Down, Hawk!" he yelled, even as he saw his second round strike home. A solid hit.

But as the driver backed the destroyer down below the ridgeline he heard a tremendous rush of air just over his head. A moment later a shell exploded somewhere behind him on a distant slope.

A moment later another round landed on the front slope of the ridgeline close to where he had appeared. Then he heard Kowaisky's second shot — followed in a moment by a round landing on the ridge where Kowalsky's vehicle had been only a split second before.

"Are you okay, Kowalsky?" he asked anxiously into the radio.

"Hell, yes. And I plugged my second one. How'd you do?"

"Got mine, too. Now we gotta get back to our other positions. It didn't take the bastards long to spot us, did it?"

"Hell, I bet we could get us another one if we shifted around some more."

"Ix-nay on that, ol' buddy. I promised the colonel — once they spotted us, that was it. Back to our old position. We got four for four — a pretty damn good record to report, I'd say."

Colonel Berrigan had already arrived at his C.P. when he heard the high velocity shells tearing almost directly over his C.P. That had to be Sergeant MacKay's two improvised tank destroyers. Quickly he bounded up a flight of stairs to the second-story room on the east side of the building. At the east window he scanned the further ridge with his field glasses, even as he heard the third and fourth rounds blast past. He had to adjust the focus — and then he saw them. Four tanks sitting dead — two of them burning furiously.

By God, he thought, I knew it! The sergeant had simply

gone ahead and done what the colonel himself had always advocated. And there was the evidence. Four for four!

Now if the sergeant wouldn't push his luck and get his two "experimental models" knocked off right away, the colonel would know he had a good ace in the hole for when those tanks came pouring across the river and into town. Which they'll be doing soon enough, he thought, regardless of how many little victories we can squeeze out first.

But by God, he told himself exultantly, they're going to know they've been in a god-damned battle. Then he remembered to glance down at his watch.

The hands showed him it was only ten minutes past three. Plenty of time for them to mount a full-scale attack before dark.

And then of course there was the long night. And after that...the next day....

13

Sergeant JayCee Washington had felt a twinge of jealousy as he heard the concentrations of artillery pass overhead to land a few hundred yards to the east. That was what his battalion should have been doing, supporting this band of gallant defenders, instead of galloping off madly to save their own necks. So everybody, seeing them rushing for the rear, could look at each other and say, "Well, there go the boogies. Damn generals should have known better — no black bastards are gonna stay and fight."

Well, two-thirds of the battalion's guns and most of the men were long gone — and all those brave white bastards they put over us for officers. But at least there's four guns and a few black bastards left here — to make you eat all your "scared boogie" talk. Though of course all anyone would ever know about it would be the ones who "shagged ass." And of course they'd forget all about the white officers. Lieutenant Ransom would probably have a great time after the war — telling his Ku Klux Klan drinking buddies about those terrified black bastards, with their eyes big as saucers, that he couldn't get to stay with their guns.

Well, you couldn't control what people would say about you. But whatever the others did, his guns were at last ready. When he had got back with the ammunition he had had to ride everybody's ass pretty hard. There were only twelve men all together—counting himself and Hooley. That meant three men per gun – horribly short-handed gun crews.

But he knew they could manage it — provided everybody worked like hell and did two or three jobs at once. And with no "fifth section" to manhandle the ammunition, he'd had to unload all the shells near each gun. No time for the usual safety rules. If an incoming round should hit any one of those piles of shells stacked near each gun, there could be hell to pay. It might even set off a chain reaction — and leave shells blowing up all around them.

If they had more time, maybe they could dig some of the shells in. But all he'd been able to do so far was provide some shallow pits to hold the fuses, igniters, and powder bags. They'd be the most likely things to go up. The explosive in the shells was, after all, encased in a heavy metal jacket. It took a lot to explode them. But those stacks of powder bags, in their long cardboard casings, held together three to a cluster — one little lick of flame and...whisssh! An instant mountain of flame, incinerating anything nearby.

Well hell, if he worried about safety, how could he ever provide any support at all? If he properly dispersed all the shells and powder bags, they couldn't get three rounds off in five minutes, short-handed as they were. Instead of like real gun crews — three or four a minute, minimum. And in their peculiar position for medium artillery, right up practically with the infantry and tanks, they were going to have to move with desperate speed to meet all the emergencies they might be needed for.

He felt he had at least one trustworthy man on each gun to do what had to be done. He himself would be chief of section for the number-one gun. Which meant he would do his own job and the gunner's, checking deflection from the aiming stakes, then raising the tube and applying the quadrant to check the elevation for the range. Meanwhile one man would be readying the shell — screwing on the fuse and getting the right number of powder bags out. Then it would take two to carry the tray with the heavy shell to the gun, set it in place, grab the rammer and ram the shell home. Next, one of them would shove the powder bags in behind the shell, while the chief was fitting the igniter into the block and slapping the breech shut. Then it was ready — there'd be no time for checks and re-checks. Pull the lanyard and pray for the best.

The only trouble was, firing as close to their own infantry as they would have to, a slight error could send the hundred-pound shell right down on top of their own troops.

It was enough to make a timid man say to hell with it and take off with the others. For that way the responsibility was spread over a lot of people — and you could always blame the mistakes on the stupid lieutenant or the dumb Fire Direction Center.

But not here. Here it was all his baby — his idea, his choice of gun crew chiefs, his laying the guns parallel with nothing but the angle measurements on the gunsights (and that was a bitch; he could only hope he'd remembered his high school geometry right). It was all—*all* his responsibility.

But he knew he had good chiefs for each gun. Hooley had trained as a chief before he took over as motor sergeant. He would be okay on the number-two gun. And JayCee had trained his own gunner, Charlie Hill, to handle every cannoneer's job — so he was ready to take over as a chief of section. That left only gun number four. And JayCee prayed he had made the right choice there.

He hadn't had much choice, actually. Everybody, including Johnny himself, knew it had to be Johnny-boy Crump. Johnny had been a chief of section once, before he began to screw up, coming in late for formation all hung over, getting drunk while out on maneuvers. What he could do wrong he had done wrong. But he was such a happy-go-lucky bastard everybody liked him — and he never meant no harm. He just loved a good time too much. So they'd broken him back to buck private and he himself said he was much happier that way.

But now there was no other choice. He'd been chief, he knew what had to be done, and JayCee just had to hope he'd pull himself together and do the job.

Johnny had tried to plead off. "Let someone else do it and get the credit," he had told JayCee. "I never was no chief material. I'm jus' a good ol' buck-ass private. I'll hump the shells for ya. But let somebody else be the brain-man."

"Like who?" JayCee had asked him. And that was when Johnny Crump knew he was elected, whether he wanted it or not. There just wasn't anyone else who knew what you had to know, or had ever done what had to be done. So Johnny had grunted and groaned and finally said all right, though he'd be happy to pass on the honor to anyone else who wanted it.

The walkie-talkie that lay on the ground beside the gun squawked slightly, and then JayCee heard the artillery lieutenant's voice.

"This is Charlie Three. Do you read me? I forgot to ask what you want for a call sign. Come in if you can hear me. Over."

JayCee leaned down and picked up the compact little radio. What should he give for a call sign? He wasn't exactly proud of his battalion now — so screw them. He'd make up something.

"Charlie Three? They call the one-five-five rifles 'Long Toms.' So I guess you should call us 'Short Tom.' This is Short Tom Five, and I read you loud and clear. We just heard your ourfit's shells go over. How'd you do? Over."

"We just had us a nice little turkey shoot up here. I can't be sure exactly how many we got, because they're down in the valley between the ridges, but we've got smoke coming up from too many places to count. Now I'd like to get your 'Short Toms' registered on a point somewhere near the middle of the sector. There's a small dirt road goes off from the main road about four hundred yards from the bridge. If we can get your guns laid on that as a central point of reference, then we can switch your guns easily for any target that shows up. In fact, once you're registered I think I'll mark a number of possible concentrations on an overlay I'll give you. You can figure out the gun commands in advance. That way you can give me quick support anywhere I need it. Then if there's time to go through my own battalion, or if it's a really big concentration we need, I'll use my own guns. But for targets where we need action in a hurry, I'll use yours. And there's one other situation where it'll be better to use yours — when we want to fire in real close to friendly troops. My battalion's so damn far away they might have too big a dispersion factor. Yours should be ideal. But we'll use my outfit's ammo when possible. They can replenish and you can't. We'll save you for the tight squeaks and sudden emergencies. Is that okay with you? Over."

If it had been any other white artillery lieutenant making the request, JayCee would have suspected him of simply not trusting the "dumb niggers" and putting a good face on it. But he'd talked with this one, even gone out with him to get their ammo in a tricky situation. And JayCee just plain liked the man. This lieutenant seemed genuinely excited by the chance to have his own close-support artillery, so he wouldn't have to let some chicken-shit colonel second-guess his every fire command. And it didn't even seem to matter what color his close support came in. JayCee decided this was one white man he could go along with.

"Sounds good to me, Charlie Three. You want me to give you a round to start from? Over."

"Can you? That would be best, if you think you can do it. I don't even have a book with me that gives ranges and elevations. And we have to be careful to make sure we clear all friendlies. Over."

"I got the book on that here. And once we're zeroed in on one point, it'll be duck soup to hit anything out there you can see and adjust on. I've already figured the elevation to the bridge — and for your road junction I'll just go up another four hundred yards. Then add one hundred to be sure we start with an 'over'."

"Roger. Sounds good. Fire when ready."

JayCee had decided to keep one shell loaded, even though that was hardly conventional procedure. Lieutenant Ransom would have kittens if he knew one of his chiefs was doing that. But Lieutenant Ransom was shagging ass to the rear, so to hell with him.

JayCee had already laid the guns so they would, he estimated, hit the bridge if they were fired. He knew that was one concentration they were bound to fire sooner or later. So now it was a simple matter to check in his book for the number of mills elevation to subtract for five hundred yards. It took only a few seconds to add the single powder bag, crank the gun to the proper elevation, and make a final check on the alignment of his aiming stakes in the gunsight.

"Here we go, kiddies," he shouted to his two-man crew, who were already preparing the next shell to load.

He pulled the lanyard, felt the ground beneath his feet tremble slightly as the cannon roared thunder and fire, and heard the shell rushing away. Then he stooped quickly to pick up the radio.

"On the way!" he shouted into it.

A few seconds later he could hear the round land not far up ahead. Then the radio crackled again.

"Wow! You've really got it figured. You landed just about twenty-five yards to the right and maybe a hundred-fifty over. Try left four mills, and down enough for two hundred yards."

The total registration on the base point took less than three minutes. He could tell this lieutenant really knew his stuff. They now had a base point to go from and could bring fire on any target in the area in a matter of seconds. As a final check they had the other guns fire one round each, closed up enough on Number One to bring their shells onto the same road junction.

"They're right in there," the lieutenant's voice said triumphantly. "You straddled the road junction — and you had one solid hit. The damn tanks may have to detour around it, you chewed it up so much. I'll send that overlay back in a few minutes. Good shooting. Over and out."

Lieutenant Colonel Berrigan saw the artillery being adjusted as he stood by the eastern window of the second-story room. Serendipity, he thought. That was the word for it — the ability to make the most of accidental discoveries. Or in Army parlance, falling into the shithouse and coming up smelling like a rose. Here was a task force stripped of all the strengths an armored group was supposed to have, yet rich in the one element — medium field artillery — that no tank general would ever have dreamed of including in a field exercise. And as those smoke columns still climbing into the leaden winter sky would surely attest, they'd made the most of their unconventional "strength."

Of course he knew they'd been lucky with those first concentrations on the tanks between the ridges. The German leadership had been either too confident of success or too desperate to push their column forward in a hurry. So they had taken a chance, advancing in a closed column with minimum reconnaissance. That enemy commander shouldn't have let a closed-up column advance so close on the heals of its lead elements.

They wouldn't make that mistake again. They must have lost a lot of tanks — and in a really insulting way. Tanks should never be deployed so an enemy's artillery could cause that much damage. An artillery battalion should be able to knock out a tank or two — with a skilled observer and a lot of luck. But for artillery alone to destroy such a large part of an advancing force was almost unheard of.

So what would the Krauts do now? If it was only artillery against them the countermove was clear: simply spread out the column and push ahead rapidly. They might lose a tank or two — but before long they'd overrun the observer, and then the artillery would be blind and largely useless.

But their commander would surely know by now he had other potential problems. Nobody was going to mistake Sergeant MacKay's high-velocity rounds for artillery. They had to know now they also faced at least some direct fire — either tank or anti-tank. And if the enemy's leader was competent (and when fighting German panzers you'd damn well better assume they had competent leadership), he would know what he was facing was not the regular American anti-tank weapon. No little fifty-seven millimeter gun was going to do the damage those two nineties did.

So in anything like a normal situation the leader should slow down, get some reconnaissance vehicles out in front, and try to get a better picture of exactly what he faced.

But the colonel was betting this was not at all a "normal" situation. He felt sure what they had here was a commander *desperate* to move ahead quickly before units from the numerically superior American forces could be shifted into the area. Once that happened, the German offensive was all through.

So they had to attack again and again — until they just plain bulldozed over whatever was in front of them. They shouldn't do dumb things like advancing tanks in a closed column. But they would have to advance quickly and take whatever losses were necessary.

How would they come first? They wouldn't want to take the time to bring up and deploy panzergrenadiers yet. There might be no need for that much of a delay. He bet they would stay with the armor — only this time use something less costly. Reconnaissance vehicles — or Mark IV's at most — and keep a big space between them this time.

He knew the damage the artillery had done, severe as it was, wouldn't hold them up for long. In a major armored offensive like this, the attacker had to have overwhelming armored superiority — tanks by the hundreds. And with the low-ceilinged winter skies keeping the American planes off their backs, the German tank columns must be lining the roads like Times Square at rush hour — all the way back to the German border. They had plenty of tanks available, all right. So however they came, it would be soon.

He raised his field glasses once more and scanned the two ridgetops to the east.

At first he could see nothing but the four knocked-out tanks sitting there motionless, two on each side of the road.

Then perhaps fifty yards to the left of the road a slight movement caught his eye. Quickly he adjusted his glasses to pick out more detail.

There, just barely peeping over the ridge, was the top of a tank turret. A moment later its huge, swollen-headed gun appeared. Then another one popped up further to the left — this one also just high enough for the gun to fire over the ridge.

He was sure now what would happen next. Quickly he swept his glasses back and forth across the length of the ridge and saw more of the tank turrets appear — each barely high enough for its main gun to shoot over the ridge. They must have eight or ten tanks getting into hull-down position, he thought. So when their lighter vehicles made a rush for the bridge, those tanks with their high-velocity cannon would be there supporting them, keeping a watchful eye for any sign of an American gun firing. If they sent Mark IVs, the seventy-sixes on the tank destroyers could surely knock them out. But all those hull-down tanks were now poised and waiting, watching carefully for the tell-tale flash of a large-caliber gun being fired. And that flash would be enough to propel a cluster of high-velocity shells toward it in an instant. And we'd get the Mark IV, he thought — but we'd pay the price: at least one destroyer for each one of their lighter tanks. And while they could easily replace their tank losses — we have no replacements at all. Once we lose our few tanks and destroyers, they'll have an open road right through to their objective.

Suddenly he saw a series of flashes along the ridgetop and dove for the floor. Before he hit it he could hear the shocking blasts of the high-velocity guns striking into the solid walls of the town's buildings. After a moment he heard the spattering rain of chunks and splinters of rock and concrete on the roof over his head. With a tremendous slapping sound one huge piece of rock burst through the roof and fell only five feet away.

You dumb bastard, he swore at himself. What are you doing standing up here like a god-damned tourist taking snapshots. Get the hell out of here while you can!

He rose and rushed for the stairs, ran down them three at a

time, and shouted at Sergeant McClanahan as he burst into the C.P.

"Down to the cellar! They're going to plaster this edge of town!"

Sergeant McClanahan made for the cellar door and followed the colonel down the stairs. They were none too soon. Shells from the second volley were crashing into the buildings around them before they reached the cellar. The colonel heard one tremendously loud crack which he was sure must have blown away part of their own building.

The barrage continued for three or four minutes. Colonel Berrigan was shaken at the incredible force of the explosions.

And you had the gall, he told himself accusingly, to give knowing lectures about the emotional trauma of "combat." What the hell did you know? No imagination in the world could prepare you for the devastating force of those shells exploding nearby.

But he couldn't stay here. He had to go out to check with the men who would play the next role in the defense.

"Stay here," he shouted to the sergeant sprawled on the dirt floor of the cellar. "I'm going next door and see if the engineers are all okay. Wait two minutes, then get somewhere you can see what's happening on the road. Everybody's supposed to hold fire unless something gets across that bridge. If anything does get across, get to Lieutenant Hood's T.D., he's only a few yards over to the left, and tell him it's up to his destroyers to knock out what gets across."

"Wilco!" the sergeant shouted back, climbing to his feet.

Colonel Berrigan went up the cellar stairs two at a time and out the back door, stopping at the corner of the building by the main street.

Peering around the corner confirmed his fears. There, tearing along at nearly top speed and already halfway down the slope from the near ridge came a squat Mark IV German panzer. Behind it some distance a second Mark IV could be seen, and a third was just cresting the ridge and starting its rapid descent.

Now the lead tank was within three hundred yards of the bridge. The colonel knew he had to get across the main street to be sure the engineers were still in business. There was always a chance one of those in-coming shells had knocked out their whole operation. A direct hit in just the right place could completely ruin the next stage of his tactical plan.

The hull-down tanks on the second ridge had not let up their firing. The colonel knew what they were doing. They intended to pour the shells in until the tanks had reached and crossed the bridge.

He heard the guns on the ridge fire and two shells struck nearby. Taking a deep breath he rose to his feet and ran, head down at top speed across the open space of the main street and threw himself down behind the first building he came to.

Pausing only a moment for a gulp of air, he hauled himself through an open window of the building.

The room was deserted. He didn't understand — where could the engineers and infantrymen who had been there a short while before have gone?

"Ho! Engineers — where are you?" he shouted.

Something stirred in the adjoining room and a frightened foot soldier's face appeared around the corner of the open door.

"They all went upstairs," he said.

Quickly the colonel ran to the hall and leaped up the stairs. In the room to the left he saw one man standing back from the window, observing through field glasses. He looked to the right through an open door and saw a number of men grouped around a detonator. He entered the room quickly.

"Is it working?" he demanded

"It checks out okay," a man with buck sergeant's stripes on his arm answered. "We buried the wires pretty deep. It would take an awful lucky hit to knock it out. We're waiting to time the explosion just right."

"Stay with it," he said as he ran back into the hall and on into the front room.

One glance showed him the tank was now less than a hundred yards from the bridge.

He stood beside the other man a few feet back from the window and watched the tank approaching the bridge. The other man raised his arm slowly.

"Get ready!" he sang out.

The tank was sixty yards from the bridge...fifty....

Ca-rumphhh!

The tank never made it to the bridge. It spun sideways and slithered to a stop, one track flapping.

"Hold it!" the man by the window shouted. "He never made it. A mine got him."

Men in gray uniforms came boiling out of the tank through the escape hatches. They were trying to make the ditch by the side of the road. A machine gun from a nearby house opened up immediately, cutting them down before they had gone two yards.

"Got 'em!" the man by the window yelled. "Get ready. Here comes another."

The colonel saw the second tank had not slackened speed and was now less than a hundred yards from the bridge. It slowed as it neared the knocked-out tank. Trying to read where the mines were, the colonel thought. But those engineers did a good job of camouflaging their holes. From where he was watching the colonel could not tell where the mines had been planted.

The second tank skirted wide to the right around the knocked-out Mark IV and proceeded cautiously toward the bridge. It got ten yards beyond the first tank, then....

Ca-rumphhh!

The explosion shook the entire body of the tank, blowing off a track and leaving it sitting there, silent and impotent.

The men inside did not attempt to get out this time. They must have seen what had happened, he thought, when the men from the other tank tried it.

But it was clear the commander of this prong of the blitzkrieg was desperate to move forward. There was not even an attempt to call back the other tanks. Now the third Mark IV was nearing the bridge, and the colonel could see two more coming behind it, not even slowing down after the mine explosions.

A sudden increase in the intensity of the shelling made the colonel and the other man by the window dive to the floor. One shell struck just outside the house and sent fragments crashing through the window and up through the roof.

The colonel stood up quickly and looked at the ridge through his field glasses. Just as he had figured — the ridge now appeared lined solid with hull-down tanks. It must be frustrating to that commander, the colonel thought — to sit there with all that firepower and find yourself held up by a few mines in front of a bridge. So he was massing all the heavy firepower he could back there on the ridge.

But he was over-extending himself there, Berrigan thought. There should be a countermove the German commander had left himself open to.

A low rumbling from the west and a rush of air overhead told him the tall, scholarly-looking artillery lieutenant had been watching carefully for his chance to make a move himself. And with the tanks on the ridge-top massed nearly side by side, he had found his chance. In a moment the hundred-pound shellbursts were sprinkling down on the ridgetop.

Of course it couldn't be a slaughter like before. The tanks were massed this time in the opposite way — in deflection rather than range. There was no way to cluster those shells around the tanks. The battalion was obviously firing on a broad front — at least a hundred yards wide. It would overlap the line of tanks on both ends. But the dispersion would spread the shells out at least a hundred yards in range. No matter. They were obviously firing a large number of shells. The mathemantical odds would perhaps give them one or two direct hits—and they sure would distract the attention of those men sighting and firing the large cannon. Even as he watched the colonel saw tanks pulling back from the ridge, and the rain of shells into the town lessened.

Another explosion near the bridge told him a third tank had fallen prey to the engineers' skill in covering the mines they had laid.

There were now three dead tanks sitting on the road just short of the bridge. But the last one had managed to get within fifteen yards of it before having a track blown off. Yet now three more tanks were speeding down the same road.

Their commander knew he just had to cross that bridge — whatever losses it would cost.

"Get ready," the other man in the room shouted to those in the back room. "I think the next one may make it."

But he didn't. In fact this one hit a mine forty yards back from the bridge. It must have triggered one the other tanks had missed, Berrigan thought.

An explosion and a huge ball of fire drew his attention to the ridgetop once more. He saw it was one of the heavy tanks that seemed to be exploding from the inside. Some of its ammunition must have gone off after a direct hit. He saw a second tank was burning fiercely. And the artillery shells were still raining down on the whole area. Other tanks were now backing away from the ridgetop.

The colonel shifted his gaze to the bridge again — and saw the next Mark IV was making it past the mines. It had passed two of the knocked-out tanks and was approaching the third. Now it was passing it...was approaching the bridge...was pulling onto it and starting across...

"Now!" the man beside him shouted, bringing the hand he had raised down sharply.

There was just a moment's delay...and then the entire bridge and the tank rattling across it seemed to rise up together into the air, hang there a second — then settle. And what had been a solid structure came down as a thousand crumbling fragments. The tank sank slowly into the surrounding cloud of smoke, dirt, and crumbling fragments.

"There she blows!" the other man yelled, as the men in the back room rushed into the front room to view their handiwork from the one eastern window.

When the pieces had all settled the bridge span was completely gone. The tank sat immobile on the bottom of the river, the water lapping around it.

Glancing back at the road the colonel saw that the two remaining tanks had paused as if uncertain what to do next. Well they might, the colonel thought. Where the bridge had been there was now only empty space, with the road ending suddenly in a drop of eight or ten feet. And those banks were too steep for any tank to negotiate.

Finally, as if in hopeless frustration, the lead tank fired its cannon into one of the buildings, then turned and scuttled back the way it had come. The second tank had not bothered to fire its gun before turning — and consequently was already more than a hundred yards ahead as they both sped back up the road toward the ridge.

Colonel Berrigan felt a wonderful sense of triumph sweep through him. It was only for a moment — for he saw the sky was already beginning to darken. The short winter afternoon was ending. So he had made it through the easiest part — the "all of today" the general had talked about. Now he had to make it through the night. And with night the capabilities of the enormously superior force against him would have a freer rein. They would soon have their engineers forward to fix the bridge. They could move their panzergrenadiers up to the river and cross it anywhere they wished. There was no end to the possibilities open to them now.

And he would have only his improvised, jerry-built con-traption — "Task Force Lone Bandit." Well, it had done pretty well so far. But how many more tricks could he manage to come up with?

14

It had been fully dark for more than an hour. Lieutenant Colonel Berrigan had suspected the enemy commander would not try again until the long winter night of the Ardennes had fallen. While almost all the German losses so far had been from artillery and mines, those four precision knock-outs by Sergeant MacKay's ninety-millimeters must have convinced the commander that the Americans had high-velocity anti-tank weapons present — though he couldn't tell how many. Keeping those few Shermans and M-18 destroyers under wraps had paid off in discouraging another attack before dark.

But he knew the German commander was going to have to make a move soon. No tank leader likes to lose tanks (and this one had lost a large number in an inexcusable way), but he would know that the essence of an armored thrust is great speed and overwhelming power. And that usually meant large loses — especially at the start of an offensive. You just had to eat the losses and shove ahead. Of course that was right at the beginning when a hole was being punched through the first layer of defenses. By now, however, if everything was working out properly, the enemy would be expecting the lightning moves to be far less costly. Berrigan knew these sudden losses would be cause for worry for his opponent.

Suddenly his thoughts were interrupted when the back door of the C.P. building burst open and a soldier entered. The colonel saw it was the infantryman he had posted as a messenger by the light tank behind the building.

"They're moving tanks toward the right flank," the soldier reported. "They're still back from the river quite a bit yet. But they may be getting ready to rush the ford."

"Who'd the report come from?" the colonel asked.

"From Sergeant Bradovitch — through the light tank's radio on the right flank."

This was important. Sergeant Bradovitch had struck him as a well-seasoned tank commander. If the report was his, it was probably accurate.

Yet the report had said only "toward the right flank" — and they "might" be getting ready to rush the ford.

The colonel strode quickly to the door. "I'm going to try to get through to Bradovitch," he told Sergeant McClanahan. "I'll be with the tank in back."

He hurried out the back door and ran to the light tank posted against the back wall of the building. The tank commander was standing in the open turret waiting for him.

"Get me your tank on the right and let me have the mike," the colonel said. A moment later the man in the tank handed him the headset.

"He's on there now, sir."

The colonel took the headset and spoke quickly into the mike.

"Lone Bandit Six here. Can you get Sergeant Bradovitch

to your radio?"

"He's right here now, sir. He came over himself with his report."

"Good. Put him on."

There was a slight pause and then Bradovitch's raspy voice came on clearly.

"Bradovitch here. Did you get my message?"

"Roger. That's why I'm calling. I take it the tank sounds are not yet down by the river."

"No, sir. There's quite a few of them — but they're all pretty far back, and moving to the right."

The colonel's mind spun through the many possibilities. That could be a problem. The map showed the dirt road at the ford ran straight back to the first ridge and then turned and went to join the main road. Yet it looked as if that turn might actually be a crossroad. For a slight trace of a road -- hardly more than a trail -- continued a short distance toward the east.

But the disturbing thing was what looked like a hint of a trail leading *south* from the junction. He hadn't paid it much attention because it was not really a road — merely two dotted lines that went no more than two hundred yards and ended. Did it really end there? Or had that hint of trail been extended after the maps were made — extended perhaps to another river crossing downstream?

He had found what looked like a possible crossing — but that was over a mile to the south. And the road there on the enemy's side of the river bent away from their present battlefield and connected with no roads from that direction. But could the trail have been extended that far? Over a mile — it didn't seem likely. But if it had been...and the enemy made use of it....

"Sergeant Bradovitch, I want you to relay an order from

me to Lieutenant Brownell, who commands the infantry in your sector. Tell him to send a small patrol down river to his right for a little over a mile to the crossing there. If they can, have them cross the river and explore back a ways to see if there's any small trail coming in from this direction. And they should be sure to note whether their route along the west bank of the river is really impassable for tanks. Tell Lieutenant Brownell to send no more than a four-man patrol — and have them report back to me as soon as they return."

"Wilco, sir. I'm having some people keep an eye out in that direction too."

"Good. Keep that in the back of your mind. Though I don't think it's where you'll be hit first."

"I know what you mean, sir. And there we'll be ready with a little surprise party."

"Okay. If anything happens in your sector, get word here just as soon as you can."

"Roger. Wilco and Out."

The colonel stood for a moment considering. What should he do next? That potential threat to the right flank was serious, but it would take some time to develop — if it even turned out to be possible. So he could be sure the German commander would not just sit there and wait for a mere possibility to develop. But where would he strike next?

He heard the radio in the tank crackle and then a voice on the edge of panic spoke quickly.

"Get Lone Bandit Six. The lieutenant here wants to speak to him — right away."

The colonel answered immediately.

"This is Lone Bandit Six. Which lieutenant?"

After a brief pause a different voice spoke.

"Lieutenant Magruder here, sir. I've got something developing that may be pretty bad. Over."

The voice was slow and measured, yet at the same time tense with an underlying desperation.

A knot formed in the colonel's stomach for just a moment. Was this tall, slow-thinking man capable of leadership in a pinch? Or would he blow up under the slightest pressure? It looked like the colonel might be going to get an answer to that question sooner than he wanted.

He made his voice calm and reassuring as he answered.

"All right, Lieutenant. I'm right here, looking across to where you are now. Everything seems quiet. What do you have?"

""Well, sir — I'm not sure exactly...but we're hearing quite a lot of noise here...across the river."

"What kind of noise? Tanks?"

"That's just it, sir. No motors at all. Just men moving through the field there. They were pretty far away at first — but it sounds like they're getting closer."

"All right. Dismounted infantry we can handle. Have your men all been alerted?"

"Yes, sir. I've told them to hold their fire until I talked with you."

Dumb bastard, Colonel Berrigan thought. That guy sure is filled with initiative. But before ordering the lieutenant to open fire immediately a sudden thought came to him. Maybe there was a better way. If the enemy were making a lot of noise and moving forward without much caution, that must mean they didn't expect to find an infantry battle line there. They must think they were dealing with just a roadblock at the bridge and in the town. And there should be a way to take advantage of their lack of caution. After a moment he spoke again into the mike.

"Do you think there's a chance they don't know you're there?"

"I had the men dig their holes under some kind of cover. And I told them to stay in their holes out of sight."

"Good. I take it the Germans aren't up close to the river yet?"

"I don't think so, sir. They don't seem to be trying to move silently — and the noises seem pretty far back yet."

"Right. Now, how close is your nearest man to the river?"

"About seventy-five yards back, sir. The cover was better there."

"Good. Now give me five minutes, starting now, before firing or sending up a flare. Don't give your position away *unless* they attempt to cross the river. When they do that you open fire with all you've got. Otherwise, give me five minutes. And keep your men quiet. Have you got that?"

"Yes, sir."

The colonel tossed the headset back up to the man in the turret.

"I'll be in the next building behind you. You can send the runner there if anything happens I need to know about."

He dashed to the entrance of the building behind them. Inside he quickly mounted a flight of stairs, then went up the second flight to a small room on the third floor. As he had suspected, the artillery lieutenant was behind his B.C. scope at an eastern window. The colonel's watch showed one minute of the five he had asked for was gone.

"We've got a real chance here," he said brusquely to the lieutenant. "But you've got to move fast. Infantry trying to go around our left flank. You can put a concentration there without adjusting, can't you?"

"No sweat, sir. We've already had a precise adjustment.

Where do you want it?"

"Put a light on this map here, and I'll show you."

In a moment they were huddled together around the map lit by a pocket flashlight.

"They're probably spread out pretty well — so you can make your colonel happy and let him fire on a wide front. Your barrage should be designed to cover this whole area."

He hastily drew a two hundred-yard square opposite Lieutenant Magruder's position. Then he glanced again at his watch.

"You have just three minutes to get them there. That way you'll catch them all in the open — they've had no warning. Can your outfit do it?"

"They can do it — if the colonel doesn't screw it up. Cordova, give them 'prepare for immediate fire mission.' Then let me talk to Major Schwartz."

While the message was being sent the lieutenant made some quick measurements on the map. He completed them just in time to take the mike Corporal Cordova handed him.

"They've got the batteries alerted, sir. Major Schwartz is on now."

Lieutenant Stallingsworth spoke in urgent tones into the mike.

"Sir, we have a tremendous opportunity here. Large formation of infantry in the open — they've had no warning. Shells must be there by...."

He paused and looked at the colonel questioningly.

"Two minutes and thirty seconds," the colonel said, looking at his watch.

"...two minutes and thirty seconds. Can you do it?"

The major's voice came back precise and controlled — but with an undercurrent of excitement.

"We can do it — Colonel's gone for dinner and I'm in control. Give me coordinates, so my crew can be working on commands."

The lieutenant read off the coordinates immediately. The major repeated them, and a number of voices could be heard in the background repeating a series of commands. Then the major's voice came again from the radio.

"Infantry in extended formation — so you want a box how big?"

"Start with a two-hundred-yard square. The coordinates are the center of the square. But keep the closest edge fifty yards back from the river. Friendly troops nearby."

"Wilco. Now, this is unobserved fire — right?"

"Only until the first rounds land. We have observation but will not use flares until then — so we'll catch them unprepared."

"Right. Now, what I'll do is give you battalion five volleys. I have it spread as you want — so the dispersion should give you good coverage. Then when you see them land, let me know if we're hitting about right. If not, give me corrections. We'll be ready to give you further concentrations as necessary to cover the target. We'll wait for word from you on that. Now...."

The major paused a moment and then continued.

"...I think the guns are going to be ready early. You want us to fire when ready?"

The lieutenant glanced at Colonel Berrigan.

"As soon as they can," the colonel said.

"Fire when ready," Lieutenant Stallingsworth said into the mike.

"Roger."

There was a wait of only a very few seconds before the words came back briskly from the radio.

"On the way!"

The colonel and the lieutenant crowded together at the eastern window, watching anxiously for the rounds to land.

The wait seemed interminable. Finally everything came at once — the rush of shells through the air, the large red-orange blossoming of the explosions off to the left just across the river, and the sudden rattle of machine-gun and rifle fire. Colonel Berrigan could tell where Magruder's position was by the beginning of the forest a quarter-mile to the north — and the shells were all landing across the river and covering the area he had designated.

As soon as the shells began landing a flare went up from the treeline and lit the entire landscape in an eerie, flickering light.

As the shells continued to land, the colonel watched eagerly for signs of the German infantry. At first he saw nothing. Was it all a mistake?

"There they are!" the lieutenant shouted. "They're right there across the river. They heard the shells coming and went down — so they're harder to see. But you can pick some out if you look careful."

Then the colonel saw them — little sprawled shapes visible when he put his field glasses on them. It was hard to tell precisely how extended their formation was, but he was sure he could see some bodies much further back from the river — perhaps four hundred yards. And the formation appeared to overlap the opposite tree line by fifty to a hundred yards.

Before the colonel could speak the lieutenant was talking into the radio urgently.

"Shells right on target, sir! Pour it on — the whole sixty rounds. Then move the center of the box one hundred yards to the left — part of the formation is out that far. Give me five volleys again if you can. Then we can really clean 'em out if you can give me five volleys with the range increased one hundred yards. The formation extends back a little farther than we hit. And I bet we're going to have heavy traffic running to the rear just about the time you fire that last concentration. That whole rear area's going to be jammed up with soldiers trying to get out fast."

The flare died out suddenly and the night again went black. But only for a moment. Then a second flare blossomed and floated downward, once again lighting the area across the river with its flickering glow. The colonel could now hear the sputter of regular small arms fire — especially the slow, measured ta-ta-ta-ta of American machine guns. There must be more than one by the sound. Then he realized the light tank must be firing its machine gun also. There was the occasional ripping sound of a German machine pistol answering — the bullets spitting out at a much faster rate of fire. But the answering fire was surprisingly light. Those panzergrenadiers must be suffering under such a concentrated barrage, the colonel thought. They'll have taken nearly two hundred rounds of one-five-five shells when the third concentration is completed. That's enough to unnerve even veteran troops.

Private Lucas Hatfield had been lying in his hole shivering when he heard the noises coming from across the river. That meant it was going to start again finally, and he would have to pay heavily for his hot coffee, his warm meal and dry socks. You got nothing for nothing from this army.

But he had been close enough to the light tank to hear the lieutenant talking with the colonel on the radio. The lieutenant's voice had been tight with tension — but the colonel's was reassuring. He knew that in a few moments he might be once again engaged in a desperate struggle where reassurance from higher officers would mean little. Still, it was good to know that somebody up there at least thought he knew what he was doing, and that they had at least a chance for success.

Then he thought of the soldier in the hole only a few feet away. The kid was probably shivering and fearing the worst. Hatfield remembered how it had been for him the first time they had been attacked in the darkness of the Hurtgen Forest.

But of course he had had the feeling of trust in Sergeant Forte then to keep him going through the darkest of nights.

"Hey, ol' buddy," he said softly to the figure in the hole a few feet away, "looks like we're gonna have a chance for a turkey shoot."

The words seemed unnatural to him. "Turkey shoot" — that was something Sergeant Forte might say. Yet it had come out rather naturally from him. Not that he could *feel* that way about it. But then, maybe the others who talked that way didn't *feel* that way either. Perhaps it was just a pose they all put on to convince themselves they were tough enough to take whatever was coming — even though deep down they knew they feared it.

He was just close enough to the other hole to see the young soldier raise his head to look toward him. His face gleamed palely in the dark.

"Are they going to come across the river?" the young soldier asked in a shaking voice.

"Hell," Hatfield answered, marveling at how natural the curse word had sounded in his mouth, "didn't you hear? We're gonna unload a buncha artillery on 'em. That'll make 'em think careful about crossing any river."

Then the huge artillery shells were rushing in to explode a short distance away on the other side of the river. For a moment Hatfield watched, enthralled by the giant red and orange bursts.

He ducked his head down as he heard the whizzing of shell fragments nearby. No rounds had landed on his side of the river — but he knew those shells could throw fragments a hundred yards or more.

He opened his eyes to see the light from a flare turn the darkness to a pale, grisly light. Getting enough control of his fear to look forward across the river, he could see two figures running back the way they had come.

"Come on, ol' buddy. We got some shootin' to do."

He raised his Ml rifle, and without bothering to aim carefully, squeezed off three shots. Two sharp cracks beside him made him turn his head. Damn — it was the young soldier, rifle raised and firing. However scared he might be, he had actually heeded Hatfield's words and was dutifully following instructions.

The flare flickered and went out.

"Nice shootin'," he said to the boy. "Now be ready for the next flare and we'll cut down on 'em again. Those jokers ain't gettin' over here that easy. We got artillery to beat hell, and if they ever make it through that, then they got us to get through. And that ain't gonna be no pushover, neither."

Again he marveled at how tough his voice sounded. Hell, no one could tell how scared he was inside. He couldn't really believe it...but was it possible all those tough-talking old soldiers were just putting it on too — like he had just done?

Colonel Berrigan saw the panzergrenadier attack had been stopped. There were still a number of gray-clad figures up close to the river — though how many were still-active attackers and how many merely bodies or wounded awaiting evacuation it was impossible to say. But there was no doubt about the general direction of movement — back up the slope and out of that persistent artillery barrage.

If those were panzergrenadiers — and he was sure they were — they should have been good troops. It was hard to believe they had been stopped so easily.

But everything had fallen just right for the defenders. They had been alerted by the sound of the attackers, there had been no cover in that open area across the river for the enemy to use, and the artillery barrage had been prompt and accurate — and then sustained long enough to be effective. No troops, no matter how experienced, could move into and ignore artillery fire like that. And as bad as regular artillery was, these one-five-fives, with their hundred-pound shells, were even more devastating.

So the colonel's motley collection of stray units had once again frustrated the attackers. But just as the suddenly blocked flow of a rushing river gathers force, he knew with every passing minute his opponent was gathering power, as eager units from the rear piled up on the heels of the blocked force. And all the while higher commanders would be raging at the delay and diverting ever more resources to clear this obstruction out of their path.

A sudden storm of small arms fire directly across the river told the colonel the enemy commander had not been pulling an isolated attack on the left wing. These shots were coming from no more than a hundred yards away. While the Americans had been concentrating on that attack a half-mile to the north, the Germans had worked troops right up to the bank of the river opposite the center of the town!

15

Lieutenant Lee Beauregard Hood had been dreading what was surely coming. All his young life he had looked forward to that moment when he could show himself worthy of his name and ancestry. For bearing a name so filled with the grandeur of Southern tradition was a proud responsibility. And he had never doubted that he possessed the qualities for fulfilling that duty.

And yet as he had come closer to the actual moment when he would be locked in deadly combat with the experienced enemy panzers, everything had begun to change. It had actually started to change on him the moment he left home for the Army.

He had been only in his first year of college when his family had found a way for him to enlist with a near-guarantee that he would go to O.C.S. immediately after he completed basic training. All that had been perfectly appropriate to the picture he had had in his mind of himself (the dashing Southern cavalier, born and bred for command of a band of devoted retainers — common country stock, eager to subordinate their untutored actions to his natural leadership ability).

But with his entrance into the Army, nothing seemed to work out as it should have. Rather than having his natural leadership ability immediately recognized, he seemed caught in an anxiety dream turning rapidly into a nightmare. In basic training, rather than leading the way at every challenge, he had found himself far back in the pack and having to exert desperate efforts to meet the minimum demands. He limped in last on the final twenty-eight mile march with rifle and full field equipment. He nearly passed out when he had to march through the double line of medics jabbing needles into various parts of his anatomy. He had done an awful job of disassembling his Ml rifle — and never did get it together again (a disgusted sergeant had finally grabbed it and put it together for him). He half-knew (though he never let his mind think about it) that he never would have made it to O.C.S. without the greasing of the skids his family had provided. Somehow he could not see himself ever becoming even a corporal among the rough, callous louts with whom he had gone through basic training.

But he did get to officer's school, he did graduate (though he nearly flunked out twice), and he did receive a commission. And with that, everything changed back to the way it was supposed to be. Home on leave in his sparkling new uniform, he was clearly a person deserving of respect from his family and adoration from his young female acquaintances. He was finally in position to live up to the Southern tradition of military glory that his very name symbolized.

Then the leave was all too quickly over. He found himself shipped overseas as a replacement officer and immediately sent up to command a platoon of the latest tank destroyers. Then once again everything had begun to go all wrong. The outfit he was sent to had trained together for over a year. The non-coms and men all knew each other well — and he was the lowly outsider, ignorant of all the battalion's rules and procedures, dependent always on his sergeant to see that things were done properly so he could stay out of trouble.

The training period hadn't been long. They were not slated to be put into the line for at least another month — then this German offensive had hit and he found himself being pushed inexorably forward for some great challenge for which he felt himself completely unprepared.

During that first experience that he had told the colonel about, when they had been ordered forward to help shore up a hopeless situation, he knew now he had been almost frozen with fear and anxiety. He was literally incapable of giving a command —certainly not a reasoned and sensible one. He had been grateful that Sergeant Whipple had been willing to take over the decision-making. What excused it all and made it seem perfectly acceptable to the lieutenant was that horrible sickness that had come over him as he approached the front. His whole insides had just suddenly rebelled, and for a time there he had been almost incapable of doing anything except ride in his destroyer, suffering pains and nausea and hoping when the need arose he would be able to climb out with his shovel and role of toilet paper in time.

He thought he had been lucky because his sergeant hadn't minded making the choices and giving the orders. And at the time the sergeant had always seemed, to the young lieutenant, to make such logical and reasonable decisions. Only after talking with the colonel, after seeing the doubt in the colonel's eyes when the lieutenant had explained about the excellent qualifications of his sergeant — only then did he suddenly have a new vision of how it all sounded to someone unfamiliar with precisely how it had happened.

And now here he was, about to undergo some horrendous

challenge — and not even sure he could trust his sergeant, the one firm star in his scrambled universe.

When the firing broke out he had been standing in the turret, wondering if the cramps in his intestines had really begun to ease a little. But when the machine pistol opened up straight ahead of him just across the river, all sensations were lost in the first paralysis that seemed to seize every muscle in his body.

He heard glass tinkle nearby and realized the machine pistol's bullets were striking the second-story window in the building behind him. Then other guns opened up along the river. Along the section of the farther bank that was within his view, sparks of fire were dancing for nearly a hundred yards. The building behind one corner of which he had parked his destroyer cut off all view to the right, but he could hear the guns firing there too.

"Jesus, Lieutenant, the god-damn roof's caving in! We've got to get the hell outa here while we can!"

It was Sergeant Whipple's voice, tight with fear, crackling from the radio. Lieutenant Hood had no idea what he should do. His main mission was to destroy tanks, and there were no tanks, so far as he could see. But the persistent small arms fire, now rising to a crescendo, told him the enemy were there close in front of him in overwhelming numbers.

"Lieutenant! Jesus, are you hit? Come in if you're not! We gotta do something fast. They'll be cutting us off. Anybody with information on the Lieutenant, come in. And everybody get ready to march order outa here."

The lieutenant still felt as if his whole body was an alien substance over which he had no control. And what could he do anyway? Those soldiers behind the flickering sparks along the river — they would soon be all around them, shooting into the open-topped turrets, throwing in hand grenades. Certainly Sergeant Whipple was right. Get out while they still could.

But even as his voice was trying to give the order, something told him to wait. He remembered what the colonel had told him about making the decisions himself — about not trusting Sergeant Whipple's judgment. But how could that be? Sergeant Whipple at least could speak, could give commands. And he seemed to know what had to be done. The lieutenant, on the other hand, hadn't the slightest idea what he should do — even if he could muster the will to do it.

"All right, everybody," Sergeant Whipple's panic-filled voice came again through the radio. "The lieutenant must have been hit. Sergeant Whipple here – we're pullin' out!"

With a tremendous effort the lieutenant forced himself to speak into the radio. He hardly knew what he was about to say before he heard himself saying it.

"This is...lieutenant here. Wait. Hold your positions. Sergeant Whipple, I'm okay. Not hit."

There was a moment's pause before he heard Sergeant Whipple's voice again. Although the tightness of fear was still there, now it was mixed with anger.

"Okay, Lieutenant. But for God's sake get us the hell out of here. We're not made to fight infantry. With these open turrets they can knock us out with a god-damned hand grenade. And where the hell's *our* infantry support? I bet they're half a mile down the road already. They just took off and left us holdin' the bag."

The lieutenant's head cleared just enough for him to hear other sounds of firing. Had the Germans crossed the river already? This firing was coming right from the buildings around him.

Then he realized — of course. That's what it was.

"Nobody's left us," he said into the mike. "You can hear them — that's our infantry firing now. Everybody — hold your positions... we have to stay and support them."

Now a tremendous amount of fire was pouring out of the buildings at the enemy, and the firing along the riverbank had slackened.

"Jesus, Lieutenant! What the hell are we supposed to fight them with? Our seventy-sixes are made for *tanks* — not infantry."

The lieutenant was intimidated by the belligerence now in the sergeant's voice. He stuck out a hand to steady himself and saw it was resting on the fifty-caliber anti-aircraft machine gun mounted above the turret.

"Use your fifty-calibers," he said. "That should do the trick. But only if you have to. We don't want to give our positions away until we have to.

After a moment's pause Sergeant Whipple's voice came back, this time more controlled.

"Lieutenant — I officially request permission to withdraw from an untenable position. Now! While we still can save our destroyers."

Lieutenant Hood quailed inwardly at the tone of his platoon sergeant. He had a feeling of being lost in a world of violent men and bellicose acts of which he knew nothing. The controlled quality of the sergeant's voice was more frightening than the previous near panic. It seemed to be telling him the lieutenant was behaving absurdly, and everyone was building a case to prove him ignorant and incapable of command.

Yet the infantry were now directing a hot return fire from their positions in the buildings. He couldn't go off and leave them — even if he was making absurd demands on his own men. He would just have to tell the sergeant that what he wanted was no good.

"Permission denied, Sergeant Whipple. Everybody stay in position and fire if you have a clear enemy target. This means *everyone*. If a withdrawal is necessary, I —repeat, *I* alone will give the order."

Then, before he thought of what it implied, he had added, "All units please acknowledge."

The radio remained silent for many long seconds. Then Sergeant Whipple's grudging voice replied, "Roger, Whipple." One by one the other three destroyers acknowledged the message.

To his surprise the lieutenant found that actually making a decision and giving an order had a remarkable effect on his whole outlook. His last assertive speech had come out with none of the breathless fumbling for words that had bothered him moments before. Was that what "command function" was all about — acting as if you knew perfectly well what you were doing and hadn't the least doubt you were right, all the while suspecting you might be totally wrong and hadn't the vaguest idea of what you would do next? It was not at all what he had been taught to believe about those great battle leaders of the Confederacy. But what he had been taught to believe had left him a paralyzed lump of fears and pains -- instead of an inspirational leader.

Maybe, he thought suddenly, "inspirational leadership" doesn't have much to do with the kinds of "battles" we fight today. If it ever did have in those other, more heroic battles.

Feeling almost light-headed and pleased to note his intestines had been remarkably free of cramps in the last few minutes, he turned his fifty-caliber machine gun toward a flicker of light where a machine pistol had just started firing. Before thinking of the restraining orders he had just given, he squeezed off a short burst. It was close enough to cut short the flickering light immediately. What the hell, he thought, maybe it was against Standard Operating Procedure. But it sure felt good.

Colonel Berrigan knew he had to get up to the buildings near the river where most of Lieutenant Kolinski's infantry were posted. That first line of buildings in the town was scarcely a hundred yards from where all the enemy fire was coming. He didn't have any idea what kind of leader Lieutenant Kolinski was — but he knew that troops collected as those had been, from units dissolving after a futile, losing battle with a powerful attacker, could rarely be depended on. He was afraid if they were left without firm leadership they might drift away in a matter of minutes.

But before he could leave he had to see if they could get any help from the artillery.

"Can you do anything to support us?" the colonel asked the forward observer urgently.

"My battalion is so far back," the lieutenant said, "they have to shoot charge seven, and close to maximum range. The shells come in on too low a trajectory — and with too much dispersion — to fire that close to friendly infantry. If I adjusted them on the riverbank, you'd be bound to get some shorts hitting the closest buildings. And that's where most of your infantry are."

"We don't want that — at least not yet," the colonel said. "That would really drive them out fast. Any other suggestions?"

"I think I can adjust the four guns Sergeant Washington put in position right close behind us. Their range is so short they'll be more accurate — and I'll use a creeping adjustment so we won't get shorts."

"Right," the colonel said. "Get 'em started as soon as you can. I've got to check on the infantrymen up there."

"Yes, sir," Lieutenant Stallingsworth said, picking up the walkie-talkie which lay on the floor beside him. As the colonel was leaping down the two flights of stairs he heard the firing commands already being given through the walkie-talkie. He passed his C.P. and then one other house before coming to the first row of buildings where most of Lieutenant Kolinski's men were posted. He ran doubled over and close up against the wall of each building as he passed it. He could hear streams of bullets tearing past him and on down the main street.

Arriving finally at the last house before the open space by the river, he paused as he saw two men come charging out the back door. He raised his arms and neatly caught one with each arm.

"Easy does it, men," he said, making his voice calmly encouraging. "Firing positions no good back there. Much better here. Let's get back inside and watch us dump a shitload of artillery on 'em."

Surprised and held back, the two men allowed themselves to be propelled by his arms back into the building. Inside, the colonel saw a number of men firing from the windows on the east wall. He noted with relief the walls of this building were of heavy stone. The only bullets that were entering the room were coming through the shattered windows and ricocheting from the back wall. That was why everyone was as close to the floor as he could get, he thought. Just then a full stream of bullets burst through one window and splattered like buckshot when they hit the back wall. He dropped to all fours himself, seeing the two men he'd brought back in do the same.

"You two take that window over there," he said, pointing to the one window from which no one was firing. He stayed crouched beside them until they got up and scurried to the window he had pointed to.

"Where's Lieutenant Kolinski?" he shouted at a man firing from the next window. The man turned his head back to look at him a moment, then gestured to the floor directly above. The colonel ran crouching to the stairs and leaped up them as another stream of bullets came through a window and ricocheted with a pinging sound off the rock walls.

On the floor above he tried the first room on the east side. It was the right one. Lieutenant Kolinski was crouching by one window, pointing out something to a soldier kneeling beside him. The colonel stepped quickly to crouch by the opposite corner of the window.

"What have they got?" he shouted to the lieutenant.

"Just panzergrenadiers so far," the lieutenant replied. "At least I don't see any tanks yet. About company size, I guess. But I think they brought some engineers to work on a temporary bridge. One man said he thought he saw them carrying a couple of pontoons by hand."

"They don't want to waste any more tanks in that artillery," the colonel said. "They'd rather do it on the cheap. If they can get a temporary bridge up, they'll figure on rushing a few tanks across before we can get an adjustment on them. But they'll do it the hard way if they have to. And that's the way we've got to make them do it. Have any of the panzergrenadiers got across the river yet?"

"Can't really say," the lieutenant answered. "If they have, they're being pretty quiet about it yet."

"Have you got any flares?"

"A few. But not enough to use them until we really need 'em."

"How are your men positioned — do they cover the whole front?"

"Pretty well, sir. I've got forty men — split even, half on each side of the main street. Almost all in the buildings nearest the river, where they can fire on anyone trying to cross. But on both sides of the town we have a small squad in the second building back. That's to cover anyone crossing down the line and then trying to come in on our flank. There's a quarter-mile of open space out there for them to come across. Captain

Bergoff said we didn't have enough men to occupy it all. So we decided to cover it by fire. If they try coming across the open area, we'll have them between my flank squad on one side and either Magruder's or Brownell's men from the other. And Captain Bergoff's small reserve can help out if they start to get through us and toward the rear. That's the best we could figure, sir."

"It sounds to me like you figured pretty good, Lieutenant. Now, have you seen any tank — "

Whhissst—*baroom*!

The high velocity tank shell hit before they could drop to the floor. A scream came from somewhere below them. For a moment everyone froze in position.

Lieutenant Kolinski was the first to recover.

"Stay here and watch those bastards on the river," he shouted to the men by the windows. "I'll see how much that one hurt us."

The lieutenant ran to the stairs and bounded down them.

"Did anyone see where that shot came from?" the colonel asked quickly.

"I think I did," a short figure posted at the farthest window said. "Way up there — at the top of the ridge."

Colonel Berrigan looked at the diminutive soldier who had spoken.

"What was it—a big flash?"

"No, sir. Just a little spark-like."

"The first ridge—or the second?"

"I couldn't see that for sure, sir."

The colonel had been wondering when it would start. With all that firepower sitting back there, the German commander had to try at least another hull-down firing. Only this time they would be firing under cover of night — and thus be much harder to spot and adjust fire on. But the colonel was glad the enemy commander was still leery of putting tanks up where they could be clearly spotted by direct fire weapons. That must mean, Colonel Berrigan reasoned, he still thinks we're keeping a lot of heavy anti-tank fire in reserve. Sergeant MacKay's "secret weapons" have made him a cautious man, and he doesn't know how many of those big ninety-millimeter tank guns we have. Let's hope the hell his caution stays with him. Sergeant MacKay's wonder-tanks are fine for occasional use — but in an all-out duel between our monsters and theirs, we'd probably go at most three shots before five or six of theirs would skewer us.

He wished he had some kind of communication with Sergeant MacKay. He definitely didn't want him to give away his position yet — but there might come a time when MacKay's guns would be the last resort. So how could he tell the sergeant to forget his colonel's previous instructions and blast away?

He knew the answer to that. He just had to trust Sergeant MacKay's judgment. And strangely enough, merely from talking with the sergeant briefly, the colonel felt he probably could.

Two more tank shells blasted into the building next to them — and then a third struck their own building. For a moment the colonel thought it had hit the room he was in — but after the shock of the ear-shattering explosion had passed, he saw no one had been hurt. And he knew if an eighty-eight had hit that close there wouldn't be many soldiers in that room left in one piece.

"God-damn it!" the other man by the colonel's window shouted, "that one hit the next room. This ain't such a smart place to be."

"You're right," the colonel said quickly. "Everyone downstairs." He noticed one of the men was wearing the three stripes of a buck sergeant. "See if you can find a cellar in this building, Sergeant. If there's one with any windows to fire from, get your men down there."

"Yes, sir!" the sergeant answered briskly. "All right, you guys — let's haul ass outa here while we still got an ass to haul."

All in a rush the men poured from the upstairs rooms and went clattering down the stairs. The colonel paused at the top of the stairs and then went quickly to the room in which the shell had struck. He saw there had been two men in the room. There still was one whole body and part of another. He checked the whole body and found a large fragment had torn into the side of the man's head, leaving only a grayish, oozy mess. He knew there was no use examining further.

He went back into the hall and ran down it to the one room on the front he hadn't been in. Very much aware another shell might plow into the building at any moment, he opened the door and looked in. This was a much smaller room than the others, with only one narrow window in the east wall. He hesitated a moment — then decided to stay. He knew he shouldn't risk himself unnecessarily — but the window gave an excellent view of nearly all the areas he wanted to see. And the room was only about eight feet wide — with solid stone walls on all four sides. It was almost a rock-walled foxhole, he thought — unless they put a direct hit in through the narrow window. Then the problems of the Task Force would increase — and his would cease altogether.

"On the way," Cordova yelled above the noise of small arms fire and the shelling of the buildings up ahead.

Lieutenant Stallingsworth waited without realizing he was

holding his breath. He was eager to see where the black soldiers' first round would land. It was rare an artillery officer had a chance like this — with his guns so close, no superiors to get in the way, and a target so near and carefully mapped out ahead of time. Sergeant Washington had his own map overlay with his guns and the bridge site plotted on it. And the sergeant impressed the lieutenant as a very intelligent young soldier. The sergeant's guns were going to give him a first round two hundred yards beyond the bridge. That was a safety margin in case they'd made a mistake somewhere — in the distance or the angle. Or a fault in the powder bag, or a sudden gust of wind, or.....

It was no use going through all the factors that might cause a miscalculation — two hundred yards was all he could allow. They needed the fire too much for more delay.

The shell in flight seemed to take forever. It should have landed already. Why hadn't he asked Sergeant Washington to check the book for the "time of flight"? Why hadn't he —

The shell blossomed in its huge red-orange glory right in front of him — just beyond the bridge perhaps a hundred and fifty yards. He reached down to take the walkie-talkie from Cordova.

"Okay! It's right where we figured. A little less than two hundred yards over. Drop it down a hundred yards so we can creep in carefully. But hurry. I think they've already got some kind of emergency crossing almost ready to use."

He handed the radio back to the corporal. It was only five or six seconds before Cordova sang out again, "On the way!"

Jesus, how could they have done all the things necessary to load and still be ready that soon — short-handed as they were?

"Sergeant Washington says he's keeping all guns loaded and following commands," Corporal Cordova said. "This is number two gun firing. Closed on number one so it should be in about the same place."

Now there's a man who knows what the hell he's doing, Lieutenant Stallingsworth thought. While he stood waiting by the window two more tank shells hit into the first row of buildings up ahead. He thought he had caught the telltale sparks coming from a distant ridge — whether the first or second he couldn't be sure. He really ought to do something about them. If those tanks were allowed to sit back there and plow shells into the buildings by the river, it wouldn't be long before the Americans would run out of infantry. If he could only tell which ridge they were firing from, he could —

The second shell landed, sending up its tower of flame and dirt.

Once more he took the radio from Cordova and spoke into it directly.

"You're right on for deflection, range about twenty-five over — a little more, maybe. Go down fifty yards on the next one— and if that's close or a short, then we're in business. Fifty should give you just enough safety margin for friendly troops."

Sergeant Washington's voice came back after a very brief pause.

"On the way, number three gun. All other guns loaded to fire for effect when ready."

This should be it, Lieutenant Stallingsworth breathed. Be in there, be right in there — for the honor of the artillery and the lives of those poor bastards up there in the buildings by the river.

The next eruption was different — muffled, less sweepingly colorful. Then with a leap of his heart he knew why.

He grabbed the radio and shouted into it. "You're on! You're on! Landed right in the god-damned water, down where I couldn't quite see it hit. Go right one mill — I couldn't tell exactly but I think you're hitting the target just left of center. *Fire for effect*! Give me one volley and then I'll correct you as necessary."

"Three guns on the way!" the voice crackled from the radio.

While he was waiting for the shells' long time of high-angle flight, the lieutenant remembered guiltily the tanks firing from one of the ridges. Their shells were still plowing into the buildings up ahead.

"Alert the battalion to a fire mission," he said to Cordova.

The corporal turned to the larger radio and picked up the mike.

The lieutenant, scanning the area where he was sure he had seen the tanks fire, suddenly spotted the same brief flashes of light again. Two of them. He couldn't be certain, but he was almost sure they were even lower than they had been when he had fired at the others in the afternoon. That would mean the tanks were firing from the first ridge. He decided it was too important to delay further. Better to waste a few shells than to let the firing go unanswered.

"Battalion ready for adjustment," Cordova said.

"Give them the coordinates I marked for Concentration B," the lieutenant said.

Then he saw the three shells Washington's men had fired land, one just beyond the river, one slightly short, and the third again muffled by an underwater explosion.

"You're right on!" the lieutenant shouted into the walkie-talkie. "Keep them coming!"

"Can you adjust battalion?" Cordova said from where he crouched by the radio.

"No time!" Lieutenant Stallingsworth shouted at his radio operator. "Tell them to fire battalion one volley on a hundred-yard front. That'll be close enough to start. Friendly troops need immediate support!"

One more round landed squarely where the bridge had been. While Cardova was repeating his words into the radio he pushed the button of the walkie-talkie.

"You're fourth gun is right on — exactly. Now give me Battery five volleys. That'll give them twenty shells right up the nose."

"Major says he'll give you the one volley," Cordova said, "but please try to observe and give corrections for follow-up."

"Give 'em a 'Wilco' on that. Jesus, are we in business, or are we in business."

Colonel Berrigan had seen the shells land around the bridge and felt a great wave of relief sweep through him. His task force might be miniscule compared to the forces arrayed against him — but while communications stayed in and the ammunition held, that artillery was giving him a real ace in the hole. It was like a giant arm holding off a dangerous fighter — reducing him to wild, futile swings at empty air.

Don't overdo your ecstasy, he told himself. Just remember those two soldiers, or parts of soldiers, down there in the other room. The enemy didn't hit empty air that time.

Then he saw, further away, the eruptions of shells at the crest of the first ridge. With so many shells landing at once, he realized that had to be the full battalion firing.

More shells plowed into the bridge area. My God, he thought, the artillery lieutenant must be firing two missions at the same time — one with his own battalion, the other with the black soldiers' "close support." If he had ever had any prejudice against black troops, they had cured him of it fast enough. All they had to do was to follow orders and they would have been out of all this mess. But they themselves had chosen to put their lives at risk.

A flare suddenly illuminated the night with its ghostly glow just as a whole cluster of shells landed. With the help of the flare the colonel could clearly see many shells erupting all around the top of the nearest ridge.

The enemy's tank shells were no longer striking into the buildings around him. Then he saw why. The tanks were rapidly withdrawing, hastily backing away and getting behind the ridge. Even as he watched he saw one shell appear to strike a turret. Immediately the tank stopped and men began to erupt from the escape hatches.

The barrage continued as the tanks withdrew. Again and again a tank would appear to be hit — only to recover and hurry on for the safety of the other side of the ridge.

Then they were gone — except for the one he had seen hit, which sat, forlorn and powerless, near the top of the ridge. A moment later shells burst just in front of Berrigan. They came in to land all around the bridge area, many apparently striking right on top of the men working on the temporary bridge. The flare had now gone out, but the exploding shells cast their own snapshots of light — with fleeing men outlined briefly against the fiery red-orange blossoms.

The shells continued to *whump-whumph* in with devastating regularity. The eruptions of those landing right in the bridge area appeared to toss up structural apparatus of some kind — lengths of planking or steel, and occasionally even what appeared to be parts of pontoons.

After twenty or thirty shells had landed, a sudden silence fell. Artillery explosons and the ripping sound of machine guns all ceased.

A flare cast its unearthly light over the whole landscape. Near the river nothing moved. Further back scattered figures were retreating, moving with the slow pace of men whose purpose has drained, leaving nothing but despair.

16

Colonel Berrigan sat at the table staring at his map. It was the first time he had sat down since — he couldn't even remember. For the moment everything was quiet...no, not just quiet...completely silent. Too quiet to be reassuring. Something was surely just about to break open.

Yet he had nothing to confirm that premonition. And just the sudden sinking down into the chair had once again made him aware of how tired he was. Yet he felt there were a hundred tasks undone, and he should be up and doing them. But what were they?

He had checked by radio with both flanks only five minutes before, and they had both reported everything temporarily quiet. Bradovitch's tank positions were still apparently undiscovered. At least no one had disturbed them. But the colonel had a suspicion the next attack would come there. After all, the Germans had tried the center and the left — the probability was they would attempt next the one route still to try.

That was only elementary tactics.

But why was the German commander taking so long? There was no question he had strength enough. He must know all he had to do was bear down hard and then refuse to let up. Then this paper-thin defense would crack like a piece of stage scenery.

But he suddenly remembered a line from one of his lectures on tactics.

"You'll always imagine the enemy is stronger than you," he had told his students. "And you'll always be certain the enemy is aware of your weaknesses. But remember, 'facts' always look different from the enemy's point of view. For every man you have, the enemy will imagine ten. It's only natural. You'll recognize the tendency in your own reactions to him. Your situation and the way the enemy imagines your situation are never the same."

Maybe it was good advice. He had always thought so.

So what would it mean here?

Maybe it would apply here as well. After all, his force had given the enemy plenty of reason to magnify its elements. The Germans had tried to advance quickly without caution — and had many of their armored vehicles destroyed by a quick and devastating artillery concentration. They had tried to rush the bridge and been frustrated by the engineers' mines and demolition. They had tried to deliver supporting fire from hull-down tanks — and only lost more tanks for their pains. And then they had tried that outflanking movement by a large number of panzergrenadiers — only to have the formation torn to bits by more artillery. And their attempt to reconstruct the bridge had been frustrated by both artillery and infantry.

My God, he thought, maybe we haven't done so badly after all. Maybe they *do* have a need to proceed carefully against such a "powerful" foe. He glanced at his watch. It was nine-thirty. And most of the night lay ahead....

Running footsteps pounded up to the door. A moment later it was thrown open and the soldier he'd posted by the tank outside the C.P. stood in the doorway.

"Sir, the light tank reports the patrol you sent around the right flank has just come back. They want to talk to you."

The colonel leaped to his feet and followed the soldier out the door and around to the tank parked behind the building. The tank commander handed him the headset.

"Okay, this is Lone Bandit Six," he spoke crisply into the mike. He knew there was always some chance of the enemy intercepting a radio message. But this information was so important he had to take the risk. "Go ahead. What did you find?"

"We had a bad time, sir. Sergeant Wolinsky was killed — or I'm pretty sure he was. Corporal Williams was hit in the shoulder, but we managed to bring him back with us. It was a mess."

The voice sounded on the verge of panic — almost like that of a young boy in a state of shock.

"Easy, now," the colonel said in a calming voice. "You made it back all right. Now it's very important for you to tell me exactly what happened."

"Yes, sir. Well, after Sergeant Wolinsky was hit...."

The colonel used the uncertain pause to break in quickly.

"No. Tell me everything in the order it happened. After you started out."

"Yes, sir. We started out with no trouble. The going was kind of tough in the dark, but then we found a sort of trail and it went faster."

"Could vehicles — or tanks use the road?"

"They might, sir. Except in a few spots they might have to

fix, or knock down some trees."

"Does the trail come all the way to our position?"

"No, sir. We used it coming back and it peters out maybe...a quarter mile or so from where we are."

"All right. Go on and tell me the rest — as it happened."

"Well, sir, we got to the river-crossing. We couldn't see anyone there, so after awhile we decided to go over for a look. We got across all right, no problem. We found a sort of rough road going back a hundred yards or so. Then it branched off, one part going to the right away from us and the other fork slanting back to the left. That's the one Sergeant Wolinsky said we should take. We must have gone three or four hundred yards. We took our time and went very careful. We knew we were getting back toward where the Germans are."

"How was that trail — passable by tanks?"

"The same as the other, sir. Much of the way they might make it O.K. — but with lots of bad places they'd have to fix."

"Did it seem to go all the way back to their position?"

"No, sir. At least it narrowed down to a little one-track trail. We were about to turn back, because Sergeant Wolinsky said we must be getting close to their positions."

"How far had you gone then? A half-mile?"

"Maybe. No more. Probably a little less."

"Then what happened?

"Well, we thought we could hear some other people. We heard voices. Talking German, I think. Sergeant Wolinsky had us set up an ambush, and we waited quite a while. But they didn't come toward us much. They...they seemed to be some kind of work detail. At least we heard somebody chopping with an ax. Then Sergeant Wolinsky sent Corporal Williams ahead to take a look. He was gone quite a long time. Then we heard some shots. Sergeant Wolinsky went up to take a look. Then there were some more shots. Then Corporal Williams came back in pretty bad shape with a bullet in his shoulder. He said Sergeant Wolinsky came up in a little different place and he never really saw him. But the Germans must have had a lookout who saw the sergeant and cut down on him. Corporal Williams said he just heard the shots. But he was sure they got the sergeant. They were looking around for any others who came with the sergeant, so he knew he had to get out of there. He just managed to get back to us and collapsed."

"Did the Germans come looking for him?"

"I couldn't say, sir. We took on out of there as fast as we could. Corporal Williams could travel if we helped him. When we got back to the river we made a stretcher to carry him in. I guess we should have gone up to try to find Sergeant Wolinsky...but Corporal Williams was sure they got him...and we were afraid we'd get caught and couldn't get back

"You did just right, soldier. It was important for you to get back with what you've told me. Where's Corporal Williams now?"

"Two guys said they'd bring him back to the aid station in town."

"Good. Now, tell Lieutenant Brownell and Sergeant Bradovitch all you've told me, then come on back to the kitchen and get some hot coffee. You and the other soldier on the patrol. You did fine — just what you should have. Over and out."

The Colonel stood for a minute thinking. There was no doubt this could be bad. But how bad? It seemed obvious the Germans had discovered the possibility of another route. And they'd certainly try to make use of it. But it all depended on how good that "trail" was. He couldn't be sure, but from the soldier's report it appeared there would be a lot of work needed before they could use that route to bring tanks around for an armored attack. Would they be willing to take the time?

But of course they could already use it for infantry — and an infantry attack on the right flank could blast a way for their panzers to get across the river. And with the right flank gone they should be able to roll up the entire defense in no time. All of which meant he had to do something to try to prevent it. Except that he didn't have enough force to set up defenses against all eventualities. But he'd just have to do what he could.

He didn't dare take the time to go over there himself. He might arrive and find everything going to hell here in town — with the whole position collapsing before he could get back to do anything about it.

Yet it was too complicated to handle over the radio. He'd have to send someone. Once again he cursed his lack of staff. Well, he'd just have to send Sergeant McClanahan.

Returning to the C.P. he quickly recounted for the sergeant what he knew about the possible threat to the right flank.

"I want you to go over and see what you can do about setting up some kind of defense there," he said. "It can't be much. Lieutenant Brownell has only a very short-handed platoon to start with — and he's just lost two men. But see if you can get a reliable non-com and four or five men to make responsible for that flank. They won't be much more than a tripwire. But tell them to go out a few hundred yards and send out a scout another couple hundred. The idea is to have them shoot up a storm — make the enemy think they've run into a main defensive position. That should at least give Lieutenant Brownell and Sergeant Bradovitch time to shift over a few men and maybe a couple of tanks. Then they won't be caught with somebody coming in behind them and cutting them off. It's all going to be pretty flimsy — there's no way to get around that. But see what you can do. Then come on back to the C.P."

"Yes, sir," the sergeant said. The colonel noted the sergeant's manner and voice appeared less ironic now. If he wasn't learning to respect his new commander, at least he was taking his responsibility seriously. And that was what mattered.

He suddenly realized he had not heard for some time from either of the light tanks he had sent back to patrol the parallel road two miles behind them. That was an oversight he'd better correct immediately.

Hurriedly he went back out to the communications tank

"Have either of the light tanks on the road behind us reported in recently?" he asked the man in the turret.

"I haven't been able to raise the one that's out to the right," the tank commander answered. "But I talked to the one on the left just a few minutes ago. He was getting kind of worried. He's out there about a mile or more, and he believes things are going to heat up over there."

The tank commander stopped, listened to his headset a moment, then stripped it off and handed it down to the colonel.

"This is him now, sir. He wants to talk to you."

Colonel Berrigan slipped the headset on and spoke into the mike. "Lone Bandit Six here. Go ahead. Over."

The answering voice came through faintly — but clear enough for the colonel to sense the uneasiness there.

"We think we're going to get hit with something pretty soon, sir. I wanted to be sure you knew."

"Have you been fired on yet? Or seen any tanks?"

"No, sir. No tanks have shown up yet. But we can tell there's a big battle going on over there somewhere. Sometimes we can hear a lot of shooting — when the wind is just right. Then about half an hour ago the sky to the north started to glow and light up. There's a town over there somewhere, and they must be having a helluva battle there. Lots of flashes — like big guns firing. And that glow is even bigger now. Like maybe the whole town is on fire. I thought you ought to know."

Colonel Berrigan took his map from his pocket and shined his light on it for a moment.

"There's a good-sized town out there all right — about three miles from where you are. We have friendly units there that must be putting up quite a battle. Now, what we have to worry about is this: if they take the town, they may send a sizable force down the road toward you. From what you've reported, I'd guess they're in the town already. What I want from you is *immediate* warning when there's any indication some of them have turned in this direction. So if you can, move up another half-mile or so. *If* you feel it's still safe to do so. Then be sure to report immediately when you make contact with *any* units—friendly or hostile. Is that clear?"

"Yes, sir. All clear."

"Right. We're all depending on you to give us adequate warning. Over and Out."

He was about to hand the headset back when another voice, much louder and clearer broke in suddenly.

"Lone Bandit Six! Lone Bandit Six! Brownell Force here. We're going to be hit big! Repeat: we're going to be hit — and plenty big. Tank motors moving up to the ford. They must have sneaked them up somehow without us hearing. But they're coming in fast now — a bunch of them. We're going to need help fast! Come in if you hear me. Over."

Once again Colonel Berrigan felt that cold hand closing around his chest. So it was finally coming. And there were no tricks for him to use here — and very little he could do to control any of the action. But he had to do what he could — and hope the men doing the fighting could somehow provide the strength to hang on.

"This is Lone Bandit Six," he said, striving to keep all evidence of the fluttering butterflies inside him out of his voice. "I read you loud and clear, Lieutenant. And we'll give you all assistance possible. I'm going to have a load of artillery dumped in behind that ford — plus some more of our close support mediums directly on the ford. Be sure your men and the tanks stay at least a hundred yards back from it. If the enemy has a heavy force coming, that'll discourage the elements coming up in support. But you and Sergeant Bradovitch's big boys will have to handle those that break through. Are all your men alerted?"

"Yes, sir. I think we'll put up a good fight. But if they send some Tigers this way and Bradovitch's big boys can't handle them, I can't guarantee there's anything we can do against them."

"Easy does it, Lieutenant. Nobody's asking you to fight Tigers with your bare hands. Forget the Tigers — I doubt if they'll send those awkward things into that muddy crossing. But leave the tanks to Bradovitch and us — just be sure your men get any infantry that accompanies them, is that clear?"

"Yes, sir. All clear."

"Good. Now I'm going to get that artillery support coming your way. Over and Out."

He handed the headset back to the tank commander and started toward the artillery O.P. building, but the tank commander's urgent voice halted him.

"Sir, it's the other light tank — the one patrolling to the left on the road behind us. He says there's a column of armor heading straight down the road toward him. He wants to know what he should do."

Jesus, the colonel muttered to himself, so do I. So the hell do I.

The flare lit up the whole area with a pale glow. Bradovitch peered eagerly through the sight, saw the squarish bulk right in the middle of the ford. Just as he'd thought — a Mark IV. They wouldn't waste V's and VI's over in this mud. The tank's turret was rotated a quarter right, firing at something there. He quickly brought the cross-hairs to the exposed side of the turret. There, you bastard, he thought as he sent one shot home, saw it hit and penetrate, followed it with another, saw that one hit too, then yelled for his driver to back away — before the shell from the second German tank blasted a tree behind the spot they had just vacated. Then the flare flickered and died.

"Pull back and to the right," he told the driver. "That'll keep the tank I just hit between us and the other one. We'll get him when he tries to pass."

The tank motor roared as the driver gave it power. They were in among the trees — but here so widely spaced they had plenty of maneuver room. He looked eagerly for the second tank but could see nothing in the darkness. Then a second flare burst, illuminating the night around him and clearly revealing the tank he had blasted — and, just beyond, the front of the second tank beginning to emerge. Its gun was swinging toward him, searching for him among the trees. Then the gunner must have spotted him, for the gun swung more quickly — but stopped as it hit the gun of the blasted tank. Sweat, you bastard, he muttered to himself as he calmly brought the cross-hairs just where he wanted them, while the German tank first tried to swing wider to clear the other tank — then started to back furiously as the Sherman's gun came to bear. He let the round go while the other tank's treads were spinning in the mud of the creek bottom, saw it hit just as he had planned, under the first tank's gun-barrel and into the second turret's exposed side. Then he followed it with a round of H.E. and felt a glow of triumph when both tanks burst into orange flame.

"Back off," he yelled exultantly to the driver. "They're

gonna have a tough job gettin' more tanks past those two we just knocked out. Those two carcasses block most of the whole god-damned ford."

"Infantry coming around the tanks," the man beside the driver shouted over the intercom. "Should I blast them with the machine gun?"

Bradovitch saw the gray-clad figures struggling to move quickly past the tanks through the hip-length water. Despite their attempt to hurry, their legs moved through the water with the lethargic grace of figures in a slow-motion movie.

"Hell, yes! Blast the bastards!" Bradovitch shouted. "Everybody who can see 'em, blast 'em."

He rotated the turret until his coaxial machine gun was pointed toward a group of the struggling figures pushing through the water, then cut loose with a prolonged burst. He saw two of the figures and then a third crumple into the water. He could hear machine guns all around him sputtering with sustained bursts.

Then suddenly a large gun to his right fired.

"No," he yelled desperately. "Machine guns only! There's tanks over there looking to spot a seventy-five — "

Somewhere on the other side of the ford a gun fired, the projectile whishing past Bradovitch's tank to strike almost immediately something further back.

Jesus, he cursed inwardly. That little mistake just cost us a tank. One down, only four left. At least it was armor-piercing and didn't set the Sherman on fire. Maybe some of the men would get out.

"No more big guns unless you're on a tank," he shouted into the mike. "I think they just got Harry. Use your god-damned machine guns on the infantry."

He saw another wave of infantry enter the water. They were illuminated starkly by the light from the burning tanks sitting dead in the middle of the ford. He turned his turret to bring his machine gun to bear. Other machine guns were firing all around him. The gray-clad figures slumped into the water before he had his own gun lined up.

Another flare high above him suddenly lit the whole scene. He saw the scattered figures slogging through the water, and behind them more figures in two files proceeding toward the ford. But it was what was between the files that made his heart jump. There, lined up almost bumper to bumper, was what looked like an endless line of squat, ugly tanks. The shorter gun and the square, squat look told him immediately they were Mark IVs.

"Mark IVs across the river," he shouted into his mike. "Make sure you're lined up good before you fire — then move fast, or they'll be on you — "

Then, without warning, he saw a whole cluster of large, red-orange bursts flower all around the line of tanks. Still lit by the flickering light of the flare, the double line of infantry scattered, some running, some being heaved up by the bursts themselves. One and then a second tank burst into flame. Then the flare went out and only the burning tanks were visible. After a few seconds, more shells began to burst all around the tanks, setting another one afire. Still they whished in, not all together now but in a nearly continuous chain, with one or two explosions shattering the night every few seconds.

Now the burning hulks of tanks gave so much light to the scene he could make out the dark, squat tank forms even when the flare had gone out.

"Okay, get on 'em," he shouted into his mike. "They're too busy trying to get the hell out of that packed line to worry about shooting back now. Go first for the ones turned side or back to us. Give 'em hell!"

He heard two Shermans cut loose with their main guns, then he was lined up on the side of another tank desperately fleeing from the packed formation. He saw his armor-piercing shell strike in the middle of the side's thin-armor, knew it had penetrated, swung his turret to pick up another one, saw that one struck by somebody else's shell before he was fully on it, and searched wildly for another.

Now the enemy tanks had scattered so much the light from the burning tanks no longer illuminated them. But the Shermans around him were still blasting away.

"Cease firing!" he yelled suddenly into the mike. "Once they're back out of the artillery they'll start looking — "

But he knew he had spoken too late. A cluster of spark-like flames reached out from higher up the ridge, and then he heard two more solid smacks behind him, telling him two armor-piercing shells had hit home. Hell, he thought, I was just too damn slow both times. So now we've lost three.

But at least, he thought grimly, there's a helluva lot of Mark IV's that'll never parade for the Fuhrer again.

Colonel Berrigan had only been able to shout a brief message to the tank commander before continuing his run for the artillery O.P.

"Tell them to try anything to slow them down a little — without getting knocked off themselves. Maybe a thirty-seven shell to the leading tank's turret — if they can shoot from a corner they can back around in a hurry. I'll get right back to them."

Then he was at the door of the O.P. building and leaping up the two flights of stairs. What a hell of a message, he thought. Just imagine what that poor son-of-a-bitch in the light tank must be thinking: Try anything hell — how'm I going to stop a whole armored column with a thirty-seven that can't even dent a Mark VI?

But there were times when you had no solution for the big problems and just had to deal with the little ones in front of you and hope for the best.

Then he was at the top of the stairs and hastily explaining the importance of getting all possible artillery on the attack on the right flank.

Lieutenant Stallingsworth had already alerted his own battalion and Sergeant Washington's guns. He listened carefully to the colonel's explanation and before he had finished was already giving Corporal Cordova commands to relay to the battalion.

"Call for Concentration W immediately," he said. "Enemy tank attack! Request five volleys. Will adjust as necessary for follow-up fire."

While Cordova was urgently repeating the commands into the larger radio, the lieutenant was shouting others into the walkie-talkie. Then he turned briefly toward the colonel.

"I'll plaster the other side of the river with everything my own battalion will give me — then adjust our four close guns on the ford itself. They'll be more accurate."

"Good," the colonel said. "I'll be back — got an emergency to attend to first."

Then he was leaping down the stairs, bursting out of the building and running back to where he had left the jeep. Jesus, it's sure lucky I didn't send McClanahan off with the jeep, he thought. With no god-damned communication to most of my own task force, I'd be lost without it.

He desperately wanted to stop at the light tank and ask what was happening now on the road behind them. But he had nothing to offer that would help them yet — he would just be satisfying his own curiosity for information. It was better not to bother the tank commander, who had plenty to think about already. The thing to do was to get some real help out to him as quickly as possible. And the Colonel could think of only one way to do that.

Then he was climbing into the jeep, backing it out and speeding back up the road through town. He had to watch carefully for the spot to turn off. It was hard to tell in the dark, but he thought he remembered the right place. He pulled off the road and bounced and jostled over the rough ground until he saw the hulking mass of Sergeant MacKay's tank destroyer looming up ahead.

"You've got to pull back to the main road behind us," he shouted up at the sergeant the moment he saw his scarecrow figure outlined against the sky. "Just you. Leave the other destroyer here. Go back to the crossroad, a little over a mile back, turn left, then go on out as fast as you can until you meet one of our light tanks. He should be retreating toward you. I can't tell you how far out. But you'll have to be careful you don't over-shoot him, because there's a German armored column coming up the road — and he's trying to delay it all he can. Your responsibility is to take over the job. Play it as careful as you can. Because if you're knocked out they'll have a clear shot to cut off the whole task force. The important point is to *delay* them. Your gun can knock out anything they've got. But your problem is you have to knock out whatever will make them slow down, and then get away to set up another trap. You're going to be giving them territory for time. Have you got all that?"

"Yes, sir! I'm sure we can put the fear of God into them. This old ninety will make 'em slow down fast enough."

The tank destroyer backed up quickly, swung around and headed for the road. Colonel Berrigan followed him with the jeep, turned left at the road and a few moments later was entering the town again.

All the way down the dark street he was wondering what

had happened at the ford. He had seen the flares and heard the machine guns and tank cannon. Then there had been that heavy concentration of artillery. By the number of rounds that had landed in the first concentration he knew it must have been a full battalion firing. Shortly after he had seen the flashes in the sky that indicated Sergeant Washington's guns were adding the close-up support. But now on the whole right flank everything was remarkably quiet.

He parked the jeep behind the C.P. and hurried inside. There he was relieved to find Sergeant McClanahan had returned.

"What happened over there?" he asked the sergeant.

"The Krauts were pulling an all-out attack on the ford," Sergeant McClanahan said. "Infantry and a whole line of Mark IV's. Our tanks got two of them halfway across the ford. They also had infantry trying to cross. But our Shermans stopped them. Then the artillery dumped all over them. The bastard running the show must really want to get across bad. He had Mark IV's all lined up for a parade. That artillery battalion made them scatter. Then those black boys got their guns laid right on the ford. God damn — pinpoint accuracy. They must have put in twenty rounds — all in the water or within ten yards of it. There were two knocked-out tanks in the middle of the river, and those guns got so many hits there must be pieces scattered for a hundred yards on either side. That ford is one god-awful mess. As anxious as he wants to cross, I don't believe the Kraut commander's going to try that route again for awhile. There must be eight or ten tanks knocked out over there."

"How about our loses?"

Sergeant McClanahan's enthusiasm suddenly evaporated. "It cost us, all right. Three Shermans knocked out. Infantry casualties not too bad. But we're left with only two Shermans to hold up what looks like half the god-damned German army."

The colonel had been dreading that. A couple more of these "victories" and he'd have no anti-tank defense left at all.

"How about the flank outpost — did you get that set up?"

"Roger. I think I got a good non-com in charge. And he knows what he has to do."

"Good. If they send tanks by that route we'll just have to pray they're held up trying to make the trail passable."

The Colonel sat down by the table and once more felt exhaustion sweep over his body. It was wonderful to relax for a moment. The trouble was, if he let himself relax completely, he knew he'd be asleep in thirty seconds. Yet even a few seconds' relaxation was a luxury.

He needn't have worried about having thirty seconds to fall asleep. In less than ten he heard the rush of incoming artillery — then shells were exploding all around him. Running footsteps approached the door. It burst open, revealing the messenger he'd posted outside by the tank.

"Mark Vs or VIs coming down the road, sir! Toward the bridge. And there's a lot of infantry or engineers down there by the river. It looks like they may have rigged some kind of bridge."

17

Colonel Berrigan couldn't understand what his opponent was doing. He had tried the middle and both flanks, and now he had to try something else. But why a straight rush down the road where artillery had already cut one such assault to pieces? He had to have more tricks in his bag than that.

Of course the German commander had his artillery up now, and that would make it a lot more costly for the defenders. But something in the back of his mind kept telling him this wasn't right.

Right or not, it had to be dealt with. The obvious danger point was the bridge. If they ever got a temporary crossing in there so tanks could roll across, just a few of them could crush the town's weak anti-tank defenses. But as long as they tried to cross in that same spot that was already zeroed in, the artillery might be able to stop them.

"Stay here," he said to Sergeant McClanahan. "If you can contact Captain Bergoff, tell him to check the state of the infantry platoon up front, and if they've been hit bad and need replacements, feed a few in from his reserve platoon. I'm going up to take a look at things — and I guess the best place for that is the artillery O.P."

"Yes, sir," Sergeant McClanahan answered. "But now they've got artillery, they'll be flattening that O.P. before long. There's only a few three-story buildings in town — and that one towers above everything else in the neighborhood."

"I know," the colonel said. "But we have to hope they won't think of it for a few more minutes."

When he was barely outside the door, he heard a shell whishing in. He dove flat on his stomach, heard it explode into a nearby building, then jumped up and dashed for the door of the next building behind the C.P. He made it to the door of the house with the artillery O.P. before another round landed, leaped up the two flights of stairs as he heard a whole volley approaching, and reached the top of the stairs just as two shells cleared the house and struck into the building behind it. A jagged piece of metal came crashing through the rear window and embedded itself in the wall three feet away.

"You're going to have to clear out of here, Lieutenant," he said. "But first we've got to drop another concentration on that bridge area. They may have some kind of temporary crossing there."

"I've already got our four close-support guns on it. They're almost ready to fire."

"On the way," Corporal Cordova announced, holding the small walkie-talkie close to his ear. "Firing two volleys. Adjust and we'll repeat as necessary."

"How about your own battalion?" the colonel asked. "Can you get them on the tanks coming down the main road?"

"I can put some shells over there — but they probably won't do much good. It may sound like a lot of tanks coming down that road, but so far they've only sent two or three — with big intervals between them. There's not much chance to hit anything while they're moving like that — unless they jam up at the crossing. But I'm sure just our four close-support guns can knock any bridge out before they get much stuff across. We zeroed in Sergeant Washington's guns on that bridge area before. That's what bothers me. They're not stupid — they know we can knock it out. So why try it again?"

A flare went up from the forward infantry position, lighting the road from the river to the first ridge. The colonel could see what the lieutenant meant. There were now only three tanks proceeding down the road — with intervals of a hundred yards or more between them.

Then the shells from the four one-five-fives hit, all exploding in the bridge area. The colonel watched intently as they landed, trying to see what had been constructed as a temporary bridge. In the brief flash of the explosions he couldn't see anything there for sure. Then four more shells hit, grouped in the same area as the others.

The lieutenant grabbed the walkie-talkie from the corporal and spoke urgently into it.

"You're right on, Sergeant Washington. Give me three more volleys in the same spot to make sure."

Colonel Berrigan suddenly realized he had seen almost no infantry or engineer troops in the area. Yet they must be there if they had constructed a crossing. He turned abruptly and started for the stairs.

"Keep on that bridge area until you're sure no tanks can cross," he said as he started down the staircase.

Shells were still pouring into the nearby buildings as he ran down the street toward the forward infantry position. He arrived outside the building just as a flare flickered out. He saw two hunched-over figures by the corner nearest the street and changed direction to join them. He recognized one of them as Captain Bergoff, the chubby-faced staff officer he had placed in command of all the infantry.

"What's going on over there?" the colonel asked.

"We've sent a scout up to the riverbank to try and get a look," Captain Bergoff replied, his plump face quivering from the tension. "He should be back shortly."

Just then they heard running feet and a soldier, panting for breath, burst around the corner.

"Jesus," the soldier sputtered, "I thought I was a goner. God-damned artillery from both sides, and then a bastard with a burp-gun saw me."

He stopped, still breathing heavily.

"Did you get a look at the bridge site?" the captain asked.

"I got one good look before I had to take off."

"What'd they have? A low pontoon bridge we can't see?" the colonel asked.

"Shit! They ain't got shit! I saw two or three guys just hammering away on a piece of wood. There's nothing down there. It's all a god-damned fake!"

The colonel felt like smacking himself in the head with the palm of his hand. Of course! And he'd been sucked in on it so easy.

"Captain Bergoff," he said abruptly, "Get all your people in firing positions. You'll have to leave some men here in the center to protect against an infantry attack — but move all you can to both flanks and prepare them for enemy crossings out in the open areas. They'll have infantry and probably tanks too. Keep the men in buildings so the tanks can't overrun them. Have your men concentrate their fire on the infantry — I'll try to get something else on the tanks."

"Yes, sir," the captain said, then turning to the man who

had been waiting with him he added quickly, "Sergeant, you go over and get those on the right started while I take care of these on the left side of the street."

Colonel Berrigan had already risen and was running to the left behind the sheltering building.

Was I stupid, he cursed himself as he ran. I knew something was wrong, but I just didn't think it through. And it was so god-damned obvious. Banging on pieces of wood! Play-acting in the center — just to cover what they were really doing. So now the big question: was it too late to stop it?

He passed two buildings and then paused behind a third when he saw the tank destroyer looming up ahead.

"Lieutenant Hood!" he shouted up at the startled figure peering down at him. "Alert all your men. Tanks will be coming across the river out in the open spaces somewhere. Probably both flanks. There may be quite a few before we can get their crossings knocked out. Tell your men to try to get in a flank shot if they're Panthers or Tigers. And tell them to take their time and line up a good shot before giving away their positions. Have you got any flares?"

"Yes, sir."

"Then use 'em. Look for the bridging site. And tell your right-flank people to do the same over there."

"Yes, sir."

He didn't have time to wait to see his orders carried out. He'd just have to hope this late-blooming son of the Confederacy could put his romantic ideas of warfare behind him and do what had to be done.

Then the colonel was running again back toward the center of town. He hoped the hell the artillery lieutenant had figured the ruse out too and was getting somebody's guns on the crossings — wherever the hell they were.

Lieutenant Stallingsworth, watching intently from his third-story window, could tell as soon as the flare illuminated the area that there was no crossing at the old bridge site. And he had managed to stop the guns before they wasted any more ammunition on a fake attack.

So what were they doing, sending those tanks rushing up like that to a river with no crossing? It had to be a mousetrap play, he thought — getting us to center all our attention in the middle, while they made their real move somewhere else. But where?

He peered with his glasses all along the river, searching for any telltale piece of evidence that might reveal the site. Away from the center of town his angle of vision was too small for him to see any bridging placed down low between the raised banks. And except for the slight activity around the bridge area, nothing appeared to be moving anywhere along the river. He raised his glasses to observe the first ridge. Nothing there either. Desperately he turned his glasses to the main road leading into town, saw the first tank approach the original bridge site — then turn off and proceed cross-country toward the left. Now he knew where to look. But was it too late?

"Fire mission," he shouted to Corporal Cordova. "Just the four guns. New bridge crossing area. Have the guns loaded and I'll give you the exact location in a minute."

He swept his glasses over the length of the river from the bridge site to the forest a quarter-mile away on the left. Still nothing. Desperately he raised his gaze to scan the first ridge to the east. That was when he saw it.

Just emerging over the ridge, clearly visible in the light from another flare that had just burst, was a peculiarly awkward-looking tank. And right behind it was a second tank, this one a standard Mark V. He watched them just long enough to see they were moving straight ahead for the river. So that was the spot — about three-quarters of the way over toward the forest. The tanks were obviously going as fast as they could in the rough, cross-country terrain.

He glanced down at his map, turned his pocket flashlight on it, and saw the spot on the river the tanks would soon reach was between two areas he had marked on the map as concentrations M and P.

He still had seen no crossing site, but he had to start somewhere. And it might as well be there.

"Enemy bridging site on the river midway between concentrations M and P. Will adjust guns as before — using all guns in turn. Fire number one when ready."

He expected a considerable wait while Sergeant Washington found the map location and then converted range and deflection into actual commands for the guns. To his surprise less than ten seconds had passed before Corporal Cordova's "Number one on the way!" rang out. That Washington's no slouch, he thought. He's worked out some system of nearly instantaneous conversion.

The lieutenant knew he would have a few seconds' wait while the shell took its high-angle route to the target. He glanced back at the road leading to the bridge and saw the second tank approach the river and then turn off suddenly – *in the opposite direction!*

"My God," he exclaimed. "They've got *two* of them!" Then he remembered the shell he had about to land and swung his glasses back to the left — just in time. The explosion came nearly a hundred yards to the left and perhaps seventy-five yards beyond the spot he had projected as the crossing site.

"Go right six mils, decrease range one hundred yards," he

said to Corporal Cordova, who repeated it immediately into the radio.

The lieutenant saw the awkward-looking tank coming cross-country from the ridge was now only about a hundred yards from the river. And in the light of a new flare he saw the reason for the awkward appearance. It was caused by a huge blade affixed to the front of the tank. A bulldozer tank — of course! The temporary bridge had been built low to hide it, and now the dozer-tank would simply knock down part of the bank on each side of the river. Then the tanks could stream right across.

"Number Two on the way," Cordova sang out.

Waiting for the long time of flight, the lieutenant shuffled through possible ways to deal with the second crossing. Two guns on each site, adjusting them simultaneously? Not nearly enough rounds landing to assure an early hit — what with the dispersion factor and the built-in error from a hasty adjustment. Fire the battalion at the target on the right? Twelve guns, much greater margin for error. But he had already told the colonel of the dangers of using a distant battalion to fire so close to friendly troops. God — he was damned if he did and damned if he didn't!

But *were* there friendly troops that close? He remembered the colonel had left a large area on both sides of town without defenders — the area to be covered only by fire from the flanks. So there should be no friendly troops for two or three hundred yards on either side. *If* the crossing was somewhere near the middle of the open area.

He swung his glance back to the left just in time to pick up the explosion of the second adjustment round. He was glad to see it landed just short of the river, about thirty yards to the right.

"Go left two mils and increase range two-five yards. Fire entire battery one volley."

He knew that would probably not be exact, but he wanted to get some solid fire going in there as soon as possible. Hitting exactly on target was going to be a matter of playing the odds anyway. He could waste ammunition or lose a few seconds — and the loss of a few seconds was clearly the greater danger now.

The nearly continuous use of flares let him see the whole thing clearly. The dozer-tank had already arrived at the new bridging site and had the eastern bank nearly leveled. The second tank was only about fifty yards from the site, and the tank that had gone down the main road and turned off was now approaching from the side. Further back he could see a whole group of tanks, arranged in a spread formation, cresting the ridge and proceeding down the gentle slope toward the river.

Jesus, he thought, how the hell can I get those crossings knocked out in time?

He strode quickly to Corporal Cordova and grabbed the walkie-talkie from him.

"Get battalion on the big radio," he said. "Tell them it's an emergency fire mission. We've got to fire the whole battalion at a point right on the river."

Back at the window he raised his glasses with his free hand and scanned the ridge to the right of the road. There! A second dozer-tank was headed straight toward the river, midway between the main bridge and the ford-crossing.

"Emergency!" Cordova repeated into the mike. "We must have fire immediately. To plug that river crossing before the tanks get across!"

Maybe, the lieutenant thought, Major Shwartz is running things himself at Fire Direction Center. If so he'll give me what I've asked for. I hope the hell he does — or we've just lost the god-damned battle.

Glancing back to the left he saw four rounds land nearly

simultaneously. Three were just a few yards to the left and slightly beyond where the dozer-tank was crossing the river on something just below his line of vision. The fourth was short of the river and a few yards to the right. It was a pretty good bracket — but no cigar. The dozer-tank was now across the river and knocking down the near bank. Across the river the second tank was poised to cross as soon as the dozer-tank had cleared the way. The tank which had come down the main road was only fifty yards to the right of the new crossing site. And back up the slope the whole swarm of heavy tanks in open formation was now almost halfway to the river. Jesus, he thought, we'd better have some luck pretty soon.

Then the second volley landed. Two over, one short, and one landing squarely in the middle of the river. But all four were slightly to the left of the bridge site.

Damn! In his haste to start firing for effect he'd been a little off and hadn't had any luck.

He spoke quickly into the walkie-talkie. "Go right one mil and decrease range one mil. Keep firing for effect until I tell you to stop. You're bracketing it and you're almost in there. Hurry."

The lieutenant looked once again to the right. Hell yes, the same god-damn deal. The dozer-tank was halfway across the river already, with a large number of tanks spread out behind it — all moving rapidly toward the crossing. And still no shells from his battalion!

God, he thought, they're going to be across in droves on both flanks before I can stop them.

"Third volley already fired before we got your change," Sergeant Washington's voice came from the walkie-talkie. "Making adjustment now."

After a pause of only a few seconds he added, "Corrected volley on the way'"

Lieutenant Stallingsworth shifted his gaze again to the left and saw the last four rounds at the old setting land: one short, one over, and two in the water — both just barely to the left of the improvised crossing. Damnit to hell! Not the slightest bit of luck. One shell had been so close that he could see part of the bridging surface bounce up into his view.

He counted the tanks that had crossed already — three, with a fourth just starting across.

"Battalion on the way!" Cordova shouted. "Give sensing and we'll be loaded to fire whole battalion again."

At last! Now the problem would be to get them adjusted as quickly as possible. He turned to look at the crossing on the right, praying his guess of the location would turn out to be accurate. He saw the dozer-tank had crossed already and was pulling away, while a second tank was about to enter the crossing. Two more tanks were within a hundred yards of the hidden bridge..

He didn't know which rounds would arrive first, so he lowered his glasses and kept shifting his glance between the two sites, praying he would be looking the right way when the shells landed.

Then he heard steps pounding up the stairway. He wondered who it could be but didn't dare turn his head to look. Those shells were due any second now.

His eyes had almost reached the left site when the four shells landed there. He saw all four explode. One over, one short, one left and — the final one just to the right. A god-damned perfect adjustment — but still not good enough! When the hell was he going to have any luck at all? Now there were five tanks over and a sixth starting across. Another two minutes of bad luck and he would have lost it for the whole task force.

Nothing for it but look for the shells landing on the right crossing and pray for a better break on Washington's next volley.

Then he saw one round from the battalion land nearly half-way up the slope on the right. Jesus Christ Almighty! Way off! Was it him or the god-damned battalion?

Then the other eleven landed, grouped together, closer to the target — but the center of impact a hundred yards over and at least as much to the right..He felt some kind of jinx must be at work on him.

"All right, Cordova. One hundred over, one hundred right, important to fire entire battalion, closed on no more than two-five yard front. *Repeat! Important to fire all guns. Tanks already crossing!*"

Feeling as if his insides had just dropped out of him at his failure, the lieutenant looked back to the left and saw with dismay, clearly visible in the light from a fresh flare, there were now seven enemy tanks already across the river, with the eighth just pulling onto the crossing. What the hell could he do? He had a perfect adjustment. If the gods were just determined to give him no even break at all, if they were determined he was going to shake box cars on every throw....

The next four rounds came in at the same moment. One was slightly left, just barely off the bridge. One was short, though it hit the near bank. But it was the other two that made his heart jump and a sudden shout burst from his lips. One had hit the bridge itself just in front of the crossing tank — and then the fourth, as if guided by a benevolent god, had struck precisely on the turret of the tank on the bridge.

The tank twisted sidewise and slid off to the right. Pieces of bridge decking and supports, cast up by the explosions, were now showering down all around the tank.

The lieutenant shouted exultantly into the walkie-talkie he still held in one hand. "You god damn did it! Square in the center, blew it all to hell. Throw in two more volleys to make sure there's nothing left of that bridge but a pile of junk."

He was surprised to see Colonel Berrigan standing there beside him by the window. Then he remembered the steps pounding up the stairs.

He felt the sudden urge to stop for a back-pounding celebration of their clear destruction of the bridge — but he knew he still had to stop those tanks pouring across the river on the right side of town..

"Aren't they on the way yet?" he asked Cordova impatiently.

"They're on the way, Lieutenant. I guess you didn't hear me because of the exploding shells."

The lieutenant quickly turned his eyes to the crossing on the right and kept them glued there. There were now four tanks across and a fifth just pulling onto the bridge.

Then the battalion's shells came in with a rush — five bunched together just beyond the river, three short, two straddling the bridge and sending up a gusher of water — and then, blessed be whatever gods were in charge of such matters, two squarely on the passageway itself, one barely over and one just short of the tank now crossing.

Then before there was time to tell the battalion of its success, the lieutenant heard a rapidly approaching rush of incoming shells, followed by an ear-shattering explosion that seemed to knock the world askew. He was lifted up bodily and tossed backward —ending up sprawled on the floor. He noticed the colonel too had been blown backward and was lying on the floor beside him. Corporal Cordova, who had been kneeling by the larger radio, was less affected by the blast, but a slashing fragment had ripped into the lower part of the two-sectioned radio, penetrating the metal casing and leaving a jagged opening, through which some of the inner contents were oozing out.

Lieutenant Stallingsworth lay there a moment, his head reeling and his ears ringing. He at first was afraid to check whether all parts of his body were still properly attached. Then he looked down, saw gratefully he still had all his legs and arms, and began to realize that somehow he had escaped injury.

"God-damn," he heard Cordova's startled exclamation, "I thought that one had all our names on it. The damn thing must have hit just below us downstairs."

The colonel was now getting to his feet. He too appeared unhurt

"I think they've got you zeroed in," the colonel said. "You better get the hell out of here before their next volley."

"I hear you talking," the lieutenant said, closing the B.C. scope in one motion and picking it up. "It's lucky we blew the second crossing up on that last volley. Now our damn radio's gone."

18

Lieutenant Lee Beauregard Hood felt he was wearing some kind of metallic vest so tight he could barely breathe. So now it had all come to a head — all his years of dreaming that someday he would take his place among the Confederates whose names he bore. Except he had never known he would feel like this. No splendor, no romance — only this horrible sense that an awful moment was coming and he must stay here and accept it. For now he was clear about only one thing — this time there could be no escape. He felt inadequate, nearly helpless, 'in' way over his head — but somehow this time he had to stay and take whatever fate was awaiting him.

He had alerted all his destroyers, told them his plan, instructed those on his side of town to wait for him to fire first, and those on the other side to fire only after Sergeant Whipple had. They'd all given him a nervous, determined "Roger."

All except Sergeant Whipple. After the others had all responded, Sergeant Whipple had tried to give him an argument.

"It's all wrong," the sergeant had protested in an assertive, yet somehow uncertain voice. "You'll just get us all knocked off. Once we fire, we'll have had it, Lieutenant. They'll just pick us off with their bigger guns. It's your responsibility to see we're used properly — that we have a chance to get out with our destroyers. Maybe if we pull back now we can stop back of town somewhere and get a few shots in — without being cut off — like we will be here. You're too new at this, Lieutenant. I been at it longer than you."

Lieutenant Hood had absolutely no faith in what he had ordered. It probably *was* all wrong. All he knew was he had to stay — the colonel had made that clear to him. And he remembered what the colonel had said about Sergeant Whipple's combat experience. So he couldn't even discuss his orders with the sergeant. He was sure anyone could find a hundred examples of his own incompetence in them. So all he could do was set himself in a frozen stance and somehow make his body carry out his brain's orders — however incompetent.

He hadn't trusted himself to speak more than a very few words. He couldn't explain or defend anything. He just had to make clear what they would all have to do.

"Sergeant Whipple," he had said, not even taking time to think what words he would use. "Shut the hell up and follow the god-damn orders."

He had been horrified himself at the words when he heard them pour out.

To his surprise, after a few moment's pause Sergeant Whipple's voice had come back with a weak, surprised "Yes, *sir.*"

He had seen the first tank cross the river and move straight ahead. Then the flare that had been lighting the scene had burnt out and he had momentarily lost the tank. But he had been able to see it was a big one — no Mark IV. That meant he had to try for a flank shot — that much his scattered senses remembered. So when another flare burst brightly and he saw the tank, now fifty yards further ahead and still proceeding straight across the open area, he had held his fire. He had been far from certain this was the correct move, but after an indecisive moment he had decided to wait. Three tanks were now across — and they were all moving straight back, rather than turning toward the town. If that was their plan, wouldn't it be better to wait till all three were further back, so everyone could get in the necessary flank shot?

Now he was even less sure. For in waiting till the three tanks got lined up better for all his guns, he had neglected to consider that more tanks would be coming across every few seconds. Now there were six tanks out there, proceeding steadily toward the rear. And he had heard nothing from the other section with Sergeant Whipple. Had they all run away, or were they just waiting too?

Another flare burst and he saw the seventh tank leave the crossing and move forward. Now it was surely too late. He should have shot earlier, when the odds were not so heavily stacked against him. He'd done it all wrong! It was no good! He'd surely do nothing but get all his men killed!

Then he remembered the colonel's words. In combat everyone was "scared shitless." But that wasn't what mattered, only doing what you had to do as well as you could.

He flinched and ducked as an artillery shell struck a building to his left, then a second round landed a short distance in front of him. He heard a fragment strike the heavy metal on the front of his turret, then ricochet off. The incoming artillery only made him feel more terrified and helpless — although he knew he was safe from anything except a direct hit. How did the infantry manage to stay out in the open under it? He pulled his mind away from the thought. He had enough to do to concentrate on his own duty.

The night had gone dark again. He picked up the flare pistol he had loaded earlier and placed where he could reach it easily. Come on, he told himself. Just shoot it and then line up one of the tanks in the cross hairs.

"All you on the left side of town, get ready," he said into his microphone, trying to keep his voice low and even, but hearing it go jumpily falsetto at the end.

He raised the pistol and fired. The flare shot out and up, then burst into light to hang there, sinking slowly and illuminating the open space before him in its flickering glare.

He saw there were now more tanks moving across his front. There was no time to count. Desperately he swung the turret until he could see the mammoth image of a Mark V tank in the sight. It was moving fast, though the rough cross-country terrain kept it from making top speed. He moved the turret left again to keep up with it, increased the elevation slightly so his cross hairs were squarely on the side of the turret. He didn't have to worry about the shell's trajectory at this short range. But he remembered he would need a very slight lead for a target moving across his front like this one. So he fixed the cross hairs just sightly forward of the point he wanted to hit. Then...fire!

He kept his eye glued to the sight. It seemed only a fraction of a second and then the armor-piercing shell was striking exactly as he had planned — just behind his point of aim. His first shot had hit — in spite his feeling that all this world of destructive power was completely beyond his control. And he was sure the round had penetrated. Yet for a moment the tank continued to move forward. What was wrong?

Something had obviously happened inside. The tank first wavered slightly, then slowed to a stop. He knew Mark V's would not "brew up" as often as a Sherman. But with an armor-piercing round penetrating and ricocheting countless times off the metallic walls, there was not much chance for the tankers inside the turret.

Then in the front section of the lower tank he saw escape hatches open and two men come scrambling out. They ran a few yards and threw themselves to the ground.

The escape hatches from the turret, however, remained shut. For just a moment in his mind he saw them, two men alive and whole a moment before, their bodies now torn and bloody masses of flesh.

He pulled his mind away from the image, forced himself to look once more into the sight as he rotated the turret to the right, looking for another one of the squat, powerful German tanks.

As he did so he was aware of one and then a second high-velocity cannon firing. That would be the other two destroyers in his section. But there was no time to see whether they had hit. He was now on another target — this one back near the river. Even as he was lining it up in his sight he had a glimpse of artillery shells exploding all around the crossing site. Had they destroyed the bridge? No time to look — he had to concentrate on that one tank.

Just as his loader tapped him on the shoulder to signal the gun was ready to fire, he fastened his cross hairs to the mammoth tank and tracked it. Then he saw it suddenly stop and swing its huge, swollen-headed cannon toward him.

He hastily rotated the turret slightly to the right until the German tank was squarely in the middle of the sight. He wasn't sure the elevation was correct, but he could see that swollen-headed cannon now pointing almost directly at him.

He fired in a quick convulsive movement, then yelled into his intercom to the driver, "Back up, Johnson! Quick!"

His forehead hit against the sight as the whole destroyer jerked convulsively backward. Almost at the same moment something whished past in front of him and struck the wall of the building to his left, bringing a large section of it crumbling down.

"I think you got him, Lieutenant!" his loader shouted excitedly. "Below the turret. Maybe he can still shoot, but he damn sure can't go anywhere."

Lieutenant Hood took his eyes from the sight and saw his driver had backed them perhaps twenty feet into the alley between two rows of buildings. From there he had such a limited view he could see none of the tanks. But he could hear the guns from both his own destroyers and the enemy tanks cracking away. Other explosions, less sharp than those of the high-velocity guns, were scattered in among the cannon shots.

Then it was dark, and for a moment he longed for it to stay that way, so he could curl up in that safe darkness among all the shattering explosions.

But he knew he had to force himself to move back where the explosions were tearing to shreds any illusion of safety.

"Move back up slow," he told the driver, "while its still dark. But go as far to the left as you can — so we don't come up exactly where we were before. As long as it's dark he can't see us with the buildings around us."

"Okay, Lieutenant," the driver said. "But get that god-damned gun on him as quick as you can. The bastard's probably waiting for us. And these god-damned Heil-Hitler fanatics fight all the way down to hell."

Then the destroyer eased forward and to the left. The lieutenant could see nothing yet, as the building on the right blocked his view of the area where the tank had been. Then he saw it, vaguely outlined against something burning at the river crossing. He could see the tank's lower body and turret — but no gun! That meant the gun was pointed directly at him! Yet a calmer part of his mind told him the gunner should not be able to see anything as he looked at the dark buildings.

Lieutenant Hood knew he must move fast before another flare burst. He rotated the turret until he knew his gun was centered on the enemy's turret. Then he realized his shell would be striking the tank's heaviest armor — the very center of the turret around the base of the cannon. He moved the gun down slightly, hoping to strike close to the point where the turret joined the lower body.

"Okay, Johnson," he instructed his driver, "As soon as I fire, back off as fast as you can."

"Right," the driver's tense voice answered.

The gun belched fire, the motor roared and the tank shot suddenly backward. But Lieutenant Hood kept his eye to the sight and saw, before his view was shut off, the enemy tank flower into flame.

Sergeant Bradovitch had heard high-velocity firing east of town and knew a tank battle was going on there — but he had more immediate worries.

"Swing around so we can take them head-on if we have to," Sergeant Bradovitch told his driver. He knew they were going to be in for it when that tank dozer made it across the river. But he had kept his tank back in the trees so he wouldn't be picked up right away by the German tanks as they poured over their new crossing.

"How 'bout those damn T.Ds in town?" his driver asked as he started to bring the tank around. "Aren't they supposed to cover that area? We're supposed to cover the god-damned ford — right?"

"We're supposed to cover where the shit's flyin'," Bradovitch shot back. "An' that's the only place I see any shit flyin', so that's what we'll god-damn cover."

Jesus, he thought, every PFC wants to make like a god-damn general.

"All right," he said on his channel to the other tank commanders. "Get turned around so we can take them on when I give the word. Stay back in the trees if you can. They'll have trouble seeing you there in the light those flares give. If we can, we'll let the god-damn T.D.s get a shot at them first."

"Their seventy-sixes got more chance than our short seventy-fives," the other tank commander said.

"Yeah," Sergeant Bradovitch growled, "but don't bank on nothin'. When it's all over, I'll bet it's us with our short-ass seventy-fives that do the job. So we might's well get used to the idea. But let 'em have the honors an' shoot first. After they shoot and the damn Kraut tanks turn to return their fire, we'll be right where we can give it to 'em up the ass. Let them T.D.'s bounce a few off their heavy armor — while we're sittin' here lookin' at their tin-plated threadbare assholes. Even a short seventy-five can penetrate there."

"Bradovitch, you sneaky son-a-bitch," the other tank commander said, "remind me not to let you ever cover my ass."

"You wanta be a dead hero, go ahead and shoot," Bradovitch said. "But if you'd rather be a sneaky live son-a-bitch, do like I'm tellin' you."

"Hell, jus' call me sneaky," the tank commander's voice replied quickly. "I'm with the live son-a-bitches every time."

Bradovitch counted three of the tanks now across the river. Why in hell hadn't the T.D.s fired? When it was still light he had seen two of those M18's go into position on the southern edge of town. They must still be there. Were they playing sneaky son-a-bitch too and waiting for him to fire first? Then he saw a fourth German tank come off the crossing. Somebody was going to have to fire pretty damn soon, he thought.

After his losses in the fight at the ford he figured it was fair to give his own men the break. But if those T.D.s were going to go chicken on him, he'd have no choice but to fire. The lead tank was now some distance from the river, and it couldn't be allowed to break through and roam free back there in the rear.

In the end it was a T.D. going chicken that turned out to be the Shermans' good luck. A flare suddenly lit the whole area, and Bradovitch saw clearly the foremost M18 backing up between two buildings, stopping a moment as it struck a stone wall, then pulling ahead to clear it. The moving T.D., clear in the light of a flare, was obviously seen by other eyes also. The third German tank in line immediately rotated its gun toward the retreating T.D. and fired. The shell of the powerful cannon caught the T.D. squarely in front, and a moment later the destroyer was a mass of flame.

High-velocity shells immediately spat forth from further back in the town. One caught a German tank in the side, penetrating and bringing it to a halt. But Bradovitch could see another American shell deflect off the heavy frontal armor of a German tank and shoot skyward.

All the shooting and the flaming American T.D. had now attracted the attention of the remaining German tanks, for they had all turned toward the town and were shooting at the exposed T.D.s.

"All right, kiddies," Bradovitch said into his radio. "Praise the Lord for that gutless bastard, he just saved your no-good ass. Now get 'em while we got 'em ass-end-to."

He fired immediately, his armor-piercing round catching the tank nearest the river squarely in the rear of the turret, blasting inward and bringing it to a stop. He felt sure that one was a gone duck, so he shifted to the next one on the left, cursed as he realized that was the one the T.D. had already knocked out, shifted further to the left, saw a shell glancing off the top of a turret that was turning to face the new threat, hastily put his cross hairs on the rotating turret, fired quickly, saw his shell hit and penetrate, but not before the mammoth cannon had spat fire once. He knew it should be all over in less that a second after seeing the gun fire. But it wasn't — he was still alive! That bastard's last shot must somehow have missed!

A quick check showed him all four of the German tanks that had crossed the river had now been knocked out.

"Good going," he said into the radio. "That's all of the bastards. "Tommy, you keep an eye on the ford and the river-crossing sites. I'll go back an' keep a look-out on the flank. If you see anything that might mean another crossing, let me know pronto, an' I'll come runnin'."

"Wilco," the voice from the other tank replied.

God-damn, Bradovitch thought wearily, it's still me and Tommy — out of a company of seventeen Shermans. Two more of us to use up and they'll have got full return on the dollar outa this god-damned outfit.

Colonel Berrigan felt he had been juggling sharp-edged axes and suddenly found himself with just one too many in the air. They'd been damn lucky they'd all come out alive from that artillery burst in the room below them.. But they'd all made it down to the ground floor, the lieutenant even saving his B.C. scope and his walkie-talkies. And he was glad the artillery officer was still in the battle. Of course, with the radio shot out he'd be without the fire of his twelve-gun battalion. But he could still shoot the black soldiers' four guns. If they had any ammunition left — he knew they'd been using it pretty freely. He'd have to remember to check on that soon. But for now he had to get to the room above his C.P. and see if the attack had really been stopped.

He ran up the last few steps to the second story and stepped quickly to the east window. Scattered artillery was still coming into the town, but apart from that, a strange lull covered the whole area. Both river crossings had been destroyed by the artillery fire, and he was sure all the tanks that had got across the river had been knocked out. He'd told Sergeant McClanahan to get a report on his own losses from the light tank behind the C.P. as soon as possible. He was sure he'd lost some Shermans and T.D.s, for he could see burning hulks on his right flank, and undoubtedly had more he couldn't see on his left. But he should have a few left yet.

So it looked as if they'd weathered another major attack. But not by much. They'd been lucky about those crossings. No — not just lucky. Having that artillery there wasn't just an accident. Talk about juggling — it had been enough to make your head spin to hear that artillery lieutenant adjust fire from the two sets of guns on different targets at the same time. And the mere fact of having that extra battery in close support wasn't all luck. Those black soldiers had made a superhuman effort to save their guns and keep them in action. They deserved a unit citation — except that they, like all the rest of this "task force," were a jumbled mess of thrown-together pieces. There wasn't a single total unit among them to "cite.".

As he looked out over the dark terrain across the river, he could hardly believe everything over there was quiet. He knew there was an impatient, angry commander there somewhere, making ready his next all-out effort. But for the moment he found the peacefulness pleasantly relaxing....

Too much so. A few more moments without a crisis and he'd be asleep on his feet. Yet he felt there had to be more unmet crises he had just forgotten about.

Then he remembered. There was not only the possibility of an attack from the right flank by that trail the patrol had discovered — there was also the more immediate problem of the road to his rear. How had he forgotten about that? You forgot it, he accused himself, because there wasn't a damn thing you could do about it. He'd sent Sergeant MacKay out with his mystery weapon — one gun to slow down a whole column. He should have sent much more, or at least pulled back his main force to keep them from being cut off.

But he didn't have any more to send. He really shouldn't have spared that one. And he couldn't pull back — because if he tried to move back even a tiny part of his terribly overtaxed little band of mismatched cast-offs, the rest would probably disintegrate like a rope of sand. And without that riverline, how the hell could he build another defense?

He glanced down at his watch. It was still only 12:23.

19

Colonel Berrigan jerked awake and guiltily looked at his watch. How many crises had overtaken him while he slept — perhaps for hours? He breathed a sign of relief as he saw it was only twelve-thirty-three. Ten minutes, that wasn't too bad — though he felt he could ill afford the waste of time.

He should have realized if he sat down at the table and let his eyes close, he would be gone. What had awakened him? He had a sense of having just heard some noise. Then the sound of footsteps approaching and McClanahan's voice told him it was probably just the outside door closing when the sergeant came in.

"It took a little while, sir — but I finally got through to everybody. Losses are only one Sherman and one T.D. The light tanks are still all okay. I guess that means they had enough sense not to shoot at anything with their pea-shooters — so nobody shot back. The infantry in town's taken some casualties from the artillery. The two platoons here have lost seven men, all told. Mostly wounded who will probably make it okay if we can get them back where there's a doctor. Both infantry platoons on the flanks have lost two men each."

"How about Sergeant MacKay?" the colonel asked anxiously. "Last I heard he had a whole armored column headed straight for him."

"I was just coming to him. I talked with the light tank commander that's with him. He said MacKay put one round into the lead tank, probably a Mark IV — and would you believe it, that stopped them."

"Knocking out one Mark IV stopped a whole German tank column? That can't be right."

"Well, sir, turns out it wasn't a real tank column. It sounds like a recon patrol — mostly lighter stuff. A few half-tracks, two or three lighter tanks. They beat a quick retreat back around the corner when that ninety-millimeter blasted the leading Mark IV."

How lucky can I get, the colonel thought. But if that was a recon outfit....

"They must have plenty of power behind it," Berrigan said. "Nothing's followed up in...how long ago was it?"

"Nearly half an hour, sir. I know it sounds crazy. Maybe they didn't have much behind it."

The colonel thought of the most reasonable explanation — and wondered if he could be so lucky.

"That could be a part of the major drive going on south of here. They must have broken through and wanted to keep driving west — which is where they really want to go. But they could have sent a small recon force out this way just in case they should be so lucky as to find nothing here. Sergeant MacKay's ninety-millimeter must have convinced them there's something here all right, so they won't waste time on us. They figure if they drive on west they'll have whatever's left here cut off anyway. Which means we've lucked out — temporarily. As soon as they hit something solid on their western front they'll send something more convincing this way."

"In which case," Sergeant McClanahan said, "we better wish them good luck — at least for a few hours."

"A few hours' good luck might be all they need to make their whole operation work," Colonel Berrigan said ruefully.

"Damned if we do and damned if we don't," McClanahan said. "It looks like we can't even wish for good luck any more."

"I guess all we can think about is holding this position a few more hours," the colonel said, "and forget the god-damned luck — all kinds. There's something I'd like you to take care of, though. You said we've got about eleven wounded?"

"Eight. Three didn't make it. Plus maybe some that might have made it out of the Sherman and the T.D."

"See if you can get the wounded back to where the kitchen was."

"Is — not was," the sergeant said with a grin. "You know that god-damned kitchen crew is still there? They've been putting out hot coffee for anybody wants it. I told the mess sergeant he could take off when he wanted. But he said he'd stay a little longer."

My God, the colonel thought — somebody turning down a perfectly good excuse to get to the rear? And all that artillery falling around them, too. You might expect morale like that in an outfit that had trained together three or four years. But this collection of battle debris — could they develop morale like that? In less than...fourteen hours?

"Tell them the men and I appreciate their staying. And if there are any of those other trucks still there, use one of them to get the wounded out. Then come on back here. I imagine our friends across the way will have thought up their next ploy by then."

"Yes, sir. Oh — if you want to see the artillery boys, they said tell you they're across the street and two houses on down toward the river.

"Thanks, Sergeant. If I'm not here when you get back I'll be over there with them."

After the sergeant had left, the colonel tried to keep his sleep-muddled mind on his immediate problem.

But there was absolutely no way of telling what would come next. The attackers had tried every route through the position and been stopped — with rather severe losses. But he knew those losses would mean nothing in a situation like this. If they were to succeed, the enemy column had to keep moving. They couldn't afford to slow down and be cautious. They would know there'd be little remnants of units trying desperately to delay them. They just had to keep bearing down on those little remnants — no matter what the cost.

So they had to launch their next attack just as soon as they could get new troops into position. So where would they come?

If that commander was any good — and no one but a fool would assume he wasn't — he'd know his opponents had had to take some losses to stop those attacks. And since the Germans would now have ample numbers of troops coming up, the best way to knock out a ridiculously over-matched defense was to pull out all the stops — attack anywhere and everywhere, searching for the weakest spots. He would know there were bound to be plenty of them, with the defenders over-extended like this. And the moment any part cracked – he would pour everything he had through the hole.

So where did that leave Task Force Lone Bandit? Answer: up shit creek without a paddle.

He rose wearily and walked to the door. He knew one big factor in stopping the other attacks had been the quick and accurate concentration of artillery fire on the key spots —

mostly the river crossings. Except now with the shattered radio, most of that artillery would be cancelled out.

Yet the artillery lieutenant was still here — and apparently, since he had set up a new O.P., he was figuring to keep on playing a role in the battle. The colonel decided he'd better go talk to him right away, to see just what — if anything — he thought he could do when the next attack came.

But before the colonel had crossed to the other side of the main street, a tremendous flurry of firing broke out across the open space on the left flank.

Private Hatfield flattened himself against the cold, hard earth of his foxhole. He felt his body begin to shiver involuntarily. Above him he could hear the bullets from a burp gun slicing the air. They were in for it now. He could hear the Krauts crossing the river in force. Some of them must be already in among the foxholes, for somebody had got close enough with a panzerfaust to take a shot at the light tank behind them.

"Get up an' open ya goddamn eyes, soldier! Ya here t' fight, not curl up 'n' cry 'Mummy'."

The shock of the voice so close, so clear in his head, pulled him up and opened his eyes. Staring around, just the top half of his head above ground, he saw by the light of the tank burning behind him a German helmet only six feet away. Then he saw the dark bulk of the body attached to it. Instinctively he raised his Ml and put two quick shots just below the helmet, heard the thud of bullets hitting flesh and bone, then ducked down a moment before the burp gun threw a stream of bullets over his head.

"That's better," the voice said. "He's ahead and a little to the right. Watch for a grenade now!"

Then he heard it land on the edge of his hole and bounce in, felt it hit his shoulder and lie there against it. Convulsively he jerked up, fumbled frantically with his right hand, found the handle, grasped it, and in a quick motion flipped it back the way it had come. The explosion followed before it had travelled far, but he felt only the sting of a small splinter in his shoulder. Then a split second after the explosion he grabbed the Ml again and rose up, peering ahead and to the right. There — a bulky form was trying to heave itself up, grunting heavily with pain. Then with a groan it fell back. As the tank fire flared up again he saw three other forms running now, bent over, back toward the creek bank. He squeezed off the rest of the clip toward them, saw one stagger and go down, then another, while the third ran on to disappear over the bank.

A flare shot skyward, fired from somewhere near the lieutenant's hole. A moment later it was alight and settling slowly earthward, casting its ghostly light over the area. Now gray-clad forms could be seen clearly on the near side of the river. It was only a few yet — perhaps a small first wave. And they quickly went to earth as the flare clearly revealed them. But across the river the slope seemed alive with the same gray-clad forms. As he watched he saw more of the forms rise up from the near riverbank, run a few steps and fall to earth. He knew they had to be stopped before their number increased.

"Come on," he yelled at the young tow-headed boy in the hole next to his. "Get 'em while they're still down by the river. Use your Ml."

As he shouted he was aiming his own rifle at new figures looming up from the riverbank. He felt a desperate need to turn whatever power he could against those gray-clad forms before their numbers grew and they came closer. He emptied his clip at them as he heard his tow-headed companion's rifle cracking away. Then paused just long enough to slip in a fresh one.

A machine gun opened up somewhere to his left. He could tell it was American by its slow, methodical tu-tu-tu-tu. The faster German-burp guns were answering it. He saw fire spitting from one right by the riverbank. In a spasm of fear and anger he emptied the second clip at the spot where he had seen the spurt of fire. He thought he saw a body heave up a moment and fall back. Had he got him? No way to tell. He put another clip in his rifle and watched carefully for any more gray-clad bodies rising from behind the riverbank.

As the flare flickered and went out he saw a form suddenly rise up only ten yards away and run toward the river. Even in the dark Hatfield could glimpse the bulk of the man against the slightly lighter sky. He swung his M1 to take aim at the man. Before he could fire he heard the rifle of the boy beside him cracking five times, saw the man stagger and go down.

"You got him!" he shouted encouragingly as he scanned the riverbank, looking for another target.

Then the burning tank, which had momentarily died down, flared up again.

"Let's get that fire out before it sets off some gasoline," a voice shouted. "It's only a bedroll strapped on the outside."

Hatfield turned and saw the tank was about twenty yards behind him in the edge of the trees. He didn't like leaving the shelter of his foxhole, but he knew that flame had to be extinguished before it drew more fire.

Taking his M1 and entrenching tool with him, he rose and sprinted toward the tank. A burp gun opened up and he heard bullets whipping past him. Then he was close beside the tank and throwing himself to the ground, breathing heavily. Running feet behind him startled him, and then another body dropped heavily beside him. Glancing over he saw it was his tow-headed friend copying his motions. Hatfield reached back and unhitched his entrenching tool. Keeping his body low he scraped some loose dirt and snow up and threw it at the fire — which he saw now was indeed just a bedroll. He scooped up another shovelful of dirt and snow and rose just enough to throw it squarely on top of the bedroll, where the flames seemed to be concentrated. He crouched down and was aware of another figure rising up to repeat his motions. The fire appeared to die down a little. Then he slipped out of his overcoat and rose again, using it to beat at the few remaining flames. Once, twice, three times — then he fell back quickly as he heard a burp gun opening up again. After a moment he saw the figure behind him, aping his own motions, rising up and beating at the dying flame. The fire went out just as the burp gun fired again, and he jumped up quickly and pulled the boy down as he heard bullets striking the tank a short distance to his left.

"Okay, okay, we got it," Hatfield breathed into the boy's ear as he held him down. "Now let's get the hell back to our holes."

"Good going, soldiers," another voice said. "Now — you in the tank — let's get on that god-damned radio and get some fire support over here."

Hatfield recognized the voice of the non-com who had been placed in charge of his improvised squad. But he knew that wasn't the voice he had heard first, warning him of the man who threw the grenade. That had been a much gruffer, more familiar voice.

Colonel Berrigan lay on his stomach until the barrage of incoming artillery rounds stopped momentarily, then jumped to his feet and sprinted for the house down the street. A shell had blasted a hole in the near wall, but the stone building seemed structurally undamaged. He ran into the open front door, leaped up the steps to the second story, and found the artillery lieutenant in the first room he entered on the east side.

"Tell 'em to get the lead out," the lieutenant was shouting disgustedly, "they need some help over there bad."

The colonel wondered just who was being shouted to — since there was no one else in the room besides the two of them.

"Get the god-damned lead out, they gotta have some help quick!"

The colonel recognized Cordova's voice coming from somewhere on the back side of the building.

"I thought that shell ruined your radio," the colonel said. "Are you shooting with just the black soldiers' guns?"

"I don't want to shoot them any more than I have to," the lieutenant said, glancing back for a moment at the new arrival. "Their ammunition supply's too limited. And I want a walloping big barrage on these guys. Look at them! The god-damned slope over there's covered with them."

The colonel joined him at the open east window. By leaning out just a little he could see the ground sloping down to the river far to the left. Then another flare burst and under its light he could see the swarm of gray-clad forms covering the slope for hundreds of yards."

"I see what you mean," the colonel said. "They need a helluva lot more than four guns over there. But how are you getting through to your battalion with a busted radio?"

"That shell fragment cut right into the bottom section," the lieutenant said, "but it didn't touch the top section. The bottom section's the battery pack — the radio's all in the top part. When we leave it in the jeep. we can run it off the jeep's battery. No problem — so long's we can get the jeep close enough to relay the commands by voice. The radio's all right — the problem's that god-damned Fire Direction Center. Though it's probably not their fault, either. It must be the god-damned colonel hanging around and getting in Fire Direction's hair. Major Schwartz would give me what I ask for, if it was up to him."

"On the way!" Cordova shouted from the back of the house.

The lieutenant leaned out the window and raised his glasses to scan the left flank area carefully.

"I'm having them plaster the whole further slope — four concentrations, each a square two hundred by two hundred yards. I already had an adjustment on one of them earlier — now they just have to hit it again and then tack on the adjoining squares. I asked for battalion five volleys on each square — that would really plaster them good. But that's battalion twenty volleys all together — two hundred forty shells. And firing that much all at once on a mere lieutenant's say-so — it must have made the colonel wet his drawers. But I guess the major convinced him. I just hope it's in time. I think the Germans have some men across already — and from what you told me about our strength over there, we must be down to about fifteen or sixteen men to hold off a whole god-damned battalion."

Then Colonel Berrigan heard the shells come in with a rush to land near the riverbank. By the light of a flare the colonel could see the shells exploding above a large group of attackers nearest the river. The devastating explosions went on almost continuously for what seemed like a long time.

"I asked for proximity fuses," the lieutenant said. "They have a kind of built-in radar that's supposed to tell the shell it's the right distance above the ground to burst. When they work right they give you air bursts — ideal against troops in the open. One shell can give you casualties up to a hundred yards away — and none of the fragments get wasted blowing into the ground. Just look at those babies pepper the landscape!"

The colonel looked through his glasses and saw what the lieutenant meant. Every time a shell burst above the soldiers lying prone on the ground below it, by the light of a flare he saw pieces of soil being cast up by hundreds of widely-scattered fragments. And it was obvious many of those fragments were hitting more than soil and snow.

After what seemed an interminable time there was a brief pause — then it all began again, only this time the shells were covering a square two-hundred yards closer.to the watchers' position.

"I asked them to fire the squares closest to the riverbank first," the lieutenant said. "That way we'll get first those who are the biggest threat to the defenders. And then after a barrage that heavy there's going to be a helluva leakage, maybe even a rush to the rear. The next two barrages should come just about right to catch those bastards running back."

It was dark for a few moments — then another flare burst. The colonel saw that now almost none of the troops were going forward. Many were walking or running toward the rear. And many gray-clad bodies simply lay there, inert and unmoving.

Next the shells began to fall in an area further back. The colonel could see the lieutenant had been right. These shells, landing further up the slope, were bursting over a now jammed and totally confused mob of panicky figures.

"By God," the artillery lieutenant couldn't help from shouting, "are we on or are we on! The Krauts threw in the goddamn kitchen sink that time and they still couldn't break through. I bet that little band of poor foot-sloggers over there aren't making dirty cracks about the gold-bricking, rear-echelon artillery now."

And that goes for me too, Colonel Berrigan thought. He

couldn't imagine what roll of the heavenly dice had given him this beautiful madman of an artillery observer. No matter – take it and be grateful. Just no telling where you'll find some lowly shavetail who gets swept away by his own enthusiasm and turns out to be kissed by the gods.

"Keep it up lieutenant," he said. "Trust your own instincts. You're writing a new book here on the imaginative use of artillery. I'm going to stop a minute at your radio and encourage your battalion commander to give you all you ask for — you've been right on every time."

"Thank you, sir," the lieutenant said, apparently surprised at such unexpected praise.

But twenty minutes later Colonel Berrigan realized his moment of relief was over. He had just returned to the C.P. and gone out behind the building to check the light tank's radio communications. The tank commander had been talking with the Stuart patrolling to the north on the parallel road in their rear when an urgent voice broke in.

"Lone Bandit Six! Lone Bandit Six! We are about to be hit by a full scale attack! They're coming in on our right from *this side of the river!* Come in, Lone Bandit Six!"

"This is Lone Bandit Six. Easy, now — what specific evidence do you have to verify the attack? I don't hear any heavy firing going on over there."

"No firing yet, sir, because we had an outpost a long way out, and he pulled back without firing when he first heard them advancing toward him. They're coming rather slowly, he said — playing it very cautious. When the outpost came back, they were sent to report to Lieutenant Brownell. The Lieutenant's already trying to get some reinforcements to send to the right flank, but he said to fill you in and request any additional help available. He says it looks like a full-scale attack — probably big enough to overlap the little flank line we put in — by plenty."

This was the bad news the colonel had been afraid of hearing ever since his patrol had got back from their mission around the right wing. This surely meant his opponent now had sufficient strength up to attack anywhere and everywhere he wanted. And he realized if enemy troops came in on his right, overlapping that short defensive position the right flank had put out, there would be nothing to prevent them from walking right into the rear of his main defense line. And there would go the ballgame.

So far he'd been lucky in being able to break up both tank and infantry attacks through a happy combination of the river barrier and excellent artillery support. Against this attack, the river was cancelled out — and it was highly unlikely artillery could be much help against a force driving into his flank and rear. They'd be so closely intermixed with his own troops it would be next to impossible to call down artillery fire on them.

So what could he do? What possible advantage did he have to put into play?

Maybe sometimes you don't have any advantage, he thought, and you just have to save what you can and get the hell out — *if* you can still even do that.

But he knew it was too soon for that if he was going to accomplish his purpose — keeping this enemy force from breaking through before the division coming up somewhere behind him had arrived.

His opponent had made the proper move — when your armor is being held up by an effective though heavily outnumbered defense using a natural tank obstacle, send in an infantry attack of such breadth and power it simply overwhelms the defenders.

What were his opponent's weaknesses here? He had to have some.

Well...he wouldn't be able to use any of his armor — at least initially. And infantry attacking in the open without armor did run certain risks, even if they had overwhelming numbers. Their weaknesses were twofold — they were extremely vulnerable to both automatic fire and artillery. And of course they were open to an armored attack themselves.

The only trouble was — he had no reserve armored force to use for attacking, and he'd had to rule out the artillery already.

Something vaguely familiar about this situation caught on the edge of his attention. Then he remembered. This situation was somewhat similar to one he had used in his lecture on "examining your assumptions." When you'd ruled out all the possible solutions, it was time to go back over your assumptions one by one and see if they were as final as you had thought.

For example — no reserve armored force. Was it really true? Well, he did have some armor, but it was already stretched far too thin. But was it? It wasn't being used anywhere right at the moment. Of course it might be needed at any time — but he might have to gamble on that. *If* he could use it quickly and effectively and get it right back into position afterward....

It was a gamble all right. But it was something. And if he could just find a way to divert that attack so the artillery — or at least the black soldiers' four guns — could be used. And if he mustered *all* his automatic fire where it would do the most good....

By God, he thought, I'm going to try it. It could be a disaster, but if I do nothing, that's an unqualified catastrophe. And what the hell, it just might work.

20

It had taken two minutes to get Lieutenant Brownell to the radio. The colonel had used the two minutes to examine his map, carefully noting the contour lines and trying to remember the exact shape of the landscape in the open area on the right. He found the spot he wanted — a slightly elevated knoll about four hundred yards back from the river. It was well out of the trees and had clear observation on all four sides.

Then he had sent one of the crew members from the light tank to get Captain Bergoff, who he hoped was still with the infantry in the building up ahead. That had left him just time enough to explain to the light tank commander what his role was to be.

As he finished he heard Lieutenant Brownell's voice on the radio.

"Lone Bandit Six, this is Brownell. Over."

"How much time do you have?" the colonel asked quickly. "Your best estimate."

The lieutenant responded after only a brief pause. "Our outpost discovered them pretty far out. And they've been working their way up very carefully. We've given them no warning that we know they're moving up, so they probably want to go slowly to get in position for a surprise attack. In which case I'd say we have anyway fifteen minutes.."

"Good. Now, we're going to be ready to give them a hot welcome. And your troops will play a key role here. I'm going to be coming right over there to give you detailed instructions. Meanwhile, check to see that all your men have good deep foxholes — and that they can fire to their rear as well as their front. If they can't, tell them they've got fifteen minutes to scrape a hole deep enough so they can get totally below ground — and can fire toward the west as well as the east. This is very important — their lives are going to depend on it. Is that clear?"

"Yes, sir. Very clear."

"Good. I'll see you over there shortly. Out."

He had just signed off when he saw two figures looming up in the darkness.

"Colonel Berrigan, sir?"

It was the pudgy-faced Captain Bergoff, breathless from hurrying his slightly plump body at an unaccustomed speed.

"Ah, Captain Bergoff — good. Now, we've got a tight situation here — but it's going to give us a real opportunity. Put your map under this light and make careful note of everything I tell you — for you're going to have to carry out the orders precisely. And there's no time to repeat them. Do you understand?"

"Yes, sir," the captain said quickly. In the glow of the pocket flashlight the captain's pudgy cheeks were trembling slightly. But his voice seemed firm and purposeful.

It took just ninety seconds to give the captain his specific instructions and have him mark the precise positions on his map.

"Now, exactly how many men do you have back there in

the houses as a reserve?"

"Twenty now, sir."

"With one machine gun?"

"Yes, sir. Plus two Browning Automatic Rifles."

"Fine. Be sure to have them take extra ammunition from the supply point by the kitchen. When it comes time I want those twenty men to throw lead like they're two hundred. Here's the story: Your men have to get to their assigned locations as quickly as possible, dig like hell till the enemy attacks, and then shoot up a storm once the action starts. And be very sure they have a clear field of fire to the east. All clear?"

"Yes, sir. Very clear, sir."

"Good. Then get them moving immediately."

As the captain was hurrying away, Colonel Berrigan was glad to see a now familiar figure approaching.

"Sergeant McClanahan, let me give you the crisis in thirty seconds and tell you what you have to do. Do you know where all the T.Ds are located?"

"Yes, sir."

"Then you're ready to go as soon as I fill you in on a few details."

Whatever ironic smugness had lurked in the sergeant's eyes at their first meeting, the colonel was glad to see they were all business now. It took less than thirty seconds to give him his instructions.

After the sergeant had left at a fast jog toward Lieutenant Hood's tank destroyer, the colonel handed the headset back to the tank commander.

"You can start off now," the colonel told him. "I'll be down as soon as I speak to the artillery observer. You'd better not use that road by the riverbank — too many Germans just a few yards away across the river. And even if they can't see you, they'll hear you. They might get lucky with a panserfaust or even a hand grenade. You'll have to pick your way cross-country. There's no real tank obstacles there. Once you start, go as quickly as you can. You'll just have to take the chance of someone sending up a flare. If they do, just go all out for the river until it burns out. Chances are they won't get zeroed in on you in that short time. That's the way I'm going in the jeep."

The tank commander saluted and told the driver to back out onto the main street. Colonel Berrigan climbed into the jeep and drove down the main street to the building now beiing used as the artillery O.P. There he stopped and got out to enter the house and run up the stairs to the second story. Lieutenant Stallingsworth, as he had expected, grasped the concept in a few seconds and made his own recommendations immediately.

"Okay," the colonel said. "That sounds good. We'll leave it up to you and the black soldiers to handle it. Though I'd love to have your own battalion in on it too. Their fire power would be awesome — but you're right. It would be too risky for them to fire that close. So they'll get a by on this one."

"Not completely," the lieutenant said. "I'm going to have them loaded and ready — then if some of those tanks across the river decide to get into the act as fire support, we'll dump all over them again. At least they won't have a pleasant few minutes' target practice at our expense."

"Good idea," the colonel said. "Now, have your close-support guns got enough ammo for this job?"

"Plenty," the lieutenant said. "I just checked with them on that, and they're still in good shape."

"Okay. Have the guns ready for when it blows open. Have you got observation on that area?"

"Absolutely," the lieutenant answered. "I've already

checked and there's a window on the south side that will over-look all the action."

"Then it's your baby," the colonel said, glancing at his wrist-watch. "I've got to get down there now. This is a real opportu-nity — if we play it right."

And also a good chance to blow the ballgame, he thought as he was leaping down the stairs, if some little thing doesn't get done just right. But what the hell, you always told your students war is one activity where, if you refuse to gamble you automatically lose.

Colonel Berrigan could feel the tension within him build-ing. The most immediate chance for disaster would come if the enemy didn't give him time enough to coordinate this com-plicated operation. It would have been a damned difficult ma-neuver to pull off if he had had time to get the commanders of all the separate parts together for a lengthy planning session. But done this way, with the pieces patched together, catch as catch can, and the enemy able to shoot the starting pistol any time he chose, ready or not — you'd have to be a manic opti-mist even to attempt it.

But if the estimates of the enemy's jump-off time were any-where near correct, he was sure he could pull it off.

His biggest worry right now was whether they would give him the few more minutes he had to have to bring the whole operation together. He jumped into the jeep, backed up and swung it around, then drove rapidly back up the main street.

It was only four minutes later by his watch when he started his own risky trek across the open space on the south side of town. It had seemed like forever. When he had arrived back at the kitchen and supply area he had first had trouble locating the three-quarter-ton vehicle he'd thought was there. With the seconds pounding by in his mind like the clock of doom, he had searched for it to no avail, and finally let out a desperate shout for anyone who knew where it was — after which a sleepy-eyed soldier ran up to say he had parked it between two buildings a few houses down the street.

"Do you know where the T.D. with the big ninety-millimeter gun is in position?" Colonel Berrigan asked while the driver was still trying to explain where the truck was.

"Er...I...I'm afraid I don't — " the hesitant driver started to apologize.

"Never mind," the colonel said. "I'll tell you. You go there and deliver this message. Then come back here."

It took two minutes for the driver to get the message and location straight enough to repeat it back. Then the colonel slapped him encouragingly on the shoulder to start him on his way. Painfully aware of the seconds rushing past, he jumped into the jeep and drove quickly to the southern edge of the town. He paused just once to get his bearings, then set off across the open space.

Driving out away from the buildings, the colonel looked up at the sky and noticed a sudden rift in the constant clouds that had thus far enclosed his task force's lonely little struggle. It was hard to realize that under this same sky people back home were living ordinary lives, following desperate actions like this as if they were taking place on some alien planet. And there were plenty of soldiers here on both sides, the colonel thought, who probably wished that's just where the hell they were taking place — and not in their world.

Despite the darkness, he could see well enough to make fairly good time. As he drove he became gradually aware the silence was not as complete as he had thought. The noises were not loud — but it was clear to anyone who listened carefully there were many surreptitious activities going on.

First he heard the light tank's motor, some distance ahead of him, progressing toward the river. Then a rustling and trampling noise from his left alerted him to movement there. In a few moments he could make out a double column of soldiers moving forward. They were loaded with entrenching tools and rifles, and one group of men carried a light machine gun broken into two parts. A number of men carried cases of ammunition. As the column passed in front of him he noticed a short but somewhat bulky figure leading it. He waved at the figure briefly and received back a half-wave, half-salute. Captain Bergoff may have been a lethargic staff officer living in a fur-lined rut, but he certainly was taking hold here as if he'd had a long career as combat leader.

The ragged column moved past and disappeared into the dark toward a higher bulk of land looming up to his right. Next he was aware of heavier motors further to his left. They were moving slowly and cautiously, and obviously were trying to escape detection. He would like to have seen how the latter-day flower of the Confederacy, Lieutenant Lee Beauregard Hood, was holding up under the pressure. Was he all horseshit and hot air? Maybe. Certainly he hadn't looked like much a few hours before, walking out of the trees with his roll of toilet paper and shovel. And he might go hopelessly to pieces as soon as the lead started flying. Still...it may have been the colonel's wishful thinking, but he had felt ever since his last conversation with the boy that he did have what it took to hang in there and do his job — once all the romantic bullshit about war had been driven out of his head.

For a few moments these motors dominated the night sounds — then they were still. They must have reached their positions, he thought. So they at least were set.

When those motors were cut he became aware of other

motors, some distance to his right and far forward by the river. One or more had the roar of a medium tank. That would be Sergeant Bradovitch's remaining "platoon" of tanks — now numbering all of two. Lieutenant Brownell must have got the message to them all right. One tank — that would be Sergeant Bradovitch's — was moving far down the gentle slope toward the river. The other appeared to be climbing the slope and heading in a direction that would bring it into contact with the infantry reserve that had just crossed in front of him.

So far, so good. Now if they'd only give him a few more minutes, Lone Bandit Six's ability as a master tactician would soon get a true test.

What was the enemy thinking of all this activity? The colonel was banking on two things: first, that those soldiers over there across the river, most of whom were trying to grab a little long-overdue sleep, wouldn't hear most of it; and secondly, that the leadership would be so concerned about getting their troops on this side of the river into position for their surprise attack, they'd welcome every other sound as cover for their own preparations.

The colonel was now nearing the river. He knew there must be enemy troops only a short distance away. They certainly could hear his jeep. Then he thought of the beautiful irony of it — they had probably been instructed *not* to use flares while their own troops were trying to maneuver into position for their surprise attack.

"Halt! Who goes there?"

He pulled the jeep to a quick stop and waited until a soldier loomed up out of the darkness. He knew how dangerous these night encounters were. He waited with both hands out before him on the steering wheel until the soldier approached and peered at his face closely.

"I'm Colonel Berrigan," he said quietly, "Where's Lieutenant Brownell?"

The soldier, apparently satisfied, motioned with his thumb toward the southern end of the line.

"He's down there close to the ford."

The colonel kept his own voice quiet so it wouldn't carry more than a few feet.

"Where does your line start on this end?"

"It didn't go this far, sir, but Lieutenant Brownell had us move it this way about a hundred yards further."

"Has every soldier got protection against fire coming from that way?" he asked, motioning back up the open slope he had just traversed.

"We've been digging like hell for the last fifteen minutes, sir. The holes may not be much to look at — but they ought to do the job. The guys who stayed further down toward the ford could use the holes they'd already dug, and they're in better shape."

"Good. I'm leaving the jeep here and walking down to see Lieutenant Brownell."

"Yes, sir."

The colonel eased the jeep carefully onto the dirt road and left it there. The road here was somewhat below the riverbank, so it was out of sight from across the river. Then he walked along the road toward the ford, keeping well bent down and out of sight of anyone on the opposite riverbank. As he went he saw the men were evenly spaced along the road, the first three in hastily improvised foxholes, the remainder in deeper, more carefully dug holes. All the men seemed awake and watching carefully for any activity on the slope down which he had just come. It took him only a few minutes to reach the ford.

As he neared the ford a figure approached and spoke very

quietly.

"Colonel Berrigan? I'm Lieutenant Brownell, sir."

"Are your men ready, Lieutenant?"

"Just about, sir. I extended my line a little toward the town, and those holes are the best we could do in the time we had. For the rest, we're really in good shape. As you suggested, I've got a good solid hinge here on the southern corner."

"Where's your machine gun?"

"Right out there about twenty yards, sir. He'll have a good field of fire over the whole slope — and he can also fire straight south to protect the hinge itself. And he's protected by riflemen around him. I've got one BAR close to the ford who'll watch for anyone attacking the hinge — and also to keep an eye on the ford, to see they don't hit us from there at the same time."

"Fine. I don't think they'll want to run the risk of a night attack from two directions. They might get tangled up with each other. But you're wise to be sure. Did you get word to Bradovitch and his two tanks?"

"Yes, sir. Sergeant Bradovitch himself is a part of the hinge here. He's pretty well concealed, but he's only about forty yards over that way. He sent his other tank up to the high ground to the west — to serve as a solid support base for the infantry moving in there."

For a moment the colonel felt the knot inside his chest loosen just a little. So they were ready — or at least as ready as you could get in such a short time. But the knot tightened again quickly. Now the question was whether it was going to work — despite all the little things that could still go wrong. And if anything went wrong now, that was the end of the line.

Sergeant Bradovitch stared carefully into the darkness. He thought he'd seen something move there between the trees, off to his right front. "Let anything off to your right go on through," the infantry lieutenant had told him. "You've got to be the traffic cop here on the corner. They probably want to drive on past and get behind our river line. Let them do it. Don't fire to the right at all in the first stage. But anything that comes directly at you — and especially if it tries to pass between you and the river — shoot the hell out of it. Use every god-damned machine gun you have, including the fifty caliber on your turret, unless you have to button up. We want to encourage them to go through the 'hole' to your right. And remember you're not alone here. On this corner we've got one machine gun, one BAR, and four riflemen. Plus all your guns. So you should be able to make 'em pass to the west of you. And they won't have any tanks or self-propelled guns. So don't use your seventy-five unless you actually have to. Some of those eighty-eights across the river might see it and decide to risk taking a shot at you. But do whatever you have to do to keep them from advancing on this corner of the line."

Bradovitch wasn't too sure about all this fancy footwork. He'd always been a stand up and slug it out man. But he had to admit this was a damned tricky situation — and when somebody had you outnumbered by plenty and was trying to pull a tricky-dicky on you, you'd better tricky-dicky him one better. And he had to admit it was a great idea — if it worked.

Nothing further moved in the spot he'd been watching, so he shifted his gaze to the right. There! He was sure that was a Kraut creeping forward. Should he blast him? The advancing soldier was almost even with the Sherman, but perhaps thirty yards to the west of it. That was pretty close — but he decided to let him go. He was definitely moving on past the Sherman. Let someone down the line take care of him.

"Jesus, there's a whole line of the bastards," his loader said tensely into the intercom. The loader had taken Bradovitch's place behind the coaxial machine gun, and he obviously wanted a chance to cut loose with it.

"Yeah," his assistant driver's excited voice came through the intercom. "A whole god-damned line of them, and we're sittin' right on their flank. We could blast shit out of them."

"Hold your fire," Sergeant Bradovitch said urgently, without raising his voice. He looked further to the right and saw what they meant. Some freak of light and shadow made the forms in this one patch of less intense darkness more visible. There were many figures moving carefully in a staggered line that started close to the man he had seen and went off toward the west until it was lost in the darkness. Then he saw other figures following on behind the first group.

"Hold it," he warned his men quietly. "That's just where we want the bastards. As long as they go around us — let 'em go."

"Hey, there's one we better keep an eye on," his loader said. "See him? He stopped and flopped down facing this way. There's another one with him. I bet he's settin' up a god-damn machine gun, pointing right at us."

Bradovitch had seen him too. It almost certainly was a machine gun. The sergeant shifted his fifty caliber until it was pointing directly at the spot.

"I got the mother zeroed in," he said. "Everyone who can see him — get on him. But don't fire unless he does. We want to suck as many of those bastards on through as we can. But once the firing starts — that's the first baby we'll take out. We'll put all three guns on him to settle his weener-schnitzel fast."

But this was getting pretty touchy, he thought. We've got the drop on them now — but how many god-damned Krauts do they want running around behind us?

He switched over to his other channel and spoke quietly into the mike.

"Tommy, you still hear me?"

After a moment the answer came back in a voice as carefully subdued as his own.

"I hear you, Brad. But I'm talkin' low 'cause I got about half the god-damned Kraut army paradin' past."

"Jesus, you too? How close are they?"

"Maybe fifty-sixty yards. We were afraid they were goin' to lap us, but they didn't quite swing out enough to do it."

"They're even closer down here. I think somebody better open up pretty god-damn soon. The order is to let 'em go so long as they go on past. But hell, I wasn't figuring' on playin' Sergeant York in this god-damn war."

"Wait a minute, Brad. I think we're gonna have to open up. I think I see another wave comin' in — right for us. I don't want the bastards to get too damn close. One of 'em might have a god-damned panzerfaust. I'll get back to you later, 'cause back here the main show's about to start."

"Get ready, kids, Tommy's gonna start the god-damned war," Sergeant Bradovitch said into the intercom.

It seemed to him the German infantry had been passing for a long time. He hoped the hell his own infantry support down the line didn't chicken out and run — or try to button up in their holes. If they did, his tank was going to be swallowed up like a cabin in the path of a god-damned avalanche.

Suddenly the silence of the night was split open by a machine-gun burst. It came from some distance to the south. As if that were a signal, guns all up and down the line opened up.

Sergeant Bradovitch ignored the pandemonium breaking out all around him and concentrated on that one darkened little mass he was sure was a machine-gun position. He brought the fifty-caliber slightly to the left, and as he did so saw a sudden spurt of fire shoot out from the very spot his gun was on. He fired immediately and held the burst for a good four or five seconds. Then the dark mass suddenly split into two figures rising up and falling backward.

Those big fifty-caliber bullets really tear the hell out of a man, he thought. Those Krauts won't be going anywhere — except maybe on a one-way ticket to hell.

He became aware of his tank's other machine guns rattling away below him.

"Okay," he shouted into the intercom. "That bastard's done for. Now pour it on anywhere in the open area. Just keep your aim down — we got troops up there on the high ground a few hundred yards away. But everything between has gotta be Kraut — so make it Kraut sausage. Those guys are caught out there without any protection. Make 'em wish the hell they'd stayed home on this one."

Colonel Berrigan had jumped into a hole abandoned by one of the soldiers who had been ordered to extend to the left. There he had waited impatiently until he had finally seen the first German infantry making their way behind the American line. While he had told everyone to hold their fire as long as possible, he had never expected the German infantry would penetrate this far without triggering a reaction. Perhaps it was too far? From the number of vague forms he had seen, the enemy had really committed a large force. He had been expecting perhaps as much as a company — but this could be even more. With the troops still back in the trees — there could be as much as a full battalion involved. Could his few defenders take on so large a force?

But when the machine guns had opened up he was reassured. A heavy curtain of fire was now pouring out into that open space, where men completely without protection were having to take it from two directions at the same time. Fire like that could drain the offensive spirit out of a man in a hurry. And if the operation worked as he had planned it, those men had much worse to come.

For just a moment he sensed what it would be like for the commander of the unit caught out there. Here he was about to launch a state-of-the-art surprise attack, cutting off the defenders from behind. And then suddenly it was his own troops who were caught in a deadly vice, and his men were falling all around him.

But the colonel told himself it was not his job to feel sorry about the enemy's problem. It was his job to make the problem worse. And the next step in his plan would do that.

"All loaded and ready to fire, sir."

Sergeant Washington's eager voice came reassuringly loud and clear through the walkie-talkie Lieutenant Stallingsworth held to his ear.

"This is going to be tricky, Sergeant, so tell all your gunners to be absolutely certain they're not even a millimeter off — their bubbles leveled and aiming stakes lined up. Tell them there's friendly troops surrounding the area on every side."

"Yes, sir. I've already made that very clear. I'm sure they're laid right where you want them."

"Okay. We'll try your gun first for a trial shot. I don't like doing this without an adjustment first — but here goes. You figured the range and deflection exactly to the coordinates I gave you?"

"Yes, sir. Precisely."

"All right. We'll try the first one right in the middle — where you'll have a few hundred yards leeway in all directions. Fire when ready."

The sound of the big one–five-five howitzer firing reached him at the same moment as the sergeant's prompt "on the way."

This should really be interesting, the lieutenant thought as he continued to stare out the south window at the open space, where now countless spikes of fire were driving into the central area. Not much fire was coming back out of the area. Small wonder, he thought — considering what those troops, now nearly surrounded with rapid-fire weapons, were having to bear.

This was another one for the books. He'd never heard of a one-five-five firing high-angle fire at such a close range. And in a tricky situation like this, you hated to be playing around with experiments.

He prayed the shell would not land too short or too long — and spread its deadly fragments over either of the defending lines. But with as much leeway as he had, it should be safe enough to try one round —

The shell exploded with an ear-shattering *Ca-rumppf*! By God, he couldn't have planned it better.

"Okay! All right!" he shouted into the radio. "You're right in the god-damned middle of the whole area. Exactly where we planned. Now, give us battery one volley — use that round as the centerpoint. Is that all clear?"

"All clear sir."

After a brief moment the eager voice came again.

"Battery on the way. Firing a hundred-yard front."

Again the wait that seemed forever for such a short distance, then....

The four shells hit at nearly the same moment. The lieutenant felt like dancing a jig. The shells had made a perfect pattern — and all were well contained within the very center of the open space.

"Okay! Okay! Perfect! Now work it over just like we planned. Each gun five rounds to start. Just tell your gunners to be sure to stay within the safety limits."

Barely five seconds later came the response: "Guns laid and ready, sir."

"Then fire at will. Let's clobber the hell out of the whole area."

Lieutenant Lee Beauregard Hood waited nervously as the criss-crossing fires flared in front of him. Things had been happening all too fast for him to think clearly about anything. When the sergeant had suddenly appeared and told him the colonel wanted all his destroyers deployed on the other side of town to help stop an infantry attack, he'd had time only to radio his three remaining units to pull out immediately and meet him there.

Since he'd been assigned to tank destroyers he'd somehow never thought of himself fighting infantry. It was the chivalric battle between two mounted noblemen — a combat of armored knights — that had captured his imagination. He remembered vaguely being taught that in a crisis situation the firepower of a tank destroyer could be used against regular infantry. But the instructors had made him very much aware that T.Ds were not tanks. Not with that open-topped turret just begging for an infantryman to throw a hand grenade into it.

But he knew in this situation they had to use everything they had, regardless of what the "normal procedures" would require. They had to stop an infantry attack — and the colonel, for whatever reason, had decided to use the T.D.s to do it.

So here he was, his destroyers lined up approximately fifty yards apart and facing the wildly exploding open area south of the town.

"Are we supposed to go down into that mess?" someone said on his radio. He recognized the voice of one of his sergeants.

"We're supposed to stay here and close off any advance into the town," he said into his mike. He cursed the quavering, apologetic tone in which he had spoken. Why couldn't he be properly "commanding" — like the colonel, or even Sergeant McClanahan? Others gave commands in voices that sounded like they expected to be obeyed. Why couldn't he? He decided to try again.

"So we'll stay here for the time being," he said, relieved that his voice sounded firmer — and without his usual question mark at the end. "If you see any infantry approaching, fire on them immediately with your machine gun or individual weapons. I'm free to order a forward or retrograde movement if the situation appears to require it. So we'll stay here giving fire support with everything *except* our seventy-sixes. We don't want any muzzle-blasts to draw anti-tank fire. Now let's get on those fifty calibers. Fire anywhere in the open space — but not toward the river or the high ground on the right. Any questions?"

For a moment he couldn't believe there were none. Had his voice sounded *that* authoritative?

Then the short bursts of the powerful fifty-calibers to his right told him that his men were doing what he had ordered — just as if they assumed he knew what he was doing.

Suddenly he heard the rush of artillery shells about to land. Then they began to hit. First four at the same time, then one every few seconds. He marveled at the way the shells were working over the whole area. For a moment he wondered what it would be like to be out there in that holocaust — then quickly turned his mind away from the thought. Better not play with challenges he didn't have to face.

The shells continued to rush in and explode, working over the whole area systematically. He fired his own fifty a short burst every few seconds — though he rarely saw anything specific to shoot at. It was only after a number of minutes had gone by that he saw the first group of enemy infantry running desperately toward his line of T.D.s. Only a few at first — then he saw more emerge from the area that was being pounded mercilessly by exploding shells and streams of bullets.

Some soldiers were obviously getting through the hail of artillery fragments and machine-gun fire. And he could tell the shells were being carefully kept away from his own position. Even the streams of automatic fire that crossed in front of him never actually approached his T.D.s.

This then was his responsibility. And he would have to meet it himself — with no one to make the decision for him. Those enemy soldiers must have sensed this was the only safe way to come. Should he and his men just sit there and fire their fifties at any figures they could see — and run the risk of a single soldier creeping up on them in the dark to throw a hand grenade into a turret?

He made his decision quickly. It came surprisingly easy, though he was far from certain his decision was right.

"All units," he said into the mike, "we're going to pull a limited attack. Drive straight ahead, firing your machine guns as you go. We'll stop this attack by fire and movement. When they see us bearing down on them, they should go back the other way. Guide on me in the middle. *But be sure not to go more than two hundred yards..* We want to be sure we don't get into that free fire zone. Get ready and go on my command. Then listen for my command to halt. All units acknowledge. Over."

It was amazing to him how quickly they all acknowledged his orders. So that's the way it was done. To command you just had to forget about doing the "proper" thing. You did your best to do what you thought was right. But right or wrong, you and your men just had to do it all together. And if you acted like you expected them to follow you — apparently they would.

He was not at all sure how many of the enemy had come through the heavy fire zone and now faced him. Though it was possible to see vague forms out in the open area, it was too dark to see anything clearly there. But from what he had seen, he knew there could be a large number now in front of him. So it was like those Civil War battles where the out-numbered Confederates simply went ahead and charged anyway — and because they acted so sure of their own superiority, the Yankees would usually decide they must be right.

"All right, here we go!" Lieutenant Hood shouted into the mike. "Fire your machine guns as you go — and stop when I stop."

He pointed his fifty-caliber at one of the vague forms ahead and fired a long burst as the destroyer jerked ahead. He aimed the machine gun at one form after another, firing separate bursts with little intervals between them. In the jerking and bouncing turret he doubted if he was hitting many of his targets, but maybe that didn't matter. He kept the heavy machine gun firing almost continuously — perhaps that would have the right effect.

He had covered the first half of the two hundred yards when he glanced briefly to his right to see how the rest of his platoon was doing. He could tell by the rapidly firing machine guns they were all nearly abreast of him and lined up as if for a parade. He felt strangely exhilarated as he saw them following his lead so automatically. By God, this was the first moment since his joining the army that the reality could approach his former dreams.

But he knew it was not like what he had dreamed. These men were indeed following him, manning their weapons exactly as he had ordered. Yet this was only a moment — and he knew what these men *really* wanted was not to go down in glory but to live to go home. They had pushed themselves to this glorious moment (just as he had), but it was not a way of life for them. Nor for him, either.

Now he must have come the full two hundred yards. As he continued to fire the fifty he shouted into the mike: "Far enough! Halt in place but keep firing!"

He continued firing his extended bursts at each dark mass or shadow that might have been a man. He saw two prostrate forms just ahead. Had they already been killed? Or were they merely cowering for protection? No time to worry about it. He moved the gun up and fired a quick burst at a vague figure running back toward the heavy fire zone. He couldn't tell if the figure fell or disappeared into the dark.

He saw another figure incongruously standing up, jumping up and down and waving something. Crazy fool — what was wrong with him? Did he think this was a time to wave banners? What was wrong with these damned Nazis?

He suddenly realized what the man was waving was not a flag but merely a small piece of cloth — perhaps a handkerchief. That didn't matter. What did was that it was white. Of course! What was the matter with him?

He ceased firing immediately. "Take over the gun," he shouted to his loader. "But don't fire unless you have to. I think there's some guys down there that want to surrender."

"Be on the look-out for soldiers trying to surrender," he shouted into the mike. "If they want to surrender, have them leave their weapons on the ground and then collect the men in a group around your destroyers. Don't kill anyone trying to surrender."

Then taking his Thompson submachine gun he jumped down and walked toward the man who had been waving the piece of white cloth. The man seemed relieved at his approach.

"You kamerad?" he asked curtly.

"Yah! Yes. I...kamerad...surrender."

"Speak any English? Leave your gun there. Come with me. Anyone else kamerad, commen mit...come with me."

He saw other forms rising up in the darkness, their hands raised, some clutching a white handkerchief in one hand.

Now he had a group of more than a dozen soldiers clustered around him. He turned back to the man he had spoken to, saw he was some kind of non-com, and spoke in as commanding a voice as he could.

"You. Line them up. No guns. Leave all guns. Single file. Follow me. Versteh?"

"Yes," the man said eagerly. "I understand."

Then he turned and barked some orders in German to the other men around him. With a precision that the lieutenant had never seen American soldiers use, even on parade, the men quickly formed in a single line. There seemed to be more than twenty now — and even as he made a quick estimate, other figures were rising from further back, nearer the heavy firing zone and rushing forward to join the group.

The non-com who was forming them up barked orders at the others as they came forward. In a few short moments the scattering of men had become an impressive line of soldiers, all standing at attention in the dark.

The non-com turned with precision, faced the lieutenant, and saluted smartly.

"Alle...all formed...sir."

Lieutenant Hood tried to hold himself stiff and speak with a precision to match the German soldier's.

"Very well. We will leave in a moment."

He turned to look up at his loader standing behind the long-barreled fifty-caliber with what must have been intended as a threatening scowl — though he was probably as surprised at the turn of events as the lieutenant.

"Check with the other destroyers," the lieutenant said. "See if they've got prisoners too."

The loader turned away to speak into the mike, listened to the answers, and then relayed them quickly.

"Two say they've captured a few — the other says they've a god-damned shithouse full of them. They want to know what to do with them."

"Line them up, leave their guns, march them back to town — single file in front of the T.D.s. Tell them to make it fast — we don't want to be caught out here if somebody sends up a flare."

He turned back to the non-com and spoke with a voice which had somehow developed a surprising air of authority.

"Keep single file. Hands on der kopf. Follow me."

He turned his back on what struck him now as a large group of German infantrymen to stride, without a glance behind him, back toward town.

Colonel Berrigan knew at some point the enemy was going to shoot up a flare. He had hoped they would delay for some

time for fear of showing too much of their attacking force —
completely exposed in the open. But as soon as the commander
became suspicious that things weren't going as planned, he
would probably chance it. The colonel was only surprised that
it had taken so long.

By the time the flare burst the attacking force had been badly
decimated. The colonel could see very few of them still moving — and for those who were, all movement was to the rear.
And all over the open area to the west he could see gray-clad
forms lying tight against the earth. Most of them were motionless — although some were moving with spasmodic twitches.
A very few were crawling back in the direction from which
they had come.

Far to the right, however, he could make out a strange force
just approaching the first row of buildings in town. There were
the T.D.s — each following a line of gray-clad figures march-
ing in single file, hands raised and placed behind their heads.

My God, he thought — so that's what was happening when
they came out with their fifty-calibers blazing. And that little
blond-headed, squinty-eyed grandson of the Confederacy was
making it all happen.

He turned and looked to his left. He was glad to see no
Shermans stood out at first glance. Because he knew just where
to look, he eventually could pick out the Sherman down near
the ford, and then one of the light tanks nearer the river. The
flare went out before he had time to look for the other Sherman
across the open area on the higher ground.

I hope the hell that T.D. lieutenant gets his destroyers and
prisoners back into town and under some protection fast, he
thought. That commander over there is going to be foaming at
the mouth, and except for the T.D.s herding the prisoners
there's almost nothing for him to shoot at.

He had told the T.D. lieutenant to stay out where he could

close the box on those attacking infantry only as long as they were a continuing threat. After doing such a fine job, would the young man have sense enough to know that the attack was beaten — and with flares lighting the landscape, if he didn't get his destroyers out of sight quickly they'd be knocked out in no time?

Then as he waited, a second flare burst, and he saw with relief the prisoners had all disappeared in among the buildings, and only two of the T.D.s were still visible, hurrying for the shelter of the nearest houses.

A sharp crack behind him told the Colonel one of the German tanks had picked up the targets and was trying for a quick kill. A moment later the shell struck the wall of a building on the edge of town, just behind one of the T.D.s as it scuttled for safety between the buildings. As he watched, the last T.D. disappeared from sight in among the buildings. He breathed easier knowing they had all made it at least to a temporary safety.

Not so the tank which had fired the shot. He saw the little twinkle of fire on the ridge way back behind the town, and a moment later the ninety-millimeter shell struck the tank which had fired, turning it into a burning mass of metal.

Sergeant MacKay's sidekick had been primed and ready, he thought. That would make the enemy commander a little less certain of how vulnerable this task force really was.

But there still was one thing the German commander could do — and a few seconds later the rush of incoming shells announced he was doing it. Explosions from artillery shells landing in town reverberated in the night air. Shortly after, a second volley came in to explode with such force the colonel knew they must be at least one-fifties. It's the only place he can shoot the artillery, the colonel thought. If he shoots anywhere else on this side of town, he runs the risk of hitting his own infantry. Though even in the town, he might hit the captured German soldiers. But he obviously wasn't too concerned about them.

Now that it looked as if the large-scale infantry attack had been clearly beaten off, the colonel knew he would have to be getting back to his C.P. and preparing plans for the rest of the night. A glance at his watch told him it was now one fifty-six.

21

"They've gone way down to the left and crossed into the trees."

The infantry lieutenant's voice coming through the light tank's radio contained just an edge of panic. The colonel had hurried out to the light tank, now in its former position behind his C.P., the moment he had been informed the slow-talking Lieutenant Magruder insisted on speaking to him.

"Are they attacking you yet?" the colonel asked, keeping his voice calm. If old cold-molasses Magruder was getting panicky, the situation must be bad. But he didn't want the dour-faced lieutenant falling apart on him. That skimpy left-flank cover force had to hang on a little longer or they were all down the tubes.

"No, sir. Not yet. Not even any shooting yet. But they've crossed in large numbers way off to our left flank. I had a patrol out that confirmed it. I'm sure they're working their way through the woods toward us. And once they get close, there's nothing we can do against them. They'll outnumber us by plenty, and they'll be coming at us out of tree cover. We'll be out in the open and sitting ducks for them."

So it was here at last. The colonel had known there would come a point at which there were really no more tricks left in the bag, and vastly superior numbers and better weapons would finally pay off.

Well, all he could do was try every stalling maneuver possible while he attempted to think of what to do.

"Look, Lieutenant Magruder," the colonel said, "here's what you're going to do while I prepare our response. You've got to slow them down as much as you can. What do you have for automatic weapons — a machine gun and one BAR?"

"That's all, sir — except for the light tank."

"Okay. You're going to send out a light patrol — just six men, but including the two automatic weapons. And be sure they all take some hand grenades. Make it very clear to them they are to move slowly and carefully. Have them go out about three hundred yards — unless they hit some opposition first. Then stop and wait for the enemy infantry to run into them. Tell your patrol it's not their job to stop anybody — just convince the Germans they've hit a real line of resistance out there. Make them take their time getting ready to assault it. Tell your men to throw some grenades before the enemy are close enough for it to do any good. We just want your men to make a lot of noise. Have the automatic weapons open up for a few short bursts — long enough to make the Krauts cautious. Then your men should retreat slowly back to your main position, putting up a good bluff all the way. You'll hear when the shooting starts. Then call me and I'll give you our next move. Have you got all that? Over."

"Yes, sir. I'll start them right away. Over and out."

The colonel hoped he had read the lieutenant's voice right. It had sounded less panicky at the end, even a little relieved after being given something specific to do. That ought to tamp down the erupting crisis for a few minutes.

But he knew he had to make some major decisions very quickly now. The position was becoming completely untenable on all sides.

Just twenty minutes before, word had come from Sergeant MacKay that something besides reconnaissance forces were moving in on his position on the parallel road behind them. And a thrust from the right rear could cut off the whole task force. Then almost at the same time the light tank patrolling the same highway to the left called in to say there had been a big battle some distance down the road to the north — and now an exploratory column was pushing in from that direction.

All the colonel could do was send a message to Sergeant MacKay through the light tank that was with him, telling him to radio his other T.D. to come back to help out. Sergeant MacKay would be responsible for the highway in one direction, while his buddy with the other ninety-millimeter covered the other. Then it was up to both of the T.D.s to retreat as slowly as possible — knocking out what they could as they went. They had about two miles leeway to the left, and perhaps a mile and a half to the right. But the colonel knew how fast an armored column could cover that — if it ever discovered there was nothing but a thin screen in front of it to stop it.

And I used to enjoy bluffing in a poker game, the colonel thought. If I ever get out of this mess, I swear I'll never play a hand of poker again.

He had looked at his watch then and discovered it was six minutes past three. And that was when the other beautiful piece of news had come through. Sergeant Bradovitch had called in from the light tank near him to say they were hearing tank motors – *on this side of the river*! The Germans had obviously cut a path along the trail the patrol had found and were somewhere within a quarter-mile of breaking out of the trees. And to make matters worse the enemy had moved in with a tank retriever and pulled out those two knocked-out tanks that were blocking the ford. So there was another avenue of approach opened up.

God, the colonel thought, now all I need is for someone to tell me they're getting some more bridges across.

Sure enough, he'd no sooner had the thought than Captain Bergoff came back to tell him he'd heard sounds of Germans working on a number of crossing points — and he was sure they'd have them completed in a very short time.

And now the god-damn left-flank infantry platoon — the smallest force he had, yet the one that had held out against the greatest pressure — was about to collapse against hopeless odds. So what the hell was he supposed to do about it, anyway?

He knew the approved answer to such a desperate defense situation. You had to rob Peter to pay Paul. Only what did you do when you had already robbed Peter blind — and Paul was no better off? What simple little school solution did you have for that?

He glanced at his watch again. God-damn that minute hand. Why didn't it move a little faster?

When there's absolutely no answer, he could hear himself lecturing, go back and examine your assumptions.

Okay, smart boy, he answered himself, what assumption can I question? I have to stay and defend this position through the night and maybe "part of tomorrow." That's the only assumption — and that's an air-tight "given."

But was it?

Hell, he thought, I've got shrunken, tiny little forces spread all over hell and starting to fall apart — front, flank, and rear. And if I leave this position — there goes my last natural barrier. No more river, no more anti-tank barrier.

But with the enemy already across on both flanks — with infantry *and* tanks — what the hell good was his "natural barrier?"

Answer — no damn good at all. So?

So get the hell out, while you still can get *something* out. And bring your scattered forces together where you *may* be able to hold the attack up a little longer on at least one route.

Of course. Why was he wasting his time here waiting for the ax of doom to fall? Shit on that noise. It was time to grab the god-damned ax of doom by the handle and start swinging.

"Sergeant," he said curtly to the commander of the light tank, "go inside the C.P. and send Sergeant McClanahan and Captain Bergoff out. Then go across the street and down two houses and tell the artillery lieutenant to come to the C.P. immediately. I'll meet him there as soon as I send a few orders out on your radio."

Suddenly his spirits had lifted. Those men who had fought so hard already deserved a commander who didn't crawl into a shell mouthing old chestnuts like "fight to the last man."

Jesus — just the *thought* of doing something made him feel better already.

Private Lucas Hatfield could tell they were getting close now. The grenade explosions had started some distance away, and the sound of the machine gun had been muffled by the distance it had to travel through the forest. But now the explosions were insistent, the machine-gun and rifle fire less than a hundred yards away.

A voice behind him made him turn and see the tall, solemn-faced lieutenant standing beside the light tank and talking into the radio's microphone.

"Yes, sir. They've slowed them down a lot — but they're almost back here now. I thought I'd better let you know."

The lieutenant listened to the headset a moment, then spoke again.

"Yes, sir. We'll move out right away. Over and out."

Hatfield turned his rifle toward a sudden crackling in the edge of the trees — only to see a soldier carrying a light machine gun run toward him and fall flat a few feet away. Then three more men ran from the trees and dropped down as a stream of bullets from a burp gun clipped leaves from the nearest trees.

"Jesus, I think they got old Lonnie," one of the men muttered.

"Tomkins too," the man beside him said. "He was trying to help old Lonnie and carry his BAR too and that god-damned burp gun stitched him across the middle."

"Where's the god-damned lieutenant?" the man with the machine gun asked Hatfield.

"Over by the tank," Hatfield answered.

He watched as the remaining men from the patrol hurried over to the lieutenant, still standing by the tank.

Three minutes later all the men of the left-flank force were crowded together around the lieutenant.

"I called you together because we're pulling out of here," the lieutenant said, his voice tense.

"Jesus, about time," somebody muttered. "How we going — straight across to town?"

"No," the lieutenant said. "We'd be out in the open all the way. We're going straight back over that little rise a couple of hundred yards behind us. From there we'll be out of sight from this position. Then we'll go straight back till we meet a dirt road that runs over to the road into town. When we start, move fast and keep going. Stay out of town. We'll all be pulling back on the main road beyond it.

"Don't worry 'bout me," somebody said. "I seen enough of that god-damn town to last me the rest of my life."

"And if we don't get the hell outa here quick," somebody else said as a stream of burp-gun bullets cut the air overhead, "that won't be very god-damn long — for any of us."

"Here's the order of the retreat," the lieutenant said. "The tank and one squad will stay behind and shoot up a storm to screen our retreat. Then the squad will pull out, and then the tank last. The tank is to shoot all its machine guns a good long burst before it goes. That ought to hold them here a little while."

"All right, already," somebody said impatiently. "Let's cut the god-damn strategy and get the hell out of here."

"Sergeant," the lieutenant said to Hatfield's squad leader, "Your squad will stay with the tank for about five minutes. Then you follow us. Remember to have your men really shoot up a storm."

Hatfield's spirits slumped as he heard this. Why did it have to be his squad?

Yet somebody had to stay, he told himself. Just put everything else out of your mind and do your job as Sergeant Forte would want you to.

A few moments later Hatfield crouched in his hole and saw the vague forms of the other men disappear in the darkness to their rear.

"Okay," his squad leader said. "All you guys heard him. Shoot a god-damn storm. Convince the bastards they don't want to come this far for a few minutes yet."

Hatfield lay in his hole and pointed his Ml toward a part of the trees where he thought he had seen a muzzle flash when a burp-gun had fired.

There. He was sure he had seen it that time. Methodically he emptied his clip toward the flash. Other rifles were shooting around him. He glanced over at the tow-headed young boy, who was emptying a clip of rifle ammunition into the darkness of the trees.

Private Hatfield emptied two more clips toward the same general area. The tank was also firing its machine guns now. Maybe this will be enough, Hatfield thought, to keep them from following us too close when we take off out of here.

"Atta boy," he said in a voice intended not to carry beyond the young boy in the foxhole beside him. The kid had just shot another clip and was loading a new one. "Pour it on 'em. Make 'em want to stay hidden in them woods."

The boy glanced over at him, apparently proud at the praise.

"Okay, here we go," the squad leader said in a voice just loud enough for the squad members to hear. "One at a time from the left. Take off."

Hatfield saw that would leave him and his friend as the last to go. Well, at least it wouldn't be much longer.

He watched the other members of the squad get up in turn and run in a low crouch past the tank and on into the darkness.

"Okay," he said in a low voice to his friend, who had just emptied another clip. "Your turn. Take off."

The boy looked over at him, gave him a rather jaunty thumb-and-finger okay, then rose and ran crouching toward the tank. But as the boy neared the tank, a burp gun much closer than the others had suddenly opened up. Hatfield heard the bullets whistling past. The boy appeared to stumble a moment, took another step, then went down.

Private Hatfield waited for him to get up and go on. A cold

hand seemed to close around his heart as the boy lay there unmoving. As if seized by a convulsion of anger and terror, Hatfield raised his rifle and poured the whole clip at the area he thought the bullets had come from.

Then he rose from the hole and ran to the young boy's side. He turned the boy over, looking hopefully for some sign of a wound, praying it was not bad. He could see nothing for a moment. Then he tilted back the helmet that had fallen slightly. forward, and under the sweat-smeared hair saw the two small holes low on the boy's forehead.

He knew without checking further it was no use. The young boy, who a moment before had been giving him the jaunty okay sign, was dead.

It always happens, he thought numbly, sooner or later. With Sergeant Forte, with the young boy, with all of us sooner or later.

"Let's go! Let's go'"

Was the voice Sergeant Forte's? He looked up and saw the tank commander's face sticking out of the turret. "Come on," the tankman went on impatiently. "It's too late for him. Get going — I'll be right behind you."

Private Hatfield, who had raised the fallen soldier's upper body in his arms, gently laid the boy back on the ground, wiped a spot of dirt from his cheek, then rose and stumbled on into the darkness. Behind him he heard the tank's machine guns rattle away for a long burst, then the sound of the motor revving up told him the tank was coming behind him — also leaving the small, vulnerable form of the young boy who had become his special friend for... not even one full day, he realized.

Sergeant Washington, the black artilleryman, entered the C.P. and took his place in the group assembled there. That should be all of them, Colonel Berrigan thought. There's no time to bring anybody in from the ford area, and Magruder and his small force were already retreating and out of contact. He'd arranged for Sergeant McClanahan to brief the right flank forces immediately after the council-of-war broke up. And if the enemy attack came before then? Well...he hoped it wouldn't. After the way the right flank had fought off all the attacks that had hit them, it would be a damnable dirty trick to go off and leave them there. But if the enemy attacked in the next few minutes, there wouldn't be much he could do about it.

"I wanted to get you all together for just a couple of minutes," the colonel said as they sat on the floor or kneeled in front of him, "first, to tell you what a great job you've all been doing. We've held up a much larger enemy force, including panzer and panzergrenadier units — probably some of Hitler's best. And we've done it with very little strength of our own that is supposed to be able to defeat such units. You've used courage and ingenuity in place of proper weapons and equipment — and you've somehow made it all work."

He could see they were pleased at these remarks. Well, they deserved to be — but they'd probably much rather have a guarantee of getting out of there alive.

"We've held on to our special advantages in this position far longer than any reasonable leader would expect was possible," he continued. "But we've taken losses, we've been forced to spread what strength we have too thin, and the position is finally about to fold. The key now to continuing our defense is getting out of here at the right time — so we can consolidate our strength and continue our defense in another position. Well, gentlemen — the right time is now."

The tired and strained faces before him brightened visibly at the news.

"We're going out," he continued, "and we're going out together, in proper order, and according to *our* plan — not the enemy's."

He paused a moment and was glad to see they were listening intently — and hopefully, so far as he could tell.

"They're getting ready to engulf this position from every direction," he said. "And we're going to let them stick their nose in the beehive — only they're going to find the honey's all been taken away, and all we've left behind for them is a few stinging bees for their pains.

"Here's the way we'll do it. We've already collected all the wounded in the kitchen area. They're being loaded right now in the transportation we have left. Fortunately our trucks just came back from their previous run with the wounded, and we've unloaded everything else that has wheels — even the gasoline in our supply trailers. So we have enough space to get them all out.

"Now, as soon as we finish here, Sergeant McClanahan is going over to the right flank and start them back, infantry first, then tanks. The left flank is already moving back. And Captain Bergoff, you will begin moving your infantry back immediately. Leave about a quarter of your men as a rear guard in case the enemy attack jumps off before we're all out. Your route will be back through town and down the main road to the rear. Proceed to the next crossroad two miles behind us. I'll get instructions to you on our dispositions there. Tell your rear guard to give you just ten minutes' start — then they can follow. Now — Lieutenant Hood —"

"Yes, sir!"

The smartness of the response startled everyone. The colonel could see, despite the exhaustion in the young man's features, that his eyes were alert and his attention was screwed up to a fever pitch.

"You and your men did a wonderful job in helping stop

that last attack. Now, you're going to have to play a key role in our withdrawal. Did you get all those prisoners taken care of already?"

"Yes, sir. We scrounged up some rope and tied their hands behind them, then we got a longer rope and tied them all together in a line — each one around the left ankle. That way we could send them back with only three men as guards. They left about ten minutes ago."

"How many were there of them, for God's sake?"

"Fifty-eight, sir."

"Great. Now, your T.D.s are going to be the last unit leaving town. And you have some very important duties to perform. Are all four of your remaining T.D.s fully operative?"

"Yes, sir. Completely. Guns, machine guns, plenty of ammo, and we recently filled all tanks with gas cans from the supply trailers."

"Excellent. Now, your two destroyers on the north side of town have an especially important job. The flank there is completely open since Lieutenant Magruder's withdrawal. Your two machine guns should be able to keep the attacking force that has moved in there from getting across the open space — nearly a quarter-mile with no cover. Try not to use your big guns unless you have to. You can be sure anything that moves on that flank is unfriendly, so blast away at it. Your other two destroyers on the south side of town have to use more judgment. There will be friendly units withdrawing back across the open space there. Tell your men there to be careful not to fire until all friendlies have gone past. Then it's their responsibility to break up any attacking force following our retreating units. Have all your destroyers try to stay for a full ten minutes after all friendly units have passed through. And you may have to deal with tanks as well as infantry."

"Yes, sir, the young lieutenant snapped again.

"Right. Then when you take off, you will follow the retreating force as the rear guard. Now, I think that completes our main components — except for the artillery. I want all the rest of you to get back to your units and begin the operation immediately. The artillery people will stay behind a minute for instructions. Are there any questions?"

He waited a moment but no one spoke.

"Very well. It is now," he raised his wrist to look at his watch, "three-fifty-five. You will have your first units begin the withdrawal by four-fifteen. That should put all units well out of the area before daylight. Good luck, and I'll see you back at the crossroad — where we'll have some more little surprises for the enemy."

The men rose and made for the door without delay. I don't blame them, the colonel thought. They have a hell of a lot to do in the next twenty minutes — and how well they do it is going to determine how many of their men live to get out of here.

Sergeant McClanahan and the two artillerymen were waiting expectantly for their instructions.

"Sergeant McClanahan," he said quickly, "I want you to go over to the right-flank force as quickly as you can. Find Lieutenant Brownell first and have his men begin to pull back as soon as he can start them. Tell him to be sure his men move very quietly —straight back across the open space, and then over to the main retreat road in the middle of town. Got all that?"

"Yes, sir."

"Fine. Next find Sergeant Bradovitch and tell him his Shermans and the light tank are the rear guard. Have them give the infantry fifteen minutes to clear, then he and the light tank can pull back by whatever route seems best to them. They'll join us at the main crossroad to our rear. Tell him to have his other Sherman maintain its position on that knoll in the rear until he retreats past them — then it can follow him.

"Now — as soon as you've relayed the orders, try to get back into town as quickly as possible. Your last job is to be sure all units in town except the rear guard have got the word and pulled out. Then come back on the main road until you find me. I'll be near the tail end of the column. Clear?"

"All clear, sir."

"Good. Then take off, and good luck."

The colonel's stomach muscles relaxed slightly. Now at least the main units were all taken care of – *if* the enemy didn't attack too soon. In which case, he thought, it will be one hell of a mess.

Next he turned to the two artillerymen.

"I wanted to see you two," he said, "to thank you for the way you've supported us. Without you we never could have held out this long. Now — do either of you have any ideas on how you might help out further during the pull-back?"

The artillery lieutenant spoke so quickly it was obvious he had been waiting for the opportunity.

"Yes, sir. First, I'd like to order my battalion to shoot a number of missions on the areas where the enemy may be assembling for the attack. Especially that area on our right flank where they're already across the river. We know they have tanks across, too — and by now they must be within a few hundred yards of breaking into. the open. I'll keep the concentration a quarter-mile away from any of our troops, so it should be safe enough to use my own battalion for that.

"Then we can put a solid concentration down on the left flank's former position. Since our troops are well out of there by now, the place will probably be loaded with enemy infantry."

"Sounds good," Colonel Berrigan said. "Tell your commander I urgently requested those missions. Anything else?"

"Yes, sir. But this is up to Sergeant Washington's judgment. If he doesn't need all the time for march-ordering his guns, I'd like to have him put down a few volleys right near the river one more time. That'll take their attention away from our troops pulling back — and if they're massed and about to attack, it can cause them some serious casualties. But this all depends on Sergeant Washington's troops being able to fire these missions and still get their guns out in time. That high-angle fire can really dig in a howitzer's trails and make them hell to pull out. How about it, Sergeant Washington — can you shoot the missions and still get your guns out in time?"

Colonel Berrigan turned to the black soldier questioningly. Sergeant Washington thought only a moment before answering.

"We've got a plan already worked out. We're so short-handed we knew it would be tough to march-order in a hurry. But we have one tracked prime mover with us still — so what we'll do is hook up the gun furthest from the road, using all the cannoneers to do it, and let the track pull it out. Then we'll go to the next one in line. I've briefed the men already, so we can be out by the road and ready to go in five minutes flat. We managed to scrounge another three-quarter-ton weapons carrier to serve as a prime mover for our third gun. But we're still short of something to pull our fourth gun."

"When I come past in my jeep," the artillery lieutenant said quickly, "I can take it."

"And I still have my jeep," the colonel said. "If anything goes wrong and you still need a tow, just let me know when I go by."

"Then that's it," Sergeant Washington said, obviously relieved. "I'm sure we can handle the missions and still be ready in time."

"Fine," the colonel said. Then he turned back to the lieutenant. "Just one more thing, Lieutenant. Is there anything we can have your battalion do to delay the enemy's follow-up? It's not going to take the Germans long to figure out we're gone, and if they follow too fast they can catch us on the road — when we'll be most vulnerable."

"There's one thing I was going to suggest," the artillery lieutenant said. "If you've noticed, there's a choke-point in getting out of this town — back where the buildings and terrain funnel everything down the main street. There are a few ways around, but in the dark they won't be easy to find. So I propose that as soon as all our elements have cleared out of town — and whenever the German tanks move in — we lay down a very heavy barrage over the whole town. It can clog up the streets and make tank movement difficult — and possibly knock out a tank or two. It can even force them to stop and wait for bulldozers to clear a way for them. And then if I adjust a concentration exactly on the last few buildings at that choke point — we can make them waste half an hour finding a way around in the dark."

"A great idea," the colonel said. "By all means try it. But how will you adjust the concentration once we're going all out for the crossroad behind us?"

"There's a ridge a few hundred yards west of town where I can stop and adjust the fire. No sweat."

"I think I'd be sweating if I hung back that close," the colonel said. "But if you think you can do it, by all means try."

"There's one more thing," Sergeant Washington put in eagerly. "We've got some leftovers I've been trying to think how to use. We have seven charges of powder that comes for each shell. We only use as many of the seven as we need to get the proper range. And with the short ranges we've been shooting, we have *six* powder charges left over for every round we've fired. And that's a helluva lot of powder — we had to keep making new piles that were away from the guns. It won't explode out in the open air — but it sure burns like hell. If we leave some of it at key places along the road when we retreat, and then arrange to light it when their tanks catch up, we can maybe burn a tank or two all to hell and make their advance a helluva lot more cautious."

"It's a fine idea," the colonel said, "but how in hell are you going to light it without staying around too long?"

"I think we can work something out," the sergeant said confidently. "Maybe use a trail of powder for a hundred yards or so. Or gasoline — I see we've still got lots of gas cans from those trailers they've been unloading. In a pinch we might even fire a fifty-caliber tracer at it — maybe the hot end of the tracer would ignite it."

The colonel marveled at the ingenuity of the proposals. By God, he thought, how did I end up with so much ability from the dregs of a defeated army?

22

Sergeant Bradovitch stuck his head out of the open turret and stared intently at the ford. Was anything moving down there? It was impossible to tell in the dark. He thought he had seen something a moment before through the gun sight, but he hadn't been sure.

Hell, they'd probably get hit by a full panzer attack just five minutes before they were scheduled to pull out. That was always the way. Put a god-damned Sherman in for rear guard. Here we are riding around in a god-damned tin-plated firetrap — and we're supposed to be supermen.

But he could see the logic of it. To a poor foot soldier with an M1 rifle and no armor at all, he thought, we must look pretty god-damned privileged.

He looked at his watch. It was four-eighteen. According to the schedule the infantry was pulling back by now. He'd told the light tank commander he could start his retreat at four-twenty. Bradovitch intended to stay until four twenty-five —

and then he was going to haul ass. If those bastards would just hold off another seven minutes.

A sudden sound of tank motors to his right made him turn and look toward the edge of the trees. Bastard! Had they found a way to get tanks through the god-damned woods already? If they had they would be thrusting right into the flank of the retreating infantry. Not to mention cutting his Sherman off completely.

"Tommy!" he barked into his radio. "Do you hear them god-damned tank motors?"

"I hear 'em," Tommy's voice came back over the radio. "And if it's what I think, you better get the hell out of there. They're going to come right in behind you."

"Too late, Tommy. I'm better off here on their flank. I'll shoot from this flank, and you give 'em hell from the other one, and we'll see what we can do. We can take their attention off the infantry, anyway. Those poor bastards are probably out in the open and scattered over the whole god-damned slope now."

"Go down the road by the river, then. Jesus, Brad — give yourself a god-damned chance."

"I can hear motors down by the river, Tommy. They'll be coming across that way too. Besides, our mission's here, remember? God-damned rear-guard heroes, that's us. We might as well give them the best we got. Hell, most of the company took it yesterday — so we got to live an extra eighteen hours. Look, Tommy — we'll be on both their flanks, and I bet they didn't send their Mark V's or VI's around that half-ass trail. Probably they're all Mark IV's. From the flank we can really chew those bastards up. And if you think we got it rough — think about those poor bastards in the Stuart. With their pea-shooter they can hit dead center and it won't even give the bastards a headache. Get ready, Tommy — I think they'll come full speed once they're out of the woods."

The roar of tank motors had increased. There must be a lot of the bastards, he thought.

Then he saw one. It was just an obscure lump of heavier darkness moving out from the trees and cutting across behind him. He quickly ducked into the turret, pulling the hatch shut over his head, and settled into his seat by the gun. He rotated the turret quickly one hundred and eighty degrees, watching intently through the gunsight.

And there it was.

No doubt about it now. It had moved out away from the trees on higher ground than the Sherman, so the turret was clearly silhouetted against the sky.

Jesus, Bradovitch muttered, what a beautiful god-damned target. He put his cross hairs just behind the forward edge of the turret, held it a moment there, then fired. His shell hit the right side of the turret, penetrated easily, and a moment later the tank came to an abrupt stop.

"Move left and swing around!" Bradovitch shouted to his driver on the intercom. The tank jerked ahead and then began to turn to the left. Bradovitch rotated his turret to keep it pointing back up the slope as the tank reversed directions.

Jesus, he thought — what beautiful luck! They can't see me against the low ground, but as long as they're higher I can see their silhouettes against the sky.

Now he could make out three more of them, all moving across the slope toward the town.

As he hastily rotated his turret to bring his gun to bear on the closest tank, he saw a sudden lick of flame from high up the slope — then he heard the shell hit squarely. A moment later a tank higher up the slope was engulfed in flames.

"Got the bastard!" Tommy's voice came from the radio.

But Sergeant Bradovitch was too busy to reply. His cross hairs fixed on the nearest tank just as the gun started to move in his direction. Hurriedly he fired, hoping to catch it before the Mark IV's heaviest frontal armor turned toward him. The shell caught the turret while it was still partly turned away. He knew immediately he had penetration. Then that tank too burst into flame.

"Bingo!" Tommy's voice shouted. "You got him, Brad. Now watch me get — "

Bradvitch had seen the remaining Mark IV rotating its gun to point directly at Tommy's tank. He suddenly realized the Mark IV would now have Tommy silhouetted against the sky. Desperately the sergeant tried to bring his own gun into position to hit the Mark IV before it could fire. He was almost on it...just a little more...

His gun spat flame — but he knew he was too late. He had seen the streak of fire lance out from the German tank toward the knoll, even as he fired into the vulnerable rear end of the turret.

A moment before his shell hit he saw the German shell drive straight into Tommy's tank, now silhouetted on the knoll. Then his own shell hit the German tank, and both tanks burst into flame.

"Quick," he shouted into the intercom. "Turn left and get into the god-damn trees."

Even as the tank turned again and sped for tree cover, Bradovitch saw another muzzle flash further back in among the trees — then heard a sudden rush of air as the shell whished past his turret, missing by inches and striking somewhere down by the river.

Lucky we were on lower ground he thought. They're having trouble picking me up down here in the dark. But what the hell am I going to do when more come across to cut me off —

and they spot me by the muzzle blast when I shoot?

"Tell them to break off the other mission," Lieutenant Stallingsworth shouted down to Cardova, who was stationed by the jeep just outside the building. The lieutenant's battalion had been firing the left-flank mission when he had heard the tank guns on the right flank. He had reacted immediately. Although the colonel was there in the O.P. to observe the later stages of the withdrawal, it had never occurred to the lieutenant to ask someone else's opinion when a hard life-or-death decision was called for.

"They say they've completed that mission now and are ready to adjust for the next one," Cordova's voice called up from below.

"Tell them negative on the adjustment. Friendly forces need immediate fire. Battalion five volleys on a two-hundred yard front — use the coordinates I just sent as the center."

There was a delay of more than fifteen seconds, during which the lieutenant cursed impatiently to himself.

The colonel looked at his watch.

"The infantry may still be retreating across the open slope," he said. "Where are you calling for the fire?"

"About two hundred yards back into those trees," the lieutenant said. "Even at this range there won't be much dispersion in deflection. So it shouldn't be near enough to hurt any friendly troops."

Finally Cordova's voice came up from below.

"They'll give it to you if it's essential — but the colonel dislikes investing sixty rounds in unadjusted missions."

"Jesus, what is he — a god-damned banker?" the lieutenant snorted. "We're not in business here for a god-damned profit. Just say it's essential."

"On the way!" Cordova shouted up a moment later.

"What can you make out of what's happening down there?" the colonel asked.

"I'd say the tanks they sent around the flank finally got through and are attacking. And we had a couple of Shermans there to give 'em hell."

"It looks like we've knocked out about three of theirs," the colonel said. "But I'm afraid they've got one of ours already — and it looks like the other's cut off."

"Yeah. Look — he just got another one! He may be cut off but he's acting like he thinks he has *them* cut off."

"He's got them against high ground," the colonel said. "They can't see him but he can pick up their silhouettes. That's a damn smart tankman down there. I wish we could do more to help him out."

"Come on! Come on! Those shells are taking forever," the lieutenant pleaded impatiently.

"Ah — here they come," he added as he heard the sound of the big shells rushing through the air. A moment later they were bursting, bright red-orange in the darkness, among the trees on the near side of the river.

"That'll give the attacking force something else to worry about, at least," the lieutenant said with satisfaction. The shells kept coming, one or more every few seconds. In the momentary flashes of light with each explosion he thought he could pick up a glimpse of the Sherman tank — at first on the low ground by the river, but as the barrage continued he was sure he saw it turn suddenly and start up the open slope.

"He's making a break for it while the barrage is on," the lieutenant said excitedly. "He might make it, too — if we can keep his cover coming."

He leaned out the window and shouted urgently down to Cordova.

"Tell them the fire's very effective — and it's urgent to repeat another five volleys immediately. Friendly unit withdrawing needs cover. Hurry!"

He heard Cordova's voice repeating his words in between the continuing shellbursts.

Now, you over-cautious, rank-conscious son-of-a-bitch, he prayed silently, don't have a god-damned committee meeting about it. Just do it!

The shells were still landing a few hundred yards to the south. But he knew the concentration must be nearly completed. If the god-damned colonel will just go ahead and order the mission now, he thought, there won't be much of a break in the shelling — just enough for the first volley's time of flight; But if the colonel played his usual game and his only worry was covering his ass....

A final few shells landed, followed by a strange stillness. In the sudden silence he could clearly hear the motor of the Sherman as the tank raced across the open space.

He leaned out the window and shouted down to Cordova.

"Ask them if they've fired yet. Tell them retreating friendly unit desperately needs the fire."

He knew his message was way out of line. Observers didn't ask if the battalion had fired yet — they just waited for an "on the way." But how could he make them see how important every second was?

The colonel stepped over to the window to stand beside the lieutenant. Both officers waited impatiently for an answer. The racing tank motor now was much nearer — but the lieutenant knew it had at least another two hundred yards of open terrain to cover.

It seemed forever until Cordova's voice shouted up to them.

"Colonel says he has to clear using that much ammunition on an unobserved target with higher headquarters. He'll get back to you as soon as —"

"Oh, Jesus Christ Almighty!" the lieutenant wailed, pounding his fist against the window sill.

The colonel leaned out and shouted down in a voice trembling with a violent anger.

"Tell him this is Lone Bandit Six — and if he doesn't order those guns to fire immediately, I'll personally drag his ass up to 'higher headquarters' and make them roast it for Sunday dinner!"

The lieutenant could hear Codorva's voice repeating the message with a definite pleasure, using not only the colonel's exact words but his angry tone of voice as well.

There was a short wait while both officers stared out over the open slope trying to pick up the retreating tank. Then at last the voice shouted up: "Battalion on the way!"

But was it in time? A high-velocity shell exploded somewhere on the open slope. Then two more tank guns fired.

They knew the Sherman was running away, the lieutenant thought — but they couldn't spot him yet.

Then, with what struck the lieutenant as an obscene brightness, a flare arched upward and burst, covering the whole open slope with a flickering glare. Now they could see the Sherman, still a hundred yards short of reaching any kind of cover.

Almost immediately a series of sharp cracks came — some from the closer line of trees, but also many from the ridge across the river. A fraction of a second later a whole cluster of shells struck about the tank. Three were direct hits. In a moment the entire tank was engulfed in flame. The two officers watched anxiously for someone to climb out of the escape hatches.

But no one did.

A few moments later the flare burnt out, and except for a flickering glow around each of the burning tanks, the slope once again was lost in darkness.

Neither of the officers spoke as the artillery shells, now that it was too late, rushed in to explode every few seconds on the extreme right flank.

"He almost made it," the lieutenant finally said as if talking to himself.

The colonel appeared to rouse himself with a great effort.

"He did more than that," he said. "He was in a tough situation, and he played it for all he was worth."

"If I could just have got that second concentration down in time..."

The colonel's hand reached out and fell on the lieutenant's shoulder. It lay there for a moment with a friendly, reassuring pressure.

"We can't be sure what causes what out here," he said quietly. "If somebody hadn't decided to shoot that flare just then, he probably would have made it. In war some things get done by people you can blame, but mostly things just happen — and there's no sense blaming anyone. Except maybe the goddamn war itself."

He was silent a moment and then continued.

"Anyway, by the burning tanks back in the trees, your battalion's concentration must have hit at least three or four tanks back there — and maybe a lot more. Better inform your gun crews — they deserve a little encouragement for the job they've been doing."

"Yes, sir," the lieutenant said listlessly. Then he straightened up and leaned forward attentively as he heard tank motors suddenly roar far to his left.

"It looks like they've got tanks across the river on the other flank now," he said. "Cordova — fire mission! Another enemy tank attack! Alert the battalion and I'll give you the coordinates."

He turned on his pocket light to examine his map.

"Get on them as soon as you can," the colonel said as he strode quickly to the stairway. "I've got to go see how the T.D.s are going to handle this. Just remember — don't delay too long before you pull out. The rear guard will be leaving in just a few minutes now."

Then he was gone down the stairs two at a time.

"Can you see them yet?"

Lieutenant Hood's voice revealed his anxiety. Both he and the commander of the other T.D. on the north side of town had heard the tank's motors — but neither had a clear target yet to fire at.

"Not yet," the other T.D. commander's voice replied. "It's just too dark to see anything that far away. Should we send up a flare?"

Lieutenant Hood couldn't remember whether the colonel had said it was all right to use flares while the retreat was going on. Would a flare reveal the retreat to the enemy? He cursed his failure to find out such an important point.

"We'll wait just a bit more," he said indecisively. Then he heard the shells rushing in to land a quarter-mile away to his front.

"There!" he said with relief. "I saw one against a shellburst. See if you can line one up that way."

The shells were coming in regularly now, briefly illuminating an area around each burst.

"I think I'm on one," the other T.D. commander said. "If I can just get another burst behind him...."

Lieutenant Hood's eyes were glued to the sight, searching desperately for a familiar silhouette to fasten on. For a moment he thought he saw one — then another shellburst showed him he was mistaken. There! He was sure it was a German tank, and a big one too. A Mark V or VI. It had been moving slowly to his left. By the time he had the cross hairs on the spot it was dark again. He rotated the turret to the left, trying to remember just how fast the tank had been going. Then three artillery shells burst nearly at the same moment. There it was again! He had been slightly behind it. He rotated the turret more quickly, picturing in his mind where the tank would be...and fired. A moment later he shouted out triumphantly. He had a hit! He was sure his high-velocity seventy-six could penetrate that thinner side armor. The licks of flame spurting up around the hull assured him he was right.

He heard the gun of the other T.D. blast once, and then again.

"Did you get him?" Lieutenant Hood asked eagerly."

"I got him on the second shot!" the other commander answered. "The first was –"

Lieutenant Hood saw a flick of flame in the gunsight. Then he heard the armor-piercing shell strike — and knew someone had taken advantage of his subordinate's mistake. He never should have fired twice from the same position, he told himself. I should have made sure he knew that.

But his training had taken place long before I joined the outfit, he thought.

Stop thinking about it, he told himself. Things are happening fast, and I have to keep my mind clear for the next move.

"Pull over to the left," he told his driver through the intercom. "Then stop on the back side of that building. We've got one tank for sure — let's try for another."

The artillery shells were now whumping down in a tighter pattern closer to the river. They must be trying to take the bridge out — wherever it is, he thought. He wondered how many tanks had come across already. He thought he had seen the silhouettes of four or five against all the shell bursts. So there probably were two or three left — and maybe more.

"You on the other side of town," he said into his mike. "Have you got any action there yet?"

"Nothing we can see yet — not since they shot a flare and got our Sherman."

"Then leave one destroyer there and bring yours over here. We've got at least two enemy tanks running loose over here — and they just got Sergeant Hickey."

"Okay. I'm on the way."

Just then Lieutenant Hood, watching carefully through the gunsight, saw another tank silhouetted against two shellbursts behind it. Although it was off the cross hairs, it had not been moving, and he decided to chance a shot after placing the cross hairs on the spot where he thought it had been.

The shell sped away. A moment later another artillery shell landed nearby and in its brief flash of light he saw men climbing out of the escape hatches. Another hit! Was he really becoming a combat veteran — even after his shameful performance in the past? If he was, it was not what he had always expected it to be. It certainly wasn't glorious and inspiring. It was just a matter of doing simple things mechanically, without emotion, without any sense of significance.

That's when he saw the short lick of flame far to the left in his gunsight. And that strange feeling of doubtful satisfaction was his last sensation — for he neither heard the high-velocity shell strike his turret, nor felt it as it ricocheted off the inside walls, chopping up the bodies of the young lieutenant and his loader as it passed.

Colonel Berrigan met the two men running wildly back toward the main street of town. They pulled up when he saw them and words spilled out of both men simultaneously.

"Hold on," the colonel said. "You — what unit are you with?"

"Tank destroyers, sir. Lt. Hood's platoon."

"Where's Lieutenant Hood?"

"Back there, sir. The damned eighty-eight chewed him all to…"

The man seemed to be unable to complete his statement. Colonel Berrigan made his voice sharply demanding.

"Tell me precisely what happened."

The man stopped, swallowed, and went on in a slightly more coherent voice.

"They got tanks across the river. Big ones. Lieutenant Hood got two. Our other T.D. got one before he got hit. Then they got us. Eighty-eight penetrated the turret. Chopped the two in the turret all to hell."

Once more he could not go on.

"How many tanks are across the river?"

This time the other man spoke up.

"At least four or five — before we started shooting. There's still some left — one or two anyway."

"Are they attacking toward town?"

"I…don't think so, sir. Not after we started knocking them

out and the shells started falling where they crossed."

"Good. Now you two men go on through to the main street and then hurry back out of town. Go fast and you'll catch up with the rear guard."

"Yes, sir."

With no further urging the men broke into a run toward the main street. Colonel Berrigan felt strangely empty. But he had no time for feelings. He carefully listed the things he had to see were done. Check to see those two remaining tank destroyers had the word to get out — they might wait for a radio message from their platoon commander. See if the light tank had gone yet — if not, use his radio to check on what was happening on the highway in the rear. Maybe, he thought, the Germans have already taken that crossroad we're trying to get back to.

Maybe. But maybe not, too. And if maybe not, then he had to pull what was left of Task Force Lone Bandit into some kind of a defense for that crossroad.

Some defense, he thought grimly — main tanks all gone, tank destroyers almost gone, infantry badly clobbered and probably as good as gone. So what does that leave? Me and those little thirty-seven millimeters on the light tanks. Man, that ought to scare hell out of them.

But one part of his brain wanted to think about the blond, curly-headed, innocent-faced tank destroyer lieutenant.

So he had turned out fine — so far as the army was concerned. He had knocked out two heavy tanks before losing his own under-gunned T.D. And, incidentally, his life.

And he had turned out fine for his family too. They now could add his name and faded picture to that treasured family album — replete with glories of their heroic past.

But something in him cried out for the bloody pulp lying back there in the turret of the T.D. It just seemed the boy deserved more of a future than that — no matter how inglorious it might have been.

"Come on, JayCee," the motor sergeant urged, "that's enough of them there. Save a little for some place down the road."

"Just a few more, Hooley," JayCee said, refusing to hasten his arrangement of powder bags around the place where the main road narrowed to a bottleneck as it left the town.

"Jesus, everyone's done gone already, ain't they? The T.D.s and that light tank — and the colonel himself. There's just me an' you left. Except for all them German Tiger tanks comin' in from every which way. Let's get the hell outa here."

"That artillery lieutenant hasn't left yet."

"Hell, what I hear about him he'll probably wait to take out one of them Tigers with a grenade."

"Take it easy, Hooley. Here he comes now. I didn't want to scatter that gasoline around till he got his jeep out of here."

Hooley looked back up the street and saw the lieutenant's jeep racing toward them. JayCee stepped out quickly into the middle of the road with his hand raised. The jeep braked to a stop a few feet in front of him.

"Watch it going through here, sir," JayCee said. "There's powder bags all over the place — and we don't want anything setting them off yet."

The lieutenant looked around and saw what the sergeant meant.

"Great idea, Sergeant," the lieutenant said approvingly. "You must have a hell of a lot of them, too. How you going to set them off?"

"I was going to use a train of powder and gas — but I think it's too far to the closest spot where we can get any cover. I got a better way. We got our guns all march-ordered, but we're leaving one in position by a turn in the road. One round ought to set it off."

"If you put it in the right place it will."

"Don't worry about this one, sir. When we got that ammo, I took a few rounds of W.P. When that hits it'll spread pieces of hot white phosphorous for a hundred yards. One little-bitty piece of that and this place will go up like a god-damned volcano."

"I see what you mean, Sergeant," the lieutenant said with a grin. "One round ought to do it, all right. Better hurry it up, though. They've got tanks coming in now from every direction."

"Right behind you, sir. Just gotta leave a few powder bags in the road after you go through — then knock over a few open gas cans to help the whole thing along."

"Jesus, you aren't leaving much to chance, are you?" the lieutenant said as his driver picked his way through the narrow part of the road.

"No, sir. What *can* go wrong will go wrong, they say. But nothing's gonna go wrong with this."

"There it is, sir," Corporal Cordova said, pointing straight ahead.

The artillery lieutenant peered intently through his horn-rimmed glasses until he saw a mass loom up by the side of the road. It was a one-five-five howitzer, trails spread and ready to fire, with two men waiting beside it.

The lieutenant quickly scanned the position. There was a clear field of fire toward the entrance to the town, although in the dark he couldn't see any details of the street or buildings. And the howitzer was in position just off the road, with a few branches placed in front of it. It would be hard to pick up, even under the temporary light of a flare, unless you knew just where it was. A few feet behind it the road bent sharply to the left to go around a slight rise of ground. So if they moved sharp they could hitch up in just a few seconds and pull around the corner and out of view of anyone coming from the town. The position would have been too risky in daylight — in a very few seconds another tank might appear and turn its gun on the prime mover before it could tow away the howitzer. But as long as it was still dark, the chances were good the artillerymen could pull it off.

"Stop when you get around the corner," the lieutenant told Cordova.

As they rounded the corner the lieutenant saw another jeep was parked there. Two figures were standing on the slight rise the road curved around. Cordova pulled the jeep to the left of the road and parked there, just behind the other vehicle.

The lieutenant sprang out of the jeep and ran up the rise to join the other men there. He saw they were Colonel Berrigan and Sergeant McClanahan.

"What do you think his chances are?" the colonel asked.

"He can sure make that bottleneck a hot spot any time he wants," the lieutenant said. "The way I saw him scattering powder around, that's not going to be any small bonfire."

"Can he set it off any time he wants?"

"If they've already trained the howitzer on the spot it's a cinch, sir. That W.P. will touch off any powder within a hundred yards."

"That powder won't explode if it's not compressed into a

gun tube, will it?"

"Not explode, sir. But it'll burn so damn fast it's almost an explosion. And I'd hate to be in a tank with a lot of that stuff burning around me."

"Good," the colonel said. "If that will close off the bottleneck in the street for a while, it's going to be hard for them to find a way around in the dark. The buildings there are too close together for tanks to go between them. It might hold them up a quarter — maybe even half an hour."

"We'll make it even tougher for them," the lieutenant said. "As soon as the sergeant sets off his little holocaust, I'm going to have my own battalion put a concentration on the town that'll blow it to kingdom come. Between what the sergeant will start with his powder bags and gasoline, and what a heavy barrage of one-five-fives will do — that town's going to be a very unhealthy place to be for awhile. Even inside a tank."

"Great. If you're going to stay here until the fireworks start, I'd better get going and find out what sort of positions we can set up at the crossroad. Be sure you make it back, lieutenant. We're going to need your help there rather badly, I'm afraid."

"Yes, sir. I'll be there. I'll come back with Sergeant Washington's men. They're going to pull a few more tricks to delay the pursuit."

"The more time you can give me, the better. But don't push your luck too far."

Ten minutes later the two black sergeants drove up with their three-quarter-ton vehicles. One was still loaded with powder bags and the other now had gas cans thrown in the back.

"Any sign of tanks in town yet?" the lieutenant asked from

the rise above the road.

"Not yet," Sergeant Washington said. "They've been shooting into the buildings near the river some, but I think they're kind of leery about rushing in without working it over some more first. They must have a number of crossings over the river now —so it won't be long."

Lieutenant Stallingsworth had already radioed in his request for a concentration on the town, to be fired only when he called for it. The C.P. had told him they would give him all he wanted. In fact, they said if they had a few minutes warning they might be able to bring in some other battalions on it — communications had now improved enough to make such a concentration of fire possible. So he was getting anxious to see the first German tanks reach the bottleneck in the road.

They all waited quietly by the howitzer for some minutes, listening for the sound of approaching tanks.

"I think I hear something," one of the men said.

They all listened carefully. The lieutenant could hear only the sound of muffled tank motors in the distance.

"That's just the tanks approaching the town from the other end," Sergeant Washington said. "I been hearing that for some time."

"No — listen," the first man said, holding up his hand. "It's different now."

Again they listened. The lieutenant suddenly could distinguish a separate, more insistent roar of motors.

"I think that's it," he said. "I bet that's a whole column coming down the main street."

"Whooee — come to mama," Sergeant Washington said. "I'll shoot a flare to see where the hell they are."

He raised the flare pistol, pointed it out over the town and fired. After a few moments the flare blossomed in the sky and then burned steadily. In its brilliant glare they could see clearly the entrance to the town. There were no tanks there yet. The lieutenant raised his field glasses to look. Then he saw them, magnified and headed straight down the main street toward him.

"There they are," he said. "A whole damn column of them. The first one must be almost at the bottleneck."

Sergeant Washington, who had stepped quickly to peer through the sight of the howitzer, whistled triumphantly.

"Atta baby...come on...just a little more...a little bit...more....

Suddenly the howitzer roared and spat flame. There was a moment of silence while the shell sped on its way. Then it seemed to the lieutenant that an entire fireworks display had been suddenly ignited.

The shell must have struck squarely in the middle of the tank, for in the light of the shellburst he could see the tank shake with the force of the explosion. But it was the aftermath of the explosion that was so terrifyingly beautiful. Little fingers of fire spread out from the tank to the buildings around it. Then a moment later came a series of gigantic flare-ups — each filled with a pulsing core of brilliant flames. Then these separate cores coalesced and formed a single wall of flame that appeared to screen the tank, the street, and even the buildings around it.

"Jumping Jesus!" one of the men exclaimed, "what the hell'd you do — pour powder over the whole god-damned town?"

"It don't take much of that stuff," Sergeant Washington said. "But we left enough."

Then the black sergeant roused himself from the spell under which the sudden pyrotechnics had held them.

"Bring up that three-quarter-ton! Let's hitch this gun up and get the hell outa here."

The men around the gun sprang to action. The artillery lieutenant jumped up and ran back to his jeep. Now it was his turn for a few pyrotechnics. He quickly grabbed the microphone.

"Charlie Three here. We're ready for that concentration on the town now. We've got a whole column of tanks bottled up there on the main street. Give us everything you can — as quick as possible. It's a chance of a lifetime."

After only a moment of silence he could hear Major Schwartz's voice answering, its customary calm shaken with suppressed excitement.

"On the way, Baker Three. We were loaded and ready for you. Three other battalions will join us. Their shells should begin arriving within one minute. You're getting enough to cover the entire town — with a big concentration along the main street. Over."

My God, the lieutenant thought triumphantly, it's working like it's supposed to for once. And this I've been waiting to see ever since I left O.C.S. in Fort Sill, Oklahoma.

23

Colonel Berrigan slowed the jeep as he became aware of weary figures plodding along on either side of the road. This would be his infantry — what was left of it. And a sorry, exhausted lot they were. Well, his job as commander was to "inspire" them all with...what was left? Damned little, so far as he could see.

"Just a little further, men," he said, trying to sound cheerful. "Kitchen truck's at the crossroads up ahead. Hot coffee and pancakes for everyone. The 'Lone Bandit' looks after its own."

Had he seen two or three faces look at him and brighten slightly? Perhaps. But most of them just continued plodding along as if only their vacant bodies were there, and the rest of them somewhere far away.

He was glad he'd told the mess sergeant earlier to set up his kitchen a short distance behind the crossroad. The kitchen crew still had enough supplies to fix another meal for everyone (especially with the "everyone" now a lot fewer). He wondered

idly if the mess sergeant had done as he had been ordered —
or just kept on going when he arrived at the deserted crossroad. He had a sneaking suspicion that kitchen crew might
still be there.

He slowed the jeep again as he came to the head of the
column and saw a slightly plumpish figure leading it.

"Captain Bergoff?" he asked tentatively.

"Yes, sir," the figure answered in a voice trying to sound
alert but unable to hide its weariness.

The colonel kept his voice low — no sense advertising the
bad news to everyone.

"Can you give me a report on your strength now?"

"Yes, sir. Lieutenant Brownell has about sixteen men, Lieutenant Kolinski lost about half and has around twenty. Lieutenant Magruder's platoon was the smallest and has only ten
men left. I had to steal some men from my reserve platoon for
replacements but I still have a small squad of nine left."

About fifty men — less than half what we had yesterday,
the colonel thought.

"Okay. When you come to the crossroad, somebody will
be there to take you to your positions. Then send half your
men back to the kitchen for a hot breakfast."

"Yes, sir. They can use it."

Colonel Berrigan knew he would soon have to think about
how to build some kind of defense out of his pitiful remnants.
But considering the apparent hopelessness of the task, maybe
he could allow himself just a few more minutes before tack-
ling it.

Sergeant JayCee Washington could just barely pick out the gun in the cold, dark, pre-dawn light. He hadn't wanted Hooley to stay behind with his howitzer. After all, the whole idea of further delaying the German panzers had been JayCee's. Then at the first spot they'd found for laying the next ambush, Hooley's gun had been the last one in line — so he said he'd do that one while JayCee went ahead and looked for the next likely spot.

"Let me take this one and you take the next one," JayCee had protested.

"Go to hell, JayCee," Hooley had replied. "Just because you had a granpappy wore the blue, you think you deserve all the god-damn medals? You get along while Lonnie an' me take this one."

So JayCee had gone ahead and found another good spot to put his gun in position.with two quick bends in the road about a hundred yards apart. It had taken only a few minutes to put the gun in position, loaded and aimed and hastily camouflaged.

"I'll leave you here with the gun," JayCee had told the cannoneer. "I'll just take the three-quarter-ton back where I can see how Hooley makes out."

He couldn't help feeling guilty for getting Hooley in that position. He knew if anything went wrong there wasn't much he could do about it now anyway. He just *felt* better seeing for himself.

That little fireworks display we gave the Krauts back in town sure must have been a big success, he thought. That was over three-quarters of an hour ago — and they haven't got even this far yet.

Now they'd need no flares in the gray morning light to tell them when the enemy poked around the corner. But that wasn't necessarily an advantage. For now the German tank could see the howitzer sitting out there in the open, its shiny tube brightly obvious, in spite of the branches laid over it for camouflage.

He's got two or three seconds, JayCee thought. The tank will probably come around the corner slowly, its gun loaded and the gunner scanning the road ahead for a target. If Hooley gets the round off, that will probably take care of the first tank. So that will give them just time to limber up and pull the gun around *their* bend — before another tank can get up there to fire at them. That was the point of having *two* bends together. That way the second tank would have a bend to get around before he could spot the howitzer's position. And after what that one-five-five will do to that first tank, you can be pretty damn sure that second tank's going to come around his bend mighty cautious. So it *could* all work out – if everyone did what he was supposed to and nothing went wrong. But if anything did — there was no margin for error.

Hell, he thought, if you want no chance for anything to go wrong, you shouldn't be volunteering for combat units like this. Well, his great-granpappy had volunteered, and in those days they had had it even rougher. But JayCee was going to make him proud, by God — proud he had a great-grandson who could live up to what his great-granpappy had done.

Then he'd recognized the spot and turned the three-quarter ton around and parked it well back from Hooley's gun. He couldn't get any closer. He had to keep his vehicle out of the action – otherwise what would the cannoneer he'd left back with his own gun do for something to pull it with.. He crawled up to a sheltered spot from which he could see the howitzer and the two crouching figures.

From the grinding sound of an approaching tank he knew he'd arrived barely in time. He couldn't see the bend in the road the tank would be coming around. But he could tell by the tense figures crouched behind the gun's shield that the tank was nearly there. Hooley had the lanyard in his hand. He looked once more through the sight and waited.

At the last minute Hooley appeared to be motioning with his free hand to the cannoneer to get back away from the gun. After a moment the cannoneer rose and ran the few steps to the other side of the road and fell prone there. Now why did he have him do that, JayCee wondered. Did he have some kind of premonition?

Then JayCee could tell by the tense, crouching figure by the gun that the tank had finally poked around the corner. Hooley held back a moment, his right arm tensed and ready to pull the lanyard. He's letting the tank get to just the right spot, JayCee thought. Then the arm jerked back in a sudden pull on the lanyard.

And nothing happened.

Misfire! The god-damned primer had been faulty. Get the hell out of there, Hooley, he breathed to himself. It's only a god-damned howitzer! Take off! Come on back and I'll get him with my gun down the road a ways.

But JayCee could only lie there helplessly and watch while the scene played itself out to its tragic end. Hooley was going through the proper motions a good cannoneer was trained to do for a misfire. First he jerked the lanyard twice more. Still nothing. Then he reached over, quickly unscrewed the device that held the primer, jerked it out, threw it aside and replaced it with a new one. While JayCee watched as if seeing a slow-motion scene in a horror movie, Hooley yanked his arm back, the gun roared, flame shot from the barrel — at the very moment the howitzer appeared to explode and jump into the air. JayCee saw a body being lifted and blown tumbling, as limp and unreal as a stuffed scarecrow.

Hooley"s cannoneer jumped to his feet and ran to where the body had been blown, stopped and stared down. Then he turned and ran quickly back around the bend, jumped into the three-quarter-ton, started the motor and sped back to where JayCee was waiting.

JayCee jumped out into the road to wave down the three-quarter-ton. JayCee could see the man's face was contorted with horror.

"God-damn misfire," the man sobbed. "It was going great — and a god-damned misfire. The one time it shouldn't! Ah... Jesus!"

"You checked him out?" JayCee asked.

"I checked him out...blew him all to hell."

JayCee could think of nothing to say. After a moment the man went on.

"And he *still* got the god-damned tank. If he'd just fired a half-second sooner. If...ah hell. And he told me to get out of there — or I'd of got it too."

"That's Hooley for you," JayCee said quietly. But he couldn't just sit there with his own voice echoing hollowly in his ears.

"You better take off," he finally said, jumping down and turning back toward his own vehicle. Blindly he started the motor and drove quickly to where his own shiny-tubed howitzer waited. Patiently waiting, he thought numbly, their common fate. And maybe then somebody would be kind enough to say, "That's JayCee for you."

Private Hatfield looked up dully as he approached the crossroad. There was a time there he never expected to make it back this far. And here he was. It didn't seem to matter what you did. You either made it or you didn't. And if you made it, you just dug yourself another hole, with the lead-colored sky sitting down over your head like a gray blanket, and tried to get ready for the shattering explosions and terrifying moments to come. And if you didn't make it, they left you lying there, like a discarded rag doll with the sawdust spilling out — until the graves registration team, your own or the enemy's, cut off one of the two dog-tags, threw you in a shallow hole, covered you over, and left you there with only the dull gray sky to witness the end of all your days.

He jerked to a sudden stop to prevent from walking into the soldier in front of him. He roused himself to look around. The column had halted in the middle of the crossroad. The tall, awkward-looking Lieutenant Magruder was standing in the middle of the road between the two files of his platoon.

Some "platoon," Hatfield thought grimly. Put the two ranks together and they'd almost make up a squad.

"All right, men," the lieutenant said, taking off his helmet and scratching his balding head. "The left file's going with me to start digging in our new position. You men in the right file," he added, indicating the line Hatfield was in, "are going straight down this road a few hundred yards till you see a kitchen truck on your left. There you'll have a hot breakfast — hot coffee, pancakes, ham, the works."

"Knock it off," he added as the men in the left file groaned disgustedly. "Soon's they're back, the rest of you'll get your turn. You men in the left file, follow me and we'll get digging us some holes."

As he continued to plod forward on the road straight ahead, Private Hatfield felt a slight stirring of warmth inside him. He knew it was his stomach anticipating those hot pancakes covered with waxy melting butter and thick corn syrup — all washed down with great gulps of hot coffee. Perhaps it wasn't much to look forward to — but it was enough to fill his whole horizon now.

He hadn't heard that voice in his ears for some time — that voice that he clearly recognized as Sergeant Forte's, even as his mind told him it couldn't be. But something had sure made him *think* he'd heard the voice — and just in the nick of time, too.

It was going to be lonely without the sergeant — who he realized with surprise had been gone less than twenty-four hours. And it was going to be even lonelier whenever he thought of that young boy with the tow-colored hair, who just at their last meal had been quietly weeping by himself when Hatfield had walked over and sat by him. And now he was lying back there, alone and lifeless.

Yet it was kind of nice to think how the boy had wanted to stick close to him, his new-found friend — how he had even overcome his fear enough to empty the clips for his Ml like a veteran. And because he and some others like him had done that, they'd held out and prevented the left flank from collapsing. That boy had been doing all right, Hatfield thought. He was coming along fine. It was hard to realize that Hatfield had known the boy all together for little more than half a day.

Well, he thought, sometimes in this war you lived your life like a speeded-up movie — and a year's worth of living (and dying) took only a few minutes.

Still, it was all right. He didn't feel so lonely, somehow. It was sort of like Sergeant Forte and the tow-headed boy and maybe eventually all the others would always be with him now, under whatever gray blanket of oppressive sky, or in whatever shallow grave.

Colonel Berrigan stood in the middle of the main crossroad and wondered where in hell he could put the few anti-tank weapons he had left. Not a favorable terrain feature in sight. In fact, the whole damn thing looked hopeless.

Stop folding up just because the terrain doesn't match your needs, he told himself. So last time you got a river that let your disorganized rabble stand off a good chunk of a German armored division for much longer than it ever should have. So you think you're entitled every time?

Well, if he'd had his good luck, this was where the gods of war evened things up for him. There's nothing, he thought — not a god-damned thing I can anchor to anywhere near this crossroad. Front, rear, or either flank. Stick anything big enough to challenge a heavy German panzer any place in this flat, open strip and it would stick out like a running pimple on a movie star's face — and get itself knocked out in a few seconds flat. And there was nothing on either flank to tie in to.

Well, so much for crying in his beer. Now as to what he *could* do. That flat, open strip — maybe that could be a plus? If the enemy could see him, then ipso facto, he should be able to see the enemy too. Think of that wide open stretch as a barrier. Perhaps he could find some positions back behind the road where he could place some of his....some of his what? What the hell did he have left to position? What in hell among his remaining "force" could possibly knock out a Panther or Tiger? His Shermans? All gone. Including that Sergeant Bradovitch he'd come to have so much respect for. The T.Ds? He had all of two of them left — and their seventy-sixes wouldn't do much against a flock of eighty-eights.

And that left him the one *full* platoon — of those.pitiful light tanks with their tiny thirty-sevens.

For a moment he felt like throwing up his arms to that damnable gray-flannel sky and screaming oaths at the indifferent gods. Then he noticed the vehicles approaching from the east.

This would be the last of them. And at least he could be glad they didn't seem to be coming in a panic-stricken rush. Which meant they didn't think the enemy was hot on their tail. Or were they just too tired to care?

First in line was a tractor pulling one howitzer. It was followed with a jeep towing a second.

"Where are the other two?" he asked the artillery lieutenant, whose jeep was pulling the second gun.

"Sergeant Washington has one in position a few hundred yards down the road," the lieutenant answered. "They've been doing a great job delaying the German tanks. They did lose one gun though — and the gunner. But they still got the tank."

"They're not pushing close behind you then?"

"Those lead tanks are getting pretty careful how they go poking around every bend in the road, sir. The Kraut generals in the rear are probably hot to trot — but the men on the point probably have their own ideas about that by now."

"Do you still have radio contact with your battalion?"

"Yes, sir. As long as we leave the radio to run off the jeep battery."

"Hold up here a minute, will you? I want to discuss our new defense. And tell your battalion we're going to need all the support they can give us."

"Yes, sir. I already have them alerted."

"Do our close support howitzers have much ammunition left?"

"Very little, sir. A few rounds per gun is all."

"Okay. They're still going to be key players in the next phase. I want to go up and check out our last road block up ahead. I'll see you back at the crossroad in a few minutes."

After one more bend in the road he saw the howitzer in position two hundred yards ahead. He had apparently arrived on the scene at a crucial moment, For even as he watched, a man was crouching behind the gun, his eye to the sight and one hand holding the lanyard. The man stepped back, pulled the lanyard, and the gun rocked back with the recoil as the shell sped on its way. Almost immediately the colonel heard a second, louder explosion and a column of smoke climbed above the intervening trees.

The man by the gun motioned quickly for the vehicle parked nearby to back up to the gun. The driver backed up hurriedly, jumped down to help the gunner push the trails together, and then slammed the ring into the hitch. A few moments later the vehicle was racing down the road toward the colonel's jeep.

The colonel pulled the jeep about and sat waiting for the weapons carrier to arrive. It slowed and stopped opposite the jeep.

"Looks like you got it," the colonel said.

"Dead center, sir. And I left powder bags and gas cans enough to make them think they've already entered the gates of hell.

"How many rounds do you have, Sergeant?"

Sergeant Washington glanced in the back of the weapons carrier.

"Just five, sir. One W.P. and four regular H.E."

"Then I want you to go directly back to the crossroad where you'll find your other guns. You're going to need those rounds for what I have in mind for you there."

The sergeant looked at him a moment, then asked in a voice that tried to temper his curiosity with proper military respect.

"Direct lay, sir?"

"You just did it, didn't you? Can you hit them at a quarter-mile range by direct lay?

"No problem, sir. And the shells have been doing the job all night."

"Good. I'll see you at the crossroad, then. We've still got a few tricks left in the old bag."

But a few minutes later, as he started across the quarter-mile open stretch, the hard reality of it all hit him. These men had all fought through the long night, trusting he somehow would always pull a rabbit out of the hat at the last moment to avert disaster. And somehow he always had. There had been some mighty tight squeaks, and many had been wounded and some even killed. But he'd never misled them. There'd always been a chance for things somehow to work out.

Only now it was different. Now there was almost nothing to fight with. One-five-five howitzers to stop Tigers by direct lay? Great.

Yet hadn't the black sergeant said his shells could stop a Tiger — had already done so? They certainly could — under certain conditions and part of the time. Well, he still had three of those one-five-fives. And he still had (he hoped) the two "experimental models" with the ninety millimeters. And two M18 T.D.s with seventy-sixes. And five Stuarts with (God help us) thirty-sevens. Plus maybe half a hundred worn-out infantrymen.

The only trouble was his only real weapons, the ninety millimeters, were stuck so far out on either flank they could neither support his main force nor be supported by it. Again he felt he had struck rock bottom. Yet as he pulled into the crossroad and stopped, he could see the men gathered there looking to him with — a kind of expectation? They were discouraged and exhausted and afraid of what was to come — yet he couldn't help but feel they expected him to come up with something, pull one more rabbit out of the hat.

Well, god-damn it — he would. To the best of his ability.

And without conning anybody with a lot of something he and they would know was plain bullshit.

He jumped out of the jeep, slapped his map down on the hood, and leaned over to study it again. There had to be some best way — as bad as it might be. And he owed them that. The best chance there was — with no bullshit about it being better than it really was.

Okay. First — he had to pull his little force together. And fast. Then defend this primary north-south road as long as possible.

"Sergeant McClanahan!" he shouted to the non-com waiting nearby.

"Yes, sir!"

"Get on the radio in the light tank. Tell the flank forces to come in immediately — both the Stuarts and the T.D.s with the ninety millimeters.

"Yes, sir."

The sergeant headed at a run for the light tank parked fifty yards behind the crossroad.

What next? Those one-five-fives — he knew they were now just "stationary pieces." But they had the destructive power for one final use.

"Sergeant Washington!"

"Yo, sir!"

"I want you to find positions for your three guns. Close enough to the road so they can shoot direct fire on anything advancing across the open space – but camouflaged so well they can't be seen until they fire. Park their prime movers in covered positions well to the rear. Leave what ammunition you have with the guns. Tell your men they are to fire the guns as long as they'll shoot, then leave them, get back to their prime movers and move to the rear. Is that clear?"

The black sergeant snapped a quick "Yes, sir!" and then turned to shout back at his men.

"Let's go and put these babies in position!"

The colonel stopped the artillery lieutenant for a moment as he drove past.

"Lieutenant Stallingsworth, let your driver deliver the gun he's towing. I want you here."

The artillery lieutenant leaped out of the jeep to stand beside the colonel.

"Lieutenant, I want you to find a spot where you can observe the entire open stretch out there."

"Yes, sir. I've already selected one."

"Good. Have your battalion ready to pour concentrations on anything that appears in the open."

"Yes, sir. I've already advised them. We'll have them for direct support — and first call on three other battalions that are already tied in with our Fire Direction Center."

Better than I had even hoped for, the colonel thought.

"Excellent." The colonel then turned toward the tank destroyers. "Now — who's in command of the T.D.s?"

"I am, sir."

A tech sergeant stepped briskly forward.

"Okay. Your job is to find two positions, one on either side of the road, where you can fire and then maneuver to the rear."

"Yes, sir," the sergeant said promptly. He turned to run back to where the two T.D.s were parked.

Colonel Berrigan looked up at the sound of approaching motors. It was the light tank and Sergeant MacKay's bulky contraption pulling into the crossroad. The tall, skinny figure in coveralls leaped down and double-timed to stand before him.

"Got your message and high-tailed it here," the sergeant said. "Sergeant Kowalsky should be here in a couple minutes."

"My congratulations for your excellent work out there on the flank all night," the colonel said.

"Thank you, sir."

"Now, I'll need your 'experimental models' right here with us. I want them both about a couple hundred yards or more behind the crossroad, but with good observation to the front —*and* well hidden. Is that clear?"

"Yes, sir."

"One on either side of the road. You'll stay in position to protect the T.D.'s when they pull back. Then you'll pull back as soon as you've fired. One shot — bingo! Then you're out and we'll put you in somewhere further back. Right?"

"Right, sir. Here comes Kowalsky now. We're on our way."

Colonel Berrigan leaned over to look again at his map. At least he now had everything concentrated. He would make a real effort with his shrunken little force to close off this one important road — or at least to delay and give ground as slowly as possible. But if they left him hung out here by himself for long, his little force would be quickly overrun. And how, most likely? Rudimentary tactics. If you hit a strong point — go around its flank and get in its rear.

So how would they go around his flank? No good roads for heavy tanks in more than two miles in either direction. And this side of the main frontal road, the land was to a large extent wooded and generally rougher than the open stretch east of it. But there were two small roads — more like rough trails — leading back from the frontal road. One was about a quarter-mile to the left, the other a little less to the right. The enemy could certainly use them to send infantry forces — and maybe even some lighter recon vehicles — around and into their rear. If their heavier tanks were held up on the main road, that's almost certainly what they would do. Could he coun

He heard a slight cough and looked up.

"Excuse me, sir. Where do you want my platoon?"

For a moment he didn't recognize the speaker. Then he r
membered — the commander of the tank that had been parked
behind his C.P. most of the night. The young man looked almost as if his feelings had been hurt at being the only unit
ignored.Well, where indeed could he use them?

Then it came to him. By God — that was the answer. And
these little tanks with their ridiculous pea-shooters might be
just the thing. A good commander — he remembered the passage from one of his lectures — uses *all* his troops. And if
they can't be used in the conventional way, then he finds a
way they can be used.

"I was holding back on your platoon because I have an
especially tricky job for you. We're going to fight a delaying
action on this central road — and you are going to provide
flank support for us. See these two roads — more like trails, I
guess — on the map? Notice how they parallel our main retreat road? You're going to send one of your tanks over to
each road. We'll also assign a platoon of infantry to both roads.
It will be the tanks' job to serve as the main fire base for each
infantry group. The mission in each case is to protect the flank
against any lighter recon units. The tanks' and the infantry's
weapons should be enough for a delaying action. Your own
tank, along with your other two, I want posted about a quarter-mile back on the central road as our final reserve. Captain
Bergoff," he said, turning to address the former staff officer
who had been waiting nearby, "assign an officer and sixteen
men to each of these flank forces. Let as many as can ride the
tanks do so right out to their position. Now," he turned back to
the young tank commander, "you'll keep your tank here on
the main road to provide communication with both flanks —
and to keep me posted. Both these forces will try to hold at the

road — but if forced to retreat, they will use the small ____ ____ back to this road which connects with our road about a ____ back. Is that clear?"

"All clear, sir," the light tank commander answered promptly.

"Good. Off you go then."

The colonel turned and stared back at the road to the east. Nothing there yet but empty road. Well, he was doing what he could. He hadn't lied to anyone about the situation — and he still might even be able to do something worthwhile But how much longer could he keep this up?

As long as you have to, he told himself. And beyond that there was no use probing.

"Excuse me, Colonel...Berrigan, I believe?"

The colonel turned and found himself staring at a distinguished-looking gentleman wearing a single star on his collar. For a moment he was too surprised to make his tired muscles react. Then he snapped to attention and saluted.

"Yes, sir."

"And this..." the general included the small clutter of men and vehicles about the crossroad, "is...er...the famous 'Task Force Lone Bandit'?"

"Well, sir — I'm not sure about the 'fame,' but that's our designation."

"Good. From our reports of what you've been holding up — using practically nothing to do it — I can assure you the 'fame' has already started to make the rounds. I'm sorry to have eavesdropped, but I was so fascinated by how you were going to handle an impossible situation, I just hated to interrupt. I'm General Butler, and I'm bringing up a full combat command to take over from you."

The colonel could only stare, dumfounded.

"A full Combat Command, sir?" he repeated numb

"That's right. Full battalion of Shermans, one of arm infantry, one of armored artillery. And what you see com. up the road behind me is the unit we're really anxious to s go into action against the Germans' best. A battalion of tank destroyers — but the new M36 model. Mounting a ninety-millimeter. Take on anything they've got — no problem. Now what's your situation exactly?"

The colonel was feeling as if a suit of heavy armor he'd been walking around in had suddenly fallen off. Task Force Lone Bandit was being relieved.

24

Colonel Berrigan had been dozing fitfully as he rode in the jeep. Sergeant McClanahan once again was driving. The colonel, relieved of even this burden, had tried to stay awake to make the necessary decisions for disbanding his patched together task force. He knew well enough what standard army procedure would require: all elements should be returned to their regular units as quickly as possible. But through the fog of his exhausted mind and body one perception stood out clearly — how terribly inadequate such a culmination was for the desperate deeds of the last twenty-four hours.

His command had, after all, accomplished a near miracle. They had been, for the most part, a frightened mob in wild retreat. Yet somehow they had managed to tamp down the panic raging within them, had forced their exhausted bodies to carry out orders their instinct for life cried out against, and finally had brought to a sudden halt a far more powerful foe.

And they had done it while under his command. That
what added the hollow ring to his sense of satisfied relief
that "under his command." For he now felt deeply they ha
entailed in him an obligation. What that obligation was he
couldn't say. He only knew that what they had suffered, what
they had done had goals far beyond merely following his orders, meeting certain strategic ends, and in the process perhaps (face it honestly for once) furthering the progress of his
military career.

He knew how others far removed in time and distance from
that night of terror would explain it, in terms already worn
bare and meaningless: the men under his command had "no-
bly sacrificed" themselves and their youthful lust to live out
the far greater, as yet unlived portion of their lives. For what?
Oh, how the empty, glib phrases then would tumble out: for
God, for country, flag, and honor. But those abstractions would
no longer be enough for him.

It wasn't that he had something better to offer. He didn't.
But what he had formerly assumed so easily and never questioned had shrunk, in one night's darkly terrible deeds, to a
shriveled, empty husk.

And those deeds had taken place under his command. That
somehow left him with a sense of obligation for which there
was no adequate response.

There were the few inadequate "rewards" he could convey
— and he fully intended to see they were awarded in full measure while it was still within his power to do so.

There were the "fruit salad" recommendations for the deeds
he knew about himself, and the many others known only to
his subordinate commanders. He knew those medals would
be appreciated — perhaps, down the years, even honored. But
he knew as well their terrible insufficiency, especially those
awarded to the stiffening bodies left lying back there, cold and

s against a hard, indifferent earth.

ut those fortunate enough to have escaped that fate —
at could he do for them?

That was the crux of it. For most of them — nothing. They were not "in his outfit" and must be sent packing posthaste. Yet he must do what he could. For whatever short span of time the night's long hours of madness and miracles might justifying his asking.

The jeep coming to a sudden stop jolted him back to full consciousness. He opened his eyes to see a roadblock a few feet away. It was obviously not intended to stop the enemy. There were no anti-tank guns nor dug-in positions — merely a plank resting on two boxes in the middle of the road, an officer and a sergeant wearing M.P. armbands standing in front of it.

The lieutenant stepped forward and saluted smartly.

"Colonel Berrigan, sir? The General sent instruction for you to place all your own division's elements in a suitable rest area and then report to his headquarters. We'll take charge of the men from the other units and see they're returned promptly to their commands."

The words seemed to come to the colonel from a great distance. He knew it must be from his going so long without rest, yet it was almost as if he had been thrown suddenly into a world completely alien to his experience.

He didn't answer for a moment, and the M.P. sergeant spoke as the silence was extended.

"If you'll just pull over for a moment, sir, and point out which are your own men, we'll take charge of the others."

What could he do or say? The army system, constructed to clank on inevitably in the face of whatever horrendous calamity, was reasserting its control over its flotsam and jetsam. And what could he do? A mere lieutenant colonel, on the basis of a

brief twenty-four hours of combat, could hardly ez..
lenge the authority, buck the power, and right the...
the Army all by himself. He knew that.

He turned and looked behind him. He saw first the..
lery lieutenant in the right-front seat of the jeep directly..
hind his, then the black Sergeant Washington riding bes..
the driver of the three-quarter ton. Behind those two vehicle..
came one of the supply trucks carrying worn and tired-look-
ing infantry. He noted particularly one forlorn private with
an Ml slung over his shoulder, who stood leaning against the
roof of the cab, his bleary, tired eyes fixed in some kind of
hopeless anticipation on the colonel's face. Following in line
came the rest of the column — light tanks, tank destroyers,
artillery pieces, even that god-damned kitchen truck still with
him -- all jumbled together as in some weird carnival cara-
van.

The colonel knew what he said or did now could make little
difference in the standardized, slow-grinding procedures of the
Army. But he also felt deeply those eyes — the owl-like, bespectacled eyes of the artillery lieutenant, the smoldering, intense eyes of the black sergeant, and the dull, resigned eyes of
the infantry private — all fixed on him awaiting his response
to the words he knew they all had overheard.

Though he realized it could make no difference in the long
run — could in fact cancel out that "one-leg-up" the recent
action might have had on his career — he knew what he had
to say for those men in the column to overhear, and for all
those left behind, lying in the grotesque postures of their dying, forever past all hearing. And for something fragile and
freshly sown within himself, that he could neither name nor
justify — nor need to.

The M.P. sergeant had taken down the plank blocking the
road. His lieutenant was waiting for the colonel to tell him
which men to pull out of the column.

"It's all right," he said, motioning Sergeant McClanahan to

.. "These are all my men."

t as, he added to himself, down all the years I'm
s.

A GLOSSARY OF WORLD WAR II TERMINOLOGY

Some of the following World War II terms are still in use; others, however, may not be familiar to the general reader.

A.P. - (Armor Piercing) A solid shell designed to penetrate tanks and other arnored vehicles.

BAR - (Browning Automatic Rifle) A rifle capable of single shot or automatic fire. Usually issued one per rifle squad

C.P. - (Command Post) The location at which a commande sets up his facilities for commanding his unit, howeve large or small.

H.E - An artillery or tank shell containing explosives whicl detonate upon contact. Casualties can be caused by the shock of the explosion, but most come from the shell fragments, which shatter and can fly up to a hun dred yards.

O.P. - Observation Post (applies especially to artillery) Th place to which the forward observer advances so h can see the enemy targets and call for fire on them vi radio or telephone.

Primer - The tiny cartridge inserted into the breech of a artillery piece. It explodes when the lanyard is pullec igniting the powder bags which propel the shell out c the barrel.

Tanks (American) - Stuart, usually called simply the "Ligl Tank," mounting a 37 mm cannon and machine guns Sherman, the main American battle tank, technically "medium tank," mounting (throughout most of the war a 75 mm cannon and machine guns.

Tanks (German) - Mark IV The German medium tank, abou the equal of the American Sherman. Mark V The "Par ther," mounting a more powerful cannon than th Sherman, plus machine guns. It also had much heavie

armor than the Sherman. Mark Vl The "Tiger," the larg-
est, heaviest German tank, capable of mounting the
dreaded 88 mm gun.

T.D. (Tank Destroyer) - Essentially an American "tank" designed for fighting other tanks, but with a turret open
at the top, which made it more vulnerable against infantry. There were many types and models of U.S. T.D.'s
developed during the war. At the time of the "Bulge"
probably the M -18, mounting a high velocity 76 mm
cannnon plus machine guns was most common.

W.P. (White Phosphorus) - An artillery shell containing burning pieces of white phosphorus. Used as a "marking"
shell, it can also cause painful casualties because of its
burning pieces of phosphorus.

The author in 1943

About the author:

Robert Billings lived most of his first twenty-two years in the small New Hampshire town of Dover. Upon graduating from the University of New Hampshire in 1942, he enlisted as a private in the infantry. A wise O.C.S. examining board changed his preference from infantry to field artillery, and he became a ninety-day-wonder in that branch. After a year of bouncing around as an "extra" officer, suddenly, a few days before the Normandy invasion, he had the position he had always coveted — forward observer for "B" Battery, 187th Field Artillery Battalion. He landed on Omaha Beach on D-plus-2 in direct support of the 29th Division. He served in all five campaigns in Northern Europe, and the end of the war found him in Czechoslovakia negotiating with the Russians over whose army was in the wrong place.

He returned home, took an M.A. at Boston University, and taught high school English a year before going on for a Ph.D. at the State University of Iowa. Since then (after six years at North Dakota Agricultural College and one at the University of Denver), he has taught more than thirty years at the State University of California, Fresno — ten of which he served as English Department Chairman.

Although his major field of interest has been American History and Literature, he has also, beginning a few years after the war, developed a special interest in military history and modern tactics and strategy. He has written many historical commentaries for one of the leading computer war game companies, as well as Civil War commentaries and a drama script for National Public Radio.

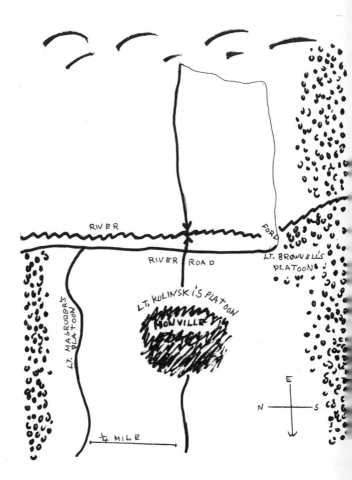